OUT OF EGYPT

Novels by Deborah Galiley

* * *

Polished Arrows

Yohana

Seeking Paradise

Out of Egypt

OUT OF EGYPT

DEBORAH GALILEY

OakTara
www.oaktara.com

Out of Egypt

Published in the U.S. by:
OakTara Publishers
www.oaktara.com

Cover design by Yvonne Parks at www.pearcreative.ca
Cover image © thinkstockphotos.ca: Patina background, David Schrader, 104310994
Author photo © 2013 by Robert Jeff

ISBN-13: 978-1-60290-353-1
ISBN-10: 1-60290-353-0

Printed in the U.S.A.

* * *

To the Mothers:
Marilyn and Esther

...and the Daughters:
Yael, Noa, Elly, Beth

* * *

"When Israel was a child,
I loved him,
and out of Egypt
I called my son....
How can I give you up, Ephraim?
How can I hand you over, Israel?
They will follow Yahweh;
He will roar like a lion.
When He roars,
His children will come trembling
from the west.
They will come trembling
like birds from Egypt,
like doves from Assyria.
I will settle them in their homes,"
declares Yahweh.

HOSEA 11:1, 8, 10-11

Prologue

1443 B.C.

IT'S BLEAK HERE, OUTSIDE THE CAMP. Every so often, when the wind blows in the right direction, I catch occasional sounds—a muffled shout, the cry of a child, the bleating of a sheep. During the day the heat is intense, and I sit in the shade of the goat hair tent, its flap open to admit enough of a breeze so as to dry the sweat off my wrinkled brow. I hesitate to look down for fear that I will catch sight of my own flesh, though only my hands are uncovered. The marks of *tzara'at*, uncleanness, cling to me like a viper hanging from its victim. I shudder, aversion mingling with remorse such that the taste rises like bile in the back of my throat. I would cry, but already the tears have wrung me dry such that there is nothing left. Nothing but time.

I cry out to Yahweh, but the heavens are as brass, and He does not respond. I grasp at the faint hope that this is not forever, but fear tracks me, settling its ugly talons into my shoulder. "I don't deserve Your love," I whisper, too hot and dry to speak louder, gritty sand settling into my throat, words barely moving the air in front of my face. Still, He doesn't respond, so different from the lavish love He has poured out on me in the past.

Terror grips my heart like a vise. What if He never speaks to me again? What if? I couldn't bear it! I've known fear before, but never like this. Fear in the past has always been tempered by His love. Without His love, there is nothing. Nothing to stem the tide of horror.

I close my eyes and lean back, and the memories crowd in clear and sharp, every image as vivid as a hawk outlined against the setting sun, every word as audible as the croaking of a frog in the delta swamp. The day it all started, the day when fear raised its ugly head. Not only I but Aaron noticed it, when Ema bartered her only bracelet for the sturdy papyrus basket and spent the afternoon meticulously coating it with tar and pitch. The child was lying on his back, giggling and cooing, on the little woven mat, blissfully unaware of the danger lurking in the street outside….

* * *

Part I

Miryam

1

Goshen, Egypt 1525 B.C.

I WAS TEN YEARS OLD, BUT ALREADY MY CHILDHOOD WAS OVER. The old king, Amenhotep, turned my people into slaves. Egged on by his wicked mother, he fretted that we would become like the Hyksos, those shepherd kings so recently vanquished from our father Joseph's time, and fight against Egypt, so he sent slave masters into our towns and villages. They rounded up our young men and forced them to toil endlessly in the hot desert sun, building tombs and monuments for their not-yet-dead. They also took our musicians, our artists, our storytellers, our craftsmen, and our older men and set them to work in the fields, planting and harvesting barley and wheat, onions and garlic, cucumbers and leeks, until their backs were so bent and blackened by the sun that they cried out in pain and distress, unable to create any more.

My father, Amram, was one of these men, revered among my people, directly descended from our father Jacob's son Levi, an old man when I was born, a shepherd and a priest, until slavery descended like an unforgiving and remorseless net, trapping everyone alive. He was put to work in the barley fields until the light within him dwindled, still there but only just. He and my mother had spent many childless years, but Elohim had mercy on them and renewed their hope by blessing them with first me, then my brother Aaron, and now the newest child, another son.

Ah, the new baby. The one who came the year after Amenhotep died. Amenhotep, who not only oppressed my people by turning them into slaves but who also devised a cruel plan to kill all the newborn male infants. The heads of the midwifery unions—Shiphrah and Puah—tricked Amenhotep, and God in His mercy stayed the king's hand. Thus it was that Aaron and thousands like him survived this murderous intent.

We had such high hopes that the new king, Thutmose, would loosen our bonds. He seemed more interested in outward military conquests than domestic terror. Immediately upon ascending the throne, Thutmose went down to Nubia, spending his first year as pharaoh quelling a rebellion against Egypt. He struck down the Nubian king in battle and attached him to the prow of his ship. When the regal yacht glided slowly up the Nile, the rotting, hacked body of the Nubian king, bloated and grotesque like some sort of obscene figurehead, stared ahead with sightless eyes, and we all felt the first stirrings of uneasiness that perhaps this newest pharaoh would not be the kindest of men. Much too soon, my people discovered that conditions were in fact to get far worse, not better.

Perhaps it was the headiness of his military victory, or perhaps it was his desire to seem stronger than any perceived weakness of his predecessor. Either way, upon returning to Thebes, Thutmose cast a cold eye in our direction and decided that our numbers continued to multiply out of his control, and that the way to stop it was by killing babies. He decreed that every Hebrew boy born was to be thrown into the Nile, but that every girl could live, thereby sentencing Hebrew women to either assimilate into Egyptian society or become concubines and slaves.

Ema was eight months pregnant when this word came down, her belly swollen such that she could barely walk. I remember the paleness of her face when Abba told her the news, the way she seemed to crumple, how he swept her into his arms and she leaned her head against his broad chest. Her tears were silent, but her determined words were not.

"I will trust my God with the life of this child," she said fiercely, already convinced she carried a son.

*

The next month was tense, as Ema tried to keep out of public sight so that none of the pharaoh's soldiers would remember a pregnant woman. Her time came at night, and Abba sent me to fetch one of the midwives, Avital, who was under the supervision of Shiphrah.

I raced through the dark streets, feeling important with my lofty mission but still a bit fearful. In the daytime these streets were as familiar as my own home, but at night they took on a different aura altogether. It seemed as though a soldier hid behind every bush and a crocodile lurked behind every house. When I finally arrived at Avital's house, she decisively grabbed her special bag, the one with the mysterious artifacts used to deliver babies. The return home proved much swifter, with Avital's reassuring presence and her warm, brown hand gripping mine, pulling me along after her.

At home, I tried to help by fetching things and holding Ema's hand during contractions. Soon enough, however, her pain became such that she bid me leave, wanting only my father and Avital. My father knelt at her side, rubbing her back and whispering encouragement while I crawled up in a corner of the hut with the sleeping Aaron, clasping his small, sturdy body to mine under our shared blanket. I didn't think I would be able to fall asleep but I must have, for all of a sudden the first pale, pink, streaks of dawn peeked through the small window just under the roofline. I blinked my eyes and pushed Aaron's heavy little body to the side so I could stretch out on the mat more fully, extending my legs as far as they could go. It was then that I heard the thin cry of a newborn babe.

Right away, I got up and peeked around the screen that separated our one-room home in half, a brave attempt at privacy. Avital had left, but Ema was propped up on her mat, attempting to nurse a tiny, red-faced infant while Abba slept next to her, one arm under his head and the other flung protectively over her lap. Entranced, I crept close enough until I could see that here was a new brother and not a sister. Oh!

"Good morning, my little Miryam." Ema's melodic voice, soft yet strong, cut through the stillness of the room.

"Ema! Let me see the new baby!" Now that it was all right to come close, I slipped next to her and stared down at this newest member of the family.

What a beautiful child. His head was very round, a downy covering of brown hair covering his skull. He had Ema's intense eyes, Abba's strong, stubborn jaw, Aaron's nose, and my generous mouth. When he stopped crying, which he did as soon as he heard my voice, I saw the intelligence in that careful look he gave me. I was smitten.

"Oh, Ema! Can I hold him?" Nodding, she gently placed the baby in my arms, making sure I held his head properly, even though she knew I understood how to hold a baby.

By now Abba had awakened. He watched me hold his new son, a sad smile playing gently around the corners of his lips. After a moment he said, "So, what do you think of your new brother, my Miryam?"

I bent my head, breathing in the soft, newborn smell, pressing my lips against his shoulder, covered in very fine down. "Mmm, I love him," I said, sighing deeply. Then the thought hit me, and I raised my eyes to Abba's. "But he's a boy," I realized. "What will happen to him?"

Abba and Ema looked at each other over the top of my head before Ema spoke. "He belongs to Elohim, Miryam. He's in Elohim's hands."

*

For the next three months everyone in our family, including the three-year-old, did an incredible balancing act of hiding the baby. Our prayer lives dramatically improved as we sought Elohim day and night about how to protect this little being with whom we daily fell in love more and more.

For this was no ordinary child. This was a beautiful child—not only physically but spiritually. I could see it in his eyes. He was aware; he was thinking. All of us were dry-mouthed at the thought of his death, but every day he became a little older and a little louder until finally the day came when his voice started to come in. Then we knew it was only a matter of time before he was so loud that he would attract the wrong attention. To cover the baby's cries, Abba made me a small, round, handheld drum—a *tof*—covered by a piece of goat skin with some bells attached. I really liked playing it and spent so much time hitting its resilient surface that Abba called the little drum a *tof Miryam*.

Two weeks later, Ema sold her last jewelry, her mother's bracelet, and bought the papyrus basket.

All afternoon long she worked on the basket, head bent, fingers busy. She coated it with pitch and tar, put it outside in the broiling sun, let it dry, and then brought it back in for another coat. Three times she did this until finally she was satisfied. In-between she nursed the baby, gazed into his face, and wiped tears off her own.

I asked as I had many times, "What is the baby's name, Ema?"

She responded as always, "I am not to name him, Miryam. His name belongs to another."

"But who?" I demanded, exasperated I could only call my perfect brother "baby" and not a real name, as this made him so indeterminate. "Who?"

Ema lifted one work-weary shoulder briefly, then let it drop. "When I know I'll tell you." As always, she added, "This baby is in the Lord's hands." She caressed the baby, holding him close to her breast. He gurgled before letting out a long happy shriek. Startled by the noise, Ema and I looked at each other, nervous. His existence had become too obvious.

*

That evening, when Abba returned from the fields, we ate our bread and beer silently. Even Aaron was subdued. After finishing our meal, Abba had us sit in a circle on the hard, earthen floor. He took the baby from Ema and kissed him, holding him aloft. Then he recited a prayer over him: "Blessed are You, O Lord our God, King of the Universe, Who has blessed us by giving us a son." He then told Aaron and me to pray to Elohim for our brother's deliverance from the evil plans of the Egyptians. He said it was time to act, and that tomorrow we would put our brother in his snug little boat/basket and bring him to the Nile. Aaron and I started to cry but he told us to hush. "You must have faith," he said. Of course, Ema was crying the whole time but I didn't point that out.

Later, after Aaron fell asleep, Ema and Abba let me know the second half of their plan. They wanted me to stay hidden in the reeds at the edge of the Nile and keep watch over Baby.

"What if someone sees me?" I asked.

"They won't if you're careful," predicted Abba.

I nodded. He was right. I'm very good at hiding.

Tomorrow came too soon. Abba could not linger in the morning because the Egyptian foremen in the barley field where he was working counted every man. The penalties for not showing up were severe. One of my cousins was hit in the head so hard for a minor offense that he went to sleep and never woke up. His young wife cried for months until she was finally married off to his younger brother.

Abba kissed each of us on the top of the head as was his daily custom, and asked Elohim to watch over and protect us. He spent extra time with Baby this morning but not so much that he would be late. Then he was gone.

Ema, Aaron, and I ate some bread and drank some water. We had beer but would save it for the evening meal, when Abba was with us. After Ema nursed Baby, she told me to bring Aaron next door to her sister's house while we took Baby to the river. She was very matter-of-fact, her eyes dry, though I knew she had cried the previous night because I heard her.

I took Aaron by the hand and told him we were going to visit Aunt Sarah. Usually he loved going there, but this morning he acted ornery. "No!" he shouted, surprising us. "I want to stay with Baby!"

It took all of my persuasive abilities to convince him otherwise, but eventually I did. Finally, I got him settled next door. I was doing all right until Aunt Sarah clasped me to her bony bosom and tearfully told me that Elohim was in control. That made me dangerously close to hysterics. I pulled myself away from her and ran out of the house and back to my own.

Ema was sitting cross-legged on the floor, holding Baby in front of her. She was talking to him in a soft voice, telling him something just for his little ears. When I entered the room, she sighed and kissed his nose. Then she was all business.

"Okay, this is what we're going to do. He'll be in this basket covered by a sheet"—she gestures to the papyrus basket at her feet—"and if anyone asks what's in the basket, we'll tell them that we're going to the river to pick some reeds. Understand?" She looked at me intently. I nodded. She continued. "Then we'll put the basket in the river, and I'll leave you there to watch over it."

"But Ema," I protested, "what about the crocodiles? What if one of them shows up? Or the soldiers?" My voice rose against my will.

"Shh," she said. "It's all right. Abba and I have prayed about this. We're going to the part of the river where the Princess Hatshepsut regularly bathes. The plan is for her to see the basket."

"But what if she doesn't? Or what if she sees it and gets mad?"

Ema turned her head and briefly closed her eyes. "Well then," she said, her voice low, "we'll see Baby in the next life."

I kept silent. I had no more questions.

Twenty minutes later, Baby had been nursed and was asleep, tucked into the basket with a sheet snugly covering him. Ema and I held hands and walked down the narrow street that separated our line of mud huts from the line opposite. Ema held the handle of the basket in her other hand. When we got to the edge of the clearing where there weren't any more huts, Ema pulled me down a path I'd never seen before—a secret path leading to a secluded part of the Nile, a part where I never went because it was visited by royalty and I was a slave child.

There was underbrush there and plenty of reeds growing out of the shallow water at the edge of the river. Ema set the basket down and pulled back the sheet. Baby was still asleep, lulled by the motion of our walk here, a trickle of dried breast milk at the corner of his mouth. Ema prayed silently, then kissed him on the top of his head. She tucked the sheet loosely over the top of the basket so the sun wouldn't scorch him but he could still breathe. After she set the basket at the very edge of the water and lodged it in some reeds so it couldn't float away, she brought me to a spot about ten meters away where it was shady and told me to stay there and keep watch on Baby. She had prepared a small skin of water for me and some bread. Neither of us knew how long I'd need to stay here.

"Ema," I said, "what if it starts to get dark, and nothing has happened? What should I do?"

"You will come home," she replied in a strangled voice. "And you will leave Baby."

We stared at each other, Ema and I. This was overwhelming for me as a ten-year-old. It would be many years before I could begin to understand the implications of what she, our mother, was going through.

Ema hugged me tightly. "We will trust Elohim," she said. "Do not fear."

She kissed the top of my head, not unlike the kiss she gave Baby, and then was gone.

I sat cross-legged on the hard ground in the shade of the reeds and waited. The sun rose in the sky and the day got hotter and hotter. Sweat formed in little rivulets and trickled down my back. Unlike the Egyptians who shaved their heads, my hair was braided into three loops and tied at the back of my head. Since I was a child, I had not yet been given clothes and therefore was naked. The ground was hard on my scrawny backside. In addition, I was terrified of crocodiles and watched carefully in case one showed up. Gratefully, there didn't seem to be any around right now. I continued to wait for something to happen.

Miraculously, it did. I had just started to doze off, my eyes heavy from staring at the basket, when I heard a light buzzing of voices in the distance. Immediately, my eyes flew open and I listened intently.

The sounds of tinkling laughter and light feet running were followed by a woman's voice raised in warning: "Wait for us, Princess!" A young girl, not much older than me, burst into the clearing not very far from where the basket was. She had the gleam of triumph, indeed even to the point of gleefully saying, "Hah!" I could tell she was happy to be alone. She looked like I did when I hid from Ema, savoring a few more minutes of play before the endless round of chores began.

This girl cannot have any chores though, I reason. *She must just want to be alone.* I squinted, studying her as closely as I could from my hiding spot among the reeds. She stood straight and very regally, her body well-fed and slightly plump. Her head was shaven except for a pony tail that draped over her left ear, clasped in several places with gold and green beetle scarab pins. She wore a linen skirt that reached her knees and nothing else. Her only jewelry was in her hair. She was here to bathe.

I kept very still, hardly daring to breathe. I didn't know what would happen to me should I be noticed. If the princess's mean old father would throw helpless babies into the river merely because they were Hebrew boys, what would he do to me? Already, I heard the sounds of grown women as three of them reached the clearing, breathing hard and scolding loudly. Two of the women were young and beautiful and the third seemed more like Ema's age, though much less weary.

The little princess ignored them. She was unrepentant about running on ahead. Now the younger women helped her take off her skirt and walked into the water with her, one in front of her and one behind in case of a deadly snake or a crocodile attack. They washed the princess and played splashing games with her, though she got more rambunctious than they liked, running back and forth in the water. It was then I heard a familiar sound: Baby, crying. The noise had awakened him.

The women were trying to shepherd the princess back to the safety of the shore, one already out of the water, when suddenly the princess grew very still. Placing one hand on her left hip, she pointed with the other directly at the basket. She had heard the crying and spotted its source.

"Look!" she exclaimed. "Amunet, go fetch that for me."

The woman who had left the water obeyed the princess. Perhaps sixteen years old, and extremely beautiful, she had long, braided hair, and had donned a white linen dress that hugged her slim figure, especially now that she was still wet from the river. Quickly, she headed to the reeds and grasped the handle of the basket, nervously glancing to both sides as if to make sure no wild animals were about. I held my breath but she didn't see me. She was too intent on returning to the princess.

When she reached Hatshepsut, the little princess eagerly pulled the sheet off the basket, ignoring Amunet's cries of, "Be careful!"

Baby was revealed in his full glory, naked, red-faced, and screaming. The earlier nursing had worn off, and he was hot and angry.

The princess gazed at him, and an indiscernible expression crossed her face, causing her to look older than her tender years. I wasn't sure what she was thinking until she said, "This is one of the Hebrew babies."

I inhaled in fear. *Evidently she saw that he is circumcised and understands what that means.* But her tone revealed compassion. Hope filled my heart and I prayed silently, begging Elohim for a miracle.

The older woman spoke. "My Princess, your father has ordered the Hebrew babies thrown into the river. Let me put him back in."

The princess scowled. "No. This is my baby. I found him." She scooped Baby out of the basket and held him in front of her like a doll. For a moment he stopped crying and they stared at one another. Then he took a deep breath, and I braced myself for the outraged scream I knew was coming.

Indeed, it came. I waited for the princess to change her mind and drop him back into the basket but she didn't. She kept holding Baby.

"What does he want?" she shouted to the older woman over the deafening din.

"He's hungry," the woman said with a sigh, obviously unhappy with the unexpected twist in the morning's routine. "He needs to nurse."

It was then that I felt an inner prod from Elohim. It was all or nothing. A little shakily, I emerged from my hiding place and slowly approached the cluster of women on the riverbank. The sun burned on my shoulders, but a slight breeze fanned my face.

"Your Majesty," I said to the princess, falling to the ground at her feet.

I could feel her curious gaze on the back of my head. "Rise," she commanded. I did, and Hatshepsut and I came face-to-face for the first time.

Up close, she was prettier than I'd thought—almond-shaped eyes, high cheekbones, a determined mouth. The shape of her skull and golden hue of her skin was pleasing. I could see she was becoming a woman by the small bumps on her chest, but baby fat gave her a small tummy. I, on the other hand, didn't see enough food to have a tummy and was painfully thin.

Hatshepsut seemed fascinated by me. *Perhaps she's never seen a female Hebrew child up close,* I thought. It was obvious she was interested in everything and had an alert intelligence. "Who are you?" she asked.

"I am Miryam, one of the Hebrews," I told her. I didn't use the word *slave.* "I heard the baby cry and thought I could be of service. Shall I go and get one of the Hebrew women to nurse the baby for you?"

"Yes, go," she answered, neglecting to ask me the most obvious of questions, which was, "What exactly are you doing here, and whose baby is this?" Instead she said, "Bring her to the palace." She turned away, dismissing me.

I hesitated, wondering what to do about Baby, but the princess had already handed him over to her maid Amunet. The older woman noticed my indecision and flashed a look of *Go!* I backed away and retraced my steps to the secret path under the reeds. Once I found the path I ran like the wind, frantic to get home to Ema.

Upon reaching home, I flung open the door and shouted, "Ema! Ema!" After the brightness outside, my eyes needed to adjust to the dark room so I was startled when Ema rose from her pallet and came toward me. She had never rested during the day before.

"Shh, Miryam, what happened?" Her voice sounded teary, husky.

"Oh, Ema!" I cried, throwing myself into her arms. "The most amazing thing has happened! Princess Hatshepsut found Baby and wants to keep him. She asked me to find a woman to nurse him."

At first Ema stared at me uncomprehendingly. Then, slowly, her face changed. Life came back into her eyes, her smile. The tension in her whole body eased and her jaw unclenched. "Oh, Miryam!" she said at last. "Oh, Miryam!" She cried with relief, hugging me so hard I could scarcely breathe. At last she settled down. "Where are we to go?" she asked. "The palace?"

I nodded.

"Good," said Ema. She unplaited her hair and re-combed it, splashed water on her face, and straightened her simple linen dress, once white but now gray from frequent use. "Come," she told me. "Let's go tell Aunt Sarah what God has done for us and see if she'll watch Aaron until we get home."

Together we walked next door where it took us awhile to extricate ourselves from the hugs and squeals of delight. It was only when Ema said the princess might change her mind if we didn't hurry up and get there that Aunt Sarah shooed us out the door. "Go, go!" she said. "I'll keep Aaron and let Amram know. Don't worry about them."

*

It was early afternoon by the time we reached the summer palace of Thutmose, significantly north of Thebes in the eastern delta region of the Nile. It was also a convenient place from which to launch his various military campaigns, mostly aimed against Syria. The complex itself was enormous, with blocks of temples lining the avenues leading to the actual palace. Several of the temples were dedicated to Thutmose's favorite god, Amun, but there were also some for Ra, Ptah, and Isis.

After the dinginess and poverty of the Hebrew section, the wide avenues and large buildings of the palace compound dazzled my eyes. Columns and piers covered in writing were everywhere, as well as pictorial frescoes and painted carvings aflame in brilliant color. I stared, mouth agape, at the drawings of scarabs, palm leaves, papyrus, lotuses, and attractive people. Ema pulled me along, intent on getting back to Baby. Already the front of her dress was stained with milk as the time to nurse Baby was long overdue.

No one stopped us until we were a block from the actual palace. Ema was so focused on getting to Baby that she practically bumped into the outstretched, oiled, sun-darkened hand of a guard. The tall, bald, muscular man wore only a knee-length white skirt but had an axe strapped to his side. "Where are you Hebrews going?" he demanded, frowning.

"To the princess," Ema responded carefully. "She asked for us."

"For you?" the guard said in disbelief. "Why you?"

"She needs a nurse for a baby," I burst in excitedly.

The guard glanced from Ema to me and back to Ema, his face skeptical. I was afraid he'd make us turn back, that he wouldn't believe us, but he beckoned us to follow him. "Let's go find out," he said, not unpleasantly.

Ema clutched my hand, and we ran to keep up with the guard's long strides.

At the entrance to the actual palace he bid us to wait. We thankfully sat under the shade of a date palm, a little respite from the oven-like heat of the day. Our guard spoke to another guard, who eyed us curiously, nodded, and disappeared into the cool interior of the palace. In a short while he reappeared, conferred with our guard, who shot us a surprised look, and then both men led us inside.

I had never seen anything so beautiful as the great hall inside this palace. Enormous murals of Amenhotep and the current Thutmose covered the walls, depicting successful military campaigns, favor from the gods, and various aspects of life as involving the gods. We Hebrews had Elohim, the one true God, yet I was fascinated and awed by the gorgeous pictures. My own life had been lived in shades of brown, with some blue and green thrown in. All this color filled my senses and made me giddy.

Ema was also enthralled, though not nearly to the dizzying extent I was. She pointed to a drawing of Thutmose standing tall over a group of bent-backed slaves who were up to his knee, toiling in a field of grain, and opened her mouth to speak—

"Come here!" The voice of a third guard cut short whatever she was going to say and we were led from the great hall into a smaller room off to one side. That room was also magnificently decorated, but I didn't have time to gawk because we found ourselves in front of the princess.

She was still in the linen skirt with the same gold scarabs in her hair, but somehow she seemed taller and more powerful here than she did at the riverbank. Ema pulled me down to the floor, and we both bowed reverentially until given the command to rise.

One of the princess's maids, holding Baby, entered the room. It appeared he was sucking on a piece of linen sopped in goat milk. I could tell he was mollified but not really happy. When he saw us, he got very agitated and started to cry, but we pretended we'd not seen him before.

The princess spoke over his cries. "Is this the woman who can nurse my baby?"

I nodded, too awed to speak.

Hatshepsut then addressed Ema. "What is your name?"

"Jochebed," responded Ema, a bit nervously.

"Take this baby and nurse him for me, and I will pay you." The princess took Baby from her maid and held him, smiling a funny, crooked smile as she studied his face.

When Baby calmed down and looked back at her, my heart twisted. I was jealous that Baby liked her. *What about me? I'm his sister.*

The princess spoke. "I will call him Moses, because I drew him out of the water."

Moses! Ema was right, Baby had a name all along but it wasn't for us to give. *Moses.* I would have to get used to the sound of that.

I sneaked a sideways peek at Ema to see her reaction. She bore no expression, but breast milk stains had expanded across her whole chest. She desperately needed to nurse Baby. The princess didn't have enough experience to notice this, but the older maidservant definitely did. She whispered something to the princess, who nodded. "You may, Inet," she said.

Inet took Moses from the princess and carried him to Ema. "Take and nurse him now," she urged as Moses started whimpering. "After, I will give you and the girl something to eat and payment for nursing the baby and send you on your way."

Gratefully, Ema took Baby—I mean, Moses—into her arms, went to the side of the room, and sank onto the floor with him. I heard his frantic sounds as he began to nurse, and then he gradually quieted. Soon there was only a contented sucking. Ema's eyes were closed, and a smile was on her lips. I relaxed.

All of us watched the scene: me, Inet, Amunet, the maid who carried Moses, and the princess. The guards at the entrance to the room resembled statues, they were so still, so I didn't count them.

Then the princess turned to me. "Miryam," she said, surprising me by remembering my name. I would learn later that her memory was impeccable.

"Yes, my Princess," I answered.

We locked eyes. I liked her face. I knew I should be afraid of her, but I wasn't. She was a girl I wanted to be friends with, and I had to keep reminding myself that she was the daughter of the king.

"I want you to bring Moses to see me once every moon when I'm at this palace," she said. "Every winter we go to Thebes, so I will send a messenger to let you know when I am here and you are to come." Her words were commanding, but there was the hint of a question.

"I would be most honored, Princess." I bowed my head before looking up.

She was grinning, and I grinned back. The princess clapped her hands and told Amunet to set-up refreshments for Ema and myself.

Baby Moses had fallen asleep in Ema's arms. He looked extremely happy but probably not as happy as Ema. She couldn't stop smiling.

When the princess walked over to plant a tentative little kiss on Moses' brow, Ema beamed at her, seemingly oblivious of the fact that this was the daughter of the tyrant who ordered the baby boys thrown into the Nile in the first place.

"Oh Princess Hatshepsut," she gushed, "thank you so much for hiring me as Moses' nursemaid! I promise that I will take wonderful care of him—"

The princess waved for her to stop. For a young girl, she was extremely self-possessed. "I am confident you will treat him as you would your own son," she said with a hint of a smile. Then she took the sleeping baby and sat with him on her lap while Ema and I were led off to a smaller room and given a meal.

I said *meal,* but I meant *feast.* A meal was a piece of bread and a cup of watered-down beer, or maybe a few slices of cucumber if you were lucky. We were given wine, fish (which I saw otherwise perhaps three times a year and it never tasted like this), bread that was lighter and sweeter than anything I've ever had plus it was dipped in honey, a bowl of big luscious dates, and a pea and bean mixture flavored with garlic and leeks. It was amazing! I ate as much as I could and wondered how I could take the leftovers without getting in trouble. Ema had more restraint than me but still ate voraciously.

We were thrilled at the end when Amunet took the rest of the dates, added more, and wrapped them up in a papyrus leaf. "Please, take this home," she said. In addition, Inet brought Ema her first month's wages, which consisted of several large linen sheets that we could use for making clothes and bedding. Not only was linen very expensive and difficult for us to get, but it was the nicest linen I'd ever seen, with a tight weave and a soft luxurious feel. I carried the linen and the dates, and Ema carried Ba—Moses.

We didn't talk much on the way home. Both of us were unaccustomed to the full, satisfied feeling that followed a nutritious meal and could barely keep our eyes open. Also, the emotions of the past days had taken their toll. We were totally and thoroughly drained.

2

AFTER WE GOT HOME, IT TOOK SEVERAL WEEKS for us to stop being jumpy and nervous about Baby Moses. The princess had thought of everything. The soldiers who patrolled our slave neighborhood had been informed that Moses belonged to her and that our family was to be protected, not persecuted. Our neighbors and family looked on us with astonishment and some resentment, but that faded as they realized that our favored status offered them a measure of protection, as well. We were careful not to flaunt our new position.

When the new month came upon us, Ema and I prepared to take Moses back to the palace to see Hatshepsut. Aaron begged to come with us, but Abba said no. "We cannot assume on Elohim's graciousness," he said. "In the process of Him saving one son, I don't want to chance losing the other." The matter was settled: Aaron would stay home. I was glad, which made me feel mean, but I didn't want to share the princess with him.

So we walked back to the palace, this time without the panic in the pit of our stomachs but to the sounds of Aaron's thwarted sobs, which grew increasingly faint as we came to the end of our street and turned in the direction of the palace. Moses was bigger now and more interactive. Ema had strapped him to her body with a piece of linen that she cleverly sewed into a baby sling, and his head swung this way and that, alertly watching everything that crossed his line of vision. He got particularly excited when he saw a cat and laughed with great joy. He was adorable.

At the palace, we were treated very differently from a month ago. Perceived as favorites of the princess, we were shocked and gratified that the same Egyptians who used to look through us as if we didn't exist now went out of their way to ensure our comfort and approval. It was quite heady stuff. We still had to wait for over an hour to see the princess, but when we were ushered into her presence, I was feeling so confident that I ran right over to her and blurted out, "Hello!"

Suddenly the room became deathly quiet. Realizing I'd overstepped my bounds, I grew afraid.

At first Hatshepsut was as still as a statue. Then she broke into a smile. "Hello."

I could breathe again, as could everyone else. Slowly the noise level in the room picked up. Hatshepsut beckoned for me to approach her, and I did. We smiled shyly at one another, not quite knowing what to say. Again, I felt that I wasn't merely a Hebrew slave child to her but an actual person of interest. That knowledge both fascinated and terrified me.

"How is my baby?" asked the princess.

Ema stepped forward and held Moses out. He was alert and cooing, eyes bright, cheeks chubby. Honestly, I didn't think there had ever been a cuter baby. Hatshepsut must have thought so too because she gave a squeal of delight and scooped him into her arms. She cuddled him tenderly, like a miniature mother. It was quite the picture: the young princess and the Hebrew baby. Sometimes life is stranger than any story even our best storyteller could make up.

The princess put Moses down on the floor so he was lying on his back, and she knelt next to him. One of her maids rushed over with a pillow for Hatshepsut to sit on, but she impatiently waved her away. *How difficult it must be to have people fussing over you continually*, I thought. Was the princess allowed to play and get dirty, or did she always have to act circumspect and mature? I suspected the latter.

Inet spoke to Ema and led her into another room to wait for Moses. I reluctantly started to follow, but Hatshepsut stopped me. She wanted me to stay and play with her and Moses.

"Why don't we play house?" I asked.

"House?" She wrinkled her nose. "What is that?"

"You know…it's when I pretend to be the daddy, you pretend to be the mommy, and this is our baby."

"Oh." She laughed. "Then we must be brother and sister as well."

Brother and sister. Like me and Aaron? What an odd thought. Brothers and sisters didn't marry, unless one counted our forefather Abraham marrying Sarah, though she was his half-sister and not his full sister. Still. I didn't know then that Egyptian royalty married siblings so as to preserve the royal bloodline. "Do you have a brother?" I asked.

Hatshepsut made a face. "I have three brothers: Amenmose, Wadjmose, and Thutmose, but Thutmose is not descended from my illustrious mother, and Wadjmose is no more."

"Which one should I be?"

The princess thought for a moment. "Amenmose," she said finally. "He is my favorite. Come, let's go out into the garden to play."

She picked up Moses and ran out a side door. I was close on her heels. Inet followed at a distance so it was almost like we were alone. When we emerged into the garden, I couldn't believe my eyes. Had I died and gone to Paradise? Though it was the heat of the day, one would never know it by the murmuring of falling water, the flower-scented breezes, and the abundance of shade under the palm trees. Smooth stones of various sizes were artfully raked into designs, and stone benches with carved lotus blossoms discreetly nestled into the sides of the many winding paths. The fragrance of roses mingled with sweet marjoram almost succeeded into putting me in a stupor, so unused was I to these delightful scents after my childhood of inhaling the rankness of poverty.

Hatshepsut, however, didn't appear to notice her surroundings. Perhaps it was too familiar. She was ready to play.

But I was so awed I couldn't breathe. "Oh!" I said and stood still.

"Come on," she prodded me. "Let's go!"

After several twists and turns on a hidden path, she led me to a secluded spot under a towering fig tree. I was good with directions but unsure I'd be able to find my way back unaided. We sat on the shady grass under the tree. Baby Moses lay on his back, looking up and making little gurgling sounds. Hatshepsut and I played house, and I was Amenmose. We fussed over the baby and then I ordered her to do something in a calm but stern voice, like I've seen Abba do with Ema hundreds of times.

I was unprepared for Hatshepsut's reaction. She immediately stuck her finger in my face and threatened me if I told her what to do again. She was like a wild cat, ready to pounce. I cried.

All of a sudden, Hatshepsut changed back into the calm little princess. "What's wrong? Why are you crying?"

I shook my head, unable to speak yet. Finally I hiccupped and said, "You frightened me."

She laughed. "I'll bet your mother never responded like that."

Was she ever right! Ema would *never* have defied Abba like that. I didn't think Egyptian women defied their husbands either. I shyly asked Hatshepsut if that was how her mother behaved with her father.

She laughed at my question. "No, of course not. But then she is not me."

She is not me? What does that mean? I wondered. The father was always in charge and then the mother. I was debating whether or not to ask her more when we heard clapping and then a voice yelling, "Princess, Princess!"

It was Inet calling. A flicker of annoyance crossed Hatshepsut's face before she composed herself. "It is my nurse. Time to go."

She picked up Moses, who was getting fussy because he was hungry and thirsty. He kicked and squirmed in her arms, which made her hold him even tighter. Oh, oh, I could tell he was going to scream soon. Maybe I could help. "Would you like me to hold him?" I asked.

The princess looked at me evenly. "No. He is mine. I'll hold him."

I followed her back to the palace proper, past banks of small yellow chrysanthemums, purple irises, and scarlet poppies. Date palms and almond trees alternated, offering a delightful relief from the intensity of the midday sun. I dragged my feet. I didn't ever want to leave.

This time, we were given a big papyrus basket filled with almonds and figs as Ema's payment. I was giddy with this food bounty—such a pleasure after our basically unrelieved sustenance diet.

When we got home, Aaron ran toward us. No longer upset that we had left him, he was wild with excitement that we were back.

Ema gave him a fig, which he examined closely. "Eat it," she said. "Go ahead, it's good."

He licked the fig, and his eyes brightened. "Yum!" he exclaimed before shoving the whole thing in his mouth. His cheeks were so full he could barely chew. Ema and I laughed at his childish greed. Of course, this didn't stop me from eating as many figs as I could before Ema snatched them from me.

"Absolutely not!" she scolded. "One a day per person." By then my stomach had started to hurt so I admired her wisdom.

*

The following day, when I was watching Moses and Aaron, my friend Tamar came to play. "Leave the baby and take Aaron," said Ema, who was kneading dough for our daily bread. "Go, go."

Tamar and I walked past the line of mud huts to the end of the block where there was a clearing. Aaron walked between us. I could tell that he was happy to be away from the baby and with older kids. Lately he'd been distancing himself from anything he perceived as babyish.

"Let's play house," said Tamar. She was shyer with me than usual. I wasn't surprised. Everyone had acted a bit odd since we'd become affiliated with the palace.

"Okay," I said. "We can make Aaron our baby."

"I am NOT a baby!" Aaron shouted.

"You are if you want to play with us," I warned.

Sulky, he stared at me.

Tamar put her arm around his shoulders. "Please, Aaron, we need you for the game."

Aaron melted for Tamar. She had that effect on people. Smaller than me, she had a round face, small nose, big eyes, and a space between her two front teeth that gave her a rakish look. We'd been inseparable in the past but lately, well, she had seemed like such a *slave* to me. I still liked her, but I wasn't sure I wanted to be her best friend anymore.

We played for a while, but I found fault with everything Tamar did. After a while she gave up. "See you later, Miryam," she said, not looking at me. "I'm going home."

Though I was ashamed at my mean-spiritedness, I didn't try to stop her.

Then Aaron confronted me. "I don't want to come home with you! I want to go with Tamar!"

"Well, you're coming with me, you little brat!" Angry at myself for being difficult, I took my frustration out on Aaron. Grabbing him by the arm, I dragged him screaming back to our house.

Tamar watched silently. I could tell she was shocked by my behavior.

When we were almost home, Ema rushed into the road. She'd heard Aaron's cries. "Miryam! Aaron! What is going on?"

Aaron broke free of my grip and ran to Ema. Clutching her around the legs, he refused to look at me. My heart ached to see him so mad, but at the same time I couldn't stand him. I was angry at everyone and everything. I pushed past Ema and ran into the house, throwing myself down in the corner on my sleeping mat.

After Ema calmed Aaron down, she came inside and sat next to me. As she stroked my hair, her touch broke through my anger. "What is it, my little Miryam?" she asked gently. "Why are you acting unlike yourself?"

I shrugged and cried silently. I couldn't answer her. I knew it had to do with the princess, but I was too young to put into words how the new world of the palace had affected me. All I knew was that nothing was the same. My world had been turned inside out. And though I didn't like what was happening, I also didn't want it to go back to the way it was.

*

After that, the days blended one into another. The only thing that changed was Moses' size. Bolstered by Ema's better diet, he was thriving. He'd been rolling over for a while and now was starting to sit up without falling over. He was so cute, and I loved him so much. By the end of the month, the palace was starting to feel far away and its grip on me lessened slightly. Soon, however, it would be time to go back.

The night before Ema and I were to take Moses to see the princess, I heard Abba and Ema talking late into the night when they were certain I was asleep.

"I'd rather not take Miryam with me," Ema murmured.

"Ah," said Abba. "I think I can guess why."

"Yes. I'm afraid she'll grow more and more dissatisfied with her lot in life. I'd cut it off now but—"

"But the princess wants her to come," finished Abba.

"The girls like each other. I think they're both fascinated by the differences in the other. Only—"

Again Abba completed Ema's thoughts. They were so annoying that way. "Only you suspect that the princess will grow bored with our little daughter long before Miryam will be ready to let go."

"Yes…leaving behind an unhappy, confused girl who no longer knows which world she belongs in."

They were both silent for such a long time that I thought they'd gone to sleep. I myself was drifting off when I heard Abba speak. Just on the edge of consciousness, I grasped for his words:

"You know what, Jochie? No matter how exhausted we are, no matter how hard these Egyptians work us, we need to pour ourselves into the training up of our children in the ways of Elohim so that their firm foundation will be built on Him, not on anything shadowy or insubstantial."

And with that I finally fell asleep.

*

The next time I saw Hatshepsut she smiled at me. "I have been looking forward to seeing you," she said.

My heart constricted with excitement. She seemed more interested in me than in Moses, though we both played with him. The princess made a show of carrying him around and calling herself his mommy. If Ema was offended by this, she didn't show it, keeping her face neutral and eyes downcast.

This time, Hatshepsut asked me questions about my life. It seemed so boring in comparison with hers that I was embarrassed. I didn't want her to know that I lived in a mud hut. So I talked instead about Abba and Ema and Aaron. I started to tell her about our father Jacob, and how Elohim sent him to Egypt many, many years ago.

"Who is Elohim?" she interrupted.

Who is Elohim? I was bewildered that she'd asked the question. Elohim had been so interwoven into every aspect of my life since birth that the thought of Him was as natural as breathing. The concept that someone as intelligent and well-educated as Hatshepsut didn't know about Him flustered me.

I answered without thinking: "What do you mean, who is Elohim? How can you not know Elohim?"

Hatshepsut's eyes narrowed and she scowled.

Realizing I'd gone too far, I stammered and tried again. "He is the God of the Hebrews," I explained.

Understanding dawned on her face. "Oh, yes, he is for the Hebrews."

Wait—that sounded wrong. I knew Elohim could not be God just for us because Abba often referred to Him as "God of all the earth." How could He be God over the whole earth but just be for the Hebrews? That made no sense.

"Actually," I said, "I think He's the God of the Egyptians too because He's in charge of the whole earth."

Hatshepsut looked perplexed. "How can that be? Is he greater than Ra? than Isis? than Amun?"

"I don't know much about those other gods. I do know that Elohim is all powerful, all seeing, all knowing, and He answers prayer." I was thinking of Baby when I made the comment about prayer.

The princess seemed intrigued. "What does he look like?"

What does He look like? "I don't know." I shrugged. "Our father Jacob saw Him many years ago when they wrestled." I thought for a moment. "Oh, and Adam and Eve!" I said triumphantly. "Adam and Eve must have seen Him after He created them."

"Who are Adam and Eve? And tell me about this Jacob."

This is getting complicated. I've never been asked to give a history of religion lecture before. I'd barely turned eleven and was in over my head. "Uh, Jacob is the Hebrew forefather who came to Egypt many, many years ago because his son Joseph was ruling Egypt under Pharaoh."

Hatshepsut lifted a skeptical brow and crossed her arms in front of her chest. "Ruling under Pharaoh? A Hebrew slave? I don't believe you."

"He wasn't a Hebrew slave back then," I added. "He told the secret meaning of dreams, and Pharaoh exalted him above everyone else…." When I realized I was losing Hatshepsut. I quickly switched to the Adam and Eve story. "But anyway, when Elohim made the earth, He placed our father Adam and our mother Eve in the Garden of Eden. They were the first people."

"Elohim couldn't have made the earth. Ra made the earth. Do you mean Ra when you say Elohim?"

By now my head was spinning. I knew that Ra was a false god because Abba had said so many times, but I also knew I couldn't insult the princess's god. So I stood there uncertainly.

At that moment I was saved by Inet, who walked up to us and informed the princess that it was time to send us home.

As she said good-bye, Hatshepsut told me that we must talk about this again. By then I could tell she was the type who never forgets. But at least I'd have an opportunity to ask Ema and Abba what to say first.

*

As it turned out, I didn't see the princess again for six months because she traveled with her family to the great palace in Thebes, on the banks of the Nile. Every year, she wintered down there, only returning to the north in the early spring. I missed the trips to the palace, but there was so much work to be done at home that the time passed quickly. Thanks to Inet, we were paid in advance, so we had baskets of almonds and dates, plus several meters of excellent linen and also a good supply of fine flour for bread. Moses, bright and inquisitive, grew quickly and started crawling everywhere. Toward the end of the winter, he took his first steps. At the beginning, he fell quite a bit, but soon enough he got the hang of it. Before we knew it, he was zipping around at knee level. He made me laugh every time I saw him.

All he wanted to do was follow Aaron. At first, Aaron was flattered by the attention. However, that soon wore off when Moses tried to follow him into the street outside the house and Ema insisted that Aaron stay right in front when Moses was with him. At four, Aaron wanted to run up and down the block, kicking at stones with his friends. But Ema was very protective of Moses, terrified of what would happen to us if we were to let him get hurt or worse. I think that if he hadn't belonged to the princess, she would still have been very protective, but since he did, it kicked up her concern a lot.

When Hatshepsut returned, we made our monthly visits as before. The princess was still friendly toward me, which was a relief. I wasn't sure what would happen after her time in Thebes, a place that seemed very mysterious as I don't know much about it other than the fact that her grandfather, Amenhotep, built a village at Thebes called Deir el-Medina. Several of our finest artisans have been conscripted to move there so as to help work on the tombs of the pharaohs. Once they relocated, we didn't see them again, which caused no end of upset with their families. When I heard "Deir el-Medina," I thought of a big black hole in the ground that sucks people in. Ugh.

Anyway, I was surprised by how happy she was to see Moses. He clung to Ema at first, but his natural inquisitiveness and happy personality won out. Within minutes of our being in the presence of Hatshepsut he toddled over to her on his chubby, sturdy legs.

"Oh!" the princess squealed, very un-princessy. "He is sooo cute! Look at him walk!"

Several voices rose in quick agreement. "Yes, he's cute, that he is."

When I said it, I really meant it. I suspected, however, that several of the ladies would agree with anything Hatshepsut said. *That would get awfully dull,* I thought. *Perhaps that's why she finds me so refreshing. Hmm, I should probably not try to wrap my opinions around hers, or I may find that I'm just as boring as the rest of the palace flunkeys.*

*

Later that summer, Hatshepsut, Moses, and I were playing in the garden when a man suddenly came upon us. He was young, strong, and good-looking, with fine dark features and a shaved head. Naked from the waist up, he was wearing a gold and linen skirt, and a golden band encircled his head, coming together in front with an intricately carved asp. The asp was golden as well, with bright blue specks of lapis lazuli for the eyes.

Hatshepsut squealed and threw herself at the man, who picked her up and spun her around. He was obviously quite fond of her, and she adored him. I guessed it was her brother Amenmose, back from one of his military campaigns.

At that moment Amenmose put Hatshepsut down and turned to look at me and Moses. "Who is the girl, my sister?" he asked, ignoring Moses.

"She is Miryam, one of the Hebrews."

"And is my father bringing Hebrew slaves into the palace now?" Amenmose spoke of me as if I were a wall hanging or a potted plant. His eyes moved lazily over me, and I stood rigid.

"No," said the princess. "Her mother is nursing my baby."

This got the prince's attention. He actually looked surprised. "*Your* baby? *What* baby?"

I had to hand it to Hatshepsut. She might be young, but nothing rattled her. "*My* baby," she said smugly. "The one I rescued from the Nile."

Now Amenmose took note of Moses. He picked him up and examined him closely. "Obviously this is the baby," he muttered.

Suddenly I was concerned for Moses, but he was amazingly good. He didn't squirm or yell. Even he seemed to understand that the prince was not one to be crossed.

"Father has allowed you to keep this Hebrew child?"

"Yes," she purred, attempting to look docile. "Father has been very kind with my requests."

At this, Amenmose slapped his thigh and laughed so loudly I was startled. At least his attention was diverted from Moses. "Ha!" he snorted. "Father is much too kind with your *many* requests! It's a good thing I am so much older than you and you are a girl, Hatshepsut, or I might not sleep at night."

Hatshepsut laughed and blushed, but I could tell she was pleased at the thought she might be competition for her adored older brother. She hugged him around the waist, hard. "I am yours to serve and obey, my brother."

He stroked her head. "We'll see what the future holds."

I knew they were talking about marrying each other, like the Egyptian royalty did. The idea was absolutely repugnant to me, but I would never say that aloud.

We went back into the palace. I followed at a safe but respectful distance. With Amenmose around, playtime with Hatshepsut was abruptly over. Hatshepsut garnered much respect at the palace, but if people anywhere saw Amenmose, they immediately fell to the ground and paid homage. He was to be the next pharaoh.

When Ema and I walked home that day, I was unusually subdued.

"What is it?" she wanted to know. "Where's my little chatterer?"

I kicked at a stone. "I don't know," I mumbled.

"Come on." Ema didn't let go. "Tell me what's bothering you."

I sighed. "It's Hatshepsut's brother. He…upset me."

Ema looked concerned. She stopped walking, pivoted toward me, and said in a low voice, "What did he do to you, my daughter?"

"Nothing! He barely noticed me." I struggled to put my feelings into words. "It was just that he didn't seem to think Moses and I were people. To him we were objects, barely slaves." Now that I'd found my voice I grew more animated. "And Hatshepsut is so taken with him. She thinks he's totally wonderful, but to me…"

Ema nodded. "To you, he is not so wonderful."

"Yes. To me he seems evil, unkind."

We walked the rest of the way home in silence.

3

When Moses was three years old, we took him to the palace and this time he stayed there. I was twelve and Hatshepsut, thirteen. "I am his mother all the time now," she declared. "I will summon you to visit, Miryam."

Back home, Ema cried when she believed Aaron and I weren't looking. I saw, though. I felt as if I could see everything. It was too much, this knowing about the adult world. My life marched forward, not back. My body betrayed me, changing shape as it prepared me to leave all aspects of childhood behind. My breasts emerged, I grew taller, and hair grew in places it never was before.

We didn't hear from the princess for a full year, a year of longing after Moses, of helping Ema, of enduring our slavery. A year of watching as Abba grew older, beaten down by the cruelty and hardship of a life of servitude. I looked at him and envisioned Hatshepsut's brother, so smooth and arrogant. *He does not care,* I thought bitterly. *He does not care that Abba is slowly dying.* I swallowed tears that rose in my throat.

On my thirteenth birthday an Egyptian messenger came to our door. The request was for me alone, not Ema. She was desperate to see Moses, I could tell, but it was enough for now that I would come back with a report. She had no choice. Summoning her courage, Ema asked the messenger when I would return. He took his time before answering, then, looking bored and put upon, shrugged. "As the princess wills," he said.

I was shocked when I saw Hatshepsut. She had changed drastically since I saw her last. She was fourteen but looked years older. Her eyes were wider, more intense, outlined in black kohl with vivid blue on the lids. Gone was the childish figure. She had to have grown almost 10 centimeters! She had become quite slender, except for breasts the size of melons that weren't there last year. She wore an embroidered linen dress, which hugged her new curves, and her head was covered by an elaborate wig. I was so awed by the sight of her that it took me a few moments to respond when she spoke to me.

"What did you say?" I croaked, finally realizing she was waiting for an answer.

"I said, you look so grown up. It's been awhile."

I looked grown up? Surely she was mocking me! But no, the princess seemed sincere and actually quite glad to see me. She stepped closer, and we gazed into each other's faces. She did not touch me, and I was careful not to touch her. I remembered palace protocol.

"How is Moses?" I asked.

"Oh, Moses!" The princess delightedly clapped her hands together. "He is a joy. Inet!" she called.

"Yes, my lady?" Inet immediately stepped forth from whatever shadowy alcove she had been hiding in. It seemed to me that Inet was acting more like a servant and less like a mother these days. The princess was obviously gaining in power.

"Please fetch Moses."

"At once, my lady." Inet bowed and backed out of the room completely before straightening up and walking forward. I watched her head to a nearby staircase.

"Now tell me what's been happening with you since we've seen each other," said Hatshepsut, drawing my attention away from the rapidly disappearing Inet and back to herself.

"Not a lot," I replied shyly, unsure of what to tell her. I mean, would she really be interested in how I make bread for the family? Or my laundering skills? Or my repentance over ongoing abruptness toward Aaron? Or perhaps she wanted to learn where I got my clothes? This last thought made me smile.

The princess saw my smile. "What?" she wanted to know. "What are you thinking?"

I suddenly understand why so many palace servants keep an expressionless face. They didn't want to be quizzed on every fleeting thought. But I was stuck, so I said, "Just that my life is so boring in comparison with yours, Princess."

"I am not a fool, Miryam," she replied harshly. "I know you live with slaves." (I noticed she said "live with" and not "are a slave." This was good.) I *want* to hear about your Ema and Abba and your little brother. I have heard enough about royal so-and-so meeting another royal so-and-so. *That's* boring."

So I told her what I do every day, and about my friend Tamar who liked me again, and how much Aaron had grown, my concern for my father (the princess didn't blink at that one) and I even got bold enough to say that we all miss Moses.

As I mentioned Moses, Inet returned with him. He was no longer a baby who was carried but an active four-year-old, and he looked like a little Egyptian prince. His head was shaved and a little side pony tail, much like the one Hatshepsut had when I first met her, spouts off his left ear. His only clothing, a blue linen belt, was loosely tied about his hips. He ran right to

Hatshepsut and bowed the most graceful bow one could imagine a small boy giving. "Mother," he said.

My heart constricted.

"Look, Moses," said Hatshepsut. "It's Miryam."

He turned and noticed me, and a frown briefly creased his smooth forehead. I could tell he didn't quite remember me.

"You lived with Miryam when you were a baby," the princess prodded. "Remember?"

Slowly, the little boy nodded. I saw that he wanted to please his mother, but that he really didn't know me anymore. I was ready to cry, but then he came over to me and looked me full in the face, his warm brown eyes examining me.

"Hello," he said, his voice tiny and sweet.

"Hello," I choked back. I desperately wanted to hug him but felt constrained.

"You're pretty," he said, still watching my face. That did it. I started weeping in front of everyone. I felt wretched and foolish but that didn't bother Moses. He tenderly wiped a tear away with his hand and asked, "Why are you sad?"

"I'm not sad," I lied. "I'm just so happy to be here that I'm crying."

Moses looked confused but accepted my statement.

"Come, Moses," said the princess, holding out her hand. "Let's go play in the garden with Miryam."

Happily, the little boy slipped his small hand into the darker hand of his adopted mother. It was clear that he adored her. I followed them outside, and we sat under one of the many palm trees. A servant approached with a ball for Moses and a board game, which he reverently set in front of Hatshepsut.

"Oh, good," she said, fingering the smooth ivory and wood finish of the board. "I love this game. Do you know how to play senet?" she asked me.

I shook my head *no*, feeling like a foolish peasant. This was obviously a game the nobility play as they wile away the hours in between feasts and entertainment.

The princess was slightly annoyed but determined to be a good sport. "It's easy. I'll teach you." She then proceeded to deliver a very fast-paced monologue about the board and its 30 holes, 3 rows, and 10 columns. The game used 7 pawns for each of us. I tried as hard as I could to concentrate but I didn't understand how to play.

"Let's just start," I suggested. "I'll try to catch on as we go."

Hatshepsut arranged the board and handed me my pieces. Once she began playing, she was quite an adept teacher. An hour later, I was good enough to capture my first pawn when a servant appeared with a tray on which were three drinks. We were all thirsty as the Egyptian heat was so very drying. He handed one to the princess, one to Moses, who had long been bored by his ball and instead was intently watching the game, and one to me. My cup had a shiny blue glaze over which were drawn figures of young women dancing with lotus blossoms in their hands. The drink was white and foamy. I took a sip. It was amazing stuff! I mostly just drank water and weak beer.

"This is so delicious!" I breathed. "What is it?"

"One of my favorites," said the princess. "Dates, honey, and goat milk all whipped together." The creamy concoction left a frothy mustache on her upper lip, which suddenly endeared her to me. *She is human,* I remind myself. *Not exactly like me, but sort of like me.*

Hatshepsut pointed at me and laughed. "You have a mustache."

I didn't mention hers but turned to Moses, who had been drinking steadily since he was served. "I'll bet he does too," I said, not quite relaxed enough to mention *her* lip adornment. When Moses finally lowered his cup, he did indeed sport a mustache, which was totally hilarious on his sweet young face.

I expected to be sent home that day but the princess surprised me. "Wouldn't it be fun if you stay tonight?" she exclaimed later as the sun edged toward the western horizon and thoughts of dinner intruded. "You can sleep in my room tonight instead of Dedi." I already know that Dedi was one of her attendants, a comely girl of about sixteen who sleeps on the floor at the foot of the princess's bed should she need anything during the night.

"What about Dedi?" I asked. "Will she be upset?"

Hatshepsut stared at me. "Upset?" she repeated, one eyebrow lifted. "What does that matter?"

I shrugged. I had no answer for such blatant disregard of another human. Abba and Ema would have been appalled. I had such unwarranted favor with the princess that it stunned me when I saw others weren't nearly so blessed.

"I would love to stay here tonight," I said.

"Good. Then it's all settled."

"Will you let my parents know so they won't worry?"

The princess airily waved a hand. "Of course. I'll send a messenger."

A little later, the princess left to have dinner with her mother and aunt. Moses was fed an early supper by Inet and then taken somewhere else. I was not allowed to sit at the table with them but instead ate after with the servants. They complained about the light fare, but I was convinced I had died and gone to food heaven. Broiled fish, vegetables with garlic, plenty of bread, and beer...I so wished Abba and Ema could enjoy this as well. And Aaron, he needed the nutrition. He was so skinny compared to Moses. I sighed through my full mouth, thinking about the difference between the two brothers. Moses was the very picture of vibrant health: bright eyes, ruddy complexion, full cheeks, no sharp bones jutting out through gaunt flesh. Would that all my family could eat like this!

Later that night I got to spend more time with Moses as he prepared for bed. He was friendly and talkative, quickly warming up to me. By the time Inet tucked him into bed, he had grown so attached that he demanded I kiss him. This I gladly did, breathing in the childish fragrance of his young cheeks.

Later that night, with Hatshepsut, I was an uneasy mix of friend and servant. She wanted to talk about the latest political intrigue at court; yet, at the same time, her very youthfulness still kept her from fully entering into the shenanigans. She saw me as someone safe to confide in, not a rival, and revealed a world so vastly different from my own it didn't seem real.

"I want to be wed to Amenmose," she finally confided to me, after playing with her pots of eye kohl while hinting at something "big" in her life.

"What does your father say?" I askd.

She made a face. "Oh, I'm sure he will agree." She flipped the braids from her wig over her shoulder in a very grown-up gesture. "I am his favorite."

"His favorite? More so than his eldest son?"

Hatshepsut put her finger to her lips. "Shh, don't say that loudly. But yes, more even than Amenmose. It is because Father and I are so much alike. Amenmose is like Father too, but he is mostly interested in military campaigns. He is not as interested in other aspects of," she vaguely waved her hand toward the outside of the palace, "life."

This didn't quite make sense to me. "But if he is so interested in military campaigns, won't he be gone for long periods of time?"

Hatshepsut looked at me, and her lips curved upwards. "You are smarter than you let on, aren't you, my little bird Miryam? If he is gone, then I will be free to live as I like, without interference." A scowl passed over her fine features. "I have seen how my mother lives and dies on every word and whim of my father, and it's not how I want to live. I want to be *free!"* On the last word, she stretched out her arms like bird wings and ran around the room laughing, an exhilarating mix of woman and child.

When I looked back on my life, that night with Hatshepsut stood out as a dividing line between my life as a slave and my future existence. I became the princess's confidante. I didn't just listen and say yes to everything but actually made some intelligent comments, enough to help her think through some of her statements. We drew close, and even though I started out that night sleeping on the little pallet at the foot of her bed like Dedi, sometime later while in the inky darkness we woke up and talked again, and the princess told me to come on her bed where we lay like sisters, taking comfort in one another.

I went home the next day, and though I was glad to see my parents and Aaron, the little mud hut looked, if possible, even dingier and poorer than before. I was ashamed to admit that several not-so-nice comments slipped from my lips over the next several weeks—comments that held Ema's cooking and housekeeping to a ridiculously high standard that compared to the superbly run and fully staffed palace of the king of the land. To her credit, Ema didn't take offense, though once or twice her eyes teared up. I had enough sense to refrain from bad behavior when Abba was around, but eventually even Aaron noticed.

One breathlessly hot afternoon he hurled himself at me and tackled me to the ground. "You are so mean!" he cried, hitting and kicking me.

"Ema, help me!" I yelled, scrabbling to get him off me, surprised at his strength for one so young and puny.

Ema merely raised one eyebrow, and I could swear she wore a trace of a smirk. "You handle this yourselves, children," she said, putting down the bowl of bread dough on the table. "I'm going out." She walked out the front door without a backward glance.

Horrified, I watched her go from in-between my fingers, which were shielding my face from Aaron's blows. Knowing I was on my own, I experienced a burst of energy and flipped him over, pinning him down until, panting from both the heat and exhaustion, he finally surrendered.

After we both staggered over to the table and poured ourselves some water, I said, "What is the matter with you, you little jerk?"

"Stop being so mean to Ema," he spat before bursting into tears.

I stared at his red, contorted face and didn't say anything. But I started thinking about how Ema had behaved, and how miserable and abusive I'd become. I felt the chastising presence of Elohim heavily upon me. I closed my eyes and tears seeped out from beneath my lashes, trickling down the sides of my face. It wasn't very long before Aaron came over and laid his head in my lap. I stroked his smooth head, and we stayed like that until Ema returned.

I heard her light step and opened my swollen eyes. "Are you two still alive?" she asked, only mildly sarcastic.

Aaron sprang up and hugged her around the waist. I slowly rose and hugged her as well, Aaron squeezed between us.

"I'm sorry, Ema," I whispered.

"For what, Miryam?" My goodness, she was tough.

I choked it out. "For being such a brat and making you feel bad."

"Do you know *why* I felt bad?"

"Because I was mean?"

"I can deal with that. No, I felt bad because you have had such contempt for our life. We may not live in a fancy palace with murals on the walls showing people being treated like animals (*ouch!*) but we know the love of Elohim here. Your father is a good man who loves God with all his heart, soul, mind, and strength. And he loves each one of us as well."

I hung my head in shame. "I'm sorry, Ema," I repeated.

My mother shook Aaron loose and lifted my face with her slender hand. "Look at me, Miryam," she commanded.

Slowly I raised my eyes to hers. We were now the same height, but I still felt so small. "I want you to listen to me. This is very important. It's not power and things that make a person important. No, what makes a person important is how she behaves in the eyes of Elohim. He expects us to do justice, love mercy, and walk humbly with Him. *That* is what makes a person important."

I nodded. "I understand, Ema."

My mother looked at me shrewdly. "I'm not convinced you do, Miryam. I want you to repeat after me. Ready?" I nodded again and in a firm, clear voice she said, "Elohim expects us to do justice,,,"

She paused and I said softly, "Elohim expects us to do justice…"

"Louder!"

"Elohim expects us to do justice…"

"Love mercy."

"Love mercy," I repeated, louder this time.

"And walk humbly with your God."

"And walk humbly with your—*my*, God."

"Good." Ema regarded me with love and tenderness in her beautiful eyes. You could drown in those eyes; they were so rich in understanding. My heart hurt with a sweet, piercing, ache. I wanted to experience life and freedom and a different reality than my childhood, yet at the same time I never wanted to leave Ema's side. I hugged her tight and rested my head on her shoulder. She kissed me on my forehead. It was as if we somehow knew that life was about to change.

*

It didn't take long. One week later the summons came. Hatshepsut wanted me to come to the palace *permanently*. Yes, I could return home occasionally, but she wanted me at the palace with her.

My last night at home was a tearful one. Abba prayed over me for a long time, while Aaron hugged my legs and Ema sat next to me, her arm around my waist, her other hand tenderly stroking my face. Both my parents were extremely concerned that I *never, never* forget Elohim. I assured them I wouldn't but still they seemed doubtful. Again and again, Abba quizzed me about the patriarchs, Adam and Eve, the land of Canaan, the promises to Abraham, and many other parts of our history as Hebrews. He cautioned me against worshiping the Egyptian gods, spitting on the ground in contempt as he dismissed them as "foul idols." Ema added some comments here and there, but mostly gazed at my face, memorizing my features.

Finally, I got impatient. "But Abba," I protested, "our father Joseph was second-in-command to Pharaoh! He spent most of his life in Egyptian palaces and never lost his relationship with God. Can't I do as well as him?"

For the first time since we had gotten the command for me to live at the palace, Abba's face crinkled into a wide smile. "Ah, my little bird Miryam," he exclaimed, clasping me to his chest and holding me tightly. "Yes, I will trust that God will keep you safe just as He protected Joseph."

I loved my family desperately, but I also knew that life in a mud hovel was not what I was looking to achieve. It was with barely concealed excitement that I said farewell the next day, bracing myself against their sadness. *I* was heading off to a glamorous life; *they* were sentenced to remaining in their dreary ones.

*

Now that I was at the palace all the time, I soon got to know everyone in Hatshepsut's family. I finally met her mother, Ahmose. Called by her title *Great Royal Wife*, she looked like an older, more delicate version of Hatshepsut. Mother and daughter could not have been more different in temperament, however. I soon saw what Hatshepsut meant by wanting to be free. Her mother was so concerned over her husband's response to everything that she lived in a perpetual state of nervous stress. She appeared to have no freedom of thought, but merely lived in a constant, daily struggle to please a man who already had the world at his fingertips. Of course, the second wife didn't help matters any.

Okay, I have to admit that I was fascinated by Mutnofret. Though the lesser of the two queens, she still, by force of personality, managed to make Ahmose cringe. Tall and buxom, she towered over her smaller rival, using her height in what I considered to be a menacing way. She favored wigs with extremely long braids that flowed down her back all the way to her waist. Slanted green eyes reminded one of a cat. No one at court was as skilled at flattery, or as charming. However, when Mutnofret decided that you were no longer necessary in her ascent to power, look out. She ruthlessly dropped people, crushing them like the worthless scum she considered them to be.

The pharaoh himself, Thutmose, seemed oblivious to the darker side of Mutnofret. She reserved the greatest amount of charm for him, dazzling him with her beauty, wit, and insidious ways. Since Thutmose was an intelligent man, I still to this day don't know whether or not he saw through Mutnofret's wiles or was completely taken in. Either way, he allowed her to run virtually unchecked, to the dismay of everyone else, especially Ahmose.

Mutnofret had one child by Thutmose: a son also named Thutmose. Five years younger than Hatshepsut, the kindest way to describe him was intensely annoying. Puny, whiny, and somewhat sickly, always with a runny nose and a querulous expression, he ran wild through the palace like the spoiled brat that he was. Hatshepsut despised him. She was constantly playing practical jokes on him, albeit so cleverly that though suspected as the perpetrator, she was never caught.

I wound up in the middle of these schemes, shaking with fear lest we be found out. It was me who slipped into his bedroom and dumped a whole bucket of beetles on his bed, and me who hid his favorite toy not once but ten times. Even though everyone knew that I only did Hatshepsut's bidding, still, I had no illusions that if I were caught I would get punished and not her. Eventually, Hatshepsut took pity on me and had others carry out her pranks. "It's not any fun with you skulking around white with fear," she told me.

Two children other than Hatshepsut and Amenmose were born to Queen Ahmose. Her second baby, a daughter named Nefrubity, died before her first birthday. I found out that there was a third child, a second son whom they called Wadjmose, who had a terrible accident at one of the construction sites the year before Hatshepsut rescued Baby Moses from the river. Fourteen years old at the time, he had talked his mother into being allowed to accompany the head foreman to the Karnak Temple Complex while his father and older brother Amenmose were off at war. Heedless and impetuous, Wadjmose apparently scampered up an older earthen ramp before he could be stopped. It collapsed, and he disappeared into the rubble and dust, his anguished screams the last sound he made in this world. Many heads rolled for that rash move, and good men still rotted in the dungeons of the Palace Guard. After hearing this story, and putting together the timing of it all, I wondered if that was why Thutmose issued his cruel decree to throw the Hebrew baby boys in the river. Perhaps he believed that others had to suffer over the deaths of their sons just like him.

Regardless, Ahmose had only two children left. She could do little more than wring her hands over Amenmose, a man by anyone's standards and not a boy to be coddled. That left Hatshepsut on which to focus her energy, and my princess decidedly did not like being overscrutinized. This led to many, many power struggles. Exhausting power struggles. By the time she was fifteen years old, Hatshepsut got the upper hand nine times out of ten. I couldn't help but feel sorry for Queen Ahmose. Her surviving children were every bit as authoritative and unyielding as their father. She didn't stand a chance.

When I looked back on that portion of my life, it really was amazing how quickly I acclimated to palace life. Though I have noticed that it doesn't take much time to get used to luxury whereas the reverse is an ordeal from which one may never recover. I shed my life as a poor slave like a butterfly sheds its cocoon. It didn't occur to me at the time that I was still a slave, only the surroundings had changed. And did I say that the food improved?

Unless you've spent most of your life eating the same dull diet—watery beer, barley bread, the few feeble vegetables Ema grew in our backyard—you cannot imagine what an intense thrill and delight it was to suddenly be fed at the table of a king. Fish, meat, leeks, cucumbers, melons, dates, almonds, garlic, exotic spices, honeyed treats, pistachios…the list went on.

After a few months on this new diet, I no longer resembled the former scrawny Miryam. Instead, at almost fourteen, I filled out enough to attract plenty of male stares when I walked around the palace grounds. My breasts never resembled overripe cantaloupes like Hatshepsut, but I got close enough. The added weight and healthy eating altered my face as well, and I developed a beauty I never realized I had.

One of the biggest physical differences between the Hebrews and the Egyptians was hair style. Even in the daunting, desert heat, the Hebrew men grew beards and kept their hair around ear length. The women grew their hair long, then braided and coiled it. In contrast, the Egyptians, men and women alike, mostly shaved their heads and then those who could afford it, wore wigs. The richer you were, the more numerous and elaborate the wigs. By the time I moved to the palace, Hatshepsut was past the childish "shaved head with a side ponytail look" and onto feminine adult wigs.

One of my best attributes when I was young was my long, black, silky hair. It shimmered down my back like a rippling waterfall. Though it was hot on my head, still, when I braided it and wrapped it in a bun at the nape of my neck, I felt that I looked so pretty it was worth the discomfort. Hatshepsut made a few comments here and there about my shaving my head and wearing wigs like everyone else, but as she gave me no direct order, I ignored her.

Two months into living at the palace, I understood the other reason for head shaving. I noticed that my head was itchy. At first, it didn't bother me very much, but after a week or so I scratched until I drew blood. One day Inet saw me rubbing furiously at my head and pulled me aside.

"Let's take a look." She parted my hair by my ears and peering closely.

"What is it?" I said.

"Don't you Hebrews get lice?" she asked.

Lice? I knew about lice, of course. How could one not? For some blessed reason, I had never gotten it. It hadn't occurred to me that what I escaped in a mud hovel, I caught at the king's palace. "I've never had lice," I said, somewhat proudly.

Inet regarded me through narrowed eyes. "Well, you have it now." She continued looking through my hair. "You have it bad, too. Come on." She took my arm and pulled me after her.

"Where are we going?"

"I'm cutting your hair to get rid of the lice."

My hair? My beautiful, long hair? "No!" I cried, attempting to pull away.

But Inet had a firm grasp on me. "Yes," she countered, through gritted teeth. "Look, you can't have lice around the princess. She'll be hysterical. Trust me. Plus, no one around here is going to spend hours each day combing through your hair." Inet stopped yanking me and looked me in the face. "Why do you think we Egyptian women shave our heads?" she demanded. "It's not just because of the heat, or because we like our pretty wigs." She shook her head. "No, it's these miserable lice. They're everywhere, and they're horribly annoying. Don't you think we would prefer to show off our own beautiful long hair and not wear those heavy wigs, if we could? But there aren't enough hours in a day to keep picking nits out of our hair." She paused, and then added, "I can't believe that you've never had lice."

As I sat miserably in a chair while my gorgeous tresses fell to the floor under Inet's relentless scissors, it occurred to me that Elohim had His hand of protection on my people in ways I had never realized. This caused me to wonder how else He watched over us, to my ignorance. This train of thought brought me back to the miracle of Moses' deliverance at the hand of my princess and what that could mean. So intent was I on this new revelation that I didn't notice that a razor had replaced the scissors in Inet's hand until she took the first swipe up my neck.

"Hey!" I yelled, startled out of my reverie. "What are you doing?"

"It's all coming off, Miryam," Inet explained patiently. "Otherwise the lice will eat you alive. Trust me."

I had no choice. Oh, what a sad day that was! At least I had relief from the horrible itching. When she had gotten rid of every last bit of hair, along with every nasty louse, Inet put some ointment on my scalp to heal the bites and covered my head with a white, square piece of linen, which she then secured by tying another piece of material around the crown of my head. My luscious, long locks lay scattered on the floor. Inet quickly swept up the hair and gave it to another servant to dispose of outside.

When I saw the princess later that day, she merely raised her eyebrows. "Lice," I explained.

"Ah." She smiled. "Now you're like an Egyptian."

Though meant as a compliment, I couldn't help but feel confused and cheapened by the comment. *Now I'm like them?* I thought. *Do I really want to be like them? Who am I—an Egyptian or a Hebrew?*

That night I had a dream. I saw Moses. He looked like the five-year-old he was, only he carried himself as a grown man of great authority. Holding a staff in his right hand, his voice thundered, "I need you to teach me the ways of our people. Do not deny Elohim!" This happened three times, and then I woke up.

I sat straight up, breathing hard. The room was pitch black and the only sound that of Hatshepsut lightly snoring. Slowly I lowered myself back down on my mat, my hand covering my racing heart. This was the most vivid dream I'd had in my young life. Suddenly I was overcome by a crushing wave of homesickness. Oh, how I wished that I could talk to Ema and Abba! Instead, I needed to work this out for myself.

A little thought pushed itself at the edge of my consciousness. I ignored it, but it pushed harder. I could—yes—I could ask Elohim to give me wisdom.

Shame gripped me. I hadn't paid much attention to my relationship with Elohim since coming to the palace. It was almost as if He wasn't as important as the Egyptian royalty. Now I knew that wasn't true, but what was true was my negligence. Before I left home, Abba made me promise to pray every morning, afternoon, and evening and to guard my heart from the evil influences around me. Instead, I had become totally immersed in all aspects of palace life. I hadn't even paid that much attention to Moses, as a five-year-old wasn't anywhere as intriguing as the shenanigans happening all around me.

I didn't get on my knees to pray as the last thing I wanted to do was wake Hatshepsut and go into a long explanation of what I was doing and why, while she stared at me blankly. Instead, I closed my eyes tightly and spoke to Elohim in my head. I repented for not putting Him first, and asked Him to show me how I could teach Moses about his heritage. "And Lord," I added at the end, "please restore my hair and keep lice far from me." No answers came to me but I felt very peaceful and drifted off to sleep.

*

The next morning, Amunet, one of the girls originally with Hatshepsut when she found Moses and now acting as Moses' nursemaid, woke up so ill that she was unable to leave her bed. Sighing deeply at the inconvenience, Hatshepsut told me to take her place. I could see the hand of Elohim in this turn of events and was amazed at the speed with which He moved. I immediately bowed to my princess and left for Moses' room, located down the hall from Hatshepsut.

Once there, I discovered him standing on a footstool, looking out his window.

"What are you doing?" I asked.

"Nothing," he answered without turning around. "Just watching."

"Watching for what?" I took a step forward.

"Anything." The little boy swiveled his head and smiled when he saw me. Then he frowned. "What are you doing here? Where's Ammie?"

"She's not feeling well today, so I'm here instead. Is that okay?"

"Uh-huh."

"Good. Can I look out the window with you?"

"Sure." Moses moved slightly to the left, and I took that as my signal to stand next to him at the window. Side by side, we stood guard, studying the early morning palace activity bustling beneath us. I said nothing, praying silently that Elohim would work things out according to His will. I didn't talk about anything important that day, but it was the beginning of a special rapport between me and Moses. We played all day and, at the end, I felt that I had made a start toward gaining entry into the little boy's heart.

*

It took another couple of months before I started telling him little stories about the history of our people. He loved it.

"Tell me again about Noah and the boat," he asked, slipping his hand into mine and standing close.

"Ark," I corrected as I scooped him into my lap.

"Ark," he repeated.

"Okay. A long time ago, a man named Noah obeyed the voice of Elohim and started building an enormous ark in a desert land far from any water…"

"Is Elohim Ra?" he interrupted. He still had some difficulty disassociating Elohim from the plethora of gods worshiped at the palace.

This was tricky. I could get in real trouble for saying bad things about any of the Egyptian gods. I took a deep breath and said quietly, "No, Elohim isn't Ra. Elohim is the God of the Hebrews. He stands alone."

Moses crinkled his brow as he tried to make sense of my politically correct answer. "I don't understand. If He's the God of the Hebrews, then what does that have to do with us?"

Oh my goodness, this boy is so smart. He's five, and I can't outthink him. "Well," I said carefully, "I'm a Hebrew."

"You?" His deep brown eyes widened in surprise.

"Yes," I said, "and," my stomach tightened, "so are—"

At that moment the door opened, and Inet came into the room. I immediately stopped talking, relieved that the decision of what to tell Moses had been taken from me. I wasn't sure what Hatshepsut wanted him to know about his birth, and I was afraid to ask her in case she forbade me to say anything to him. At any rate, the decision of what to do was put off…for now.

4

THE SUMMER AND FALL MONTHS FLEW BY. As winter approached, the palace servants began the involved task of packing up for the winter migration to the palace down south at Thebes. I was given permission to visit Abba and Ema for two days before we went. I was so grateful that I kissed Hatshepsut's feet.

"Stop it." She laughed. "Go, see your parents. Tell your mother that all is well with Moses."

Hatshepsut kept me on my toes. Some days she was as imperial as the pharaoh himself, and at other times sensitive to the needs of those around her, taking time to help them. I was never entirely sure which side of her I was going to get. That day I was thrilled it was the good Hatshepsut.

Laden with presents, I returned to my childhood home one sunny morning (they were almost all sunny). Aaron opened the door, and by the shocked look on his face, I could tell he wasn't entirely sure it was me. I was very aware of how different I looked, especially my hair, which was currently ear-length and covered by a wig, modest by Egyptian standards and outrageously extravagant by Hebrew standards.

"Aaron, it's me!" I set down my parcels, opened my arms, and he rushed into them. I hugged and hugged him, so happy to see his scrawny face.

"Who is it, Aaron?" Ema's voice preceded her to the door. I extricated myself from Aaron's hug and took a step toward her. It was so bright outside and so dark inside that at first I couldn't make out where she was, but then she stepped to the door and my heart did a flip. *Oh, how I've missed my mommy!*

"Ema!" I squealed, rushing toward her.

"Miryam! Oh, Miryam!" Ema dropped the towel she was holding and gathered me in her arms, holding me tightly. "Thank You, Elohim! Thank You for bringing my daughter back to me!" She sobbed as she embraced me. I cried, too, breathing in her familiar smell, a combination of garlic, herbs from the garden, and fermented bread dough. Finally, she pulled back and held me at arm's length, studying me. "Are you back?"

"Just for two days, Ema." I felt bad saying this because she looked so utterly disappointed. "I'm sorry. I'm leaving for Thebes with the palace staff and will be gone until spring."

Ema sighed. "Can't be helped. Come inside."

Aaron, in the meantime, was curiously examining my packages. "Don't look!" I ordered him, snatching a jar of honey away. Wait till Abba's home." He obeyed right away, which led me to believe that he *really* missed me.

Once inside, I stashed my belongings against the wall and hugged Ema again. "I've missed you so much!" I said.

Ema and I clung to each other. When we separated, she took a good hard look at me. "You have changed," she murmured. Her hand touched one of the braids from my wig. "What's this? What did you do to your hair?"

Instead of a long explanation, I said one word: "Lice."

"Lice?"

"Lice."

"Oh." I expected Ema to have lots to say about my hair, or lack thereof, but she didn't. Instead she clasped my face between her hands and gazed deeply into my eyes. "Are you okay, Miryam?"

"I think so, yes, Ema." I paused. "It's so different."

She nodded. "Tell me all about it."

So I did. I talked and talked and talked. I told her about Hatshepsut, Inet, Amunet, the Royal Queen, Mutnofret, and even that little brat, Thutmose. But mostly I told her about Moses. She was hungry for news of him, and I recalled every detail I could, describing his face, the sound of his voice, his antics, his obviously superior intelligence, our conversations about Elohim. When I finally slowed down, Ema was weeping.

"My little boy," she said. "How I yearn for him." She wiped a tear from her eye. "It's such a struggle, *beeti*, to have lost both of you to the palace, but I'm so grateful that God has given you such favor and you're able to help raise Moses."

Help raise him? I hadn't thought of it in quite those terms but now that Ema mentioned it, she was right. I *was* helping to raise him. Maybe there was more I could offer to do. *Hmmm.*

Abba returned home just as the sun was starting to sink down below the western horizon. The sky was awash in startling shades of pink and red. When he stood in the doorway, it looked like he was glowing red. I jumped off the mat where I had been laying and ran to him, clasping him hard around the waist.

"Abba!" I cried.

"Miryam? My Miryam!" Abba's bearded face broke into a huge grin. He held me to him and then spun me around, overjoyed to see me. "When did you get here?" he asked once he put me down.

"Just this morning."

Ema appeared behind me. "Don't get too excited, Amram. She's only here for two days."

"Two days, eh? Well, then we must make the most of them." He swayed a little on his feet, and Ema quickly grasped him by the elbow.

"Sit down and eat something. You must be exhausted after working all day in the hot sun."

Wordlessly, my father allowed himself to be drawn down to the eating mat. Ema propped some pillows behind him. "Aaron," she called, "get a basin of water."

Aaron took the basin and filled it up with water from a bucket he had gotten from the river earlier in the day, before I arrived. He brought it over to Abba, and Ema lifted one of Abba's feet, then the other, tenderly cleansing off the day's accumulation of dirt and sand. "Miryam," she said, without looking up from her task, "go get your father some food and drink."

I took a cup and poured some beer in it, then yanked a small packet of dates from one of my packages. Abba thirstily drained the cup, his eyes closed.

"Here, Abba," I said. "Have a date."

He opened his eyes. "Dates, hmm? More perks from the palace?"

I grinned, relieved to hear him joke. "You should see what I brought!" I skipped over to the wall where my parcels lay and hauled them over to where Abba was reclining.

"Oh, good!" enthused Aaron. "I can finally see them."

"Yes." I handed the first package to Abba. "It's your favorite."

Ema lit the sole oil lamp, shedding some much needed light in the room while Abba awkwardly untied the thin ribbons of papyrus with which I had sealed the parcel. His fingers were so stiff and coarsened from hard labor that he didn't have the dexterity necessary to complete the job. I helped him out, though I felt frightened of the bad shape he was in. Had he been like this when I'd left last spring? Surely I would have noticed if my big, strong Abba was so tired and...*elderly*. Wouldn't I? I glanced up and met Ema's eyes. She looked sad, and her mouth drooped at the corners. A few more strands of gray streaked her hair but overall she appeared pretty much the same. Abba, however, seemed ancient. Ancient and almost dead.

The package was finally untied, and honeyed almonds spilled out into Abba's hands. Inet had given us a packet of these when Ema was nursing Moses for pay, and Abba just *loved* them. Now, with shaking hands, he put a few into his mouth, chewing slowly. "Thank you, *beeti*. These are wonderful."

"Let me show you what else I brought," I said too enthusiastically, too forced. I handed out gifts to Ema, Abba, and Aaron, one by one. For Ema there was a simple gold bracelet. "To replace the one you sold," I told her. "It's actually one that Hatshepsut doesn't want anymore and gave to me."

Ema turned the bracelet around and around in her hands. "This is magnificent. It's worth so much. Are you sure?"

I hugged her, hard. "You're worth so much more."

She kissed me and slipped it on her slender wrist.

For Aaron there were two wooden balls, and last season's favorite board game, aseb. He eyed it questioningly.

"I'll show you how to play tomorrow," I promise. "It's easy."

I didn't know what to get for Abba, so I'd decided on as many food treats as I could get away with. Besides the honeyed almonds, there were dates, figs, pistachios, dried fish, and a whole long braid of garlic. (I knew how much he loved garlic.) I also gave Ema several meters of fine linen. She was thrilled. It felt so good to be able to bless my family. They looked poorer and shabbier than I remembered, but at the same time much more *real*. There was a weight and lack of frivolity to their words that I found reassuring. How I loved them.

*

The next two days sped by. It was painful to watch Abba leave for work. I wish I had thought to ask Hatshepsut to pardon him from his labors during my visit. Perhaps she could have him permanently pardoned from work? He was too old for this. How much was his body capable of handling? In between these difficult thoughts, I thoroughly enjoyed reconnecting with Ema, Aaron, Aunt Sarah and her huge brood, my friend Tamar, and several people from the neighborhood whose curiosity overcame their discretion. They stared at me and asked questions, too many questions. I realized I have learned much from Hatshepsut as I laughed, acted charming, and didn't hand out very much information at all. Even with Tamar, I was careful not to say anything that could get back to the palace and cause me to fall out of favor. I had seen how easy it was for that to happen. Looking around at the dismal row of huts and their overworked, half-starved Hebrew inhabitants, I was even more determined to escape this life. No way did I want to be sent home. I would make myself invaluable to Hatshepsut.

The night before I was to leave, Abba prayed over me. He laid both hands on my head, chanting a special prayer language in a singsong tone, a prayer language I did not understand. This went on for quite some time, until I grew weary of holding still. Suddenly, he broke into coherent words, loud and clear: "Blessed Elohim, Lord of heaven and earth and all that is, God of our fathers

Abraham, Isaac, and Jacob, I give to You this most precious daughter of mine and ask that You watch over her, protect her, keep her under your wing. Give her wisdom and discernment as she makes her way in a dangerous and confusing world. Most especially, be with her as she seeks to find ways to talk to Moses about You. Let her be as wise as a serpent and as innocent as a dove. We love and bless You always, in Your holy name. Amen."

"Amen," I repeated, along with Ema and Aaron.

I was crying the next morning as I said good-bye to Abba, Ema, and Aaron. I was not convinced that I would see Abba again. I clung to him, and he whispered in my hair, "It's all right, my little one. God is in control."

*

Thebes was amazing—no other way to describe it. Treacherously hot in the summer, it was absolutely perfect in the winter. The sweet scent of winter desert flowers filled the air, and the land on either side of the Nile was lush and green. There was a bigger variety of fruits and vegetables than up north, exotic tastes that were new to my more and more discerning palate. I was now floating down the Nile in a pleasure barge, quite unlike the much bigger boat that carried me, Hatshepsut, Moses, Inet, several dozen other people and mountains of luggage up the Nile a few weeks back. This boat had twelve slaves manning the oars, one Egyptian in charge, two soldiers, the princess, Moses, me, Inet and Amunet. It was heavenly. The princess reclined on cushions in the shade, sipping a drink while I sat next to her, watching Moses as he leaned over the side of the boat, gazing at the sparkling water as it disappears beneath our prow.

"Moses! Be careful," called Hatshepsut languidly. The river air and general laziness of the day had succeeded in drugging all of us. Even Inet had slowed down. I was close enough to Moses so that I could grab him should he slip—at least, if I could keep my own eyes open. I wasn't worried, though. Moses was a good boy—thoughtful and cautious. He wouldn't do anything reckless.

The whole area was magnificent. The city perched on the east side of the river, whereas on the west were enormous tombs and monuments to the kings and queens who had come before. Mountain after mountain faded into the distance, looking like the fingers of God pressed into the earth, culminating in *ta dehent,* the Peak. Thutmose was having his tomb prepared in anticipation of his death. He expected to head into the afterlife with his favorite possessions and vast quantities of his wealth. I knew from Abba that he was mistaken, but still I was awed by the grandeur and vastness of it all. The only thing that quenched my joy was the occasional glimpse of the slaves—sweaty, dirty, miserable—toiling endlessly under the hot sun. I knew they were mostly Hebrew slaves, and I felt pangs of guilt at living the high life while my people were suffering.

Despite my full days in the sun and the fresh air, I began to experience sleeplessness at night. Always one to fall asleep within minutes of my head hitting the pillow, this was a new, startling development. At first, I fretted and obsessed about not getting enough sleep. Finally, after a week of this, it dawned on me that Elohim was seeking my attention. It was my opportunity to spend time with Him.

So I did. Once Hatshepsut nodded off (for we talked in the dark most nights), I spent time praising and thanking Elohim for His greatness and His graciousness. I talked to Him about everything that happened during the course of the day and what I expected from tomorrow. Then I listened for the sound of His voice. Not much happened at first, but after a couple of weeks I got impressions in my spirit, as if He were telling me to say a certain thing, or do a certain thing. Once I received what He said, I fell into a deep sleep. I wasn't tired during the day anymore. I looked forward to being with Him, and anticipated our time together.

One night I heard actual words in my spirit and knew it was Him. "*Tell Moses you're his sister.*"

I gasped silently. "Oh, Lord, how can I? He'll say something, and Hatshepsut will be furious with me."

"Trust Me."

Trust Him.

"Trust..."

I grappled with this, fear rising up, a subterfuge against the love that had developed. Despite my youth, this was a major turning point in my life. I could choose what seemed to be the safe course, motivated by fear, or jump off the cliff and pray that I landed in the arms of Elohim.

I didn't make an immediate decision. I let it go for a few days, only to realize that the voice of my Lord grew fainter each night. A deep sorrow welled in my heart at the thought of losing the sweetness of my evening times with Him. On the third night I made my decision, expecting to lie awake until daybreak worrying about the possible consequences. Instead I fell asleep, dreaming of a land I had never seen, a green land of hills and valleys, brooks and waterfalls, lush and secure.

*

The next morning, Amunet was needed by Hatshepsut, and I was given solitary care of Moses. I breathed deeply, steadying my nerves, and headed to his room. His eyes brightened when he saw me, and he ran to hug me.

Bending down, I hugged him back. "You are my little brother, aren't you?"

"Yes," came the muffled response from against my chest.

"No, I mean it. You *are* my little brother."

Now he pulled back and regarded me quizzically. "You're not Mother's daughter." It was a statement, not a question. Moses was almost six years old and knew this was impossible.

"No, I am not Mother's daughter. I am her servant and her friend." I sat on the floor and gathered Moses onto my lap. "I have a secret that's just for the two of us."

He nodded solemnly, already understanding the palace was full of secrets.

"We have the same mother, and she's not Mother."

Moses' eyes widened and his lip quivered. I held him tighter. It was only obedience to Elohim that propelled me further. "You are a Hebrew—like me—and Mother rescued you when you were a baby. She loves you very much, and she is your mother now, but I am really your sister."

It was a lot for one little boy to handle. He was taking it in, up to a point, but I could see this news was enough for today.

"Then why am I a prince and you're a servant?"

Whoa. Out of the mouth of babes. Why am *I a servant and he's a prince?* "Because that's what Elohim has decided," I finally said, knowing it was indeed the true answer.

Moses accepted this. He disengaged from my grasp and stood. "Wanna play ball?"

*

For several days after that conversation, I was jumpy whenever Moses was around Hatshepsut. To my relief, he didn't act any differently and made no mention of what I told him. He was, however, more affectionate toward me. That was gratifying. As he got older, I caught glimpses of Abba and Ema in him: the shape of his nose, his smile, the way he walked, certain facial expressions. I noticed in particular that he inherited Abba's careful way with words. He didn't immediately answer a question, but thought it through thoroughly and then responded. This drove Hatshepsut crazy. She had an extremely quick wit and was highly impatient when kept waiting. But I could tell that she was trying with Moses in a way that she never did with others. She really did love him.

*

One day in late winter, a fleet of royal barges glided into Thebes. It was Amenmose, returning from his latest military expedition against the Syrians in the north. Rumors flew that he successfully fought his way to the Euphrates River. In any event, elaborate festivities were planned for his welcome.

Hatshepsut was beside herself with excitement. She was almost seventeen years old and more than ready to marry. Her father kept putting her off whenever she tried to talk to him about it. I had observed them together, and he treated her more like a junior wife than a daughter. Abba would *never* have given me preference over Ema, or run his hands up and down my arm in a suggestive way, or acted pouty and jealous if I were to talk about a boy I liked (not that I ever would have talked to him about a boy I liked anyway). Frankly, I was appalled with how the royal Egyptians treated close family members as potential sexual partners. It was disgusting. Ever since our father Abraham had married his half-sister Sarah four hundred years ago, we Hebrews had seriously cut down on that sort of thing.

Hatshepsut went all out getting dressed up for the first major feast honoring Amenmose. She chose a stunning blue linen dress threaded with real gold. The dress flaired at the bottom, and whenever she spun (which was often), flashes of light caught the gold. She insisted on wearing her wig with the longest braids, and then her new makeup girl, Tiy, tied the end of each braid with a slender strip of blue and gold that matched the dress, scooping the whole concoction up into an elaborate bun. Tiy then expertly applied blue eye kohl, exaggeratedly drawing the already almond shape of the princess's eyes into a more pronounced shape. Tiy then reddened her lips.

Next came the selection of a gorgeous gold and turquoise beaded necklace and earring combo, followed by a circlet of gold studded with blue stones of turquoise, carefully placed on her head and secured with scarab pins. Last but not least, Tiy anointed Hatshepsut behind the ears, on the wrists, and on the back of the knees with a costly bottle of lotus perfume. The smell was intoxicating.

Before the princess slipped on matching blue and gold sandals, we *oohed* and *ahhed* over her great beauty. She preened before us, enjoying the attention, even more excited about the male attention she knew would be forthcoming, and optimistically hopeful about Amenmose's response.

Amunet entered the room with Moses, who stared open-mouthed at the princess. "Mother," he said shyly, "you look like a great queen."

Smiling widely, Hatshepsut gathered him in her arms, kissing his cheek. The kiss left a perfect red imprint of her lips. Just as quickly, she released him.

I also got to go to the festivities. My dress, which I slipped into once the princess was ready, was a cream-colored linen with green trim. Though my hair had grown back to jaw-length (and I did not get lice again), I still wore a wig so as not to annoy Hatshepsut, who considered wigs to be the badge of a true Egyptian. My wig this evening had shoulder-length braids with bands of green linen every few centimeters up and down each braid. Tiy took a few minutes and helped me with my makeup, which was very kind of her. She used green eye kohl for me, and left my lips alone.

"They're already nice and red," she declared.

The final effect was thrilling. I gazed into the hand mirror and hardly recognized myself. The form-fitting dress emphasized my round breasts, small waist, and trim hips. I really looked good. Not nearly as good as Hatshepsut, of course, but really, really good.

The princess noticed. She came over to inspect me. I stood nervously, not used to this much attention. Finally, she took a step back and smiled. "You look fabulous, Miryam."

"Thank you, my Princess," I said humbly, head slightly bowed.

"You're very welcome. Don't give me any competition," she said, part jokingly, and part, I suspect, not.

"Also," she added, "take responsibility for Moses tonight and bring him up to bed after dessert is served."

"Yes, Princess," I answer.

Moses was wandering around the princess's apartments. His ears perked up when he heard his name. "Oh, good!" he sang out.

This would be his first official major party. We didn't have a clear decision from Hatshepsut before now.

"So go get him ready." She gestured for us to leave.

Moses took my hand, and we dashed down the hall to his room. I chose a gold and blue skirt similar to the material in Hatshepsut's dress. I also combed out and redid the side ponytail he sported.

As we descended the curving staircase, Moses gripped my hand. His eyes were wide, taking in all the action downstairs: servants scurrying, early guests arriving, platters of food swooping past on sturdy shoulders, heading to their final destinations whereupon they will be devoured like berries off a bush by hungry birds. I was entranced as well. This was life: heady, luxurious, exciting! I glanced down at the little boy so straight and intelligent beside me, his hand still in mine, and for the first time it occurred to me that his future was bright and unlimited. If Pharaoh hadn't tried to kill him, he would be a slave child in a small hut. But look! Look at what Elohim had accomplished!

Suddenly there was a commotion at the main entrance to the palace. I was Amenmose, arriving with a large entourage of men and women retainers and surrounded by dancing, music, and all sorts of ado. I hadn't seen him in a while, though I'd certainly heard enough about him from Hatshepsut. More than enough. He strutted like a peacock, arrogant and cocksure. I did not know a man could be so petted and fawned over. Still, he fascinated me. I stood in an alcove, hidden by a large, potted palm, clutching Moses' hand, and studied him.

"Come *on!*" Moses tugged at me, impatient to get downstairs. He'd spotted the platters of honeyed almonds and didn't want to huddle in a corner.

I couldn't blame him. "All right." I smiled down at him. "Let's go have fun."

And fun it was for the first several hours. Moses and I ate our way through the evening, and he got to run around and play with several other boys his age, sons of the nobility and another prince or two thrown in for good measure. Hatshepsut made a grand entrance about a half hour after we first came down and was immediately surrounded by an admiring throng. The place was jammed with beautiful women, but none with the commanding presence of my princess. I was proud of her. Every so often, I caught her watching the crowd, and I knew she was looking for Amenmose. He played her like a cat, though, and kept her at bay until she was just about ready to search for him. Then he appeared, bowing slightly before her, holding her hand to his lips, flattering her shamelessly.

When the sun sank below the western horizon, across the river, the torches were lit and the party took on a totally different aura. The music changed to a much faster tempo, the beer flowed even more abundantly, and legions of nursemaids gathered up their small charges. I went to pull Moses from his umpteenth intense game of tag from the gardens, walking past shadowy benches and potted palms.

Amenmose unexpectedly appeared right in front of me.

"Oh!" I gasped. "Your majesty." I bowed low to the ground, eyes averted.

"Arise." Amenmose's hand gripped me around the upper arm in a steely vise, pulling me to my feet. "You are growing up *very* nicely." He leered, his face close to mine, his breath reeking of beer. "I think I'll take a closer look." He yanked me toward the shrubbery, into the dark, one hand still on my arm and the other groping my breast. My heart was beating so hard I thought it would pop out of my chest.

"My lord," I stammer, terrified, "Hatshepsut..."

I shudder to think what would have happened if Inet hadn't briskly walked down the garden path, calling, "Miryam! Miryam!"

Amenmose cursed under his breath before releasing me.

"Oh, there you are," Inet exclaimed brightly, catching sight of the two of us. "I am so sorry, your majesty," she said to Amenmose, dropping to her knees in a curtsey, "but my lady the princess has specifically commanded that Miryam take the boy up to bed now."

"Of course." Brusquely he waved her away and left without a backward glance.

As soon as he was out of sight, Inet's whole demeanor changed. She grabbed me by the shoulders and looked into my eyes. "What happened, Miryam? What did he do?"

I was shaking, I was still so frightened. At first I couldn't respond, which made her even more determined to get an answer. We walked slowly toward the part of the garden where Moses was playing, and my heart slowed down. At last I was able to say, "Nothing."

"Nothing? Really nothing?"

"Nothing really bad," I amended.

"You must keep away from him," she admonished me. "There will be hell to pay if the princess were to find out."

"Inet, I didn't—"

"Shh, don't even say it. I know. Believe me, I know."

"But how can I stay away from him if he seeks me out?"

"You're just going to have to be more clever than him." She studied me carefully. "And from what I've seen of you, my dear," and a small smile played about her lips, "that shouldn't be overly difficult."

*

I don't know which was harder—avoiding Amenmose or hiding from Hatshepsut that I was avoiding Amenmose. She received just enough encouragement from him at the party so that she talked about him incessantly.

I never liked him before, but now I totally despised him. It was difficult to keep an interested face and not let my true feelings slip.

I tried to keep away from Amenmose and even asked Elohim for help, but there was so much interaction between him and Hatshepsut that it was inevitable we'd be in the same room. He stared at me way too much, occasionally touching his tongue to his upper lip, reminding me more of a wild cat contemplating an especially tasty piece of fish than a man looking at a slave girl.

One night Hatshepsut burst into her room where I was putting fresh sheets on her bed. "Miryam!" she practically shouted, shutting the door behind her and twirling in circles.

"Oh my goodness!" I clutched a folded sheet to my chest. "What's happened?"

Hatshepsut stopped spinning and smiled broadly at me. "Father has finally agreed to wed me to Amenmose!"

I stared at her. "No," I faltered.

"Yes!" she sang delightedly. "I am sooo happy!"

"My Princess, do you thin—"

"Think what?" she asked.

I felt wretched. What could I say? Tell her that her intended was a despicable swine? Besides, all these noble men cheated on their wives. It constantly happened around me. I didn't want the princess to turn on me, though. I had to stay here with Moses.

"Think that you're too young?" I managed.

"Ha!" She laughed. "I'm practically seventeen. It's more like too old."

She was right. At seventeen and sixteen we were ripe to be married. There was nothing I could do except hope that Amenmose would quickly lose interest in me. I forced myself to smile as wide as I could.

"I'm so happy for you, my Princess. I will pray to my God that your husband will be the most devoted and loving husband in all the world."

Hatshepsut laughed again. "We'll see what happens. Anyway, Father is announcing the betrothal tonight."

"Tonight! Already?"

She nodded. "We plan on being wed upon returning to Memphis."

Ugh.

The marriage announcement that night turned into quite the party. Beer and wine flowed like a river, and the kitchen staff worked like mad keeping up with the demand for food. I had never seen Hatshepsut happier. She sat next to Amenmose, beaming and gorgeous. He seemed taken with her, as well.

Watching them, I relaxed. *Why would such a powerful man want me, especially when he has the princess?* For the first time in weeks, I breathed a deep sigh of relief, and a huge weight rolled off my shoulders.

The party went very late. Hatshepsut drank more than I've ever seen her drink and finally staggered off to bed around 3 a.m. I helped her undress, covered her with a light sheet, and, exhausted, slipped into my own bed. I'd scarcely closed my eyes when one of the princess's guards roused me.

"Come on, wake up," he whispered, shaking me lightly.

"What?" I sat up, groggily opening my eyes. "What's wrong?"

"You're wanted in the little master's room. Those are the only instructions I've been given. Sorry to wake you so late," he added.

Moses!

Suddenly, wide awake, I quickly got up, donned a light robe, and left the room. The guard nodded at me, taking up his position at the door. I felt my way along the dark corridor, turned the corner, and was a few feet from Moses' room when I was suddenly grabbed from behind. A large, coarse hand was clamped over my mouth and I was half-carried, half-dragged past Moses' room, up the stairs, and into one of the many guest chambers. Whoever had pulled me in let go and disappeared, the door clicking shut behind me.

The room was pitch black. "Hello?" I tentatively called out. "Who's in here?" Trembling, I wrapped my robe more tightly around my chest and stood with folded arms, waiting.

A low laugh came from behind me. Terrified, I started to scream, only to find another hand over my mouth, this one smooth and smelling like expensive perfume. "Don't be afraid, my little bird. This is your lucky night."

A sick dread washed over me as I recognized the voice of Amenmose. *Elohim, help me!* I prayed.

Amenmose released his hand from my mouth. "If you know what's good for you, don't scream."

"What do you want with me?" I asked, my mouth dry.

The prince ran one hand through my hair and encircled my waist with his other. "I'm tired of you running away from me," he hissed.

"But I'm not—"

"Quiet! I will not be spoken back to by a Hebrew slut!" Abruptly, he picked me up and threw me onto the bed.

"No! Wait!" I sobbed, scooting back toward the wall.

"Shut up!" Amenmose slapped me across the face before raping me.

*

The night seemed endless. I was drowning in a nightmare. Again and again, I silently called out to Elohim, but no rescue came. At one point, I stopped crying and merely hung on, enduring. Finally, *finally*, the first weak rays of the sun peeked up over the horizon. This roused Amenmose, and he got off the bed and pulled on some clothes.

"I'm leaving." He leered. "But don't think you can tell Hatshepsut what's happened here." He jabbed a finger at me. *"You'll* wind up in the dungeon. *I'm* the next pharaoh, *I'm* her master, and she'll believe *me*."

Numbly, I stared at him. Frankly, I was so shell-shocked that his words barely made any sense. Later, I would recall what he said, blanching at the threat to my life.

Five minutes after he left, Inet entered the room. She sat on the bed and held me as I cried. "Shh, shh," she soothed. Then she took a wet cloth and cleaned me, tenderly and gingerly.

"What of Moses?" I asked when I stopped crying long enough to form words.

"He's fine. It was a ruse to get you out of your bed."

"You *knew?"*

She shook her head. "No. Only this morning, when one of the prince's aides came for me. I'm so sorry, Miryam. I feel for you. I know what you're going through." Her brown eyes were thoughtful and sad.

"How could you know?" I snapped bitterly. "How could anyone?"

Inet sighed. "You're far from the only one who has been used in this fashion. The old pharaoh, Amenhotep, took me for himself when I was even younger than you."

My eyes filled again. *What a nasty world!* "I'm sorry, Inet."

"Yes," she said. "Aren't we all."

"Has the princess asked for me?"

Inet shook her head. "She is still sleeping. I suspect that after the amount of wine she drank last night she will be sleeping for quite a while yet. However, I will tell her that you aren't feeling well, and I think it best to keep you away from her. Miryam, you can't talk to her about what happened."

"That's what," I couldn't bring myself to say the name, *"he* said."

"Well, *he's* right. She will side with Amenmose no matter what she knows to be the truth. The only one who'll get hurt will be you."

"So what do I do now?" I wailed, my voice rising on the last word.

"Now? Sweetie, I hate to break this to you, but you're a slave. Pharaoh owns you. He and his son can do whatever they want, and you can either grin and bear it, or…"

I supplied the rest. "Or die. Isn't that what you were going to say?

Inet gazed at me, brushing a strand of hair off my face in a motherly gesture that made my heart lurch. "It's a definite possibility."

"There are worse things than death," I said defiantly.

"Are there?" she said mildly. "And what of Moses?"

Moses! Of course she was right. I had a God-given responsibility to care for Moses as long as I was able. And technically, I was still able. If I weren't around to teach Moses about Elohim, then who would? This was too much, too hard, I was too young.

"Moses needs me." I sobbed.

"Yes," said Inet. "He does."

5

YOU WOULD THINK THAT I WOULD IMMEDIATELY GO TO ELOHIM and pour out my heart, but I didn't. Other than Inet that first morning, who was the closest thing to a mother I currently had, I kept the whole incident bottled up inside. It was Elohim who spoke to me first.

A week after Amenmose raped me, a frantic week of skulking around the palace and steering as clear of him as I was able, I was lying on my pallet at the foot of Hatshepsut's bed. She had drifted off to sleep, and I was unsuccessfully attempting to as well. I curled up on my left side and closed my eyes when I heard:

"Miryam!"

My eyes flew open, and I was afraid to breathe. I heard my name a second time and realized that the voice was coming from within me.

"Oh, Elohim," I breathed, and then the tears came. "Oh, my Lord, I am so frightened. I want Ema and Abba!" I sobbed into my pillow for a while, drenching it with my tears, until I heard His voice again.

"Do not be anxious or afraid. Amenmose will pay for touching My anointed."

"Me, Lord? I'm Your anointed?"

"I have set you and your family apart for My purposes and they will not be thwarted. Know without a doubt that I am more powerful than any king or pharaoh. Rest in My love, do My will, teach Moses about Me. Sleep well, My daughter."

Filled with the gloriousness of His presence, I fell deeply, soundly, asleep.

*

Amenmose didn't get another opportunity to molest me. Though she didn't act suspicious, Hatshepsut kept me close to her those next few weeks, close enough that any pursuit would have been very obvious. This son of Pharaoh was nothing if not a military strategist, and as such did not want to turn Hatshepsut against him unnecessarily.

After the entire royal party left Thebes and returned to Memphis, Thutmose got word from his messengers in the southernmost part of Egypt that there was unrest in Nubia. Scowling, he sent for Amenmose.

"Go there and teach those upstarts a lesson, my son," he said. "Show them the supreme might of Mother Egypt."

Hatshepsut threw a tantrum when she found out Amenmose was leaving again so soon. The marriage was due to be consummated the following month and would most likely have to be postponed. I used all my latent acting ability to hide my elation. I was also completely stunned with the speed with which Elohim had worked to remove Amenmose from my life. I floated on air for several days. I felt so invincible.

Less than two months later word came of Amenmose's death. A stray arrow from the enemy pierced his heart. It was said that he died instantly. I expected Hatshepsut to be inconsolable after the fuss she made upon his leaving, but she was strangely stoic.

"The gods have willed it," she said quietly.

"Why do you say that?" I asked.

She was silent for several minutes, then responded, "There is no greater warrior than Amenmose. He has no equal. No one can touch him unless the gods let them."

Frankly, I was amazed at her spiritual insight. How I longed to explain the way of Elohim to her more fully and not let her mistakenly linger in her misguided beliefs about multiple gods, but I knew enough to know this was not the time. Instead, I knelt by her feet and wrapped my arms around her. She allowed me to offer comfort, for which I was grateful. Two tears slid down her perfect cheekbones, but otherwise no sobs escaped her throat.

*

Not long after these events, I was allowed to go home for a short visit. Unhappily, I arrived to find Abba on his deathbed. Various friends and relatives did what they could to help out as he was no longer able to work and the family no longer qualified for daily rations. Ema apologetically told me that she sold the bracelet I gave her so they could buy food, adding that she was being careful with the proceeds as she hoped to be able to live off the sale for a long time to come.

I cringed when I thought about the feasting I had done as opposed to the meager existence Ema, Abba, and Aaron lived. "Please don't apologize!" I begged Ema. "I'll try to bring you more money."

"You're such a good daughter," Ema murmured as she put yet another fresh wet cloth on Abba's forehead. He looked so worn and wasted, lying on the mat in our hut. Even so, his high forehead and long nose bespoke a quiet dignity I rarely saw at court. I felt terrible leaving them but at the same time was determined to petition the princess for funds to take care of them.

Before I left, I told Ema what happened with Amenmose and how God had intervened. She sat very quietly, her eyes getting rounder and rounder. When I finished, she hugged me for a very long time, pain etched into her features. Eventually, she pulled back enough to gaze into my eyes. "I have to tell you something. I am completely convinced that Elohim has an amazing plan of salvation for our people and that it includes you, Aaron, and Moses."

"All of us? Even Aaron?"

Ema gave me one of her looks. "Yes, even Aaron."

We both peered toward Abba's bed. Aaron had fallen asleep the night before huddled next to Abba and lay there still, father and son asleep together.

"He's going to miss Abba," I stated.

"The whole village is going to miss Abba," said Ema sadly.

I placed my hand on hers. "Tell me more about what you think the future holds," I urged.

Ema sighed. She squeezed my hand. "I think," she said slowly, "that it was God's plan all along for Hatshepsut to find Moses, and also for her to take such a liking to you."

I nodded and she continued.

"It was not His will that you were harmed by that evil man." She grimaced. "We won't always be slaves. God made a promise to our fathers Abraham, Isaac, and Jacob. He promised us the land of Canaan for our own. He showed Abraham the land and proclaimed it as an inheritance for Abraham's children, who would be as numerous as the stars in the sky and the sand on the seashore."

"We're certainly that," I said, thinking about the multitudes of Hebrews, too many to count.

"Yes. I can feel in my bones that the time of our servitude is coming to an end. Our people need a leader, one who has been trained to be a leader. What are the chances that one of ours would be in the palace of Pharaoh, raised as one of Pharaoh's own? What are the chances?" Ema's eyes grew intense and she gripped my hand even tighter. "Miryam, you must guide Moses, you must make sure that he is trained like the other princes. Watch out for him, speak blessings over him. My daughter, my son." Ema began to cry, and we held each other. Her tears were not only for the daughter who had been violated, but for the son she gave up and for the husband she was about to lose, and the life that had been so terribly hard. Would that she were right and this nightmare of slavery was crumbling! Would that Elohim in His power and great might had deigned to use me and my family to accomplish His will! What honor! Suddenly, I felt so totally, utterly unworthy. The responsibility was crushing.

"I cannot do it," I whispered. "It's too much to bear the weight of a nation on my shoulders. I cannot do it."

"Not on your shoulders, my daughter." Abba's frail voice wafted across the room. Startled that he was awake, Ema and I turned toward him. "Always remember the weight is on Elohim's shoulders. *He* can bear it, *He* can perform miracles, *He* can change the direction of the world, bringing princes to naught and reducing the rulers of this world to nothing. Do not fear Pharaoh and his ilk. No sooner are they planted, no sooner are they sown, no sooner do they take root in the ground, then He blows on them and they wither, the whirlwind sweeps them away like chaff. Always, always remember that those who hope in Elohim will renew their strength. They will soar on wings like eagles, they will run and not grow weary, they will walk and not be faint. This is you, my beloved Miryam." Abba stopped talking and started to cough. He had used every last bit of energy to share his final words of wisdom with me. I noticed that Aaron had awakened and was likewise listening intently. Neither of us would ever forget these words.

I ran over and threw my arms around Abba's neck, hugging myself against his shallow chest. "I love you so much!" I cried.

He patted me gently on the back. "God be with you, my child." Closing his eyes, clearly exhausted from the effort of talking so much, he lapsed back into sleep. I kissed him on the forehead and extricated myself. It was not an easy parting for any of us that day.

*

Back at the palace, Hatshepsut generously offered to give Ema and Abba a stipend to live on as Abba was no longer able to work. This greatly relieved my mind. However, it wasn't more than a week before I received word that Abba had died. Overcome with grief, I immediately prepared to go home and sit shiva with Ema and Aaron, the seven-day period of mourning. I even worked up enough nerve to ask if I could take Moses, knowing how encouraging that would be for Ema.

Hatshepsut looked at me strangely. "Moses?" she asked. "Why?"

I thought the answer was pretty obvious but hesitated to spell it out for her. "Because," I began, about to say "it's his father" but under the princess's direct unblinking gaze, I faltered. Instead I said, "Because I love having him with me, and I know my mother would be thrilled to see him."

"No," said Hatshepsut, and in that short one-syllable negative word was the shutting down of Moses' Hebrew identity. I heard it, I knew it, and so did she. There was nothing left but to acquiesce.

"As you wish, my Princess. Thank you for allowing me to attend my father's burial." I gave a stiff bow and waited to be dismissed.

"Miryam!"

"Yes, my Princess?"

Hatshepsut sighed, and in that sigh I saw the beginning of many hard decisions, decades of difficult choices, against personal relationships and in favor of what would be best for Egypt. A long, dreary road of royal responsibility.

"It is my love for Moses that constrains me. For his own protection, he must be raised as a true prince of Egypt. Do you understand?"

Did I understand? Young as I was, I knew enough of court life to know that the other princes and nobles vied for power in a backstabbing manner held in check only by Pharaoh himself. Yes, the princess was correct. Any perceived weakness in Moses would draw enemies to him like bees to honey. The temporary joy of reuniting him with Ema and introducing him to our family was ultimately not worth the danger it would thrust him in. Yes, I understood.

"Yes," I said softly, raising my eyes to hers. "Yes."

*

I mourned for my father for several months. Even though I hadn't lived under his roof for years, I still knew that he was there, which offered me a level of security. Now, with Abba gone, that security seemed gossamer-thin. I leaned on Elohim more and more, forced to trust that He would take care of me no matter what, more aware than ever that it was only He who kept me from harm.

After my ugly experience with Amenmose, I was really careful around any potential "admirers." Even so, I had several near misses with men who noticed me. Though I didn't think I measured up to what I considered to be Hatshepsut's stunning beauty (her transformation from cute girl to gorgeous woman never ceased to amaze me), nevertheless I had—and I say this modestly—achieved a certain level of attractiveness which seemed to excite more than enough men so as to make my life dangerous.

In the midst of all this, I didn't understand why Elohim had allowed me to be abused by Amenmose. I pondered over it for a long time. Finally, I came to the conclusion that the world was filled with sin, bad things happened, and sometimes they even happened to me, but Elohim could bring me through it and make me a stronger person if I didn't give in to bitterness and anger.

Hatshepsut exuded sexuality these days. She had kept herself in check in anticipation of marriage to Amenmose, but now that that dream was dead, and no suitable alternate choice for a husband presented itself, she started looking around. I was concerned that she would get herself in trouble with her father and attempted to restrain her, but she would have none of it.

"What is the problem, Miryam?" She glowered at me one day when I had suggested a more modest outfit for a dinner party she was attending that evening.

"Nothing, my Princess. I just don't want your beauty to so overwhelm the men tonight that they lose their senses," I said, holding out a dress somewhat less see-through and low cut than the one she had picked.

Hatshepsut smiled. "If any of them do lose their senses, what of it?"

"You may find a mess on your hands, my Princess."

Hatshepsut considered me thoughtfully for a few minutes before pointing to her original dress choice. "Help me into that, Miryam. Your concern is touching but don't doubt in my ability to take care of myself." She waved a finger in my face and laughed.

Sighing, I tugged the dress over her head and stood back disapprovingly as she ran her hands over her full breasts, flat stomach, and rounded hips, emphasizing everything that could be emphasized.

"How do I look?"

"Exceedingly gorgeous, my Princess, but also like trouble."

Once again, Hatshepsut wagged a finger in my face. "Don't presume on my unaccountable liking for you," she said, but her tone was light-hearted.

I saw him even before she did. *Oh no,* I inwardly groaned. I recognized the type instantly. Even among the Hebrews we had men like that, though not too many, praise the heavens. He was really, really, really, I mean, *really* good looking, cocky, arrogant, strutting like a peacock, confident that the world was his for the asking. Of course, when one was a slave, life crushed one soon enough, but if one was the son and heir of a nobleman, like this young man, then the amount of damage that could be caused to the local female populace and beyond was staggering to contemplate. Khufu had been at court with his parents as a boy, but not in a few years. I judged him to be about twenty years old. His skin was like gleaming bronze, his perfect teeth flashed blindingly white, his facial features were absolutely symmetrical, his eyes deep and intense, his hair glossy black and *just right.* Not a gram of spare fat clung to his muscled physique, yet he was not bulkily muscular but rather lithe and sensual, like a leopard. I have to admit he was the most beautiful man I had ever seen. Every woman in the room was eyeing him, and I knew that neither would Hatshepsut be immune to his charms.

I noticed that Khufu worked his way through the crowd like a pro: a smile here, a kiss on the cheek there, a bow and a compliment to a twittering older lady here, a manly handshake to a senior noble there. He kept angling toward the princess. He had a plan, I just knew it. When he finally made eye contact with her, it was like a small explosion went off. They stared at each other for several seconds until Hatshepsut inclined her head, which was Khufu's signal to come forward and greet her, which he did.

They were inseparable the rest of the evening. When the princess finally came to bed, close to dawn, she was giddy with excitement.

"Oh, Miryam," she purred, lying undressed on her bed in the sultry summer night, "Khufu is the most magnificent man I have ever met!"

"But what can come of this, my Princess?" I asked. "You know that the law of Egypt prohibits you from marrying outside of immediate royalty."

Hatshepsut gave a low laugh. "Who's talking about marriage?" I heard the bed creak as she turned on her side. "I'm going to enjoy myself."

"But what of your father?"

"He won't know."

"Are you so sure? He seems to know everything that goes on."

"Well, even if he did find out," said Hatshepsut, her voice slightly less confident than a moment ago, "I don't think he would care that much. He does this kind of thing all the time."

But he's a man, I thought. I didn't say it out loud, though. I had given enough input for one day.

It didn't take long before my lady lost her virginity. I was terrified she would get pregnant, but she used Inet's trick of a hollowed-out lemon and managed to escape those particular set of consequences. However, she didn't escape *all* consequences.

One day, when Hatshepsut had slipped away for a tête-à-tête with Khufu, the Great Royal Wife, Ahmose, came to Hatshepsut's apartments with her entourage. It was rare that she came here, seemingly content to see her daughter when their paths crossed on more social occasions, and every so often in her own apartments, by request.

Inet was immediately respectful. "How can I serve you, my Queen?" she asked, sinking to the floor in a curtsey. The rest of us took our cue from Inet and likewise bowed down.

"I am looking for my daughter," the queen answered, her noble demeanor a contrast with her sad and anxious eyes.

"She is taking a walk in the gardens, my Queen," smoothly lied Inet. "Shall I send her to your rooms when she returns?"

The queen looked flustered. She had not expected to be put off. "Yes. Have her come immediately," she said, turning around and walking off, her entourage trailing along after her.

Once they had all gone, Inet, Dedi, and I all looked at each other nervously. "When is she expected back?" Dedi asked.

Inet shook her head. "We can't wait for her to show up." She turned to me. "Miryam, go find the princess."

Why was it always me? "But—"

"Fast!"

I jumped.

"And take Moses with you! Make it look like you're on a play outing with him."

I nodded as I quickly walked to Moses' rooms. He was studying with his tutor, a gentle, refined, short, bald-headed man named Sinuhe. They looked up when I entered, Moses smiling when he saw me, Sinuhe frowning.

"What is it, Miryam?" asked Sinuhe.

"I'm so sorry to intrude, but I need to take Moses out for some air, sir. It's almost lunchtime, and Inet would like him to take a break and spend a few minutes with his mother, the princess."

"This is highly unusual. We are not yet finished with our lesson." Sinuhe gestured to the open papyrus on the table. Lately, he had been teaching Moses the history of Egypt.

"I promise I'll have him back right after lunch. I'm sorry to intrude, sir."

Sinuhe stood. "All right." He sighed. "But be careful with my star pupil." Moses beamed when he said that, and I momentarily forgot my haste to find Hatshepsut. I was so proud of my little brother! Eight years old and already he had a reputation for brilliance. If only Abba could have seen this!

"Come on!" Moses tugged at my hand and together we headed out of the room. Like any young boy, he was delighted to be sprung a little early from school. "Did Mother call for me?" he asked eagerly.

I shook my head, sorry to disappoint him. "Your royal grandmother wants to see her," I explained. "Inet thought it best if you and I were to go get her."

This wasn't the most logical explanation ever given, but Moses seemed content with the answer. We took a private side exit from the palace that led directly to the gardens. I knew the princess's secret hiding place, and if I were to go near it and play loudly with Moses, she would hear me and meet us. I prayed she was there.

We made as much noise as we could, which wasn't hard, and presently Hatshepsut emerged on the path behind us.

"Ema!" shouted Moses joyfully.

"Hello, my son," responded the princess, appearing seemingly from nowhere, flushed and a bit breathless. She kissed him briefly on both cheeks.

"My Princess," I said, bowing. "I thought you would be interested to know that the Great Royal Wife came looking for you earlier."

Hatshepsut's eyes flickered. *Not unlike a clever snake*, came the unbidden thought. "Ah," she said. "I will go directly to her."

"I think that is most wise, my Princess."

"May I come with you, Mother?" asked Moses.

"Later, my love, later," she said, dismissing him.

Disappointed, he kicked at a pebble. Hatshepsut walked swiftly away, toward the wing of the palace that housed the Great Royal Wife.

I put my hand on Moses' shoulders. "Come on, Moses. Let's throw a ball around before you go in for lunch."

He scowled. "I don't want to anymore."

I knew he was upset with the lack of attention from the princess. Ever since she had taken up with Khufu, the princess barely noticed Moses. He really was very attached to her, and not a toy that could be set aside at will.

I sat on a stone bench under a shady palm tree. "Come here, Moses." I patted the empty space on the bench next to me.

He ignored me, glowering in the direction the princess had gone.

"Moses!" I called, more firmly.

That got him. Grudgingly, he stomped over and threw himself down on the bench. As he tended to be a most obedient child and rarely, if ever, disobeyed, I knew he must be really upset.

"Talk to me."

Silence. I put my arm around his shoulders and he shook it off, moving a little further down the bench from me.

"Look, Moses," I began. "I know your mother has been, well, *distracted*, lately..."

He rolled his eyes. I ignored him and continued. "But she loves you very, very much. She's not like other mothers, I know," again, the eye roll, "but she occupies an extremely important position in our country. She's not always available, but since she loves you so much, she's arranged for other people to be there for you. Like me." I smiled brightly.

This got him. "You?" He laughed, a short, hollow laugh. "You're my sister, not my mother."

"Shh, don't repeat that," I warned, glancing nervously around. "Remember, it's our secret."

"I remember." His brown eyes turned to mine, and I noticed they were wet. "Tell me about my real mother," he suddenly said.

I hesitated. This was the first time he had asked me about Ema. I wasn't sure how much to tell. Silently, I prayed for Elohim to direct my words. "What do you want to know?"

"Everything!" I was startled by the fierceness of his tone.

"You've been thinking about this, haven't you?"

"A lot," he admitted.

I described Ema, and Abba, and Aaron. I didn't go into detail about the harshness of our lives, or the poverty we endured. I didn't mention Abba's recent death, but Moses brought it up.

"When you left for your—our—father's burial, it was all I could think about. I wanted so much to go with you," he said shyly, not looking at me.

My heart constricted within my chest. "Oh Moses, how I wish I could have brought you!"

"Then why didn't you?"

"Because your mother—wisely—forbade it. You have to understand that this court is a snake pit. Even though you're only a child, you have real enemies out there who envy your position. They'll do anything to unseat you, and if you start attaching yourself to a slave family, it'll be your undoing. And mine. Understand?"

"Understood," he said, but he wasn't smiling.

*

When Hatshepsut came back from her meeting with her mother, she was not at all pleased. Queen Ahmose apparently knew all about Khufu and ordered the princess to immediately end the relationship. Since she so rarely disciplined the princess about *anything*, her warning held weight. "You do *not* want your father to become involved with this," she cautioned Hatshepsut.

Hatshepsut stormed and stomped around her rooms, as angry as I've ever seen her. She had tasted illicit love and was exceedingly loath to let it go. In fact, she seemed obsessed with Khufu. All of us did our best to keep out of her way. Royalty having hissy fits was not a safe thing.

"I'm going to see Khufu to say good-bye," she said the next day, when she had calmed down.

"I don't think that's a good idea, my Princess," remonstrated Inet gently. "Your mother the queen has already forbade you from seeing him. What if your father finds out about this?"

The princess pursed her lips together in a straight line. She frowned. "He won't," she optimistically declared. "And if he does, I'll handle it."

Those words struck fear into all our hearts. All our hearts, except one, that is.

That evening, Hatshepsut had a rendezvous with Khufu. I believe her intention was to let him know they had to part, but one thing led to another and they lost all control sexually. One of Thutmose's servants, doing some work in the garden, overheard them and peeked into their secret hiding place. Aghast, this loyal man let the pharaoh know what he had seen.

When Thutmose summoned Hatshepsut later that night, well past an hour when he normally would have ever seen her, we were all literally quaking in our sandals. Even my stubborn, supercilious princess was worried.

"Do you think he knows?" she asked me as I arranged a light shawl around her shoulders before walking her to the guards who would escort her to the pharaoh's private inner room.

"Probably, my lady," I said, lowering my eyes. An idea popped unbidden into my head. "Can I pray to my God for you?"

Hatshepsut sighed. "Sure. It can't hurt."

"And might even do a lot of good," I couldn't resist adding. I placed my hand on her forearm. "Dear Elohim, please bless and protect Princess Hatshepsut as she goes forth to meet with her father. May only good things come from this. Keep her safe and calm her spirit. In Your mighty name."

I looked up at Hatshepsut and was gratified to see that her eyes were wet. "Thank you, Miryam," she whispered, and then she was gone.

After she left, I knelt on my bed mat and prayed fervently that Elohim would rescue her from this mess and turn her heart to Him. I was so encouraged that she allowed me to pray for her. *Wouldn't it be wild,* I thought, *if she were to become a believer in the one true God, and free all the Hebrew slaves? Look how Elohim opened her heart to baby Moses.*

It was so late when the princess returned that I had fallen asleep sitting up. Hearing her step on the threshold of the door roused me. I sprang up to meet her.

"How did it go, my Princess?"

The princess shook her head at me and walked over to her bed, where she sat down heavily. From the light of the wall torches I could see tears streaming down her cheeks. I sank to her feet and waited.

After a while, she spoke. "I am so unhappy I want to jump off the top of the nearest pyramid."

"What happened?"

"My father was furious about Khufu. He said all sorts of hurtful things to me."

I stroked her arm. "I'm so sorry, my Princess."

"No, there's more. He's marrying me off."

"To...?"

"That annoying pest, Thutmose!" she spat, her voice harsh from tears and anger.

Thutmose! The princess's half-brother! "Oh, my Princess," I commiserated. "Surely this is far off, as the prince is barely thirteen years old!"

She shook her head, clenching and unclenching her fists as tears spilled vehemently down her cheeks. "He says he can't trust me. The marriage will take place next month." She thoroughly broke down and I sat next to her, holding her while she cried. It sounded as if her heart were breaking in two.

"Oh, Miryam!" she cried, clutching at me. "I love Khufu! I can't bear to be separated from him!"

I held her, stroking her back and making soothing sounds while she got all the angst out of her system. Finally she fell asleep from sheer exhaustion.

*

The next day, Hatshepsut arose looking hollow-eyed but determined. She refused breakfast, wrapped a robe around herself, and sat at her writing desk, furiously scratching a series of hieroglyphics onto a small sheet of papyrus. When she had finished, she blew on the ink, waved it in the air a few times to dry it, and rolled it up tightly, tying it in the middle with a piece of string.

"Here," she said, handing the tube to me. "Find Khufu."

My stomach lurched. "But—your father—my Princess—"

"I must see him one last time," she insisted, eyes burning.

Reluctantly, I took the letter and concealed it under my dress. I knew that if I were caught, life as a slave would look like a cruise on the Nile in comparison. Sighing a bit too loudly, I sought out my favorite guard, Hapu. Secretly, I thought he was perfectly named as he always seemed happy, which was not by any means a given in this life.

An older man with a family (I had discovered that he had three girls and one son), Hapu currently stood sentry outside the palace at the gate by the front walkway, the shade from a tall palm his only protection against the already intense heat of the day. Posture erect, he could have been a statue except for the slight twitch under his left eye. I approached him slowly, not pleased with my task.

"Ah, Miryam!" he said upon spotting me, a broad smile spreading across his face. "How's my favorite handmaiden?"

I couldn't help but smile back at him despite my anxious mood. He was so likable. "I'm pretty good, Hapu."

"So what brings you out here on such a hot morning?"

"Well," I said, lowering my face and glancing quickly around, making sure no one was in hearing distance, "I have a communication from the princess for a certain person. But it has to be kept secret."

Hapu's face lost some of its merriment. "Hmm. Don't give it to me here. I'll meet you when I'm on break over by the big palm in the garden. Can you do that?"

I nodded. "She'll be very grateful, Hapu." I knew he stood to earn some gold for his service.

"Hmph," was all he said.

I scurried away.

Everything went off as planned, but it was a tense time before we got back any news. Finally, on the third day, Hapu was assigned guard duty at the entrance to the princess's apartments. He motioned for me to come close. "I have some news," he whispered.

"Yes?"

His face was grim. "The message has been delivered. However, there is no response as the young man in question has been given a post in the army and is currently on his way to Nubia. He's not expected back for several years, if ever."

I drew in my breath sharply. Thutmose obviously played hard ball. At least Khufu escaped with his life and his manhood. Hatshepsut had been terrified that her father would have him forcibly castrated as a penalty for defiling the princess.

I broke the news to the princess. It was not as bad as it could have been, but the chances of her ever seeing her lover again were virtually nil. She took it better than I thought she would.

"Okay," she said, hours later, after spending much of the day pacing back and forth throughout her apartments. "Okay. I understand what to do."

I was afraid to ask. She whirled and faced me. "Ask me," she demanded.

"What will you do?"

"I'm going to marry Thutmose like Father said, but I'm going to totally control him. When he's the next pharaoh, I will take over and rule Egypt!"

I didn't know what to say to this. I mean, what could I say? I thought she was upset and delusional. While it was true that Egypt had two women rulers in her history—Neithikret and Sobeknefru—it had been three hundred years since the last one. Still, the thought *was* an intriguing one. Could Hatshepsut be Elohim's choice for freeing the Hebrews? Certainly she was sympathetic in ways most royalty weren't, what with Moses being her son and me her confidante. It couldn't get much worse than her father, Old Thutmose, tossing babies into the Nile for the crocodiles to feed on, the monster! In fact, the more I thought about it, the more I liked the idea.

"Not a bad idea," I slowly agreed.

Hatshepsut smiled, the first one in days. "We must plan carefully."

6

AFTER HAPSHEPSUT AND THUTMOSE II WERE OFFICIALLY WED, not much changed initially. The pharaoh had deemed his son too young for sexual intercourse for at least a year, and so the marriage had yet to be consummated. Politics within the palace subtly shifted with the princess's new status as she would be the next Great Royal Wife once her father went to his eternal reward. Both Ahmose and Mutnofret paid more attention to the princess. Ahmose looked to train her daughter more fully in the role she would one day fulfill, whereas Mutnofret gloried in her position as Hatshepsut's mother-in-law and sought to use it to her own advantage. The young Thutmose himself was just as much of a jerk as always. He was easily ten years away from being mature enough to be married, but then no one asked my opinion, or his either, for that matter.

The princess had a pretty good attitude about the whole liaison, seeing as how she had a master plan up her sleeve. But about three months in, even the dangling cucumber on a stick long-term reward of being the most powerful leader in the known world lost some of its allure when compared to the daily annoyance of dealing with Mutnofret and her son.

"I'm going to put an asp in that woman's bed!" fumed Hatshepsut after a particularly trying day. Inet, Amunet, and I were all attending her. Inet was massaging scented oil into the princess's neck and shoulders, I was painting her fingernails, and Amunet worked on her toes.

"Breathe deeply," urged Inet. "Relax."

"I *am* relaxed." Hatshepsut glared.

Amunet and I glanced at each other. "I saw that!" snapped Hatshepsut. We both sighed at the same time. "And I heard that," she added. All of us started giggling, and the princess felt much better, at least for an hour.

*

I had pretty much been able to keep out of Mutnofret's way, and so she didn't bother me nearly as much as she annoyed Hatshepsut, who was thrown into her path more frequently. Later that week, however, I finally saw firsthand the danger she posed.

It had to do with Moses. Suddenly, now that her son was wed to the princess, she became aware of his existence in a way she hadn't previously. I was walking downstairs with him so as to go out to the garden for his after-lunch playtime when Mutnofret and six of her regular attendants popped out of whatever room they were in and saw us.

"You!" she said loudly, pointing a finger with a long, red fingernail at me.

My heart thumped. "Me, my lady?"

"Yes, girl. Come over here with the boy."

Slowly we descended the stairs and approached her. She was very tall and imposing, using one long arm to impatiently flip several of her long braids off her shoulder. She stared at us with narrowed eyes.

Moses and I didn't say anything. We stood quietly while she examined us. Moses, though several years younger than Thutmose, had not looked up to him with the adoration younger boys have for older boys. Rather, he steered clear of Thutmose as much as possible, his instinct for self-preservation kicking in. To say that he had been less than thrilled upon learning that this was his new stepfather is the understatement of the dynasty. I could tell by the way he rigidly stood that he was acutely uncomfortable.

"So," Mutnofret said to Moses, her attendants twittering behind her, "have you paid proper homage to your new father?"

"Uh...I...," Moses stuttered, nervousness shutting down his tongue.

"Come on, boy," impatiently snapped Mutnofret. "Out with it!"

Moses gulped, his face red. "Yes, I have," he mumbled, staring at the floor.

"Good," snapped Mutnofret, and with a sigh of exasperation, signaled to her attendants and stalked off, the women following at her heels like a swarm of confused bees.

Moses and I stood in place until she had disappeared from sight. Then we clasped hands and raced to the garden, not stopping until we had reached our favorite hiding place. We were both breathing hard, and collapsed on the ground.

Moses spoke first. "I hate her."

I glanced around nervously. "Shh!"

"Why should I be quiet?" he demanded. "I'm a prince of Egypt, not a slave to be bullied about!"

I stared at him in surprise. Where was the compliant, gentle child of just this morning? When had he suddenly become aggressive? "First of all, trust me when I say you're *no* slave. I know what it's like to be a slave and you are definitely *not it!*"

He had the wisdom to look somewhat ashamed at this.

"Also," I continued, "even your mother, the princess Hatshepsut, the pharaoh's only daughter and the wife of the next pharaoh, has to suck it up around that woman. You must realize that she is extremely ambitious and will seek to destroy anyone who is a threat to her or her son." I wagged my finger in his face. "So don't do anything stupid."

Moses was relatively quiet the rest of the day. I could tell he was deep in thought, which always made me nervous. Although he was barely nine years old, I could discern in him a dignity like Abba's, and a stubbornness not unlike Ema's. I was so used to thinking of him as a small child to be protected that these first stirrings promising manhood totally shocked me. How could I protect a grown man, with all of the aggressive, violent urges men have? Especially the nobility, who have little to restrain them. *Moses won't have me as an extra nursemaid forever. In a few short years, he'll be out of my sphere of influence, learning military maneuvers and state protocol. What if he gets in a fight with someone? What if he is perceived as a threat to someone at the palace and they seek to harm him? What then?*

I had worked myself into such a tizzy by evening that I went and spoke to Hatshepsut concerning my fears. I told her what had occurred that morning with her mother-in-law, and then shared my concerns regarding Moses. At first she didn't even want to talk about Moses, so infuriated was she over yet another Mutnofret offense.

"I wish Father could see what a witch that woman is!" she exclaimed. "Her precious son is the heir to the throne. What else does she want?"

I tried not to dwell on the thought that this question came from a woman who had more than just about anyone else on earth, yet was scheming to take over the kingship from her husband. This discussion was really about Moses. I steered it back in that direction.

"I think she wants everything, my Princess, which is why," I said hurriedly, before she could interrupt with more Mutnofret insults, "I am concerned that she not view Moses as a threat, or seek to harm him in any way."

The princess's eyes glittered. "Thank you, Miryam, but don't you worry about Moses. He's mine, and I'll take care of him." With that, she turned away and summoned Amunet to help take off her wig for the night. The conversation was obviously over.

Lying in bed that night, I spoke to Elohim, talking to Him about all my concerns. I was still miffed about the princess saying Moses was *hers*, as if I had nothing to do with him, or my father when he was alive, or Ema, or

Aaron. I was unprepared for His response.

"Miryam," came the Voice. I heard it inside my head but knew it wasn't me.

Yes, my Lord?

"Miryam, I gave Moses to Hatshepsut. She is right: he does belong to her. Do not be jealous. Your job is to teach him about Me. I will protect him."

I lay in the dark, waiting, but He said nothing more to me that night.

*

The days passed quickly. Almost a full year went by, a year in which I saw Ema and Aaron only twice, but I had learned to be grateful for whatever opportunity I had to look upon their beloved faces. I shared with Ema the word I received from Elohim, and she confirmed it was Him.

"Yes, yes. I totally agree." Her fingers busily kneaded bread dough as she spoke, a wisp of hair falling into her eyes. She blew it off her face. "It is obvious to me that God has his hand on Moses in a spectacular way. You and Aaron, too," she added loyally.

"How is Aaron?"

"It's not easy. A boy without a father, and both you and Moses at the palace, well..." She let her words drift down slowly as she pounded the bread dough some more. "He's busy fetching and carrying and doing plenty around here. I try not to give him too much time to think about things. You know, though," she said, looking up at me, "that he's almost old enough to work."

Work! You mean that vicious slave labor where the Egyptian taskmasters drain every drop of vitality out of a man, under the scorching desert sun. Was it already time for my little brother to take on that daunting, thankless life? "Oh, Ema! Maybe the princess will do something for us."

"Try," my mother urged. "I'm afraid for him."

Fear, so much fear. Fear at the palace, fear at home. Yet Elohim wants us to trust Him. I know it, Ema knows it, but we are still afraid. Why, Elohim? Why can't we trust You like we should?

I thought about this as I returned to the palace, and as I went about my daily tasks. I thought about trust and fear for several weeks. I didn't want to be locked into a cycle of fearfulness. I didn't want to mistrust every man I saw, wondering if I was going to be raped again. I didn't want to worry ceaselessly about Ema and Aaron, vulnerable without Abba in the slave village. I didn't want to be afraid of Mutnofret and her minions. I didn't want to live in fear lest Hatshepsut no longer wanted me as her friend, or found out about

Amenmose and decided to blame me. I wanted to wake up every morning and be filled with joy.

So I determined that was what I would do: every morning when I awoke, I rejoiced in Elohim. I tried to let my gentleness be evident to all, though I've been told I *can* be prickly. I refused to be anxious about anything, but by prayer, with thanksgiving, I presented my requests to God, trusting that God's *shalom,* which transcends all understanding, would guard my heart and mind.

I also made an active attempt to monitor my thoughts. I tried to only think on those things which were true, noble, right, pure, lovely, admirable, excellent or praiseworthy. Obviously, I wasn't always successful, but I was a lot better off than when I hadn't made *any* effort.

Interestingly enough, the first one who noticed the new me was Moses.

"You're different," he said one day when I was straightening up his room.

I crawled out from beneath his bed where I had been gathering little missing game pieces. "You think so?" I asked, pleased. "In what way?"

"You're calmer, and happier." He seemed to be thinking of something else, but just shook his head and added, "That's all."

I smiled broadly. "That's a lot. Thanks for noticing."

"Anytime." He smiled back at me.

I floated on clouds the rest of the day, supremely pleased that the new Miryam—the joyful, calm one as opposed to the fearful, anxious one—was apparent to my little brother. I was also intrigued by the awareness and thoughtfulness Moses exhibited at such a young age. Hmm.

*

The next week, Hatshepsut had a crisis in her life such that I was involuntarily drawn into the maelstrom of her emotion and, as desperately as I tried to hang on to my new sense of well-being, it was ripped right out of my hands by the intensity of her angst.

The furor began when the pharaoh, old Thutmose, decided that it was time for Thutmose and Hatshepsut to consummate their marriage. The princess could barely stand being in the same room as her half-brother/husband and was sickened by the thought of having to sleep with him. Well, apparently the actual event was even worse than the imagined one. Having been initiated into sex by Khufu, the youthful, inept, unattractive Thutmose was, in comparison, much worse than he may have seemed under other circumstances.

Hatshepsut did her best to bear it—closing her eyes and thinking of

Memphis, that sort of thing—but could not quite control her sighs of *get it over with already, you're such an idiot.* Both were crying by the time The Act was accomplished: she with rage and he with humiliation. Needless to say, this did not move forward the agenda of controlling Thutmose. The pharaoh had another little chat with the princess, and when she returned from her father's private quarters, she locked herself in her inner room and did not emerge for hours.

"Can't be easy to have to give oneself to a little boy after that gorgeous Khufu," remarked Amunet in a break from her usual discretion.

"Mmm," I said, not sure if this line of conversation was going to get us in trouble. No matter how empty the room looked, I had learned that there were always ears listening at the palace. Amunet, however, was not to be dissuaded by my lack of response.

"I mean," she continued, "after having a *real* man, to be stuck with that nauseating twirp—"

"Amunet!" I exclaimed, glancing around, horrified. "Shh!" I lowered my voice to a whisper. "You don't know who's around!"

"Oh, Miryam!" She gave me a disdainful look. "You're a little paranoid, don't you think?"

Maybe you would be too, if you were raped by the prince, I thought angrily. Which wasn't a good thing to think, because suddenly that whole nasty incident was in my mind again, and I lost all my joy.

Hatshepsut was mean for days. It took a good two weeks for her to calm down, not to mention one late night session where I had to talk her out of disguising herself and finding Khufu in Nubia. We both knew that was a completely insane plan, but Hatshepsut wasn't entirely rational where Khufu was concerned. Time had eased her obsession with him somewhat, but she was still very smitten. And when life got difficult, as it had recently, all her longings and desires and wishes got tangled up in one packet, and that packet was called "Khufu."

"He was the embodiment of all that was perfect in a man, was he not, Miryam?" she said dreamily, while lying in bed late one night.

"He was very handsome, yes, my Princess," I carefully responded.

I heard Hatshepsut's head turn on the pillow. "I can hear the *but* in your voice. What are you thinking?" she demanded.

"My Princess, I just think that in taking advantage of you, his character was less than desirable."

"Ha!" She laughed. "No one took advantage of me. I wanted him."

"For your own good, though, he should have stood against desire."

The princess sighed loudly. "For my own good? What is my own good?"

I propped myself up on one elbow and looked across the dark room at the shape of the princess in her bed. "Your own good is what's good for Egypt. You've told me yourself that you want to have control when Thutmose is king. I think that's a good idea because, and I mean no disrespect, my Princess, but from what I've seen of the young man and his mother, I think the land will be much better off with a woman of your caliber and intelligence ruling it than with a man of the character and intelligence of your esteemed husband."

A very un-princesslike guffaw came from the bed. "Oh, Miryam!" she gasped, in between peals of laughter. "You are brilliant. Brilliant! Taking you from the slave village was the best thing I ever did. You have learned well."

Pleased as I was by the princess's praise, I did not think it prudent to inform her that any wisdom I had came from Elohim and my father Amram, and not so much from the Egyptian court, though I could not deny the court had taught me some things.

After that night, I saw a change in Hatshepsut. She gradually let go of her feelings for Khufu and turned her energies to learning about matters of kingship. Throwing her considerable charm at her father, she sought to make herself indispensible to him. And it worked. It has always been my opinion that she was head and shoulders superior in intelligence to any of the pharaoh's children, and I could tell that the old pharaoh Thutmose was convinced of that as well. He forgave her for her dalliance with Khufu (now that she was properly behaved), allowing her more and more freedom within the court.

Soon Hatshepsut was sitting beside her father during affairs of state. The youthful Thutmose was of course included, but he had little aptitude for military and international affairs, tending to fidget and complain if proceedings with various ambassadors and advisors went on for too long. Hatshepsut strongly encouraged him to be part of things, knowing that with his contrary nature this would cause him to do the opposite.

In the midst of all this, Moses was growing up. It had not gone unnoticed by the princess that here was a young boy who was blessed with all the attributes her husband/brother lacked. Handsome, healthy, strong, discreet, analytical, bright as can be, honest, thoughtful, and did I mention handsome? I was very proud of my brother, and I knew that the princess was planning for Moses to be intimately involved with all she did.

Such being the case, Hatshepsut engaged new tutors for Moses in addition to Sinuhe. Teachers of military strategy, domestic affairs, agriculture, foreign relations, geography, engineering and math kept my little prince busy from morning till dinner. Evenings found him engaged in directed play: board games that emphasized advanced thinking and forward strategy. I was Moses' opponent at first, but he quickly outgrew me. We chose his fellow game players carefully. Never was he pitted against Thutmose, though on the occasional evenings when Hatshepsut played against him, I could see that Moses was thrilled by her attention. He concentrated hardest at those times.

The day came when Moses beat the princess at a game that took quite a bit of intellectual skill. He methodically captured her last game piece, and then leaned back and looked at her with a pleased smile.

"So, Mother," he said, grinning. "Do you concede?"

Hatshepsut abruptly stood and walked around the table to Moses. For one crazy second I thought she was going to slap him. Instead, she cradled his face in her long, slender hands and stared intently into his eyes. "You, my son, are absolutely brilliant! You are my gift from the gods."

God, not gods, I mentally corrected.

Moses was inordinately pleased. His cheeks and the top of his ears turned pink, and he gazed downward. "Thank you, most blessed mother."

Of all my many memories of Hatshepsut and Moses, this is the image I cherish most: this season of love and wonder and promise.

*

The old pharaoh, Thutmose I, died the spring Moses turned twelve. It was a sudden death, for he did not seem unhealthy or ailing. Indeed, the bald, muscular, strong-featured king had been vital and energetic for a man of fifty summers. Rumor had it that his heart simply gave out one night as he lay in his bed. When his servants tried to rouse him the following morning, they found his body cold and lifeless.

My princess mourned for her father deeply. Though their relationship had been tumultuous in places, not the least of which was the Khufu episode, the last several years in which she had worked with her father, learning how to govern this vast land of Egypt, succeeded in bringing them close to each other. So close, that both Mutnofret and Queen Ahmose had shown signs of jealousy, jealousy which had only been kept in check by the old king himself.

Conveniently, Thutmose had died while we were still at Thebes, so we didn't need to travel down from Memphis in order to bury him in the Valley of the Kings. Not as conveniently, it got awfully hot down south as the seventy-day mourning period slowly wore on. I had never stayed in Thebes later than mid-spring, but now we were approaching summer. The workmen and artisans put in sixteen-hour days, frantically prepping Thutmose's tomb, which was cut into the rock in the eastern half of the valley, below the cliffs.

With the original shock of Thutmose's death, the family drew together, forgetting petty jealousies and grievances. However, as the days passed and the temperatures rose, so did the tempers. Mutnofret, apparently believing herself invincible now that her son was within sight of his coronation, picked a fight with Hatshepsut over something stupid. Their ensuing raging battle was finally ended by young Thutmose II, who wonderfully and unexpectedly sided with his queen and not his mother. This proved to be a huge turning point in his relationship with Hatshepsut. It also did wonders for the defusing of Mutnofret, as the rest of us saw that her power was not to be limitless.

Finally, the day of the burial arrived. The old pharaoh had been washed, had his internal organs removed, was embalmed, had his head covered in a gold-and-pottery cobra-designed linen cap, was covered in precious jewels, was bandaged mummy-fashion, had his hands and feet covered in gold. Finally, an ornate gold death mask, ornamented with lapis lazuli, carnelian, quartz, pieces of pottery, and topped with another cobra, was placed on his face. He lay within four coffins: the first of quartzite, the second two of wood, and the final of solid gold. The resulting enormously heavy coffin was then transported by a sacred boat to the west bank where it would be carried to the cut-out tomb in the sheer cliff towering over the so-called Valley of the Kings.

I was one of the many women thrust into the job of mourner. Loud wailing and breast-beating simply was not my style, nor was I inclined to mourn the passing of one who had been responsible for so many Hebrew baby deaths. To decline, however, was suicide. Instead, I stayed within the middle of the crush of women, wordlessly opening and closing my mouth, my silence unnoticed in the midst of the cacophony.

In the coolness of dawn, we trailed the pharaoh's coffin into the valley and up a narrow, winding path to the entrance of the newly prepared tomb. By the time we arrived, the sun had risen enough to make it hot, but still bearable. Thutmose had opted out of a pyramid; he was fascinated by the cliff formations at Thebes and wanted to spend eternity there. I strongly suspected he was spending eternity somewhere entirely different and probably much hotter than the desert at noonday, but this thought I wisely kept to myself.

It was the responsibility of Thutmose II as son and heir to be next to the priest performing the opening of the mouth ceremony. This ensured that the dead king could breathe, eat, and speak in the next life. Trembling slightly both from nerves and the fatigue of the climb up the cliff, Thutmose appeared very somber as he stood next to Kha, the high priest of Anubis, the jackal god of the afterlife. Kha was dressed in ceremonial splendor, complete with a jackal head propped on his own head, sort of a cross between a hat and a wig. It looked dreadfully hot and uncomfortable. It also made him look really demonic and creepy. I shuddered at the sight.

The funeral rites went on and on. In addition to the royal family, nobles and workers, priests from the various cults, and the mob of women mourners, there was also a caravan of items for Thutmose to have with him in his tomb, lest he be without the comforts of home in the afterlife. Wagonload upon wagonload of vases, art, bedding, cookware, food supplies, and little statues signifying the different people in his life, were pulled up the cliff by half-naked men whose muscles strained and whose bodies were slick with sweat. *Thank You, Elohim, that one of us isn't getting locked up in there with him*, I silently prayed.

I saw Moses standing behind and to the left of Hatshepsut. I couldn't help but feel that these elaborate Egyptian funeral rites didn't seem as bizarre to him as they did to me. I had had enough of a childhood immersed in the things of Elohim so as to have a natural aversion to a belief system that I was convinced was not only wrong, but downright evil. In their misguided conviction that the demons they worshipped were actual gods, the Egyptians sentenced themselves to a hell without the one true God: the God of Abraham, Isaac, Jacob, and Joseph. The God of Amram and Jochebed. The God of Miryam, Aaron, and Moses.

"Hey, Miryam! Pay attention!" hissed Amunet softly as she elbowed me in the ribs. Lost in my own thoughts, I hadn't noticed that the funeral ceremony had finally, *finally* ended, and we were lining up to march back down the cliff side. By now the sun had risen far enough in the sky such that the shadows were short, and the heat intense. Sweat trickled down my back and between my breasts, and my throat felt parched and dry. I think everyone was getting nudged and annoyed. What a relief when we reached the relative coolness of the palace, and were able to have a drink of water!

The next few hours were busy as the palace servants (myself included) attended to the needs of the royal family and their guests. Eventually, I was able to sit, eat, and relax.

Not for long, though. As I closed my eyes, slowly chewing a piece of bread topped with dried fish paste and oil, Amunet sat down next to me.

"Hey, Miryam," she said, jingling her many bracelets.

I opened one eye. "Amunet."

"You look tired," she commented.

"Yes," I acknowledged. "Hence the closed eyes."

Amunet laughed. She didn't take the hint. "Hey," she said again, a little shyly. "Can I talk to you?"

I sighed and took another bite of fish and bread. "Speak," I said grandly.

Amunet hesitated.

That was unlike her. Interested, I looked at her...really looked at her. Though we have worked together for many years, Amunet tended to keep her opinions to herself and I never felt like I got to know her. As a result, I sort of kept my first image of her in my head, when I was a terrified little girl crouching by the river and she was the very young, beautiful maidservant of the princess. Though still beautiful, she is now in her late twenties, her youthfulness faded. I see worry in her eyes, and tiny lines at the corners of her lids. Her mouth droops a bit, and the vivacity that used to come unbidden now seems forced.

I gently touched her arm. "Tell me," I prod.

"It's the old king's death," she began, twisting her hands nervously.

"Yes?"

"If I tell you something, will you keep it a secret?"

Uh-oh. Secrets are never good. "Of course," I answered, smiling at her, attempting to put her at ease.

She looked away from me as she spoke, her eyes straying to the wall just behind me and to my right. "Not long after you came to be with us, he called me to his bed." She paused and I nodded. It was not a surprising story. "I became pregnant and lost the baby," she continued, speaking very softly, tears misting her eyes. "After that, his interest in me waned but made it so that no other man could have me.

"Today at his funeral I was happy he was dead because I hate him. But it's not fair if he gets to dance into the afterlife and not have to pay for what he did. I kept hoping the priest would mess up the opening of the mouth ceremony and sew it shut instead so he would starve in the afterlife, but it all went perfectly."

When Amunet mentioned sewing the old king's mouth shut, my eyes widened and I involuntarily looked around me to make sure no one was near. Once I ascertained we were totally alone, I felt free to laugh.

Amunet smiled wryly. She leaned forward and spoke intensely once my laughter died down. "I know what he did to the Hebrew babies, Miryam. I know what he would have done to Moses. But you have such joy! I come to you because I want what you have."

I sat back in amazement. She noticed my joy! After all these years, someone noticed there was a difference about me. And it was the least likely person too. I would have thought that Inet, who knew what I had gone through, would have approached me well before Amunet. Ah, the ways of Elohim are inscrutable. Who can know them?

"Anything good you see in me comes from Elohim," I told her.

"Elohim is the Hebrew god, right?"

"Well, that's the thing. He's a lot more than just our God. He's the God of the whole earth."

Amunet wrinkled her brow. "You mean like Ra?"

I shook my head. "No, not at all like Ra." I scanned around us again. Good. We were still very much alone. I kept my voice low. "You see, Amunet, Elohim is the *only* God."

Amunet looked really confused. "How can he be the only god? There's Ra, and Anubis, and Amun, and Isis, and Mut—"

"No," I said patiently. "You don't get it. They're not gods. They're demons."

"What?" exclaimed Amunet, her mouth dropping in shock. "That's crazy! How can you say such a thing?"

"I can say it because it's true. They even *look* like demons, with their jackal and cow and snake heads. Elohim is nothing like that." I realized as I was speaking that if Amunet *wasn't* serious about finding out why I was the way I was, that I could be forfeiting my life, speaking like this. But for some reason, I didn't care. Watching the pagan customs at Pharaoh's funeral emboldened me to speak forth the truth. I felt carried along by something much bigger than myself. I felt empowered by God.

"Then what does Elohim look like?"

"I don't know."

"You don't know?"

"He's invisible. He's compared Himself to a lion, but He doesn't *look* like a lion. He's compared Himself to an eagle, but He doesn't look like an eagle, either. He did say that He made man in His own image, so perhaps He looks like a man." *Like my father Amram with his long, white beard.* "He's told us not to make images of Him. We're to trust when He speaks, and not attempt to recreate Him to fit our concept of who He should be."

This was a lot of new information for Amunet, and she nodded gamely as she sought to take it all in. I could see that she had lots of questions.

"But how do you know what He's said? How do you hear Him and not see Him?"

"That's a great question. There are people He's spoken to in the past, either through visions or by manifesting Himself in human form in a way they could comprehend. For example, our Father Abraham, who lived roughly five hundred years ago in our homeland of Canaan, often spoke to God. There's one story where God showed up in the form of three men, and ate and drank with Abraham. Then they walked and talked together, and God shared His plan to destroy the wicked cities of Sodom and Gomorrah."

"That's amazing!" exclaimed Amunet. "Has he come to you like that?"

"Not exactly. But I have heard Him speak, and He's directed me to do things that have turned out just like He said. It's faith to do those things."

"Faith?"

"Faith. That's when you don't have any assurance that something is going to go well but you do it because you're convinced Elohim said to do it." Okay, so it wasn't the greatest definition of faith the world had ever seen, but it seemed to satisfy Amunet, who wasn't exactly a scholar.

"Okay," she said, satisfied.

"So, it's my faith and belief in Elohim even though I can't see Him that makes me His child. It's not necessarily that I was born a Hebrew, because He's God of all the earth, and there is no other. I become more and more like Him as I spend more time in His presence. That's the joy you saw. It's all Him. There's no way I could manufacture that on my own."

Amunet slipped her hand in mine, and I noticed that her face was wet with tears. "Thank you, Miryam," she said simply. "What you have shared with me today is the most wonderful thing I have ever heard. Can we talk more about this together?"

"Absolutely." I smiled at her. "Only let's keep it between us and only talk to other people if they're sincere, otherwise there could be trouble."

"Of course," she said. "But I know my family would like to meet you and hear what you have to say. Will you do that?"

Amunet's family. I knew her father was a craftsman who lived a few blocks from the palace. I didn't know much else, except that I felt a nudge from Elohim to accept.

"I would be honored to meet with your family," I told her. "We just have to get the princess to give us permission."

"The queen," corrected Amunet.

"Oh that's right, the queen! That'll take some getting used to after all these years of calling her the princess."

"I imagine it won't take long," remarked Amunet dryly. We laughed and squeezed hands. After twelve years of working side by side, we were suddenly friends. It felt wonderful.

7

Not long after we returned to Memphis, Amunet got Hatshepsut's approval for us to take a day off to visit her family. "I'm happy to see that you've become so friendly," the queen said to me, one eyebrow raised quizzically, after giving me last-minute instructions before I left the palace.

"I'm getting to know Amunet much better, my Queen," I said, meeting her eyes.

"Don't forget to come back," she quipped before turning away.

"Never, my Queen," I said. *I value my head too much*, I thought. Although that wasn't entirely fair on my part. Hatshepsut had always treated me very well, with considerable kindness. Despite missing both my aging mother and Aaron, I knew that my heart was here at the palace, with Hatshepsut and Moses. I could not leave.

Amunet and I walked out of the front gate of the palace giddy with freedom. It was a nicer-than-usual late summer's day, breezy with a few clouds in an otherwise blue sky. We chatted light-heartedly, smiling and saying hello to various guards with whom we were friendly. I tended to talk to the older ones who treated me more like a daughter and less like something they might want to eat for dessert. Since Amenmose, I shied away from men who looked at me with interest. It made me nervous and uncomfortable.

Outside the palace walls, we passed through a few blocks populated by various temples, heading in the opposite direction from the Hebrew section of town. At first the homes were large and magnificent, as befit those who lived closest to the seat of power. However, by a mile out, the neighborhood became merely pleasant, with modest-sized homes. Amunet came to a halt just outside a particularly well-kept one-story bungalow, enhanced by flowers and a row of six palm trees, three on each side of the house.

"Here we are!" she announced gaily, practically skipping up the front walk in her excitement to be home. Right before she reached the front door, with me at her heels, the door flung open and an older, heavier version of Amunet came running out.

"Mother!"

"Ami!"

The two women hugged and kissed each other while I stood awkwardly by. A few tears gathered threateningly behind my lids but I blinked them back. *I would not think about Ema and feel sorry for myself!* I had so looked forward to this time with Amunet and her family and refused to sink into a trough of self-pity.

Amunet pulled out of her mother's embrace, motioning to me. "Mother, this is my friend Miryam from the palace."

Amunet's mother smiled broadly, revealing the spaces from two missing teeth. *A honey eater,* I thought. Always *trust a honey eater.* "Welcome!" she cried, kissing me on both cheeks. "A friend of Ami is automatically a friend of the family. Come in!"

We followed her into a spacious, bright living area. Plump cushions surrounded a long, low table. Colorful scenes of everyday life were etched onto the stone walls. And the delightful sounds of a lyre being plucked wafted toward us from a corner of the room.

"Hello." The owner of the lute carefully put his instrument down, stood, and walked toward me, bowing slightly and smiling. A young man in his mid-twenties, he was of average height, had pleasant, symmetrical features, short, dark hair, olive skin, and the most incredible eyes I had ever seen.

"Pawero!" Amunet intercepted the lute player, hugging him hard. He grinned at me over her head, pointing to her with his free hand (the other being crushed to his body in the hug) and mouthing the words, "My sister." I couldn't help but laugh; he was so likeable.

"Let me guess, Amunet," I said, after she had released him. "This is your brother, right?"

"There's no tricking you, is there?" She laughed in response. "Yes, this is my beloved baby brother."

"Hey," he protested. "I'm not a baby." *Obviously not. Wow.*

"Pawero, this is my dear friend, Miryam. Miryam, my brother, Pawero," Amunet said, ignoring Pawero's latest remark as she formally introduced us.

"Very pleased to meet you, Miryam." Warm brown eyes studied me with an interest that was surprisingly nonthreatening.

I felt myself blush. "So nice to meet you as well. Are you a musician?"

"Ah, the lute. Not really, though I enjoy playing. I'm—"

"He's an artist!" Amunet's mother burst in proudly. "Look at the pictures on the walls!"

"Lovely," I agreed.

"Mom," demonstrated Pawero, looking uncomfortable.

He's modest, I thought. *How refreshing after all the power-seeking hounds at the palace.*

"Come, come," said Amunet's mother, whose name, I soon discovered, was Tutu. "Let's have something to eat and drink. I'll go get my husband...ah! Here he is now."

A handsome man with short, graying hair who closely resembled his son entered the room. His eyes lit up when he saw Amunet, whom he swept into an embrace, murmuring, "My beautiful daughter!" He then warmly and graciously greeted me, after which we sat on cushions and were served by Tutu. Both Amunet and I tried to help her, but she wouldn't hear of it.

"Pah! You girls work so hard for the royal family. I'll serve you. Besides, it's just a few dishes." What seemed like seventeen dishes later, Tutu joined us, settling down next to her husband.

"This is so delicious," I told her, scooping up pickled cucumber slices and baked garlic with a piece of wheat bread.

"Good." She beamed. "Eat, eat. You're so thin."

Smiling, I helped myself to more food. Pawero poured me another cup of plum wine. "I made this," he informed me.

"Really? I am so impressed. This is wonderful!"

"My brother is a man of many talents," said Amunet, looking meaningfully at me. That's when it occurred to me that this was a set-up, but either because of all the plum wine I was drinking, or because of Pawero's gorgeous eyes, I didn't mind.

The conversation revolved around various events, not the least of which was the death of the old king and Hatshepsut's ascension to queen. Both of Amunet's parents were concerned that the drama that already swirled around Hatshepsut was going to increase exponentially and become too much for her to handle.

"Perhaps the queen will let you go so you can come home, find a nice man, and give me grandchildren," said Tutu wistfully.

At the mention of grandchildren, Amunet grew a little pink. Changing the topic, she said, "I brought Miryam home for many reasons, not the least being that I have been asking her questions about her god." Ignoring the alarmed faces of her parents and brother, she boldly continued. "I have seen strength of character in Miryam that truly astounds me, and she tells me it's because of Elohim. Everything she has said makes such perfect sense to me that I knew I had to share this with you, my beloved family."

Hau, Amunet's father, spoke first. "Who is Elohim? I don't recognize the name."

"He is the Hebrew God," answered Amunet.

Tutu's eyes grew wide, and they all turned to look at me.

"You are a Hebrew?" asked Tutu.

I nodded.

"You are the first palace person Amunet has ever brought home, so you must be something special." She looked at her husband and son and they both nodded at her. "So, please, tell us about your god."

I drew a deep breath. "Thank you. It's a privilege to be in your home. It is just recently that Amunet and I have gotten close, but already I feel as if she is my sister. We Hebrews have one God, and we call Him Elohim. He is a jealous and all-consuming God, and He doesn't allow us to worship anything else."

"So no Ra or Amun or Anubis?" asked Pawero.

"Exactly. Or any of the others. In fact, we believe that those aren't gods at all, but in fact are demons." Plunging in, I told them everything I had told Amunet. There were some questions, but mostly they listened. After about twenty minutes, when I paused to take a sip of wine, Pawero spoke.

"Let me ask you something," he said, leaning forward. "If the Hebrew god—Elohim—is as powerful as you say, then why are you the slaves? Why don't you rule us?"

Why don't we rule you? I thought, looking at him blankly. *I don't know.* But then it came to me, as clearly as if God Himself had dropped the answer into my brain. "What if," I said, "God is more interested in forming your character than in making you a ruler? What if judgment begins in the house of God? What if He seeks to purify us, and He can only accomplish that through suffering?"

Hau spoke. "Judgment? Suffering? Purification? No, God is about power and strength and prosperity!"

I looked at him with love. "You don't know God at all, do you? You haven't a clue."

Everyone seemed stunned after I said this. Hastily, I apologized. "I'm sorry, Hau, you've been exceedingly gracious to me. I didn't mean to be insulting; it's just that I *know* Him so well! He's been my comfort and my protector all my life, and I've seen Him do mighty deeds. And you're right, He *is* powerful and strong. When the time is right, He will show all of Egypt His power and great might, and there won't be any doubt He is Lord over all."

Pawero spoke quietly. "This is a description of God unlike anything I have ever heard." He turned to his sister. "What do you think, Ami?"

"What do I think? I think Miryam is right and the rest of us are wrong. I have determined in my heart to follow the Hebrew God."

A lump rose in my throat and my eyes grew misty as I gazed at Amunet's beautiful face, made even lovelier by her declaration of belief in Elohim.

"This is dangerous, my daughter," warned Hau. "The priests in the different temples won't like hearing that their gods aren't gods but are...demons."

"I know, Father. I don't plan on saying anything incendiary. I just intend to seek after the Hebrew God and see what happens."

Always dangerous with Elohim, I thought. *He's not tame.*

"Very interesting," mused Pawero, his eyes on me. "Very interesting indeed."

*

We didn't discuss Elohim the rest of the visit, though I could tell that He was not forgotten. On the contrary. However, I had a sense from Him that enough had been said for now, and anymore would be overload and unproductive. Instead, we admired Pawero's artwork, toured Hau's studio (he was a potter), baked bread with Tutu, walked around the neighborhood, and talked about a myriad of subjects.

I could tell Pawero liked me. I liked him, too. In fact, he was the first man I'd ever liked, and it was a good feeling. I had started wondering if men simply weren't part of my future, I'd felt so closed off inside for so long, since that jerk Amenmose. But now a flower was springing to life inside my chest. My heart beat faster, I smiled more, I immediately looked for him when I entered a room.

On our second and final night, Amunet and I prepared for bed in a little room off the main living area where we shared a floor mat. I was combing out my hair and she was undressing when she said, "I knew you would like him."

I paused, the comb halfway down my head. "I really like him, Ami." (I had taken to calling her by her family nickname sometime during the visit.) "I'm a bit overwhelmed by how much I like him."

Amunet pulled off her shift and lay down on the mat. It was too hot to wear clothing at night. She closed her eyes and smiled. "Don't be overwhelmed. I can tell he likes you. I've never seen him like this before. He's resisted marrying up until now because he didn't want to get stuck in a, and I quote, 'loveless marriage with a boring woman who only thinks about her next meal and whether or not to paint her nails.'"

"Ha ha. Well, I'm certainly not that."

"No, you're not," agreed Amunet, suddenly serious. I lay down next to her and she reached out and clasped my hand. "I want you for my sister."

"We'll see what happens," I said, trying to be nonchalant but not entirely succeeding.

Long after Amunet had fallen asleep, her regular breathing punctuating the quiet night, I lay awake arguing with God.

Would You really have me marry an Egyptian? Not that he's asked, of course. What about my life with Hatshepsut, and Moses? How can I disciple Moses if I don't see him?

"You're assuming too much," was the enigmatic response. *"I am giving you a gift. Trust Me."*

*

All too soon, our time off was over, and Amunet and I reluctantly headed back to the palace amid a flurry of farewells. Pawero clasped my hand firmly between his own and looked deeply into my eyes. "I will be thinking of you, Miryam. I hope to see you very soon."

"And I you," I choked, overcome by emotion. How could I pursue a romantic relationship while a slave at the palace? Which of course was irrelevant if Pawero didn't follow after Elohim with all his heart.

"I hate to break this up," said Amunet, "but we're going to be late if we don't get going."

On our walk back, I voiced some of my concerns to Amunet. "Faith, Miriyam, faith!" exclaimed the new believer, shaming me. "I am convinced my entire family is going to be saved. As for my little brother, it doesn't matter what the life of a palace slave is normally like. God can do anything."

That jogged my memory, and I repeated to her the words of Elohim about giving me a gift. "Do think Pawero is my gift?" I asked, blushing.

"Haha. If he wasn't my brother, I'd consider him a gift!"

I poked her in the ribs. "You are so obviously *not* Egyptian royalty!" Giggling, we ran the rest of the way to the palace.

*

I slipped back into my regular routine as if I had never left, the only difference being that now thoughts of Pawero occupied enormous amounts of my waking moments. Every time I started to fret about my future, I heard Elohim whisper to my heart, *"Don't worry."* Just as I was able to fully obey Him, something big happened.

Thutmose was sitting at dinner with thirty or so members from his entourage one evening, including Hatshepsut and Moses. He picked up his special gold goblet, brimming with his favorite red wine, when all of a sudden the servant behind him, not the one who had poured the wine, seized his arm. The babble of voices ceased as suddenly as if a switch had been turned, so quiet did it get in the dining hall. Twelve guards immediately rushed for the table, but the servant held up his other hand and said, "Wait! There's something wrong with this wine. I can smell it." He then released Thutmose's arm.

The young pharaoh sniffed cautiously at the wine. "It *does* smell a bit odd," he commented, before pouring some of the wine out on the white linen tablecloth. We all gasped as the tablecloth sizzled, and steam rose.

"The wine is poisoned!" shouted Thutmose, standing so abruptly that his chair knocked over. "Lock the doors!"

Thus followed an exceedingly long night in which everyone there—nobility as well as servants—was questioned and examined. Well after midnight, a minor noble with a strong hatred of Mutnofret and a misguided desire to see Hatshepsut on the throne alone was singled out. Shackled and led off to the palace dungeon, the rest of us were released to our beds, pale and shaken at the thought of what almost happened, and what would indeed happen to the poor man who had acted rashly.

Back in Hatshepsut's rooms, the queen shook with rage. "I cannot believe it!" she stormed. "That foolish man has sullied my reputation by association. What an idiot!"

"I suspect he's paying for his idiocy, my Queen," said Inet.

The queen glowered at us all. "How did he know of my plans to rule Egypt alone? Did one of you say anything?" She stared at us so intensely that despite our collective innocence, we felt guilty.

"No, no, my Queen," Amunet quickly responded. "The difference between you and Thutmose is so extreme, and your abilities so widely renowned, that it is quite clear to everyone that you are the only royal worthy to rule Egypt and take her to greater glory and splendor."

Hatshepsut continued to stare us all down. Finally, satisfied regarding our innocence, she deflated, sinking heavily down into a chair. "This is not good," she said quietly.

"Oh, my Queen!" I ran forward and kissed her hand. "All will be well. Look how fast the assassin was captured."

My words, as it turned out, were anything but prophetic. The next morning, Mutnofret brusquely requested an interview with the queen, during which she accused Hatshepsut's staff of being a party to the attempted murder of her son.

"I will not be vilified!" thundered my queen, eyes blazing.

The two women stood eyeball to eyeball, one young, beautiful, and powerful, the other older, flamboyant, and domineering.

Mutnofret backed down. "I did not mean to accuse you, my Queen," she said with a slightly mocking sneer she was unable to entirely hide. "But you must agree with me that one of your attendants may have been in cahoots with this wicked man."

"I do not agree with you at all. My attendants are all fiercely loyal to the throne. They know of my love for Thutmose, and respect for his kingship. This attempt on his life shocks me as much as you, Mutnofret. I will not hear of any more accusations."

"Yes, my Queen," murmured Mutnofret, but her cat eyes flashed with indignation.

When Hatshepsut returned from this exchange, she was shaking. "I do not like or trust that woman. I suspect this isn't the end of the matter." She put her fingers together and pursed her lips. "It's a good thing that Ipi (one of Mutnofret's ladies) reports to me."

Ipi did report back to Hatshepsut, and the report wasn't good. Apparently, Mutnofret had gone ballistic from this attempted assassination. Now that the old pharaoh, her husband, was dead, the only claim to power she had was through her son. She constantly battled Hatshepsut for control of Thutmose. He was young and sickly and seemed to become less and less robust as time progressed. She knew that once Hatshepsut had a child by Thutmose, her power would diminish even more. I was very well aware of her dislike of Moses, and her fears that he would one day usurp her line to the throne.

Apparently, Mutnofret had become fixated on the idea that one of us wanted Thutmose dead. No one else believed it, but that didn't stop her from spreading misinformation—aka, slander—and lies. Into her son's ear, and into the ear of any who would listen, she poured her diatribes. Hatshepsut did her best to counter this with Thutmose, going so far as to spend night after night in his bed, but it was an uphill battle.

"I'm really concerned," she confided in me, about three weeks after the poisoning attempt. "Right now, Thutmose agrees with me that my attendants aren't responsible for the attempt on his life, but Mutnofret is so out of control that he may be swayed at any time." She paused. "I'm also not convinced I can keep Moses safe. I think it best if he were away from the palace so as not to attract Mutnofret's notice."

Moses! Out of the palace! My heart constricted. "But where, my Queen?

Where would he go?"

"Military boarding school," came the decisive response. "There's a fine school south of Thebes. All the royal princes go after age thirteen. He's almost that now."

"But he's not thirteen yet!" I protested, sick at the thought of Moses so far from me, so far from my influence.

"Miryam," admonished the queen, "he's close enough. But he is going to need someone completely trustworthy as his servant. Someone who will sacrifice his life for my son, if necessary."

She sat back and closed her eyes, pondering. An incredible thought struck me, a thought I knew had to be from Elohim.

"My Queen! I know!"

She opened one eye. "Yes?"

"My brother Aaron. He's three years older than Moses, and is bright and competent. I know he'll watch over Moses as if, as if—"

"As if he were Moses' brother?" asked the queen wryly.

My face colored. "Yes," I said softly.

"Hmm. Interesting." She waved me away. "You may go."

All that day, I walked around in a daze. Theoretically, I knew that sooner or later Moses would leave the palace and do the things princes do, but it seemed so far off. Under my nose, he had grown up. Of course, this woman, this Mutnofret, had precipitated matters, but still he would have left eventually. For years, I had spoken to Moses about Elohim, sharing all my knowledge. He was always interested, and exceptionally discreet. Was he ready to take this knowledge and sustain his own relationship with God away from my protective influence? Was he?

But that idea about Aaron! If Hatshepsut agreed, it would kill two sparrows with one stone, as the saying goes. Aaron had recently turned sixteen, and would soon be expected to leave field work and go with the gangs of slave laborers into the dangerous building jobs. Last time I saw Ema, she'd expressed her grave concerns.

"I just couldn't bear it if anything happened to him, Miryam," she had confided to me in a moment of uncharacteristic weakness. "He's all I have left."

"Oh, Ema," I cried. "You have me, and," I stretched out my arms wide, encompassing the neighborhood in all directions, "so many friends and family who love you!"

"I know I have you, *beeti*, but you're gone almost all the time. I never get to see you." At this, she had started crying.

"Ema!" My heart broken, I wrapped my arms around her and held my sobbing mother tightly to my chest. "I miss you so much! But we agreed it's Elohim's will for me to watch over Moses."

"Oh, I know it's Elohim's will," she'd said, smiling weakly through her tears. "That doesn't necessarily make it easy, just right."

I thought of those words now. That *doesn't necessarily make it easy, just right.* How perfectly Ema put her finger on this situation. God's plan for our lives is often the difficult path—for a season—until we drag ourselves out of the desert and see the river, shining in the sun, cool and refreshing to our parched senses.

If it were God's plan to send Moses and Aaron off together for a season, how wonderful that could be for both boys. And yet I would miss Moses dreadfully, and Ema would miss Aaron. Both of us would be forced to trust them to Elohim, though if I were to be perfectly honest, that's all we've ever been able to do. Neither Ema nor I in our own strength could have held off even one of Pharaoh's men for more than two minutes. Probably not even that, I reflected, an involuntary smile coming to my lips when I thought about taking on one of the burly, highly trained guards who filled the palace and its grounds.

"What's so funny?" Unbeknownst to me, Amunet had walked into the room, a platter of fruit balanced on one outstretched hand.

"Oh, nothing really. I was just thinking about how long I would last if I were to fight one of the guards."

"About one second," said Amunet, raising her eyebrows. "Are you seriously considering this line of action, and if so, why?"

"No, of course not. I was actually thinking about Elohim's protection on my life, how faithful He is."

Amunet lowered the fruit platter, a shadow passing over her lovely features. "I need to talk to you."

"About?"

"Your safety."

"What's going on?"

"I heard some gossip from Mutnofret's side of the palace. She's been talking about 'those Hebrews' and how dangerous they are. I think she may be trying to set you up. I know that she's been out to weaken Hatshepsut by implicating one of us."

"When did you hear this?"

"Just this morning."

"Could you tell the queen?"

Amunet nodded. "I intend to, as soon as I can get her alone." She paused. "You know, Miryam, if you ever need a safe haven, my family would gladly welcome you."

"Oh, Amunet! I love your family, but I couldn't possibly put them in danger."

"Let's see what the queen says. Can we pray about this together?"

"Definitely. Thank you for caring."

Amunet grasped my hand to pray, drawing back slightly at my words so she could look full into my face. "Thank you for caring?" she repeated, incredulous. "Don't you know how much I owe you for introducing me to your God? Don't you know how much I love you? Of course I care!"

Without waiting for my response, she immediately launched into prayer: "Lord Elohim, God of the heavens and the earth, bless and protect my sister Miryam. We know how Your hand is heavy upon her, and we trust that You will keep her safe and secure. Now we ask in Your holy name to do what is necessary to keep her from Mutnofret, and to not only preserve her life, but to prosper it. Amen."

"Amen," I whispered in agreement, blessed beyond belief by Amunet's prayer.

8

EVENTS MOVED QUICKLY AFTER THAT. Before we retired to bed that night, Hatshepsut summoned me for a private meeting. We went into her bedroom, where she motioned for me to shut the door firmly behind me. Then she sat in her favorite chair, silent.

"Yes, my Queen?" I knelt before her, sensitive to her mood.

Hatshepsut sighed. She took my hand and looked into my face. "I want to tell you something that I haven't said many times in my life." She paused, and I waited, motionless, while she collected her thoughts. "I love you, Miryam."

"Oh, my Queen!" Overcome, I gently squeezed her hand. "I love you as well." We smiled at each other.

"We've been through a lot over the years, haven't we, Miryam?"

"A great deal, my Queen. You've been exceedingly gracious to your servant."

"And you've been an exceedingly gracious servant." Hatshepsut briefly averted her eyes before meeting mine again. "I've heard rumors."

I nodded. "I think I may have heard the same rumors, my Queen."

"Yes. I refuse to risk your life. Trust me when I say this is one of the hardest decisions I've ever had to make, but for your own protection I'm sending you away."

"When, my Queen?"

"Tonight."

"Tonight? That's so…sudden."

"I know." Wearily, the queen extricated her hand from mine and stood. I stood as well. "Amunet tells me that you know of a safe place. Don't return home. It's not a good idea." She spoke faster, the emotions of a few moments ago now firmly under control. "I've asked Paser the guard to escort you." She drew an item of clothing out of one of her big clothes chests. "Here! Take this cloak and make sure you wear the hood. I don't want you recognized. Also, take these gold pieces," she said, handing me four small gold nuggets. "They'll enable you to live until I bring you back."

"You'll bring me back?"

"As soon as I can get Mutnofret under control." She sighed again. "I don't know how long it's going to take. Hopefully not very."

"Can I say good-bye to anyone? To Moses?"

The queen shook her head regretfully. "Too risky. I only want you leaving this room to go outside the palace compound with Paser. I'll tell Moses. Oh, and I like your idea. I'm going to send your brother Aaron down south with him."

So many pieces of new information were flying at me, I could barely process one thing before the next. I was still stuck on not saying good-bye to Moses. "Are you sure?" I ventured.

"About Aaron? Of course."

"No, I mean about my seeing Moses one last time?" It pained me to think how blithely I had said good night to him, fully expecting to see him in the morning.

"Absolutely not," Hatshepsut said firmly. "We're not taking any chances."

"All right. Can I say good-bye to Amunet or Inet?"

"Why don't you let me take care of that after you're safely away? Let's not have anything out of the ordinary tonight. My plan is for you to sneak downstairs during the third watch of the night. Every guard you encounter has already been clued in and won't molest you. Paser will be waiting at the entrance to the garden door. Go quickly and quietly to him, and he will get you the rest of the way to your safe place." She stopped and looked intently at me. "You *do* know what Amunet was referring to, don't you?"

I nodded, my heart too full to speak. It didn't take long for me to gather together my few belongings and secure them in a cloth bag. The gold nuggets I carefully sewed into an inner pocket of my dress. The cloak was folded neatly, placed at the edge of my mat. Everything was done. I blew out the candles, leaving only one wall sconce lit. Hatshepsut lay in her bed, and I lay fully dressed on my mat. For a while, we listened to each other breathe, neither of us speaking. I heard Hatshepsut snort.

"Come here," she commanded.

I crawled up on her bed and she put her arms around me, hugging me. We both shed some tears over this unforeseen interruption to our friendship. For even though she was technically the queen and I the slave, we had grown to love one another from the heart. It hurt us to say good-bye, perhaps she more than me since I was going to see Pawero, whereas she was to remain in this palace among very few trustworthy souls. I knew Hatshepsut better than anyone, better than her own mother and certainly better than her husband. "I'll pray for you every day, my Queen," I said softly.

"Yes, do," she replied. "Tell that God of yours I want you back as soon as possible."

"I will tell Him, though I suspect He already knows."

"Don't push it, Miryam," warned Hatshepsut in a joking tone.

We laughed, tempering our emotional mood.

A little while later, the queen kissed me and told me to go. "Don't forget to hide your face in the hood of the cloak," were her last words as we parted.

That night seemed endless. I met Paser as planned, and we managed to escape the palace without anyone stopping us. In silence, we walked to Amunet's parents' house, staying in the shadows alongside the road. When we approached the house, Paser waited at a distance in order to make sure that I got in. Hesitantly, I knocked quietly at the door, aware that my presence a few hours before dawn was not a friendly gesture. No one responded at first, and I knocked again, a bit louder, only emboldened because I could feel Paser's impatience to get going.

Finally, I heard Pawero's voice on the other side of the door. "Who's there?"

"It's me. Miryam."

Quickly, the door swung open, and he stared at me in surprise. "Miryam! What's going on? Come in." He took me by the elbow and guided me into the house, firmly locking the door behind us. "Sit down, sit down."

Pawero took my belongings from my unresisting hands, encouraging me to sit on one of the big living area cushions. Once seated, I started trembling violently. To Pawero's credit, he didn't ask any more questions. Rather, he sat across from me, holding my cold hands in his warm ones, simply waiting until I calmed down enough to speak.

"I'm so sorry to wake you up in the middle of the night," I choked out, barely able to talk, exhausted and overwhelmed.

"Shh, shh," he said tenderly, caressing the backs of my hands with his thumbs. "Never apologize for coming to me. You are always, always, welcome."

I smiled weakly. "Queen Hatshepsut sent me here. She thinks that Thutmose's mother is out to discredit her and had planned to make me the scapegoat for the attempted assassination."

"Ah, this all makes sense. The queen did not think it wise for you to return home?"

I shook my head. "This is the only safe place I know." I raised my face to his. "May I stay? I'll earn my keep. I won't be any trouble—"

"Miryam, Miryam." He let go of one of my hands to trace the path of a tear rolling down my cheek. "You have been in my thoughts and dreams day and night. I am so happy you're here that I'm pinching myself to make sure

I'm really awake. See?" He pinched his forearm before glancing up, grinning at me like a young boy.

That did it. I broke down completely, sobbing in his safe arms, overwhelmed by emotion. Hau and Tutu burst in the room, finally awakened by the commotion.

"What's going on?" exclaimed Hau, a lighted candle in one hand and a knife in the other.

"It's okay, Father," said Pawero, instinctively shielding me with his body in case his father slashed out with the knife before waiting for an answer.

"Pawero? Who's with you?"

"It's Miryam."

"Miryam!" Tutu's astonished voice chimed in. She rushed over to us. "Child, what's happened? Are you all right?"

I went from Pawero's embrace to Tutu's soft bosom, crying on her shoulder while she patted me on the back, saying, "There, there."

I hiccupped a few times, unable to speak, and Pawero took over.

"Father, Mother," he said, "Miryam showed up unexpectedly a little while ago. There are problems at the palace, and the queen sent her here for safekeeping."

"The queen!" exclaimed Tutu reverently.

"Yes. It's our duty as good Egyptians to protect Miryam from the queen's enemies. Agreed?"

"Of course," responded both parents, Tutu holding me a little tighter, protecting me from those nameless, faceless enemies.

"You will be our daughter," promised Tutu. "Everything will be just fine."

They put me to bed in the room I had shared with Amunet. Tutu strongly encouraged both Pawero and Hau to go back to bed and she sat up with me, holding my hand, murmuring comforting words until I finally drifted off.

*

I didn't awake until late the next morning, sun bright in the room despite there being only one small window high up in the wall. I sat up abruptly, my first thought being that I had overslept and was in trouble with Inet. Then I remembered where I was and slowly sank back down in the bed, my hands behind my head and my eyes open.

Tutu suddenly appeared in the doorway. "Good morning!" she sang cheerily, hands covered in flour. "Don't get out of bed before you're ready, love. But when you are, there's breakfast for you."

"Thank you," I mouthed, but she was gone, back to her bread dough, singing as she worked. Slowly, I got up, used the pee jug, splashed some water on my hands and face from the water jug (*do not mix up jugs*, I always reminded myself), and wandered out to the main family area.

"Ah! There's my beautiful Miryam. Sit, sit!" Tutu fussed over me like a mother hen, bringing soft bread, dates, sliced cucumber, and a cup of creamy goat milk. I luxuriated in her ministrations, quietly eating my bread and milk like a child. Eventually I got up the courage to ask about Pawero.

"Where is he, Tutu?"

"Mother! Call me Mother; you're like one of the family."

"Mother," I said shyly.

"He's off looking for some of the special plants he uses to make paint. He'll be back later today." She peered at me meaningfully. "You like my son?"

I could feel myself blushing. "Yes," I murmured.

"Good! Because I know he likes you." She beamed happily.

Thus began what in retrospect would be one of the, if not the, happiest periods of my life. Every day the palace receded a bit and the comforting, lovely, calm world of Amunet's family embraced me more and more. I took long walks with Pawero, helping him gather painting materials, learning about his craft. I helped Tutu in the kitchen, learning how to competently make the foods Pawero loves. I cleaned Hau's pottery shop, carefully dusting each piece before replacing it in its space on the shelves. I carried baskets of laundry down to the river, beating sheets with a stone in the cool water. I spent long evenings sitting with the family, talking about Elohim as they listened with ever-growing interest and respect. I spoke of Moses, and Hatshepsut, and Inet, and Amunet, yearning for each of them after a fashion, but still so happy that I was here and not there.

I was growing more and more dependent on Pawero for my emotional happiness. One day, I realized that Pawero so filled my heart that he was crowding out Elohim. I still spoke of Him and gave Him homage, but my prayer times were rushed and the intensity lessened. It was Pawero who set my pulse racing, Pawero whose presence filled me with joy, Pawero whose smile melted my heart and made my knees go weak. Let's face it, I was totally smitten.

One morning as I rushed through my customary prayers in a preliminary fashion so as to meet up with Pawero before Tutu and Hau were about, I heard the voice of my God:

"Do you not have one hour, Miryam?"

Elohim?

"Not one hour?"

I'm sorry. I love him. I can't stop thinking about him.

"He doesn't know Me yet."

Yet?

"Yet. But the choice is his. Set an example for him. Don't let your devotion to Me be sloppy. He won't be attracted to a lukewarm faith."

I love You, my Lord.

"Spend time with Me, My child. I rejoice in your company."

The Lord of the universe, the King of all that is rejoices in my company? Did He really say that, or did I imagine it? No, that's not the type of thing I would imagine. I pressed into prayer, worshiping my God, sharing all that was within my heart, asking Him to bless me and to bring Pawero to an unshakeable faith in the one, true God. For the first time in days, even weeks, I lost myself in prayer, losing all track of time, not hearing Tutu call me to breakfast until she entered the room and placed a warm hand on my shoulder, causing me to open my eyes, intimacy with God receding into the background as the reality of the present day impressed itself on my senses.

"Are you all right, Miryam?"

"I was praying."

"Ah." Tutu stepped back a step. Praying was a sacred duty; she understood this. "Come in when you're ready," she whispered, tiptoeing out of the room.

I realized that day that the time had come to step up my witness about the necessity and importance of putting one's faith in Elohim. Since I had moved in, the four of us had several conversations about the things of God, and I did notice that there was less and less defending of the various Egyptian deities and more questions about the actual things of the Hebrew God. As yet, though, no one had dropped to their knees, exclaiming, "I must know this God of yours and renounce those awful demons I've been mistakenly following all my life!"

That morning at breakfast, I probed deeper. "So, Tutu," I began, in-between bites of my bread spread with goat cheese, "what do you think about Elohim?"

"Ah," she said, smiling broadly. "I think He is a wonderful God!"

"Do you think He is the only God?"

"The only God?" She frowned. "I have worshiped many gods all my life, and I am particularly fond of Isis. If I were to say He is the only God, could I still worship Isis? After all, I have modeled my life on her." She looked at me beseechingly.

"Uh…no. Agreeing that Elohim is the only God means you can't worship any others. He tends to be a jealous God, and considers it adultery when we go after other 'gods.'"

Pawero walked into the room. "What's this I hear about adultery?" he asked light-heartedly.

"Miryam is talking to me about her God," said Tutu, standing against the wall, arms folded at her chest.

Pawero looked from his mother to me. "I see," he said, sitting down and helping himself to breakfast.

"What do you think, Pawero?" I asked. "Have you come to the point yet where you realize Elohim is the one true God?"

Pawero laughed. "You should be a scribe, Miryam, the way you phrase things."

"But do you?" I persisted, intent on getting an answer.

Pawero sighed. "Look, I am very seriously considering the claims of both you and Amunet. You have to realize that this goes against everything I have thought and learned my entire life." He placed his hand over mine and looked deeply into my eyes, making my insides melt. "What's important to you is important to me. Just give me time."

"All right," I said, loving the sensation of his hand on mine.

Later that day, I went with Pawero on a walk in the fields to collect more ingredients for paint. It was a lengthy walk, and hot, so after we accumulated everything we needed, we found a tiny patch of shade under a palm tree whose leaves were sparse but still visible, and plunked ourselves down.

Pawero leaned against the tree, his legs stretched out in front of him. Sweat glistened on his bare chest and his well-defined muscles. I forced myself to focus on his face (*up here*, I scolded myself), sitting down on the ground beside him. He pulled something out of his gathering bag, waving it triumphantly before me.

"Look what Mother sent," he said happily. "First of the season."

It was a pomegranate, a fruit for lovers. I blushed deeply as he split the soft, red rind with his fingernail, pulling off a section of fruit and handing it to me. I stared dumbly at the glistening ruby seeds nestled in my hand while Pawero inhaled seed after seed. "Eat, eat!" he exclaimed. "Don't you like these? Pomegranates are my favorite."

I looked at his bright eyes, cheerful countenance, kind and intelligent face, innocent enjoyment of food, and I loved him.

"Does it bother you that I'm a Hebrew?" I asked him suddenly.

"Bother me?" he repeated, surprised. He shook his head. "It's made you who you are. You wouldn't be Miryam if you were an Egyptian girl born in Memphis." He gazed at me fondly. "Why? Does it bother you that I'm *not* a Hebrew?"

"If you were, you'd be slaving under a hot sun, earning a meager existence, and not sitting here in the shade," I replied, not without a trace of bitterness, the image of my deceased father springing to mind.

Pawero's face turned grave. He reached for my hand. "I think of you at the palace with my sister, and sometimes I forget that you came out of such a hard background. I'm sorry, Miryam, for what my country has done to your people. I've seen the gangs of men—many only boys, really—toiling on the pyramids and the monuments, seen men whipped by their taskmasters, falling to their deaths off rickety scaffolding, and I've felt shame. Now that I've come to know you, that shame has deepened into anger." He pressed my hand to his lips, briefly kissing my fingers. "What can I do? What can we do?"

"We can pray," I offered, internally debating whether or not to tell him about Moses.

"Ah, pray," Pawero said. "To the Hebrew God, yes?"

"Not to the Egyptian ones, certainly."

"No, not to the Egyptian ones." Pawero absently tore off another section of pomegranate, appearing thoughtful. "Tell me, Miryam, do you think your God will demand that your people remain slaves here forever?"

What a question. "Forever?" I said uncertainly. "What do you mean? Do you think that my people will gain control over your people, like the Hyksos?"

"No, nothing like that. I'm thinking more along the lines of your people leaving Egypt."

"Leaving Egypt?" What a thought. "Do you think that's possible? What about the pharaoh?"

"Who's the pharaoh?" asked Pawero, smiling slightly. "Thutmose…or Hatshepsut?"

I stared at him. "Do you think she would, she could…?"

He shrugged. "I don't know anything. I'm just an artist. I find it very odd that you're her confidante, however. Ami has told us how fond the queen is of you, how dearly she holds you in her heart, and she's not so close to everyone. That would make a lot of sense if you were another member of the nobility, but a Hebrew slave? How odd."

"Yes," I said slowly. "It *is* odd. But there's something even odder, something only an all powerful God could bring about."

"What?" asked Pawero, interested.

"You can't tell anyone."

"I can keep a secret."

I smiled at him. "I believe that, otherwise I would never even entertain the thought of telling you this."

Pawero leaned forward. "Now you've got me really curious. What's going on?"

I hesitated. *Is it okay, Elohim?* I silently prayed. I didn't hear anything distinct but did feel an internal push to tell Pawero. *Okay, here goes.* "You know Moses? The queen's adopted son?"

"You mean the prince you take care of and always talk about? Yes."

"I don't *always* talk about him!" I protested.

"Not always. You also talk about your God."

I threw a pomegranate rind at him. "Anyway, he's my...brother."

"What?" Pawero's eyes widened in shock. "Are you kidding?"

I shook my head. "You're familiar with the command the first Thutmose gave when he became pharaoh? To throw all Hebrew baby boys into the river?" Pawero nodded and I continued. "Moses was such a beautiful baby, we could all tell how extraordinary he was, and so my mother came up with a plan to make a little boat for him and put him in the reeds at the edge of the river where the princess was known to bathe. She sent me to watch."

A knowing look dawned in Pawero's eyes. "Now I remember! Ami told us about finding the baby. She never mentioned you, though."

"Back then she was probably hoping that I would disappear." I laughed. "I was only sporadically at the palace at the beginning. It wasn't until a few years later that I came permanently into Hatshepsut's service."

"I can see why you say only God could bring such a thing about," said Pawero thoughtfully. "An abandoned baby, condemned to death, rescued by the daughter of the man who issued the decree and then raised to be a prince right under his very nose in his own home with the help of his natural-born sister, no less. What an unbelievable story! Just amazing."

"You see why it's so important to keep it a secret?"

"Of course. Does Hatshepsut know?"

"Most definitely," I confirmed. "We've only skirted the issue and never said outright...she's very committed to being his only mother."

"Ha!" said Pawero. "I can see that. She's not the type to share the light."

"No, but she's been extraordinarily kind," I said loyally.

"So what's happening now, with Moses?" he asked.

I sighed, biting into a seed. "As far as I know, he's off to military boarding school down south with our brother Aaron as his personal servant. I miss him."

Pawero raised an eyebrow. "The pass off? From one sibling to another? Does he know who he is?"

"I've told him many things over the years, but we've always had to be very careful. It's hard to say where Moses is in his thinking, he's still so young. I know he loves Elohim, yet he also has to attend many ceremonies involving other gods. He's interested in the family he came from, yet he's extremely attached to Hatshepsut. He gets along well with just about everyone, but instinctively knows who to avoid, like Mutnofret and the first Thutmose."

"He avoided Thutmose?"

I nodded. "Even as a very small child, he didn't feel safe around him. He would be very quiet and docile if the pharaoh showed him any attention, but I could see the strain. I'm very excited about his time with Aaron. I think Aaron can influence Moses in ways I can't, and with Moses approaching manhood, it's time for a change."

"Just amazing," said Pawero again, shaking his head. "That you spent all these years at the palace and now your other brother is picking up where you left off, and both of you slaves…it boggles my mind. You know, Miryam, more than anything else you've said, this convinces me that the Hebrew God *is* an all powerful God."

My heart leapt. "*The* all powerful God," I couldn't resist adding.

Pawero laughed. "You're unsquashable, aren't you?" he said fondly. "Give me some time. I will pray to your—to Elohim—and see if He answers me. If He does, then I will swear to Him my allegiance."

"That's very fair, Pawero," I said, trying not to sound too eager. On the inside, however, I was jumping up and down with joy. *Oh that my beloved would love my God!*

Pawero was true to his word. He refused to discuss Elohim for the rest of that week and I used all my self-control not to push him. Soon enough, he came to me and told me we must talk. "I have sought Elohim," he said, "and I have heard His voice in my heart."

"Oh, Pawero!" Impulsively, I threw my arms around his neck. Mistake. He grabbed me around the waist and spun me, hard. The next thing I knew we were kissing, the first real kisses I ever had. Mmm. My body melted into his, the feel of his soft, warm lips flushing me with desire. Gasping and laughing, I feebly attempted to push him away, only to have him kiss me even more. Finally, we both came up for air.

"That's not the way your walk with Elohim is supposed to begin," I said hurriedly.

Pawero drew me close. "I don't mind," he said, reaching for me.

I smacked his hand playfully. "You should."

The next several weeks saw the flowering of our love in lock step with the moving forward of Pawero's new faith. Even his parents came on board, showing more and more interest. We talked about getting married, something that seemed like a dream I'd never even dared to hope for coming true. But now that Pawero had made a commitment to Elohim, two more obstacles popped up: Hatshepsut and Ema.

"I should take you to see my mother," I remarked one evening while we took an after-dinner stroll in the rosy glow of the sunset, a relief from the heat of the day.

"I would like that."

"It's just that…"

"That what?" asked Pawero, holding my hand and swinging it just enough so as not to be annoying.

I winced. "Well, she may have a hard time with you being Egyptian. Are you offended?"

"Offended? No. I don't blame her for not wanting to hop in bed with her oppressors."

"Yes, but it's more than that. We Hebrews have always sought to marry within our tribes. There's a stigma attached to going to the nations, so to speak."

"Even if the person in question believes in your God?"

"Well, obviously that *does* change things. I'm sure she'll love you like I do," I said, trying to hide the slight doubt in my voice.

*

We went to Goshen to see Ema a few days later. Amunet had told us that Mutnofret was no longer a threat to me, though the queen thought it best that I stay away from the palace and not remind her of my existence, something I myself was eager to do. We sent word ahead to Ema, and she was waiting for us when we arrived, peering expectantly out the door.

"There you are!" She threw herself at me and wrapped me in her thin arms. I clung to her, both of us thrilled to see each other. When we let go, I saw that her eyes were wet.

"This is Pawero," I said proudly, introducing the beautiful Egyptian man standing next to me.

"Hello," said Ema, with some reserve. She and Pawero bowed politely to one another before she led us into the cool recesses of the house.

It was strange. When I came back from the palace, the difference was so vast that there was no point in making a comparison between lavish luxury and clean poverty. Since being at Pawero's home, however, my childhood house seemed so much smaller and dingier. It didn't seem right to leave Ema in this place.

Ema was talking, pulling me out of my thoughts. "I've heard from Aaron," she beamed. "He's with Mos…er, Prince Moses." She glanced at Pawero.

"It's okay, Ema," I said. "Pawero knows."

"He…knows?"

"About Moses. Being my brother."

Ema's face blanched and she looked horrified. "Miryam!" she scolded. "How could you?"

"It's okay, Jochebed," quickly inserted Pawero. "I'm safe. Don't worry."

Ema looked at him, and he looked at her. My two favorite people in the world sized each other up. This was highly stressful. I held my breath.

"All right," Ema finally said. "I believe you."

I closed my eyes in relief and let out a long breath. They both looked at me and laughed at the same time.

Things went really well after that. We sat and ate and Ema told us about Aaron and Moses and all the exciting military maneuvers that Aaron was learning. "The boys have really bonded," she enthused. "They're forming a friendship that has lifelong implications."

"That's fabulous," I said, but not without a slight twinge of jealousy. It was time to let Moses grow up and form new attachments. I was certainly doing that. "Ema," I said abruptly. "Pawero and I want to get married. We came here for your blessing."

To her credit, my mother didn't look at all surprised. She nodded slowly. "How will you live, my daughter? Like a Hebrew or like an Egyptian?"

I glanced over at Pawero, and he motioned to me with his fingers as if to say, "You talk, I'm with you."

"I'm not sure how it's all going to play out," I said slowly. "We're determined to follow Elohim, but we're going to live in the Egyptian section of town."

"And your children?" asked Ema.

"We'll teach them about the one true God," I said, coloring.

Pawero nodded his agreement.

"It sounds wonderful," said Ema, drumming her fingers on the table. "But I suspect you two are very naïve. Don't you think that your family will be subject to all sorts of persecution if you don't worship other gods? And what of Hatshepsut? Has she agreed to give you up, Miryam?"

Hatshepsut. That's a sore subject. "Uh, I haven't actually gotten her permission yet."

Ema shook her head and pursed her lips. "Good luck," she said grimly. "That one will never let you go."

"Ema!" I exclaimed hotly. "Don't be so negative!"

"Ladies, ladies," cut in Pawero. "Let's not get upset. The only way to deal with this is to pray and let Elohim work it out."

Ema and I both stared at him. My mouth dropped. When did Pawero become a spiritual leader? He didn't wait for our response, however. Reaching out for Ema's hand on one side and mine on the other, he started to pray: "O God, King of the universe, Lord most high, we come before You to pray Your favor on our marriage. If it be Your will, please soften the heart of Hatshepsut so that we get permission to wed. Your will, not ours. We love You."

"Amen," I said, after a short silence.

"Amen," agreed Ema, somewhat tentatively. Still, she said it.

The rest of the visit went well. I think Pawero did an amazing job winning Ema over.

By the second day, she seemed to have forgotten that he was The Enemy and he became just Pawero. To my way of thinking, this was a great accomplishment. By the time we left, she was hugging him good-bye and reminding us to give her plenty of notice about the wedding date.

"You're amazing," I said on our way back.

Pawero merely grinned and kissed the tips of my fingers.

9

"ONE DOWN, ONE TO GO," I muttered the next night as we ate dinner with Hau and Tutu.

"Ah, yes, our Hatshepsut," commented Tutu, spooning more sliced cucumbers onto my already full plate.

"Thank you." I smiled up at her.

"What does Ami think?" asked Hau, washing down a mouthful of bread with half a cup of beer.

"She seems relatively optimistic. What do you think?" I turned to Pawero.

I caught him midchew. He swallowed before answering. "I think that we need to be in prayer about this and not do anything before Elohim tells us."

My heart swelled at his words. What a godly man! Our marriage must be approved, it must! Would Elohim have let so many things fall into place only to frustrate us at the last moment? I needed to trust Him, but my heart was so filled with longing for Pawero that I couldn't relax. "Maybe we should fast too," I suggested.

Pawero met my eyes. "Don't worry, my little Miryam," he said, speaking more to my thoughts than my actual words. "God will not let us down. We're meant to be together. Just trust."

Just trust. Such simple words, yet so hard to do.

Praying for the queen to approve our marriage drove me to my knees several times a day. I don't remember ever praying so much in my life, and that includes all the Moses prayers.

*

Two weeks later, Amunet came home for a short visit. She had the complete attention of her parents, Pawero, and me as she told us that Hatshepsut and her supporters had succeeded in undermining Mutnofret to the point where the former Second Wife of the old pharaoh was significantly marginalized.

"She wants to keep Moses where he is for the next two years and then bring him back to the palace."

"And what of me?" I asked with trepidation. "Does she know of my plans to marry?"

Amunet looked at me. "I felt a push from our God to broach the subject the other day. I told her how happy you and my brother are, how delighted with one another. I could see by her face that she was struggling. On the one hand is her need for your complete attention, and on the other is her genuine love for you. So I suggested a plan."

"A plan?" said Pawero, all ears. "What plan was that, my sister?"

"I suggested that you return to the palace as a day worker, but that you get a special provision to go home to your husband each night."

"And, and…?" I was beside myself with excitement.

"And," said Amunet, obviously enjoying herself as she drew this out, "she agreed!"

"Ahhhh!" I screamed, jumping up at the same time as Pawero. He grabbed me around the waist and spun me around and around, until, exhausted, we fell into a heap on the floor, laughing and giddy.

That was one of the best days of my life, so young, so happy, so excited about the future. The promise of all to come! How could I have been so blessed, to have been plucked from the midst of slavery: me, Moses, now Aaron? What was so special about our family that we were exalted above so many thousands of other Hebrew families? What was it?

It had to be the faith of Ema and Abba, their total reliance on Elohim, their teaching the next generation (us) to have faith in Him no matter what. When I stopped to really think about it, we were relatively unique among the Hebrews. Sure, most people gave lip service to following Elohim, but when push came to shove there was plenty of bitterness, anger, discontent, sexual sin, adherence to Egyptian ways. It hit me all of a sudden just how incredibly lucky I was to have the parents that I did. They provided a godly lineage worth more than all the gold in the old pharaohs' tomb.

Marriage ceremonies in Egypt were simple affairs. Pawero and I were wed at his home, with less than fifty people in attendance. Ema and my Aunt Sarah were there; the rest of the people were friends and family of Pawero. Moses and Aaron were still down south but sent warm greetings via a messenger. Hatshepsut didn't come (she would have totally upstaged me) but sent a gold and lapus scarab pin for my hair. Tutu loaned me her wedding gown: a long, white dress with a beaded sheath and flashes of silver interwoven in the material. My hair was just past my shoulders, and instead of a wig, Amunet swept it up in a bun and secured it with the scarab pin. She also did my makeup and hennaed my feet. My cheeks were naturally flushed with excitement and my eyes bright with the anticipation of not just the marriage bed but the life that lay before me. I say in all modesty that I looked beautiful.

Pawero apparently thought so, too. When I entered the room and he saw me dressed as a bride, his jaw dropped and his eyes glistened. As I approached him, he grasped my hand and murmured into my ear, "So beautiful, my sister, my bride. There is no flaw in you."

I smiled back at him, my beloved. "Nor in you," I mouthed silently.

The ceremony, though brief, reflected our love for Elohim. It was the first public proclamation of this new faith of Pawero's family, and was met with some puzzlement and raised eyebrows. Everyone, however, was too well-mannered to make a fuss during the wedding. That would come later, in spurts and stops over the years, many relationships strained and tentative due to our faith.

Ema stood next to me throughout the ceremony, looking ten years younger in a dress that Amunet had practically forced her to wear. She had finally relented and allowed us to make up her face and hair. I don't know why she put up such a fuss; she looked fabulous. I could tell that she missed Abba, though. As much as she liked Pawero, his not being a Hebrew made her nervous. I kept telling her that it was faith in Elohim that counted, but she wasn't really buying it. Tutu made a tremendous effort to draw Ema out of her shell and integrate her into the excitement of the day. I made a mental note to thank Tutu later.

Later, after dozens of conversations, many well-wishers, whispered advice from Aunt Sarah, more whispered advice from Ema, not so quiet advice from Amunet, jokes, prayers, stories, food and drink, Pawero and I were at last alone in his room, which became our room until we could afford our own place. I'd told him about Amenmose, and together we prayed that I would approach our wedding night like an *almah*, a virgin, since what happened before was forced on me. Still, I couldn't help wincing as we consummated our marriage. My new husband was very gentle and understanding, not to mention extremely handsome. Did I mention extremely handsome?

Each time it got easier. We kept laughing, so happy to be together. This dream was unlike any dream I'd dared to dream. In fact, I was so happy that I was afraid for what may happen.

"Shh, shh," said Pawero, placing his fingers on my lips. I nibbled at them. "Let's trust that God has good for us and not evil. Enjoy this day and don't worry about tomorrow."

"Yes, you're right," I said, forcing myself not to consider anything beyond this current magnificence.

We were given two weeks to settle into our new roles as husband and wife, two weeks to be gloriously, deliriously happy before I was summoned back to the palace, to my old job in a new wineskin, to my queen.

Pawero came with me on my first day back. He had never officially met Hatshepsut, despite Amunet's many years of service. When we approached the palace gates, I was inundated on all sides by greetings from guards, palace employees, even nobility. Everyone seemed thrilled to see me. I was astonished by my own popularity.

Inet rushed at me and clasped me in her arms. "Miryam!" she cried, hugging me tightly. Pulling back, she acknowledged Pawero, looking him up and down. "This is the husband, yes?" She grinned.

"Yes," I said, while Pawero bowed slightly in respect.

"Come," she said. "I will take you to the queen."

We walked through familiar rooms, so much bigger and more magnificent now that I'd been gone for a while. They were not so familiar to Pawero, and he studied the artwork swiftly as we were ushered through. At last, we got to the inner chamber outside Hatshepsut's apartments. Inet bid us wait, and we sat. "I'll come get you when *she's* ready," we were told, and then she was gone.

"Stunning," said my husband.

"Thank you," I replied demurely, eyes downcast.

He laughed. "You too, my love, but I was speaking of the art in this place." He sighed. "I'd love a commission here."

"Hey, you never know. I understand you have a contact at the palace who's crazy mad in love with you." I nudged his knee and we laughed, just as the door opened and Inet returned.

"Come with me," she said, one eyebrow raised. We quickly got up and followed her. I was suddenly nervous at the prospect of seeing my queen. I prayed she hadn't lost her affection for me. I'd never really understood why it existed in the first place, other than unmerited grace. Smoothing my dress, I walked next to Pawero and behind Inet. She opened the door to Hatshepsut's private chamber, the room outside her bedroom, and stood to the side as we entered.

Hatshepsut was sitting in her regal chair, the one with the leopards carved into the armrests, waiting for us. She was as gorgeous as ever, her abundant figure perhaps a bit fuller. She and I stared at each other for a moment—it had been so long—until I gathered my wits and knelt before her. "My Queen," I said.

"Posh, Miryam," she responded, rising. "Come hug me."

With a squeal of joy, I ran into her arms and we hugged. For a few moments we weren't queen and servant but two girlfriends thrilled to be reunited. Then she pulled out of my embrace and the queen mask slipped back on.

"This is obviously Pawero," she remarked, her eyes coolly appraising my husband.

I felt a twinge of jealousy. "Yes, my Queen," I answered as Pawero knelt before her, bowing his head in obeisance.

"You may rise," she told him. When she turned to me, there was a slight smile on her lips and she winked.

I relaxed. Approval! She bid us sit, and we three talked for several minutes. Hatshepsut was a busy lady, and very soon she was off to a conference with one of her advisors. Pawero kissed me good-bye, leaving me to acclimate to my old job.

The first day was pretty easy, mostly retelling the story of my marriage again and again. Still, by the time I got home that night, escorted in a chariot courtesy of the queen, I was exhausted. It took a week to get my stamina back. I basically had just enough time at home to have dinner with Pawero and fall asleep in his arms before repeating everything. Every seventh day was a day of rest. I got so tired from the routine that I found myself living for that day of rest, that Shabbat.

It didn't take long for Hatshepsut and me to realize that both of us had changed. Neither of us qualified as a young girl anymore. I tended to be more cautious around her now that she'd amassed so much power—power that seemed to rival Pharaoh himself, her husband, Thutmose II. I also took care not to make too much of my loving relationship with Pawero. I was very aware that it was something she'd never experienced and quite possibly never would. Khufu was a wild, sexual obsession, not a companion. And Thutmose was a sickly, half-grown man to be endured. My queen was restless and unhappy. She loved me as well as she loved any other, but I could count only on the will of Elohim to sustain that. Capriciousness has long been a characteristic of those who rule.

My new husband was very understanding, but he wanted more time together. We both did. As hard as this working schedule was, I could only surmise what Abba and Ema must have gone through as slaves. This was so much better than that. Still, by the end of six months, we were crazed from the pace.

One morning, as I sleepily stumbled out of bed so as to be ready for my pick-up by the royal chariot, Pawero pulled me back down. "Don't leave," he said, half-awake.

I enjoyed being back in his arms, but within a few minutes I was nervous. "I really must go," I fretted, observing through our small bedroom window the ever-increasing brightness of the morning. "The chariot will be here any minute."

"Damn the chariot!" exclaimed Pawero.

I was shocked. My husband never speaks like this. "Pawero!"

"I mean it." He sat up, fully awake now. "I hate seeing you leave like this. Just quit. Stay home and have babies."

My heart constricted. How I would love to do just that! "Honey, you know I would stay back in a second if I could, but I don't work for just *anyone!* She's the queen, and not only the queen but sometimes I think maybe she's the pharaoh as well."

My husband made a hollow, choking sound. I think maybe it started out as a laugh but got changed along the way. He pounded one fist into an upturned palm. "I understand all that, Miryam. I've been trying to come up with a solution but my only solution is to plead with Elohim to change things somehow. I feel so helpless."

I sat back on the bed and wrapped my arms around him. "But we're always helpless! We never have control, just the illusion. I totally agree with you that the only way to change things is through prayer. Can I pray with you?"

He held me tight. "Of course."

So we prayed. We asked for blessing, protection, and a change in our current situation such that we would have more time together, even be able to have children and properly parent them. We prayed for God to move quickly. We thanked Him for His generosity and kindness toward us. We praised Him for all He is and all He does. And then I grabbed my bag and flew out of the house because the chariot driver was banging impatiently on the front door.

It was interesting what happened. God didn't immediately change our circumstances; first He worked on our hearts. Over the next several weeks, independently of one another, He taught both Pawero and me to be joyful. This was a lesson I had learned, but then I didn't have to work at it because life became naturally joyful. I needed to turn my heart to embracing joy even when it wasn't immediately apparent.

Next, He moved us to pray continually. I hadn't been praying as often as had been my daily practice because I was so caught up in my new husband and then the business of life at the palace. Now I willed myself to speak to Elohim about all that was on my mind as it occurred, trivial or significant, I knew that my heavenly Father cared about it all. As I spent more time in prayer, setting my face toward joyfulness, I discovered to my joy that my heart was overflowing with thankfulness.

This then was the third lesson that God taught us: to be thankful *in everything*. I glimpsed the spiritual power inherent in constant thankfulness. As I joyfully and in prayer thanked Elohim not only for the good things but especially for the annoying and difficult ones, obstacles and problems in my life were overcome and resolved in miraculous ways.

The most exciting thing that happened was when I mentioned to the queen about Pawero's desire to use his artistic skills at the palace. She hired him on a trial basis to work on a mural in the first floor antechamber leading to the throne room. Even better, she assigned us a small apartment right on the grounds. We no longer had to travel back and forth, plus we were able to have our own place (much as we loved Tutu and Hau, it was *really* nice to have the privacy) and between the two of us working, we were compensated quite handsomely. We were able to provide Ema with all the necessities of life, plus some of the luxuries. In turn, she blessed friends and family. Her generosity was such that we hoped she kept at least some things for herself.

During this time, Moses returned for a visit. At fifteen years old, he resembled a man and not the young boy I remembered. I cried when I saw him, longing to throw my arms around his neck but was somewhat intimidated before this prince of Egypt. My brother stepped forward and kissed me on both cheeks, briefly hugging me.

"It is so good to see you, Miryam," he smiled, thoroughly in command of the situation.

Behind him stood Aaron, who at eighteen was now most definitely a man. Tall and broad-shouldered, a faint beard shadow outlining his strong jaw, happy and self-assured, glowing with the health that three years of good food and hard, physical military exercises had wrought, he barely resembled the scrawny boy snatched from the slave village to accompany Moses.

"Aaron?"

"My sister!" he exclaimed.

This time, I didn't hesitate but threw myself into his arms and hugged him hard. We chatted, and they congratulated me on my marriage to Pawero, expressing interest in meeting him later that day. I noticed the easy camaraderie between the brothers, and Aaron's deference to Moses' superior position despite his being the older brother. I caught no resentment on the part of Aaron; just delight at being part of Moses' life.

When Moses and Aaron did meet up with Pawero, a few days later as it turned out, they really liked him and he them. I wasn't sure if Aaron would resent my marrying an Egyptian, but he took to Pawero right away, thrilled that he knew Elohim. Moses especially found my husband fascinating, the perfect blend of Egyptian and believer in the one, true God. It hadn't occurred to me that Pawero was just the right person to reach out to Moses, who was caught between two wildly divergent worlds. I saw an animation in Moses' face the likes of which I had never seen. That night at bedtime, I got on my knees and thanked God for the masterful way He brought all things together for the good of those who love Him according to His perfect will and plan.

Pawero entered our small bedroom just as I got up off my knees. I quickly crossed the room and buried my face in his chest. "Thank you, my love," I murmured into the smooth, brown skin.

"I receive that," he said, enveloping me in a warm caress. "But why?"

"My brothers. They adore you."

He laughed. "You have fine brothers. I am delighted to finally meet them."

I raised my face to his. "But did you see how Moses responded to you? You have pulled together the Egyptian thing and belief in God in a way neither Aaron nor I could ever have done. It was truly gratifying!"

Pawero wrinkled his brow. "Excuse me, the 'Egyptian thing'? What does *that* mean?" He tickled me in a sensitive spot, causing me to scream and run away. Pawero dashed after me (neither of us had very far to go in that room), catching me so that we collapsed in a heap on the bed, laughing uproariously.

*

The marriage of Hatshepsut and Thutmose was not what one would call "close." My queen paid him only as much attention as was absolutely necessary to accomplish her goals and not a gram more. Yearly, she grew in power while he became more and more sickly. Though only a young man of twenty-one, Thutmose appeared more like a middle-aged man on the verge of death than someone who should have been at the peak of his vigor and strength. Thin to the point of skeletal, he spent more days in bed than not. In startling comparison, Hatshepsut was bursting with health and vitality. She had put on some more weight and was positively bursting out of her clothes in a still attractive way. Her eyes flashed, her color was high, and her step firm and purposeful. So it was a great surprise to us all when Thutmose suddenly announced that he was taking a second wife.

The pretty, quiet daughter of a court nobleman, Iset was also one of the attendants of Mutnofret. It seemed that Thutmose's mother had thrown the pair together at every opportunity and nature, helped along by Mutnofret's detailed directions, had taken its course. This established Mutnofret in a higher position and shuffled court power plays quite a bit. Hatshepsut still had the upper hand, but she had to work at maintaining control. Suffice it to say that her good mood suffered while all this transpired, and the rest of us suffered along with it.

This, however, was small onions compared with the hysterics in our section of the palace when Iset's pregnancy was announced. Hatshepsut was beside herself with outrage.

"That awful bitch thinks she's won," she raged, speaking of Mutnofret. "But she will not succeed!"

Not surprisingly, my queen threw her unashamedly awesome powers of seduction into bedding her previously largely ignored husband. Not the biggest whiz at cause and effect, Thutmose didn't stop to analyze this new attention: he just enjoyed it to the hilt. After their nights together, Hatshepsut came back to her rooms, stripped off her clothes, called for a bath, and scrubbed herself. She allowed herself an hour of silence and brooding before putting on royal dress plus the crown with the serpent and striding forth to embrace her duties as monarch.

Three miserable months of this and my queen announced her pregnancy. To his disappointment, the nocturnal visits to Thutmose ceased due to the queen's "exhaustion."

In her defense, it wasn't all a ploy. Pregnancy was indeed hard on Hatshepsut. She gained too much weight, her ankles swelled, and her face grew bloated. The first several months she didn't seem to think about the actual child at all, content instead with the accomplishment of producing an heir. Toward the end of her term, she did think more and more of the actual child in her womb. In the meantime, Iset gave birth to a healthy son, who was given the name Thutmose, as in Thutmose III.

I was the unhappy servant chosen to bring Hatshepsut the news. "You'll be able to soothe her better than any of us," I was told, though I wasn't sure I was buying it. Pawero and I had time for a quick prayer, and then I was off to the queen's chambers, knocking hesitantly at her door.

"Come in," she commanded.

I entered the room and found my lady propped up against numerous multi-colored linen pillows, feet elevated on a pillow, a young girl rhythmically fanning her with a big bundle of peacock feathers.

"Yes, Miryam?"

"It's about Iset, my Queen." I curtsied.

"Yes?" The word sounded natural enough, but I knew Hatshepsut so well that I could see the flicker in her eyes, the slight increase in stillness to her persona.

"She's had the baby, my Queen. A boy, named Thutmose."

Hatshepsut moved her hand so that it rested lightly on her bulging belly. I saw it all in that gesture: the resignation, the protection, the hurt, and the determination to turn this baby into her trump card.

"Thank you, Miryam. You may extend my congratulations to Thutmose on the birth of his son." Though the words were steady and calm, I detected the tremor of emotion beneath the surface. I looked at her, my eyes saying, "Do you need me?" I saw the imperceptible shake of her head, those full lips forming the word *later*, the girl with the fan oblivious to it all.

It *was* later, later that night after Pawero and I had long settled into sleep that I was summoned to my queen's rooms. I disentangled myself from Pawero's sleepy embrace, whispering that I would be back as soon as possible, and he reluctantly let me go. The guards who came for me hurried me along silent corridors, not pausing until we reached the outer chambers of Hatshepsut's apartment. I let myself in, familiar with the surroundings such that I could walk with ease in the dark, and dark it was. Hatshepsut waited for me at the entrance to her bedroom, opening the door herself. After I entered, she closed the door so that it was only the two of us. It was then that the mask came off. Her face crumpled as she held out her hands. "Miryam," she cried, brokenly.

"Oh, my Queen!" I held her closely, cradling her in my arms like a child as she sobbed and sobbed and sobbed.

Every so often she would hiccup and whisper, "I was so close," only to be overcome by another spate of crying.

We sank down to the floor, sitting on the plush wool rug, my back to her bed and her head in my lap. I stroked Hatshepsut's hair, and for the rest of that night she allowed me to comfort her. I did not attempt to strategize or point anything good out to her; I merely allowed her to grieve: for her father, for Khufu, for her girlhood, for the marriage like mine that for all her wealth and position she could never have. Eventually, she fell asleep, and I covered her with a light sheet, making her as comfortable as possible. I prayed over her as she slept, lightly touching her shoulder as I asked Elohim to bless her and bring her to Himself before going to sleep myself on a pallet, like the old days.

*

The next morning, Hatshepsut seemed renewed. She smiled at me before dismissing me. I quickly retraced my steps throughout the palace halls until I came to my private quarters.

"There you are!" exclaimed Pawero, standing dressed with a paintbrush in his hand, obviously about to go to work. "How is she?"

"She'll make it." Wearily, I crossed the room and slipped into my husband's warm embrace. "Have I told you lately how much I love and appreciate you?"

"Tell me again."

"I love and appreciate you." I held onto him tightly. "Don't let the palace corrupt you."

Pawero kissed the top of my head. "We'll stay close to Elohim."

*

Egypt went wild with the birth of Thutmose III. Thrilled by a male heir who ensured the continuation of the royal family, the people danced and partied in the streets for a week. Life settled down after that, but only until Hatshepsut gave birth to her daughter, Neferure.

The birth itself was uneventful. My queen was a strong, vigorous woman; the baby small and in the correct position. All went as it should, for which I was very grateful.

What could I say about our first glimpse of Neferure? The round head, the black hair that stuck straight up, the tiny flower bud mouth, the dimples in each cheek, the determined chin, the delicate ears, the soft eyes, but mostly the indescribable, utterly fetching quality to her persona. I aided the midwife, cleaning off the baby and wrapping her in a blanket, stopping to gaze into her sweet face, only delivering her to Hatshepsut when my queen grew impatient at the delay. "Miryam! The baby!" she demanded from the bed, her voice weak yet still authoritative. Reluctantly, I handed the little princess over.

Hatshepsut's eyes glowed when she beheld her daughter for the first time. "Oh, she's so beautiful!" she exclaimed, awed.

Later that day, Moses came by to see his new sister. By then, the queen was washed, hair brushed, propped up in bed and feeling better. She even insisted that we apply eye kohl. She held little Neferure close to her breast, transfixed by the tiny face. "Moses, my son," she said when he arrived. "Come see your new sister."

Moses pulled a chair up to the side of the bed. He looked like a man these days, tall and handsome. My heart swelled at the sight of him. Carefully, he touched his finger to the baby's cheek. She opened her eyes, and they looked at each other. I know it's impossible for an infant just born to smile, but it really looked to me like she smiled at him. He certainly smiled at her.

That little girl changed our lives. The queen nursed her baby, though there was a wet nurse on call. I had the pleasure of taking care of her for part of each day. This totally changed my attitude about work. I couldn't wait to go each day and see little Neferure, or Nef Nef, as we called her.

"Is it time for your own baby?" asked Pawero, amused by my utter devotion.

I wasn't sure how to answer. I had such mixed emotions about having children of my own. Growing up in a slave village, not seeing the end of torment for my people, I was reluctant to potentially bring a child into that life.

"Our children will be safe," promised my husband, answering my unspoken concerns. "They'll be Egyptian."

I shook my head. "Anything can happen in this life. Who's to know?"

"That's what I love about you; you're such an optimist."

"Hey," I said, throwing a pillow at him, "a *practical* optimist."

We didn't speak of children again for some months. I was fully invested in taking care of Neferure, and Pawero was working on a huge mural in the banquet room that called into play all his creative skills. I knew how fulfilling he found his work and was so glad for him. Every night he relayed his progress and weekly took me to see the ever-expanding mural. Bright and colorful, it celebrated the joys of eating and drinking, complete with pictures of royalty and servants. I *oohed* and *aahed*, so proud of my talented husband, assuring him it was absolutely perfect for a room dedicated to feasting.

Both royal babies flourished. Little Thutmose grew strong and sturdy, unlike his delicate father. From the time he could sit up on his own and grab things, everything was a weapon. Everything! Obviously, this one was destined for military greatness.

Baby Nef Nef, on the other hand, was born with people skills. She charmed everyone, including her own mother. I've never seen Hatshepsut so fierce about someone before, even during the most obsessive Khufu days. She adored her child. The other person who was completely smitten was Moses. He showed way more interest in that baby than young men his age ever do.

Unfortunately for Moses, even though he was a prince—or maybe in spite of it—his time was not his own, and he couldn't stay endlessly at the palace. He and Aaron were back and forth to Thebes and various outposts even further south. There was talk of building a military compound northeast, toward the Euphrates River. If it happened, Moses told me he wanted to be in on the ground floor of the design. It appeared he had an interest in architecture. He kept Aaron with him all the time. They had grown so close during these last several years. As I watched them banter back and forth, my heart swelled with happiness.

More and more, Aaron reminded me of my father. He was quick to discuss theology, often drawing Moses into debates on Elohim versus the Egyptian gods. Though Moses had expressed faith in Elohim, still, I knew that he attended many of the temples of the different gods for every royal ceremony and celebration. I wasn't clear how he reconciled that in his own head, and indeed where he stood. After all, he was still very young. I prayed that Moses would grow close to God despite the unholy pantheon that swirled around him. I knew that Ema prayed for him fervently, day and night. More and more, it was the influence of Aaron that gave us hope.

*

When Neferure turned two, I gave birth to my first child, a girl. We named her Abigail, as both her natural father and her Father in heaven were rejoicing at her birth, not to mention her mother.

I was every bit as entranced by my daughter as Hatshepsut was with hers. "Don't tell the queen," I said to Pawero, "but I think we got the cuter baby."

"That's only because she looks like you," he answered, as besotted as me over our new daughter.

"Maybe this child will live to see a free Israel," I said, wondering what the future held for the next generation.

"She might," agreed Pawero. He fondled Abigail's tiny foot, peeking out of the linen blanket I used to swaddle the baby in. We both gazed at the little girl, overcome with love.

Ema, Hau and Tutu had nearly given up on grandchildren, it had taken us so long to have our first child. But the timing felt right to me. At almost thirty years old, I was secure in who I was, plus, even more importantly, Hatshepsut had let me know that I could work minimal hours if I had a baby. She was so thrilled with Neferure that she had suddenly become aware of my barrenness. We discussed it one day.

"So, Miryam," began Hatshepsut idly as I hung up dresses in her closet.

"Yes, my Queen?"

"Why haven't you and Pawero had a child?"

Why haven't I had a child? Why do you think! Could it be because you want my attention every waking moment? Instead I said, "It seems that God has not yet seen fit to bless me, my Queen."

"Hmm," said Hatshepsut. "Well, I heartily recommend motherhood. I can't imagine life without Nef Nef."

"None of us could." I hung up another dress, deliberately keeping my voice light. "So, do you think Pawero and I should try to have a child?"

"Yes."

I spun around. "Really? It won't...inconvenience you, my Queen?"

"No," she said, smiling at me.

I smiled back, and nine months later little Abigail entered our lives.

I never thought I could be so deeply attached to a child. For the first time, I understood what Ema must have gone through when she put Moses into the little basket and sent me off to the river with him. What faith in Elohim! My admiration for my mother, which had grown steadily the older I got, reached a new level. How relieved I was that I could raise this child without fearing for her life. I praised God for His faithfulness and blessings.

Hatshepsut was extraordinarily generous. She let me stay back from work for the first three months of Abigail's life. After that, she put me on half-days, sending Amunet to watch Abigail when both Pawero and I were unavailable. Amunet loved this arrangement, cooing over her niece continually. Unlike me, she had never married, and Abigail helped fill a hole in her heart.

*

My life for the next two decades was full and happy. Abigail and Neferure basically grew up together, inseparable for ten years and in close contact after that. Altogether, I raised three children, two girls and a boy. When Abigail turned ten, I retired from palace work, and Pawero and I moved back to his parents' home, building an annex onto it to make room for our young family. Hau and Tutu were thrilled to be intimately involved in the daily lives of their grandchildren, and we were able to help as they aged.

Ema maintained her independence until her death, just after Abigail's thirteenth birthday. How I mourned for her, the slave woman who gave birth to a prince. Jochebed will not easily be forgotten.

When Thutmose III was five years old, his father died. Once again, we endured the long voyage down the river to Thebes, the funeral procession to the Valley of the Kings, the ceremony of the dead. My queen shed some tears, though I suspect they were mostly for show. In reality, she was secretly relieved to be rid of Thutmose as he was a hindrance to her plans to rule the country. With him out of the way, and herself declared regent for Thutmose III, it was full sails ahead for Hatshepsut.

Not surprisingly (at least, not to me), my queen made an excellent pharaoh. She ruled wisely, initiating trade expeditions and extending Egypt's influence far and wide. The famous mission to Punt was her brain child, resulting in the introduction of myrrh to Egypt. Pawero actually worked on one of the murals commemorating the trip. He particularly enjoyed doing the depiction of the boats loaded with trees. She led successful forays down into Nubia, and up to Syria and the lands around the eastern Mediterranean. Moses and Aaron were in on some of those battles, which caused my prayer life to get very active. Elohim faithfully brought them safely home, to my great relief.

Hatshepsut went wild building. Perhaps Moses and his preoccupation with architecture added to what became an obsession with her. Obelisks, temples, the red chapel, Djeser-Djeseru, which was the stunning colonnade and garden portion of her mortuary temple, these were the most notable of an avalanche of building projects. It was a season of great prosperity, especially if you were an artisan like my husband. He never lacked for work.

As I spent my time immersed in palace duties and babies (my own), then home with my young children, my brothers' lives expanded in interesting ways. Aaron, first *de facto* then officially, became Moses' aide-de-camp. He also served in a capacity not unlike a temple priest: a priest of Elohim.

Moses moved forward under Hatshepsut's tutelage in a number of ways. His years of military training were put to good use when he went as the royal overseer of the Syrian expedition. Gone for over a year, the experience had a profoundly sobering effect on him. He saw much death, causing him to seek after the meaning of life.

One cloudless night, when we were still living at the palace, I had just gotten the kids to bed, and Pawero and I were taking advantage of our few minutes of alone time at the end of another good yet exhausting day. Moses had come back from Syria a few days earlier but had mostly been shut up with Hatshepsut and her advisors. Briefly, I caught sight of him in the hallways and hugged him hello.

I was in the midst of telling Pawero about something cute one of the kids had done when a knock on our door startled us.

"Oh no," I groaned. "Do you think I'm needed back at work tonight?"

"Only one way to find out," answered Pawero, grimacing slightly. He got up and opened the door, breaking into a broad smile when he saw Moses in the doorway. "Come in, come in, my Prince!"

Immediately, I jumped to my feet and went to greet him. I realized I had gotten shy in his presence, the little boy who was now the imposing young prince, the battle-hardened leader.

"Miryam, hug me," he commanded, a half-smile on his lips.

Happily, I slipped into his embrace, holding him tightly before giving Pawero a chance to hug him as well. It turned out that Moses had come to see Pawero, not me, to talk about war, and God, and Egypt. I always knew how brilliant he was, but somehow that night convinced me that the little boy was gone forever, with a *man* in his place. They talked for hours, Moses baring his soul over the horrors he had seen in Syria, and the burden of being the one in charge of decisions that affected thousands of lives. He spoke of wanting to sit quietly in a room somewhere and design buildings, while at the same time understanding his position in life and the necessity to function as a leader. At one point he laid his head in his hands and cried as he recalled the fear, suffering, hunger, and helplessness of war.

Pawero was magnificent with him, challenging him, encouraging him, pulling philosophy and theology into the discussion. I dozed off as the hour grew late, jerking into wakefulness in time to hear my husband say, "God has called you to extraordinary greatness, my brother. He will uphold you in everything you do. Seek Him!"

Moses listened intently, only to yawn moments later. "The night is far past," he said, rising. "I will let you good people get to bed." He kissed the top of my head, "No, no, my sister. Don't get up."

Pawero walked him to the door where they clasped hands and said good night. After the door had shut, Pawero came back over to me and pulled me to my feet. "Come, Miryam. Let's go to sleep."

Dreamily, I leaned against him and sleepily stumbled to our warm, inviting bed.

"What do you think?" I murmured as I lay on my side cuddled against my husband, sleep about to overtake me.

"I think," said Pawero, sounding much more alert than me, "that our Moses is in the process of working out what God wants from his life."

"And...?" I managed, barely awake.

"And I can't even begin to imagine what's coming."

* * *

PART II

MOSES

10

1485 B.C.

THE MAN STOOD SILENTLY, LOOKING OUT OVER THE BUSY COURTYARD, his eyes narrowed, his hands balled into fists. He was a handsome man, finely dressed, clean-shaven, with short, black, curly hair, noble brow, almond-shaped eyes, a somewhat prominent nose and a pleasant mouth. Usually this mouth was smiling but not today. If you knew the man, you would probably be able to tell that he was furious. If you had just met him, you would most likely assume he was perhaps on the stern side.

Suddenly, the man spotted something—or someone—in the courtyard below. His face relaxed somewhat, and a tear could be spotted at the corner of his eye. "Oh, Neferure," he said brokenly. "Neferure."

The lady in question, though there was no way she could possibly have heard him, glanced up at the window. He could not read her expression from this distance, but she lifted her slender arm and gave a partial wave, a wave of farewell, before turning and continuing on across the polished stones below. Dressed in the blue and purple embroidered white linen of royalty, her long, luxuriant black wig topped by a circlet of gold, jeweled sandals on her dainty feet, attendants surrounding her, this was obviously the princess—the Princess Neferure.

The man gazed after her until she was out of sight. When he turned away, he grabbed a small vial of ink from the top of his desk and hurled it across the room, watching with satisfaction as it shattered on the opposite wall, splattering black ink over the intricate mural and onto the colorful rug, shards everywhere.

"So have you destroyed my life, Mother," he said to the empty room, through clenched teeth.

A knock sounded on the door. When the man didn't respond, the door opened, slowly, cautiously. A man who resembled the first man walked into the room, though he was taller, broader, with a close-cropped beard and not as nicely dressed. He was a commoner, not a prince.

"Moses!" the man who just entered exclaimed. "You *are* here!" He noticed the wall, the ink, the man's face. "What happened? Are you okay?"

The man named Moses walked over to the door, shut it, and leaned against it, breathing heavily. "Aaron...Aaron."

"It's Neferure, isn't it?"

"No, no." Moses shook his head. "She's an angel. It's...Mother."

"What did she say?"

Moses sighed, running a distracted hand through his hair. "She's marrying Neferure off to Thutmose. She claims it's for the good of the kingdom, that there are no other options. Says she should never have allowed things to get to this point." He crossed his arms and looked up at the ceiling as he spoke. "She wants me to stay away from Neferure until after the wedding. Doesn't want me to 'confuse' her." He laughed mirthlessly. "As if I could confuse her! She knows she's in love with me. And I with her," he added softly. "Desperately in love."

Aaron moved to hug his brother.

"No," Moses said, putting up his hand. "I don't want your comfort. I want...Neferure."

Aaron nodded, looked at the floor, studying his feet before looking up. "I understand," he said gently.

"How can you understand?" cried Moses. "Have you ever loved a woman as if she was your own heart, with all the passion in your soul, only to be told she's off limits. Have you?"

"How can I?" asked Aaron wryly. "I've been with you constantly since I was fifteen years old."

"Ha!" said Moses, lifted briefly out of his misery.

"At least you smiled," his brother commented.

Moses flashed him an annoyed look, then started pacing back and forth, every so often glancing out the window. Aaron knelt by the damaged mural, carefully picking the broken pottery pieces off the carpet.

"Hey, don't do that," remonstrated Moses. "Get a servant."

"I am the servant," said Aaron mildly.

"Get up. Just get up and go find someone to clean that. Someone else." He waved his hand distractedly, staring morosely out of the window.

"Yes. But then come to the barracks with me. Let's have some swordplay. You can work off some of your anger that way."

"Anger? Who said I'm angry?"

Aaron looked down at his ink-stained hands and the ruined rug. "Humor me."

*

An hour later, the prince and his aide circled each other, breathing heavily, sweat pouring down their faces as they parried with wooden practice swords. Moses lunged at Aaron, only to have his target leap out of the way. A few more turns and the prince was able to pin Aaron to the ground, the dull, wooden tip of the sword at Aaron's neck.

"I concede," panted Aaron as he lay in the dust, squinting into the sun.

Later, after they had washed and changed clothes, the brothers sat in the shade of Moses' private garden next to a small pond with a waterfall that provided the pleasing sounds of rushing water, and sipped cold drinks brought to them by a slave girl.

"What you need," said Aaron, relishing the frothy milk, yogurt, and fruit concoction, "is a new project. Something to get your mind off of Neferure. What do you think?"

Moses didn't respond immediately, staring instead across the expanse of lush garden with its fruit trees, palms, streams and flowers, his expression grim. "I don't know," he said finally, when Aaron had almost forgotten the question, so much time had elapsed. "What's there to do?"

"Building?" suggested his brother. "You've always loved a new project."

Moses shrugged. "The Hatshepsut's Needle obelisk is finished."

"There are other obelisks to be done…"

"Oh you mean like that absurd failure down in Swenet? That pathetic excuse for a monument?"

"Pathetic?" said Aaron, leaning forward intently. "Not at all! That thing was *enormous!* A first of its kind. And only one broke," he added. "Not both."

Moses said nothing. Reminders of success did not appeal to him right now when all he wanted to do was drown in his own misery. Absently, he took another swallow of his drink. "Look, Aaron, I appreciate what you're trying to do here, but it's no use. I've waited eighteen years for her. She's not going to be easy to forget."

"No, no you're right. She's not."

The men sat in silence, listening as the birds called loudly to one another from the tops of trees.

"Battle?" suggested Aaron.

Moses groaned. "Yes, you know how fond I am of war." He shook his head. "Maybe I can appeal to Mother? Maybe she'll yet see my side of things."

"I don't know," said Aaron nervously. "You know that once she makes her mind up, she rarely changes it. You know that she wants Neferure to be

Great Royal Wife. There's no way that can happen if she marries you."

Unhappily, Moses nodded. His Hebrew heritage could be overlooked to a point, but the people would never stand for him to usurp the bloodline. Besides, at a very young age Thutmose was showing himself to be a military genius. His wildly successful invasion of Mitanni in the past year earned him the position as head of Egypt's armies in fact as well as in name. No, an adopted prince from a suspect lineage would be a poor choice for the daughter of the great female Pharaoh.

He knew that Neferure loved him, *really* loved *him*, but it wasn't enough. It would never be enough. Again, he felt that tug, like he was being pulled in two opposite directions. Would that never cease? Always he had been led one way by his mother and the other by Miryam, who constantly let him know in a myriad of ways that he was really a Hebrew, one of the slaves, one of *them*.

At those times when Hatshepsut had been too busy, often too busy, the loving arms of Miryam were his refuge and he had been excited to contemplate his secret identity. But then Hatshepsut would suddenly show up, embrace him, call him her son, and he would eagerly return to his role as prince, his standing as one of the royal family of Egypt.

And then Aaron entered his life, the brother he always wanted, the companion lacking from boyhood. He showed up at the end of childhood and accompanied him on the path to manhood. Together they learned swordplay, spear throwing, horseback riding. They were put through the rigorous training that made a man out of a pampered twelve-year-old boy, a boy who longed for a mother…but Aaron was not a usual older brother. He was a servant who ultimately lived or died on Moses' word.

Moses glanced over at Aaron, who was currently leaning back with his eyes closed. Faithful Aaron, a real blood brother. There was absolutely no one he could trust like Aaron. Except maybe Miryam. And Pawero.

His mood lifted somewhat at the thought of Pawero. Good old Miryam, marrying the best guy around. He'd been a combination older brother/father figure over the years, always available, always helpful. He hadn't been part of the tugging, didn't seem to have an agenda other than genuinely wanting to help Moses find his way in life. Come to think of it, Pawero had always urged caution where Neferure was concerned. Hmm.

Which of course led him right back to Neferure. Heavens, she was gorgeous! He felt a pang in his heart at the thought. It was more than that, though. There were plenty of gorgeous women around, and most of them were eager to throw, no hurl, themselves in his direction. He was a catch—he knew it; they knew it. But since birth, Neferure had had a sweetness about her. He'd been drawn to her right from the start. As she grew up, he enjoyed his role as big brother. She was such a smart little thing, always asking questions with those big, guileless eyes, slipping her tiny hand in his, ecstatic to see him after he had been out of the city for any length of time. And then five years ago, when she reached her thirteenth birthday, everything changed. All of a sudden, he didn't look at her like an older brother anymore. Her beauty dazzled him, but it was her gentleness that seduced him.

Neferure loved him back. They spent more and more time together, laughing, talking, just being. Of course they had known all along that the unspoken plan was for her to marry her half-brother Thutmose, to be his first wife and further secure the kingdom for Hatshepsut. Thutmose himself had no objections to this; he liked Neferure well enough. Besides, no one was deceived that she would be his only wife.

Who Neferure married was always going to be Mother's decision. That was a foregone conclusion. It was just that he harbored hope that she would choose the happiness of those she loved over her plans for power. Hope, that fleeting, insubstantial flame. Angrily, he gritted his teeth as he thought about how today hope had been smothered in an instant. He thought about his interview with his mother, and how she had barely been able to rise from her chair to greet him, the extra weight gained in the last ten years holding her body hostage. "Don't get up," he cautioned, alarmed at the flashes of pain crossing her face, knowing that the pain in her bones was worsening.

As usual, she ignored his advice, insisting on struggling out of the chair and standing face-to-face with him. "My son," she said, lightly touching his cheek.

"Mother." He grasped her hand and kissed it. "Please sit."

"Ah." She waved her hand in the air before sinking back into her chair—the special one with all the cushions.

Moses pulled another chair close to her, sat down, and waited.

"The reason I asked you to come," said Hatshepsut, her face expressionless, "has to do with Neferure."

Moses could tell he wasn't going to like this. "Mother . . ."

"No, let me finish." Hatshepsut shook her head. "I have always known your feelings, and I have been remiss in allowing them to continue." Moses opened his mouth to interrupt, but Hatshepsut stopped him. "I have been remiss," she said again, more firmly. "And I know that you are wise enough to understand that our personal wants *must never get in the way of kingdom business!* So I must inform you that Neferure's engagement to Thutmose will be announced this evening. They are to be married." She sat back, the exertion of this encounter causing her forehead to glisten with perspiration.

Moses' eyes narrowed. "Does this have anything to do with that story you circulated about the god Amun impregnating your mother, Ahmose, and conceiving you? Those pictures at Karnak? Am I not in the 'deity' line?"

"Don't push me, son."

Moses tried another tactic. "Mother," he pleaded, "please! Together Neferure and I can accomplish great things. Don't waste her on Thutmose."

"No!" interrupted Hatshepsut. "Do not defy my decision! It has not been an easy one to make, but it has been made. It's final."

Mother and son stared at one another for several long moments. The son was in the prime of life, strong, healthy, clear-eyed while the mother was in decline, aging, ill, physically weak. But she held the true power, and they both knew it. Finally, Moses looked away.

"All right, Mother," he said, his voice strained. "I can't fight you." He gave a stiff, cold bow, turned, and left the room.

Hatshepsut sat very still, gazing after him. "Good-bye, my son," she murmured to the empty room.

*

After Thutmose III's wedding to Neferure, Moses got serious about his Hebrew roots. Sure, he had always been *interested*, even intrigued, and yes, there had been plenty of contact with his natural brother and sister, not to mention his real mother, but an all-out desire to know more, to *identify* with the Hebrew slaves had been missing. Until now.

"Do you really think this is a good idea?" asked Aaron, after Moses let him know that they were heading to the slave village to 'get to know people.' "You're so visible."

"We'll go incognito."

Aaron raised his eyebrows. He studied his brother's clean-shaven face, glistening skin from years of perfumes and lotions, well-fed appearance, extremely short hair, spotlessly white fine linen tunic embroidered in gold, expensive leather sandals. He shook his head. "I don't think it's going to work. There's *no way* we—you—won't be recognized. Just ask me what you want to know."

"I don't merely want information. I want to get a sense of what it's like to be a Hebrew in the midst of other Hebrews."

"Moses, you really don't want to experience *slavery!*" cried Aaron. "It's awful, it's...there are no words to express the brutality and hopelessness of the lifestyle. You are so blessed that Elohim saved you from a life of degradation and pain. As I am too," he added.

"I don't want to be a slave," Moses said quickly. "I want to experience what it's like to be a Hebrew."

"You can't do that. Slavery and Hebrew have become too deeply intertwined. If only the pharaoh would set us free…."

"We've been through this," interjected Moses. "She can't. She won't. The will of the people is too strong against it." He paused. "We did talk about this recently. Before the Neferure decision."

Aaron's ears perked up. "What did she say?"

"This is super confidential…"

"Of course."

"Well, you know that she's been easing the burden of slavery somewhat."

"Somewhat," Aaron conceded.

"The work days are shorter, the food rations improved, no babies are being killed."

"It's still a hellish existence," said Aaron quietly.

Moses looked at him. "Yes. Anyway, Mother said she hopes to slowly free the slaves in the next ten years."

"Ten years!" exclaimed Aaron. "But—"

"But?"

Aaron took a deep breath. "Please understand that I mean no disrespect as I say this, but your mother is not in the best of health. Do you," he looked exceedingly nervous as he said this, "think she'll be alive in ten years? Or do you think Thutmose will be sole ruler?"

Moses sighed. "You're not being disrespectful. Merely realistic." He ran a hand through his hair. "I don't know, Aaron. Mother is sure that to free the slaves now would cause rioting and chaos. I also know that Thutmose is not, shall we say, predisposed to continuing along on the path she's set. He's military all the way and is terrified about the size of the Hebrew population and their latent ability to rise up against us. He wants to keep them enslaved, in fear, and powerless. Plus, he can't stand me."

"He knows he pales in comparison to you," said Aaron.

"You're very loyal."

"And truthful."

"Yes, that too." They both laughed.

"So, what do you want to do?" asked Aaron cautiously.

"Why don't we go out to one of the work sites and just observe?"

"Do you think we'll get into trouble?"

Moses stared at him. "I'm a prince! My mother is Pharaoh. How can we get into trouble? Besides, we're just going to watch. Don't worry."

"Okay," muttered Aaron. "You're the boss."

*

The following morning, Moses and Aaron set out early. They went to the stables and selected two non-racing horses, horses that wouldn't be easily spooked by the noise and commotion of a building site. After the grooms prepped the animals, the men rode about seven miles to a local rock quarry. When they approached, the supervisor for the project, a short, muscular man sporting a turban to keep the hot sun off his bald head, hurried forward.

"What can I do to assist you, my Prince," he groveled, bowing down such that his forehead touched the ground.

"You can arise," said Moses airily, used to such displays of obeisance. "We're merely here to observe. You may resume your duties."

"Is there a problem, my lord?" The man's eyes flicked nervously to Aaron and back.

"No. You may resume your duties," Moses repeated, this time a little stronger.

"Yes, yes, my lord. As you say," said the man politely, backing away.

"Seems nice enough," said Moses as he and Aaron watched the supervisor scurry back to the makeshift hut that was obviously the center of operations.

"Just watch," warned Aaron.

They found a small patch of shade where they reared in the horses. Then they sat and observed. The scene before them was fraught with energy. Thousands of slaves labored relentlessly under the scorching sun, spread out over a huge area. Some were busy with pick axes in the quarry, freeing shapes from stone while others grunted and heaved the enormously heavy stone onto carts and pulleys, getting it up out of the earth and off to new destinations. Everywhere Egyptian foremen cracked whips and yelled.

"It's hot," said Moses, eyes on the scene below as he reached for his water pouch. "When do they get to drink?"

"There's a water break every four hours," replied Aaron.

"Every four hours?" Moses turned in shock toward his brother. "How can they survive that in this heat?"

"Some can't." Aaron jerked his head to the side. "There's the cemetery."

Moses looked to the left and noticed for the first time the shallow indentation with two, no three, bodies flung in. "That's awful."

"That's slavery. We're considered as less than human. No need to preserve the lives of animals."

"I've not heard you speak this way before."

Aaron took a swig from his own water pouch. "Sorry. This brings back ugly memories. Our father and so many of our relatives suffered like this. It's horrible. If it wasn't for you, and of course Elohim orchestrating our lives, I'd be one of those hopeless men down there."

In silence, they watched awhile longer until Moses abruptly steered his horse around. "Come on. Let's go."

They didn't talk on the ride back to the palace. Both men were preoccupied with their own thoughts. Aaron looked sad; Moses, grim. Neither was prepared to run into the honeymoon party of Thutmose and Neferure, newly returned from the pleasure cruise on the Nile.

"Oh, no." Aaron groaned. "Look, my Prince!"

"Tell me that's not what I think it is."

"I believe it is."

"Well, let's get on with it." Moses grunted. Without speeding up or slowing down the pace of the horses, the men proceeded to the gates of the palace, where the guards cautioned them to wait while the pharaoh, his new consort, and their entourage emerged from various litters and proceeded into the palace. Thutmose, looking pleased with himself, caught sight of Moses and flashed an *I won but I still don't like you* excuse for a smile. Neferure, curious as to who her bridegroom was looking at, turned and saw Moses. Her perfect lips, painted the color of deep pink summer roses, formed a perfect "O" before she mastered her feelings, smoothing her face over so that it was a pleasant, nonemotive, mask. It was enough, though. In that split second of candor Moses saw it all: the regret, the disappointment, the resignation. She was, after all, her mother's daughter.

Abruptly, Moses steered his horse in the direction of the stables. "Let's dismount," he called over his shoulder to Aaron, who followed closely behind.

*

Over the course of the next several weeks, Moses went to several more construction sites and watched the slaves work. At first he took Aaron, but soon he started going alone. He would be gone for hours, and when he returned, he was hot, tired, and moody.

His odd behavior was not unnoticed. The predictable day came when Hatshepsut called for him. Mother and son were on better terms than when

Neferure's engagement was first announced but were still not quite as easy in one another's presence as they used to be. Moses greeted his mother with a kiss on the cheek before sitting in a chair beside her.

"How are you, Mother? Are you feeling all right?"

"Fine, fine." She waved to signify that her health was not the issue here.

"Are you in pain?" he persisted.

"I'm much better," she said, somewhat evasively. "The doctors give me things. It helps."

It was on the tip of his tongue to say, "I'd like to see you lose some weight," but he thought better of it. Sometimes it was best not to push too hard. "What else is going on?"

"I'm more concerned about *you*, my son. What's this I hear about you going out to watch the slaves? What are you up to?"

"I'm not *up* to anything," Moses protested. "I'm interested, is all."

Hatshepsut searched him with her eyes. "You're a prince of Egypt. Those people have nothing to do with you."

"How can you say that? It's where I come from!"

"Don't go there, my son. Don't assume I can always protect you."

"Have I looked to hide behind your skirts, Mother? Have I?"

Hatshepsut gave a wry smile. "It's not what you've looked to do; it's the reality of the situation. You've been protected because of me, but," and here her smile faltered, "I'm weakening. Thutmose is gaining in ascendancy. Don't antagonize him, Moses. He's itching for an excuse to destroy you."

"Destroy me? Do you not exaggerate a bit?"

"Be very, very careful." She lifted her eyes to his. "Please stay away from the slaves."

Frustrated, Moses abruptly stood. "I want to obey you, Mother, really I do," he said in a low voice. "But I'm drawn. I'm compelled—"

Hatshepsut reached out and grabbed his arm. "For me. For me."

*

Moses tried. He really did. But it was like a fire had been lit in his belly, and he couldn't ignore it. Thoughts of his people filled his head, day after day, night after night, such that they even succeeded in crowding out images of Neferure. Eventually, he returned to the stone quarry he had first visited.

This time the supervisor wasn't around. In fact, it seemed like none of the higher-ups were visible. *Probably at a meeting*, thought Moses. He tethered his horse in the shade and walked around the outskirts of the quarry. After about an hour, he started thinking about heading back to the palace and was retracing his steps toward his horse when he heard muffled screams. Quickly following the sound, he came to what appeared to be a deserted area, and saw one of the Egyptian foremen mercilessly beating an elderly Hebrew man.

"No, no," the man sobbed, collapsing into the dirt as the heavy, leaded whip landed squarely on his back again and again.

The foreman grinned evilly. "Shut up, you Hebrew bastard," he growled, snapping the blood-stained whip even harder.

Moses saw red. Every promise to Hatshepsut fled his mind as he lunged forward and grabbed the whip out of the foreman's hand.

"Hey!" the foreman yelled, swinging around with his fists balled, ready to take out whoever dared to interrupt him. His eyes widened when he saw Moses, and the fist stopped in mid-air. "S-sorry, my lord," he began, only to find himself flung backwards with Moses' hands around his throat.

Moses glanced this way and that, and when he didn't see anyone, he squeezed harder. The foreman's face turned red, then purple. Those arrogant hands that had just held the whip now flailed uselessly in the air, slowly dropping down as the life was crushed out of him. As soon as he was good and dead, Moses turned to help the Hebrew slave, who had apparently already taken this opportunity to flee.

"Glad he wasn't too hurt to move," Moses muttered under his breath. Breathing hard, he pulled the Egyptian by the feet into some bushes, picked up a discarded shovel, and dug a shallow pit in the sand. Breathing hard, he heaved the dead man in, covered him up as best as he could, and slunk around the edges of the quarry, making his way back to his horse.

Not seeing any of the leaders, Moses heaved a sigh of relief and headed home. His heart pounded, and his hands shook. He couldn't quite believe what had just happened. *But that man deserved it*, he thought.

Later that night, after a long, soaking bath and a good meal, Moses sat in his bedroom and prayed to Elohim. He poured out his heart, telling Elohim what a good idea it had been to kill that man, and how it was time to free the slaves, and that he was more than available for the job. He failed to hear anything back, however. Totally keyed up from the death of the Egyptian, it was a relatively sleepless night.

*

The next morning, his messiah complex firmly in place, Moses returned to the quarry to see who else he could protect. It was pretty quiet out here today.

Maybe they were investigating the disappearance of the foreman. Hard to tell. *Wait a minute, what's that, over there?* Moses narrowed his eyes as he peered into the distance. It looked like a scuffle. As he made his way over to it, he noticed that two slaves were involved in an all-out, knockdown, drag-out fight. When he was within ten feet of the action, he could tell that one guy was giving the beating and the other poor slob was getting it.

"Hey, stop that!" demanded Moses. Startled, both men looked his way. "Come on," said Moses. "Get away from him."

Reluctantly, the aggressor released his grip on his victim, who promptly escaped. "Why are you hitting your fellow Hebrew?" asked Moses.

Sullen and unrepentant, the man spat on the ground. "Who made *you* ruler and judge over us? Are you thinking of killing me as you killed the Egyptian?" And he glared at Moses.

Normally, Moses would have had him hauled away to the dungeons for that level of impertinence. Instead icy fingers of fear crept down his spine. How did this fellow know what happened yesterday? How many others knew? *What I did must have become known.*

Without bothering to answer, he spun on his heel and took off. Reaching his horse, he swung himself on and pressed it toward the palace.

I have two choices, he thought. *I can go home, or I can go into hiding.* He prayed about it and came to the conclusion that he should gather some things together, tell Aaron what was going on, and go into hiding until he knew how serious the repercussions were going to be.

Upon reaching the palace compound, he immediately went to the stables and handed his sweaty horse over to the groom. "I'll be back in an hour. Have a fresh horse ready for me," were his terse instructions. Next he went to his rooms, careful to avoid anyone who wasn't a servant. Since he had grown up in this very palace, he knew all the back halls and secret spots, so that wasn't difficult. Once he reached his private rooms, he told a servant to find Aaron and have him go to the stables. "Tell him to wait for me there."

"Yes, my lord." The servant bowed and left to accomplish the task, not realizing that it was the last task Moses would demand of him.

Moses rummaged quickly through his desk and his bedroom, his mind amazingly clear and alert. He packed two changes of clothes and every piece of gold anything he could find. He stowed everything in a cloth bag before scanning the rooms one last time. Satisfied there wasn't anything too valuable left behind, he closed the door behind him for the last time.

*

At the stables, Aaron waited by the horse. As soon as he saw Moses, he bowed down. "My lord?"

Moses touched him on the shoulder. "Get up, Aaron. Come with me." He led the way to a private alcove down by some of the horse stalls, away from any potential listening ears. "I'm going to have to talk fast. I killed an Egyptian foreman yesterday, and today I've realized that the story is out." Aaron opened his mouth to say something but Moses kept talking. "Let me finish. I don't have much time. I'm heading out of Egypt. I need you to say my good-byes to Miryam and Pawero and…and Mother."

"Are you sure you need to leave? Won't your mother protect you? Surely you don't have to leave Egypt!" protested Aaron, stunned by this unexpected news.

"I wish that were so. Mother warned me that Thutmose is looking for an excuse to get rid of me, and I've handed it to him on a platter. No, I need to leave. I only hope I haven't put you or our sister into danger. Be careful and lay low."

"I'll come with you! It's too much, going off alone like this."

Moses shook his head. "Much as I appreciate the offer, I can't take you up on it. I need you here to look after Mother and Miryam."

"How about if you stay somewhere safe while all this plays out? Maybe it will blow over and you won't need to actually leave Egypt?"

Moses hesitated. "Where's safe?"

"There's a friend of Pawero's right outside the city limits. You could stay there, and I'll send word to stay or go. Please. It would be crazy to leave the country if you don't have to."

Moses scratched his head. "It's not looking good, Aaron."

"Can you give me two days to catch the palace buzz?"

Moses nodded. "Two. If I don't hear from you by the day after tomorrow, I'll be heading to Midian until it's safe."

"Fair enough." The brothers studied each other sadly before saying a hurried good-bye.

"Give my love to Miryam, Pawero, and the kids," was the last thing Moses said after memorizing the location of Pawero's friend's house.

Aaron didn't answer, not being able to speak past the lump in his throat. He touched his fingers to his forehead and watched as Moses mounted the horse, steering it toward the back exit of the palace, watching until he could see his brother no more. It was only then he walked slowly back to the palace.

*

It didn't take long for Aaron to understand that Thutmose had already found out about the death of the Egyptian and that he knew of Moses' culpability. It also didn't take long for him to realize that Thutmose did indeed want Moses dead. Frantically, Aaron sent word to Moses, warning him to flee for his life. That same day, he was summoned to a private audience with Hatshepsut.

Upon entering the room, he immediately prostrated himself before her. "My Pharaoh."

"You can arise." When Aaron got up and lifted his eyes to hers, he was startled to see how much Hatshepsut had aged in the past few days. She looked old, tired and sad. "Where is he?" she asked.

Aaron saw no reason to pretend. "On his way to Midian, my lady."

"Ah. Will I ever see him again, I wonder?"

"He loves you very much, my lady."

"This is a hard life," said Hatshepsut, speaking as much to herself as to Aaron. "One can only hope that the afterlife will bring compensation for all that was missed in this world."

"It's only Elohim who can bring you true peace, my lady," replied Aaron, emboldened by the Spirit of God.

"Yes, the Hebrew God."

"*Everyone's* God," emphasized Aaron.

Hatshepsut stared at a point somewhere above Aaron's head. "Perhaps," she conceded wearily. "It's best for you to pack your things and leave the palace. My stepson...," she said vaguely. "I'll arrange for you to have a pension and, of course, your freedom."

Aaron bowed again. "Thank you, my lady. That is exceedingly kind of you."

For the first time during their interview, Hatshepsut smiled. "I am nothing if not kind," she said lightly. "Give your sister my regards. Tell her...tell her not to forget about me."

"There is not the slightest chance of that, my lady."

"Thank you, Aaron. And thank you for all you've done for my son."

"The pleasure is mine," he said, taking his leave.

* * *

Part III

Zipporah

11

1485 B.C.

THE SUMMER I TURNED FIFTEEN was a time of great inner restlessness. No longer was I content with helping Mama run the household, no longer was I content with mothering my six younger sisters, no longer was I content with my role of shepherdess. I yearned for something more, though for what I would have been hard-pressed to say.

Perhaps it was my emerging sexuality or my growing awareness of the lives of the adults around me. It's possible that the sameness of our transitory existence forced boredom on me despite the many tasks that took up my days. In any case, when Moses entered our lives, I was ripe for a change.

The day started out like all the days before it and, assumedly, like the days that would follow. Mama woke me before dawn, gently shaking my shoulder.

"Mmfh," I mumbled, burrowing even deeper under my warm, cozy sheepskin blanket, clinging to those last few precious moments of sleep.

"Zipporah, let's go. Up!" she commanded in her no-nonsense voice. "It's getting late."

Sleepily, I struggled out from under my bedding, shivering in the cold desert air that permeated our goat hair tent. Later on, the day would grow hot but not yet. Hurriedly, I slipped out of my nightdress and threw on my working robe, the one that used to be white but was somewhat dingy after repeated washings. I used the chamber pot, then washed my hands and face with clean water in the basin we kept next to it. A little more alert now, I brushed out my long hair, quickly and expertly braiding it and tying the bottom.

I heard Mama waking up the rest of my sisters (except for Nashita, the youngest, who at five years old was still two years away from going with the sheep) while I was getting ready. It was our job to take the sheep to pasture.

While my sisters dressed, I made up our food bags. Today was...the same as yesterday: barley bread, cheese, dates, and water pouches. Tonight's dinner would most likely be lentil stew with more bread. By the time we returned from grazing and watering the sheep, I was generally so hungry that anything tasted fabulous. We only got meat a few times a year, during the feasts of He Who Sees.

My father, Jethro, was the priest for our clan, which amounted to about seventy people. We were Midianites, descended from the great father Abraham, and our lives consisted of following available pastureland so that our sheep could graze. Not all the Midianites followed He Who Sees. In fact, most did not. Four hundred years ago several of our direct ancestors were involved in the purchasing of a Hebrew named Joseph. He filled their ears with talk of He Who Sees from the time they first tied him up until they sold him to a top official in Egypt. Through a mighty confirmation of his God, he became second only to Pharaoh. This little fact caused my forefathers to embrace He Who Sees themselves. After all, who can argue with success?

We of course knew the sad state Joseph's descendants came to…the forced slavery of a great multitude. Enough time had passed for us to realize that He Who Sees was no less real even if His people suffered. Instead we regularly prayed for their deliverance from bondage. So far, no movement on that issue as far as we could tell.

That morning, my sisters and I led the sheep out to graze as we had so many mornings before, my biggest excitement for the day being the promise of dinner once we returned home. If I had realized what He Who Sees had in store for me…how I was about to be blessed beyond my wildest dreams. But we don't know, do we? That's where faith and trust enter in: believing for great things in the midst of the desert when all one sees on the horizon are sandstorms.

About mid-afternoon, as was our habit, we brought the sheep to the shared well so we could fill their troughs and let them drink. This wasn't as simple a task as one might think. Quite regularly, other shepherds were there before us and we had to wait, or sometimes they tried to antagonize us by not letting us get water until they got bored and finally left. Father says it's because we're young girls that the boys play these games, thinking they're being funny. I didn't find it amusing in the slightest. I wanted nothing to do with these buffoons.

When we were almost at the well I saw a group of boy shepherds there who had pushed us aside in the past. I really was not in the mood for their antics.

"Oh, no," I groaned, kicking at the dirt with one sandaled foot.

"What is it, Zip?" asked Farah, my next oldest sister.

"Look, it's those boys," I fumed. "I so hope they're not going to bother us again."

Farah shaded her eyes with her hand and peered toward the well. "You're right," she said, studying the scene before us. "Wait, though! There's someone else there."

I peered too. "You're right. He looks like an Egyptian."

We looked at each other. "Maybe he has news of what's happening in the world!" I said while Farah simultaneously said, "Maybe he has goods to trade!" We giggled and picked up our pace.

The Egyptian sat with his back against the well, in the little bit of shade he could find. Frankly, he looked exhausted, which is how most travelers looked when they reached our out-of-the-way desert location. He was good-looking, I spotted that right off—not real young but not weathered and old either. His clothes, though travel-stained, were made from expensive linen, gold thread embroidering the edges. He didn't have a real beard, just what looked like a week's growth from not having access to a razor, and though I'm sure he was hungry, he didn't look like a man who had been food-deprived at any point in his life. Oh, and did I mention the absolutely gorgeous white horse tied up to the left of him? I hadn't seen anything this interesting in maybe forever. I stared at him, tongue-tied.

Farah stared at him also, as did Lana and Maysan. Reema immediately went for the horse while Nadira, the most delicate of my sisters, dropped to the ground and started to cry. I ignored her as this was a usual thing at the end of the day. He didn't introduce himself, and it would have been inappropriate for me, a young girl, to go over to him, so instead I nudged Farah with my elbow and we went to the well to draw water for the troughs.

One of the boy shepherds, the biggest one (and in my opinion the meanest), Layth, pushed me out of the way when I tried to lower my bucket.

"Oh, come on," I said impatiently. "Don't try this again. Just leave me alone."

He laughed at me, which was probably his pathetic attempt at flirting. "Why would I leave you alone, little bird?" he teased, saying the meaning of my name as he grabbed the bucket out of my hand and held it above my head out of my reach. "You're so charming. Isn't she charming, Khurram?"

Khurram, who seemed anything but his name (which means cheerful), sneered, saying, "As charming as a snake," after which he laughed.

Frustrated and close to tears, I would have stalked off except that I knew there was no way I could go home without watering the sheep. None of my sisters wanted to take on the boys except maybe Reema, who at seven years old would not have been very effective. Maybe she could stun them into submission with her cuteness.

Suddenly, the Egyptian sprang up from his resting place and strode over to Layth. Tall and powerfully built, he addressed the shepherd with an unmistakable air of authority. "Leave the girls alone, boy, and take your friends with you. You're done here for the day. Move along."

"Who do you think you are?" protested Layth a little nervously.

"I'm not a little girl, so I won't be easy to push around. That's who I am." The Egyptian's hand lightly rested on the hilt of his dagger. "Get going."

"We're done anyway," growled Layth, struggling to keep his dignity while nevertheless backing up. He, Khurram, and the rest of the boys turned and ran over to their sheep, leaving us alone.

I was about to thank the Egyptian, but before I could form the words he said, "Give me your bucket, please, miss."

I handed it over and stood by in amazement as he scooped bucket after bucket, filling the trough so our sheep could drink. He was certainly much faster at it than me or Farah. "I appreciate your helping us," I said shyly.

"It's my pleasure," he answered, looking directly at me for the first time. I can still remember the jolt that went through my body at his gaze. Flustered, I dropped into a slight curtsey, then spun, grabbing Farah's hand. "Come on!" I shouted to the girls. "Let's get the sheep back to the pen!"

"Why are you rushing me?" grumbled Farah. "Shouldn't we even ask his name?"

"Shh, no, keep walking!"

"Zipporah, what is the matter with you?" demanded my sister.

"He makes me nervous, that's all."

"In a good way?"

I tugged harder at her hand. "Yes. In a good way."

After we secured the sheep, we returned to our tent. Our father sat in front, repairing a tool. He looked up at our approach, surprise evident on his face. "Why have you returned so early today?"

"We had an adventure!" sung out Maysan, the nine-year-old.

"What kind of adventure?" asked Father, smiling.

"An Egyptian rescued us from the shepherds!" shouted Reema, happily blurting out the story before any of us had a chance to speak.

"Shush, Reema, let me tell Father," I scolded. "Those boys harassed us again," I told him. He frowned. "But an Egyptian was resting by the well, and you should have seen the way he chased those boys off! They were soo scared of him. Ha!"

"Zipporah, be nice," said Father, but he was smiling so I knew he wasn't angry.

"He even drew water for us and watered the flock!" added Farah, anxious for Father to know everything immediately. It was impossible to stretch a story out with *any* of my sisters around. Sheesh.

"And where is he?" asked Father. "Why did you leave him?"

"Zipporah pulled us out of there," piped up Nadira, the eight-year-old, all dimples and excitement at being able to tell Father something he didn't yet know. Apparently when someone sits on the floor crying she's still paying attention.

"Well, we need to show hospitality to strangers," lectured Father. "*Especially* strangers who have done us an act of kindness. Zipporah and Farah, I want you two girls to go back and invite him to have something to eat."

"But Father," I said, nervously, "maybe he's already left! It'll be a wasted trip. Plus I'm hungry."

"You can eat when you get back. *Go!*" he commanded.

We went.

I didn't talk much on the way; mostly I pretended to listen as Farah prattled on about this and that. I didn't understand why I was so nervous, but there you have it. I was. The Egyptian was still there, on his knees. He looked like he was praying. We walked toward him.

"Hello!" called Farah.

He looked up, then slowly got to his feet. "Hello," he responded, and I noticed for the first time that his voice was deep and melodic, his accent clearly Egyptian.

Farah spoke since I was obviously not going to, but I noticed he looked at me. "Our father asks if you would be our guest for dinner tonight, sir."

The man's face broke into a wide grin. "Praise You, Elohim, for providing for Your servant," he exclaimed.

I spoke up for this first time. "Is the One you call Elohim He Who Sees?"

"Yes, that is He." His eyes studied my face.

I blushed. "We worship Him as well."

The Egyptian untied his horse and walked with us, leading the horse behind him. "My name is Moses. You are?"

"I am Farah, and this is Zipporah," said my sister confidently.

"It's a pleasure to meet such charming women in the middle of the desert," replied Moses gallantly.

We giggled.

I relaxed a bit. He *was* easy to be around. He was also the most…manly male I had ever met. Whew.

My father and Moses hit it off right away. Their shared belief in He Who Sees sparked a common bond, despite their wildly different backgrounds. Mama was a bit shy, but not so shy that she didn't urge Moses to eat more. It was easy to see that he was extremely hungry, but he ate with restraint, like a gentleman. I was fascinated by him.

Later, after the dinner dishes were cleared away and the younger children put to bed, Farah and I joined Father, Mama, and Moses around a small fire outside the tents. Something about the dark brings on confidences, I've noticed.

I heard Moses' story for the first time, amazed that a *real, live Egyptian prince* was not only sitting within a few feet of me, but had actually spoken to me and defended me. Up to now, the most exotic man I had met was a Sabean trader who offered me a colorful scarf. Just as I had been about to say thank you, Father coldly told him no. That was embarrassing.

It was fascinating to hear about Moses' flight from the Egyptian king. "Why were you so eager to protect the Hebrew slave?" asked Father.

There was a pause, then from the shadows cast by the flickering of the fire Moses answered, "Because I am one."

What? A Hebrew? "Like our father Joseph?" I said, surprised into speaking up.

"Not exactly like Joseph," answered Moses wryly. "He ruled Egypt whereas I merely antagonize the rulers."

"Zipporah, Farah, time to go to bed," announced Mama. "It's late."

"Can we stay up a little longer? Please?" I pleaded.

"Girls," came Father's voice from the other side of the fire, "our guest will still be here tomorrow. You're not going to miss anything."

"Good night, Zipporah. Good night, Farah," said Moses, the sound of his voice saying my name making me hot and cold all over.

"Good night," sang out Farah as she traipsed into the tent.

I followed with a much softer "good night," pushing past my sister into the dark interior, greeted by the familiar sounds of five girls breathing as they slept.

Farah fell quickly asleep, but I lay in our shared bed quite awhile, mulling over the details of my extraordinary day. Eventually, I drifted off.

*

Father told the truth: not only was Moses still with us the next day, but he continued to stay. He apparently had enough gold to keep going, had he wanted, and to set up a new existence anywhere...perhaps Syria? Canaan? However, he showed no inclination to leave our small desert abode. He thoroughly enjoyed getting to know Father, seemingly thirsty for the fatherly guidance of an older man who as the priest of our community was intent on the things of He Who Sees.

I could tell that Father was also thrilled with the company of Moses. He loved Mama and us girls, true, but an intelligent, fascinating fellow like Moses who loved He Who Sees was for Father like a gift dropped straight out of heaven. I came to realize that, though Father faithfully ministered to the men in our midst, he hadn't had an equal who challenged him both spiritually and intellectually. Until now.

When Father refused to accept any of Moses' gold, Moses insisted on working for his keep. He accompanied us girls to pasture, evidence of Father's trust in his good character. This also enabled Nadira and Reema to stay home and help Mama. Having a grown man shepherd moved our day along a lot quicker. Not only was he a huge help with watering the flock and making sure no one bothered us, he also got the sheep to behave and move along so much better than we ever did.

I began to look forward to my days in the field. No longer did Mama have to push me out of bed; I positively sprang up in the morning, raring to go.

"Look who's wide awake?" teased Mama one morning, about a week after Moses appeared. Normally she would have been threatening me, and I would have had my head buried in a pillow, but now I was already dressed and braiding my hair.

"Ha ha," I answered somewhat sheepishly.

Mama slipped her arm around my waist and kissed me on the cheek. "Do you like him, sweetheart?"

I kept my face down, not meeting her eyes. "Of course I like him," I said, dodging the question. "Doesn't everyone? He's definitely the most interesting man who's ever been here."

"You know what I mean," said Mama. "Do you *like* him?"

"He's old."

"Not that old."

"He's probably going to leave anytime and find some royal court somewhere."

"I wouldn't be so sure about that," said Mama mildly.

I looked at her. "Why do you say that?"

"I've been watching him. I don't see a restlessness to keep moving. He's attracted to this place, to us."

At that moment Lana called for Mama's attention and the conversation ended, but I kept thinking about what she'd said, and that day I studied Moses even more carefully, if that were possible.

Mama was right; he *wasn't* restless. He seemed content, walking with the sheep, sitting under the shade, eating the lunch Mama packed. He wasn't especially talkative—I think Father wore him out—but he was obviously thinking. Several times I felt his eyes on me, but when I turned to look, he would only smile, not speak. I felt like our time together was a dance, only I didn't know the steps.

One day we were walking home, the other girls running ahead of us and so it was just Moses and me. We walked companionably side by side for a while, neither of us speaking. Every so often I cast a sidelong glance at him. Despite the fact he was wearing one of Father's working tunics and not the expensive clothes he showed up in, and his beard had grown in more, he still looked foreign. I liked his profile—the high forehead, aquiline nose, kissable lips. Involuntarily, I sighed.

Moses turned to me. "Everything okay, Zipporah?"

"Yes." It came out like a squawk. Clearing my throat, I tried again. "Yes."

"Tell me," he said. "What goes on in that pretty head of yours? What do you think about?"

Pretty head? You think I'm pretty? Mostly I think about you. All the time, actually. "Oh, not much," I hedged. "You know, the usual: world politics, the fate of man, existentialism in our time." The words slipped out before I could stop them.

Moses stared at me, then roared with laughter. "You're a very unusual girl, do you know that?" He wiped tears from his eyes once he calmed down.

"I'm sorry," I said, horrified that I spoke so flippantly with him. "I shouldn't have—"

"No, don't apologize. It's wonderful to talk with a girl who has actual thoughts in her head."

Wow, the girls in Egypt must have been morons. "Surely the women in Egypt have thoughts?" I asked innocently.

"Yes, but they mostly center around men, beauty, and intrigue. It gets very wearying."

I laughed. "As you can tell, there's not a lot of men, beauty, or intrigue here."

Moses stopped walking and looked at me. "I disagree about beauty, Zipporah. I see plenty of it."

My stomach dropped to my knees, and my mouth felt dry. I tried to say something witty, but nothing came out. All I could do was gaze back at him, into those deep brown eyes that held so much *life*. Moses touched a strand of my hair that had escaped from its plait. He rubbed the silky lock between his thumb and forefinger. "*Very* beautiful," he said, his voice husky.

I tore my eyes away from his. This was overwhelming for a girl whose most intimate encounters with the opposite sex had been crude teasing from Layth the shepherd boy. Moses was not only handsome, not only cultured, not only well-spoken, not only (and most importantly) a follower of He Who Sees, but he was a prince. A prince! I felt like my life had gone from deadly dull to something approaching the stuff of legends overnight. I was afraid to look at Moses, afraid I would be tempted to press my lips to his and lose his respect.

He misinterpreted my actions, dropping his hand to his side. "I apologize. I see that I have frightened you, innocent one."

I shook my head *no*, not trusting my voice. We walked the rest of the way to the well in silence.

Moses was careful to keep some distance between us once we returned home. At dinner and afterward, he made a special effort to play with the younger children, offer help to a blushing Mama, and engage in debate with Father. He only caught my eye once, and he didn't smile or speak, yet his look affected me more than a thousand words.

As I lay in bed that night, I continually replayed his words in my head, particularly the ones where he called me pretty and referred to beauty. I imagined kissing him, growing almost feverish with anticipation. Needless to say, I could barely sleep.

*

The next morning, eager to see Moses and perhaps continue our conversation, I was extremely disappointed when he didn't show up.

"Where's Moses?" I asked Mama, trying to sound nonchalant.

"He's spending the day with Father," she said, not elaborating.

"Oh."

I hadn't realized how much I had grown to appreciate Moses' company until that day. It was the longest, most excruciatingly boring day in recent memory. All I wanted to do was get home and catch sight of him.

By early afternoon, I was so crazed I was ready to scream. When Maysan inadvertently spooked one of the sheep, I almost slapped her.

"What is the matter with you?" rebuked Farah, protecting the sobbing Maysan from the evil me.

"I'm sorry. Come here, Maysan. It's okay; I'm not mad at you." I grabbed her away from Farah and gave her a fierce hug.

"Then why did you yell like that?" accused Maysan.

"I'm just a little nudgy right now. It's not you. Forgive me?"

Still a little shaken, she nodded, letting me kiss her. Conflict resolved, my little sister ran off, happy.

Farah watched me, one hand on her hip. "Tell me," she demanded.

"What?"

"Tell me."

I sighed. "It's Moses."

"Ha! I knew it!"

"If I tell you something, promise not to tell anyone?"

Farah looked offended. "When have I ever broken a confidence?"

I looked askance at her. "I'll still trust you. Let's sit down." We plunked ourselves down on a couple of rocks, which afforded us a clear view of Lana, Maysan, and the sheep. "I can't stop thinking about him."

"That's obvious enough."

"What do you mean?" I asked her, nonplussed.

"You stare at him *all the time!* You rarely talk when he's around. It's like your whole personality changed."

My mouth dropped open. I was about to deny everything, then thought better of it. "I thought I was being discreet," I said quietly.

"Discreet?" hooted Farah. "Adorable, yes. Discreet? No."

"It's driving me crazy that he's not here today."

Farah gazed at me sympathetically. She placed one of her dainty hands over my own slender, brown one. "You'll see him very soon." She squinted at the sun. "Look! It's almost time to round up the sheep and head back."

"Far-*ah!*" I moaned, dropping my head into her lap. "What am I going to do?"

My sister absentmindedly stroked the back of my head. "Let's trust He Who Sees. If Moses is for you, it will work out. If not, you'll lose interest."

"You think?" I asked, my head still in her lap, my voice muffled.

"I'm convinced of it."

Without Moses, it took longer to get the sheep back, watered, and penned for the night. It had only been a month since he entered our lives, but I felt like I could barely remember what life had been like before I met him.

As we walked up to the tents, hot, tired, and hungry from the day's outing, I saw him sitting with Father. They both looked pretty serious.

"Zipporah!" Father called to me before I had a chance to greet either he or Moses. "Get cleaned up and come find me. I want to talk to you."

"Yes, Father," I said, wondering what this was about. *Oh, I hope Moses hasn't been offended by my behavior! What if he had been testing me, to see how chaste I was, and thought that my behavior wasn't godly? What if Father is mad at me?* These and other similar thoughts swirled as I washed my face and hands, combed and rebraided my hair, and had a quick drink of water.

Hastily, I went back over to Father and Moses. "I'm here."

Moses stood. "I'll leave you two alone. Jethro, Zipporah." He nodded at Father and glanced at me, briefly but intensely. I shivered.

"Come, daughter. Sit," commanded Father kindly.

"Everything okay?" I asked.

"Zipporah," said Father, ignoring my question, "you're at an age where young ladies tend to get married." I opened my mouth, but he ignored me, continuing. "I realize there's not a lot of choice in our small community, so this is a subject your mother and I were getting somewhat concerned about—your limited opportunities to find a good and proper husband. When Moses came here and expressed an interest in staying, I cannot tell you how thrilled I was. Not only is he a brother to my heart, but it so happens that he's fallen in love with you." Father stopped talking and studied me, brown eyes twinkling.

"What? Fallen in love—with me?"

"Don't look so shocked, Daughter. You're a very beautiful, intelligent, godly young woman. Any man would be most blessed to have you."

"But Father, he's a *prince!* We're not talking about Layth."

"Don't put Layth down. That young man still has some growing up to do. He may surprise you one day."

Anything less than being on the run as a criminal would surprise me, I thought. Aloud, I said, "Did Moses talk to you?"

Father smiled. "All day. He's smitten with you, Zipporah. He's asked me for your hand in marriage."

I gasped. "Oh my goodness! What did you say?"

"I told him yes on the condition that you agree." Father put his arm around my shoulders. "I understand that this is unexpected. Take all the time you need to decide. I also know that he's quite a bit older than you, and I'm not sure if you think that's a problem or not."

Marriage! Questions rolled off my tongue, one after another. "Does Mama know? Would we live here? Did he say anything else about me? What happens next?"

"Slow down," said Father, laughing. "Okay, the answers are, yes, yes, lots, and it depends on your answer."

"What did he say about me?"

"He's in love." Father looked at me searchingly. "He seems to think you're amenable."

I blushed.

"Zippi, he's ready to settle down, and for some inexplicable reason, this place appeals to him. I don't know if it's because we're the antithesis of Egypt, if he wants to remain hidden, if He Who Sees has told him to stay, or if my beautiful oldest daughter is the draw, but he's here, and we're the richer for it."

"Father, I don't have to think about this. I'll marry him."

"I hear your answer, but I still think you need to take tonight and pray it through. If, in the morning, your answer is still yes, we'll plan the wedding."

I flung my arms around my father's neck and kissed him. "Thank you, Father. I love you!"

"I love you, too. Now go tell your mother. She's been desperate to find out about our conversation."

"Ha ha, I will." I left him and went in search of Mama, looking for Moses but not seeing him. When I found her, I pulled her to the side, away from the children.

"Well?" she said, eyeing me expectantly.

"Oh, Mama!" I hugged her, and we swung in a little circle. "I'm so excited! But Father told me to pray tonight and give him a final answer in the morning."

Mama tenderly touched my cheek. "This man, Moses, he is a gift from God! I am so very happy for you, my daughter."

"Do you think so?" I asked with some trepidation. "You don't think He Who Sees is going to say *no*, do you?"

Mama looked in both directions before answering. "I don't want to influence your decision or get your father mad at me by interfering," she whispered, "but I would be totally shocked if He said no."

We looked at each other and smiled. Then Mama kissed me on both cheeks. "So beautiful," she murmured.

Father must have spoken to Moses because that night he gave me plenty of space to pray about my decision and didn't try to influence me in any way. This knowledge that Moses wanted me—*me!*—to be his wife was like a precious secret that I hid in my heart. I didn't even tell Farah about this latest development. Somehow I got through dinner and then took a walk by myself. I tried not to let my prayer time with He Who Sees be just me gushing over Moses. When I forced myself to be still and listen for His voice, I got an overwhelming sense that not only was He willing to permit this, but that this was *from* Him. By bedtime, I was ready to tell Father that my answer was a definite yes but obeyed his injunction to give it overnight.

*

The next morning I felt even more determined that it was right to marry Moses. I arose and quickly used the chamber pot, washed, dressed, and did my hair. As I was finishing with my hair, Mama came into the tent to rouse Farah, Lana, and Maysan. I silently beckoned to her, and she came right over to me.

"Yes," I told her.

"Oh, how wonderful!" She looked about as thrilled as anyone could look at the crack of dawn. She grabbed my hand. "Let's go tell your father."

We left the girl tent and went into the "parent" tent. Father was kneeling in his traditional morning prayer time. I hesitated to interrupt him.

"I think it's okay," whispered Mama. "This is what he's praying about." She seemed a little indecisive too. We *never* interrupted Father during prayer. Fortunately, he saved us the dilemma by noticing us and rising.

"Yes?" he said.

"Yes!" we answered.

"You are sure this is what He Who Sees wants, Zipporah?"

"Yes, Father. I am sure."

"Then I give you my blessing."

"Oh, thank you, Father!" I hugged him around the waist, hard. He held me as well, kissing the top of my head.

"Our oldest has grown up," he said to Mama, who had joined our group hug with an arm around each of us. His voice had a tinge of sadness to it.

"This is probably not the time to tell you, Jethro," said Mama, "but we're a long way from done."

Father's eyes widened. "Are you...?"

Mama nodded.

"Praise You, He Who Sees my God!" burst out Father. "Praise and bless You for the glory that is You, and for all these mighty blessings that You continue to pour out on our family. Who are we that the Lord of the universe should take such notice? Praise and thank You!"

"Amen," we said.

I looked at Mama in surprise. "Really? You're expecting?"

"I'm sorry to crowd your news with my own, Zipporah," she said, slipping into the waiting arms of my father, whose broad smile lit up his face.

"Mama, the more good news the better. I am totally thrilled."

The rest of the morning was a blur. I felt like I had this great, big, wonderful *thing* inside and, on the one hand, couldn't wait to shout to the world that I was marrying Moses, and on the other hand, I wanted to hug this information to myself and ponder it endlessly. I felt very shy about seeing Moses and made no attempt to get close to him on the way to the grazing land. It wasn't until we had gotten the sheep to pasture that I came face to face with him.

"Can we talk?" he asked me, a playful smile on his lips.

I nodded eagerly, and he led me over to a private spot.

"Zipporah," he said, looking very appealing, the breeze ruffling his hair, "your father has told me of your decision. I cannot tell you how happy this makes me." He got down on one knee and clasped my hands in his. "You are a stunning jewel, hidden away in the desert, kept safe by Elohim for me and me alone. I cannot wait until I make you my bride."

"I don't know what to say, my lord," I responded, overcome.

"Say that you'll let me kiss you," he urged.

"I've never been kissed."

"That sounds like a yes to me." Standing up, he cupped my face in his hand and bent his head to meet my upturned lips, kissing me softly, again and again, lingering longer each time until I gasped for breath. Finally, he drew back and gazed at me.

"Is that what marriage is going to be like?" I wondered, dazed.

"Better," he said, kissing me again.

We didn't last until noon before telling Farah, Lana, and Maysan our exciting news. The two younger girls screamed with joy and jumped all over us, but Farah was strangely quiet.

"What?" I pulled her to the side while Moses contended with the shrieking girls.

"Nothing," she snapped, yanking away from me.

"Stop it, Farah! Don't ruin this special time for me."

"The least you could have done was tell me before *them*," she said, softening.

"I'm sorry! I'm in such a tizzy from all this, I wasn't thinking straight. Forgive me? Please?"

"All right," said Farah, mollified.

"Good. Come on. You need to congratulate Moses."

She made a face but obediently followed me back to Moses. "Congratulations," she said dutifully.

"Why, thank you, my new sister." Moses flashed such an engaging smile that she couldn't help but laugh.

That evening, when we returned home, what a celebration we had! Dinner was so much fun, everyone talking, me sitting next to Moses, his hand touching mine. I was so very, very happy. After the other girls went to bed, I stayed up with Father, Mama, and Moses, and we discussed the upcoming wedding.

"Tomorrow?" asked Moses, not really kidding.

"Sounds good to me." I leaned in his direction.

"Slow down, sweetheart," said Mama. "We have some planning to do. Don't you want a wedding feast?"

"I guess..."

"Mama's right," said Father. "We need to include our whole community in this celebration. Marriage is a covenant that lasts a lifetime. It's not something to be done hurriedly, in the dark."

"So how long, do you think?" asked Moses.

"One month," said Father decisively.

"One month?" exclaimed Mama. "Do you really think we can pull this together in only a month?"

At the same time I said, "That long? Why that long?"

"I think we have our time frame," said Moses drily.

*

That next month was wildness, getting everything ready. The girls and I were dismissed from sheep duty so we could help Mama prepare enormous amounts of food. Moses took over the sheep entirely, a responsibility which, unbeknown to us both, would occupy him for a *very* long time to come. This meant that we had barely any time alone together. I suspect this was Father's plan all along. When we did see each other, we were never alone.

"This is so annoying," I fumed in passing to Moses, after yet another day waiting to see him, only to have Mama continually want me somewhere else.

"Fuels the desire." He winked, always one with a good attitude.

"How intense does it need to be, anyway?" I boldly asked.

He raised his eyebrows, shocked but not that much. He was getting to know the real me, the one who thought outside the lines. He seemed to like it.

12

THE DAY OF OUR WEDDING FINALLY ARRIVED. It dawned, as did most days, bright and clear. Mama, Farah, and several of the women from our community took me into a tent and worked on me for *hours*. They applied make-up, hennaed my feet, washed and perfumed me, elaborately braided and twisted my long hair around an exotic, bejeweled headpiece that had been in our family for generations, covered my arms with bracelets and my ankles with ankle bracelets, and fastened necklaces around my neck and rings on my fingers. A silky red dress was slipped over my head and tied about my waist, followed by red satin slippers for my feet. I felt like royalty. Surely, the great women in Egypt were no better dressed than I.

Nervous and excited, I could do no more than take a few sips of goat milk as nourishment before shaking my head no to any and all proffered food. Even so, I needed to use the portable potty several times.

"Are you sick?" asked Mama, concerned.

"Just excited."

She looked doubtful. "All right, but that's it until after the ceremony. Will you make it?"

I nodded. "I'm good, Mama."

"I know, my daughter." Mama hesitated. "Anything you want to talk about before things get going here?"

"I think I'm good," I said patiently.

She studied me for several moments. "I know Moses is a lot older than you, but—apart from your father—I've never met a more extraordinary man."

"I know."

"God is doing something with this marriage, because the chances of it happening were so small. Stay close to He Who Sees, Zipporah."

"Yes, Mama. I will."

She kissed me and held me close, carefully though, so as not to crease my wedding finery or muss my hair. I kissed her back.

"I'm going to see if they're ready for you. Be right back."

"I'll be here," I said, breathing deeply.

After a few delays, I heard the beats of the drum and, accompanied by Mama and Farah, left the tent and emerged blinking into the glare of the day.

The whole community was assembled, eager to witness the joining together of this runaway prince of Egypt with one of their own. Moses waited for me under the *chuppah*, the wedding canopy, with my father. He stood tall, beard neatly trimmed, hair combed back, dressed in his fine linen robe with threads of gold interwoven throughout. He saw me before I saw him, so when I looked up, he was already gazing in my direction, happiness lighting up his face like a full moon on a cloudless night.

The ceremony itself was relatively short. We sang, we prayed, we shared wine from one cup, I circled my groom seven times, and then it was done. We were joined together in a covenant bond that would only end with the death of one of us. He was mine, and I was his. Oh, bliss!

We feasted and socialized for hours, at times his fingers intertwining with mine, at other times his arm possessively encircling my waist as if I were treasure that needed to be secured. Soon enough, we were led by the laughing, happy, well-fed crowd to our new tent, mine and his, alone. Father embraced Moses and then me, Mama waved a bit tremulously, my sisters smiled shyly, the shepherd boys yelled out embarrassing words of advice, and then we entered the tent and Moses firmly closed the flap behind us.

Inside was dark and quiet. The only ventilation and light came from a slightly raised wall on the side of the tent across from the mound of sheepskins that comprised our new bed. It was also on a side of the tent that was off limits to our guests. At least I hoped. Moses saw me glance in that direction and said, "Don't worry. No one will bother us."

"Are you sure?"

"Very. I made it quite clear that if anyone tries to ruin our wedding night, I will be most unhappy. And then I pulled out my sword and examined the blade."

"You didn't!" I giggled. "Was this with Layth?"

"And Khurran, and some of the others. I believe I got my point across."

"No pun intended."

"No pun intended," agreed Moses. "Can I get you something? A drink?"

I shook my head.

"You're very beautiful, Zipporah." My new husband put his hands on my shoulders and looked intently at me. "I am blessed you have agreed to be my bride."

A wave of warmth spread through my body. "I am the one who is blessed," I said in a low tone.

Moses removed my elaborate headpiece and, while I was standing, one by one pulled out the pins that held my hair in place until my long dark hair fell in a sheet down to my waist. He then removed my dress, rendering me naked before him except for the covering of my long hair. "You are so *very* beautiful," he whispered, drinking in with his eyes every aspect of my uncovered form. He gently held my face between his hands and kissed me, softly at first but with increasing passion until we fell down on the bed together, driven by our passion to consummate our marriage.

Afterward we lay locked in each other's embrace, my head resting on his shoulder, his right arm covering me. I thought I knew what to expect from sex after years of watching the sheep, but this had to be so much better than what the sheep experienced. A gurgle of laughter escaped my throat.

"What?" asked Moses, pulling me close.

"I was just thinking that I thought I was prepared for today after watching sheep."

"Not the same, is it?"

"Not even close."

Moses rolled over and stared into my eyes. "I love you," he said, kissing me.

"I love you too," I responded, as soon as I had a moment when his mouth wasn't covering mine. "But, why? I mean, you could have married anyone in Egypt. The women there are so much more interesting and prettier and better-dressed…"

"Shh," he said, placing a finger on my lips. "You have no idea how fresh and open and intoxicating you are in comparison. I forbid you from putting my wife down ever again, okay?"

I kissed his finger. "Okay," I said softly, marveling at his love for me.

Our wedding week went way too quickly. The days melted into each other as we explored both each other's bodies and minds. We talked and talked, and I learned a lot about Moses' life that I hadn't known. I found him thoroughly fascinating and couldn't ask enough questions.

"My sister Miryam would like you," he said unexpectedly one morning while we were eating breakfast. "She and Pawero, my brother-in-law, would appreciate your quick wit."

I had heard briefly about Miryam and Pawero already. "Tell me more about them." I set my cup of goat's milk aside.

"They're wonderful people." He sighed, lost in memory, eyes distant. "They've been among the select few I could always trust, who always had my back. I left without being able to say a proper good-bye."

"Maybe one day we can go back and I can meet them?" I asked eagerly.

Moses focused on me. "Zipporah," he said, and his voice though tender had a tone of finality to it, "I think that short of a miracle I'll never be able to set foot on Egyptian soil again."

Never? "That's disappointing," I managed after a few awkward moments. "It all sounds so intriguing."

My husband shook his head. "It depends how exciting you would find it to watch me hauled off and killed."

"Moses!" I exclaimed, shocked. "That would be horrible!"

"Yes, I know. That's why I'm not going back." He toyed with the piece of bread in his hand. "You forget: I watched Thutmose grow up. I know how he feels about me and about Mother. I know what he's capable of."

I came over to Moses and plopped myself down in his lap. "You're right. It doesn't matter. I only want you."

"And I you," he murmured, kissing my neck.

After our wedding week, we settled into our new life. Moses took on the task of shepherding Father's sheep and I kept house (or tent). In the beginning, before the children came, I went with him a few days a week. We talked a lot, and Moses taught me many of the things he had learned both from his tutors and general life experience. I became quite good at the history of the known world and also showed prowess with reading and writing, which we practiced by using a stick in the sand. Over time, he shared about his mother, Hatshepsut, whom he missed quite a bit. "I never got to say good-bye," he remarked sadly.

"I'm sure she understood," I said, trying to be a comfort.

"Hard to tell," he replied a bit drily.

He also spoke of Miryam, his sister. She helped raise him,and then went on to marry and have children of her own. "The kids didn't refer to me as 'uncle' as it would have been a bad idea politically," said Moses. "But I got to know them really well."

"Tell me more."

"The first child was a girl, Abigail."

"That's a beautiful name."

"She's a beautiful girl. Her first ten years were spent at the palace, running the place with Mother's daughter." His eyes had a faraway look.

"Would that be...Neferure?" Moses had alluded to his half-sister, and I had a hazy idea of some of that drama.

"Yes," he said, shortly. "They were quite the pair."

"What happened to her? Abigail, that is."

"She married very young to a fellow from the tribe of Judah named Hur. I remember Miryam was torn about her age, but all of us were really impressed with the young man so in the end Abigail received permission."

"Was she younger than me?" I teased.

Moses looked at me. "Are you that young? You seem so mature that I forget just how much of a child you are. And yes," he added, before I could speak, "she was a bit younger than you. By the time I left Egypt, they already had their first child, a son named Uri." He seemed wistful.

"Would you like a son?" I asked shyly.

"Of course. We'll set lots of time aside to work on that." He grinned at me.

Blushing, I pushed ahead with my questions. "Tell me about Miryam's other kids. Boys? Girls? Names?"

Moses sat back on his heels. "The second child is a boy named Johanan, and the youngest is another girl, Noa. I—" He lapsed into silence.

...miss them. Mentally I filled in the unspoken words. The more Moses spoke of Miryam, the more I got the impression that she was an extremely competent powerhouse of a woman whose significance in his life wasn't to be underestimated. He missed her like he missed his mother. I felt so young and uncharted in comparison to these two women. I suppose I became a bit jealous, letting that fact leak once in the midst of a teary argument. Moses immediately gathered me to himself, crushing me against his powerful chest.

"You're my *wife,*" he exclaimed passionately. "Not my mother or my sister! You're the one I've covenanted to before God, you're the one I love more than any other human, you're the one to whom I give my body. Don't compare yourself to any other woman, ever. Do you hear me?"

Already emotionally drained from our original argument, I simply nodded, burying my face in his shoulder. I loved him fiercely.

*

Our lives fell into a groove. We worked, ate, made love, slept, visited with friends and family, made love, talked, did chores, and made love. One other thing we did was talk about He Who Sees.

"Why do you call Him Elohim?" I asked Moses one day while we were eating a light supper of bread and dates in our tent.

He shrugged. "He's always been Elohim. Why do you call Him He Who Sees?"

"I'm not sure. We've always called Him He Who Sees." We looked at each other and laughed. "Well, it doesn't matter anyway," I said. "We know who we're talking about."

Moses looked thoughtful. "I think it does matter. Names are extremely significant. It defines who you are. For instance, you're a little bird."

I rolled my eyes. "Please. I've never liked my name."

"Seriously? I love your name. I think it perfectly suits you."

"How?" I demanded, starting to lose my good humor.

"You're adorable, quick, you sing beautifully, and you eat constantly."

I threw a pillow at him which he dodged, laughing. "What about your name?" I asked.

"My name defines the act that saved my life. Mother 'drew me out' of the water and rescued me, making me her own. For which I will always be grateful."

"As will I." I came over to him and wrapped my arms around his neck so I could kiss him. My Moses. My handsome, extraordinary Moses. How I loved him.

In retrospect, I was pretty sure that was the night we conceived our first son, Gershom. As Moses felt very strongly about the significance of names, he named our son a name that meant *a stranger there*, as in "I have become a stranger in a foreign land." I realized that as much as he loved me and was seemingly content with our life in Midian, still, he never forgot who he was or where he came from.

This was reflected when Gershom was almost a week old. "The Hebrews have a custom," began Moses quietly, holding his baby son in his arms, looking down at the tiny face.

"Yes?" It was early morning and I was propped up in bed, not quite up to doing anything yet, grateful that Moses had the baby.

"Have you heard of circumcision?"

I flushed red. "Is that when..."

"Yes, it's when the foreskin on the tip of the penis is cut off."

I made a face. "Sounds painful."

"Well, now, yes. But it's supposed to happen at eight days old."

Eight days? "You mean...our baby...tomorrow?"

He nodded.

"But what if he's hurt, or maimed for life?" Suddenly, I was irrationally terrified. My eyes got big, and I started to hyperventilate. "Please, Moses, no! Don't let our son be harmed!"

"I don't think he's going to be harmed, Zipporah. This has been done since the time of Abraham. I haven't heard of a casualty yet. Except," he said, growing thoughtful, "the village that got taken out by Jacob's sons Shimon and Levi after their sister was raped. All of those men died." He saw my face and added hastily, "It wasn't the circumcision that killed them; it was the swords running them through when they were too weak to defend themselves."

I stared at my husband. "You're not helping." I held out my arms. "Give me my child."

"*Our* child," he corrected, but he handed the baby over anyway, then got up.

"Where are you going?"

"The sheep haven't stopped eating because we've had a son. I'm going to work." He leaned over to kiss me good-bye.

"Well, wait," I said, holding onto his neck with one hand and Gershom with the other. "What about this whole circumcision thing? We don't have to do it, do we?"

"I'm not sure…"

"Please, my love! Please let's not do it, at least not now. He's so little."

We both looked down at the tiny baby cuddled against my breast, which was bigger than his head.

"I'll think about it," he said, but I heard the hesitancy in his voice.

I'm ashamed to say that I worked on my husband not to circumcise our son. Looking back, I'm not sure why I flipped out like that, unless it had to do with the newness of the concept combined with my being a new mother. A very *young* new mother. Plus, I didn't understand just how important this was to He Who Sees. I guess I thought it was optional.

As Gershom got older, the timing never seemed right. We did circumcise our second son, Eliezer, at eight days, but opted out of doing Gershom at the same time as by then he was a squirming, screaming two-year-old, and it seemed like a really bad idea. After that, it got away from us. This was probably the worst decision we ever made.

*

It was while I was pregnant with Eliezer that we saw our first Egyptian traveler since Moses. By then Moses so resembled his Hebrew shepherd forefathers in appearance and dress that one would have been hard-pressed to ascertain the Egyptian in him.

The traveler showed up late one afternoon as Mama and I were preparing dinner. Gershom had finally fallen asleep after some "I'm tired" crankiness, and I was rushing to accomplish several chores that I hadn't been able to get to while dealing with him. So it was with a certain level of *oh no, what now* bad attitude that I responded to the traveler-sighted alert thrown up by Maysan, just returning from the well.

"Not now," I grumbled, hurriedly beating out a rug that I meant to get to that morning. "Gershom just settled down."

My sister, now a very mature-looking twelve-year-old, stared at me in amazement, hands on her hips. "You can't be serious, Zippy! Are you really such an old married lady now that you aren't excited about strangers coming through, telling us what's been happening in the world?"

She was right. I shouldn't be acting like an old woman before I even turned twenty. "Okay," I repented. "You may as well go back and invite him to eat with us."

"Already did," she said smugly.

I lifted my eyes and saw a cloud of dust on the horizon, signifying camels.

Turned out it wasn't just one traveler but three, each on a camel. They were Syrians, returning from trade in Memphis. Two of the men were taciturn and suspicious, barely grateful for our hospitality, whereas the third was as talkative as his companions were not, flashing us a very white grin and thanking us over and over again for the dinner he had yet to eat.

After Moses came home, we sat around a small fire and ate bread and lentil stew, our visitors emitting contented noises as they hungrily gobbled down several bowls each. "So," Moses asked casually, once the eating settled down, "what's the news from Egypt?"

"Egypt?" repeated the loquacious one. "Same as always, really. Another pyramid going up, a few more battles. Good year for dates."

"Yes," said Moses, "but what about the royal family? Any news?"

The traveler squinted at my husband. "Oh, it's royal gossip you're looking for, are you?" He ignored Moses' pained expression and scratched his chin thoughtfully. "Uhh…."

"The pharaoh took a new wife after that pretty one died," unexpectedly volunteered one of the travelers who had yet to speak half a dozen words.

The first traveler brightened. "Yes!" he said, snapping his fingers. "That's right. Her name is Satuh, or Satiah, something like that. She's pretty too. They all are, lucky guy."

Moses looked dazed. "What? Wait. What about Hatshepsut? And are you speaking of Neferure? Who died?"

"You're way behind on the news, friend," observed the first traveler. "The female pharaoh died last year. Some say it was a broken heart from missing her son, the one who got involved with the Hebrews and killed someone. Or maybe it was her health. She didn't look so good at the end. At any rate, Thutmose—Thutmose III, that is—took over, and he's been running one military campaign after another. Unfortunately, he keeps looking toward Syria," he finished darkly, scowling at the thought.

"And the Princess Neferure," persisted Moses faintly. "What of her?"

"Dead. What was it?"

"Childbirth," supplied his fellow traveler.

"That's it! Childbirth killed her, just after her mother died. Babe survived, though. What's his name?"

All three travelers thought for a few minutes before the second one called out, "Amenemhat."

"Amenemhat, yes, that's it. You're good at this," he admiringly told his friend.

While this conversation was going on, Mama and I exchanged worried looks. I could see how upset my husband had become, though he hid it well enough from our guests.

Now he stood abruptly, his face pale. "I must say an early good night," he said, falteringly. "I must have had too much sun today, and I need to lie down. Nice meeting you all." Without looking at me, he turned and went to our tent.

"Nice fellow, that," commented the first traveler after Moses had gone. He held out his empty bowl to Mama. "Any food left?"

I stayed just long enough to help Mama, who whispered to me, "Leave the baby with me. See to that man of yours. He needs you."

"You're okay with Gershom?"

"Fine. I'll have Nashita and Reema watch him. They already have Hobab," said Mama, referring to my baby brother, who was less than a year older than his nephew, Gershom.

"Thanks, Mama," I said, kissing her cheek.

"I hope he's okay."

"I know. Me too. That was a lot of shocking news for him to hear all at once."

"We'll talk later. Just go."

Knowing better than to make a fuss over Gershom before leaving him, I slipped away quietly, walking quickly to our tent. I hurried inside, then stood hesitantly in the gloom. "Moses?"

"Here," he replied in a flat tone. 'Here' meant sitting on the floor, back against one of the tent walls, staring straight ahead. I walked over and sat next to him. Tentatively, I placed my hand on his knee. He didn't move or speak.

"Hey," I said. I saw a tear trickle down his cheek. "Hey," I said again, climbing into his lap, hugging him. "I'm so sorry about your mother, about Neferure. I love you."

He didn't answer, but neither did he push me away. I considered that a victory. I don't know how long we sat like that. I only got up when Mama knocked softly, calling out, "Zipporah, come take Gershom." I roused myself, opening the tent flap, and took my sleeping boy from her arms.

"Thank you, Mama." She looked at me, a question in her eyes. I shook my head, she nodded, and our silent communication ended for the night. I tucked Gershom into his bed and returned to Moses. "Come," I said to my husband. "Come to bed." Without a word, he allowed me to pull him to his feet and bring him to our bed. He lay flat on his back, hands behind his head while I lay beside him, my hand on his arm. Sometime later I fell asleep, only waking when Moses got up in the pre-dawn dark to go to work.

"You're heading out?" I asked groggily, still half asleep.

"Somebody's got to take care of the sheep."

I lifted myself up on one elbow. "Are you all right?"

"I'm working on it. Give me some time before we talk, okay?"

"Whenever you're ready. I love you."

"I love you too," he said, but he didn't kiss me before leaving as was his usual custom.

Our visitors left that morning after a hearty breakfast. Mama and I were happy to see them go, both of us breathing a sigh of relief when the clouds of dust kicked up by their camels' hoofs were no longer visible—she because of all the food they went through and me because I wanted them gone before they grew suspicious of Moses. Father joined us as we stood there.

"How's your husband?" he asked me.

I shrugged. "Upset."

Father nodded. "That was a lot of bad news all at once." He appeared thoughtful.

"Father?"

"Yes?"

"What do you know about Moses and Neferure?"

He looked at me. "What do *you* know?" he asked after a moment.

"Just that she was his sister, though not his real sister, and that she meant a great deal to him and he was really upset when she was married off to Thutmose."

Father nodded. "That's basically what I know."

"Basically? As in, there's more to know?"

Father laughed. "I taught you a little too well, didn't I?"

"Aha!" I pounced on his latest statement. "How involved were they?"

"Zipporah, don't go looking for trouble," broke in Mama with a worried expression.

I ignored her. "Well, Father?" I prodded.

"This is a conversation you should have with your husband. Suffice it to say that the news of her death was probably almost as upsetting as the news of his mother's death." He gazed at me sternly. "Enough, all right?"

"Enough."

Father put his arm around my shoulders, holding me securely within his grasp, reminding me of when I was a small girl and those arms promised protection from every problem. They still did a pretty good job, truth be told. I laid my head on his shoulder, not noticing when Mama quietly left, presumably to check on the children and proceed with the morning work.

I went about my day completely distracted. Previous to now I had considered my husband's past as just that: past. Glamorous, yes, fascinating, yes, emotionally powerful, no. Sure, he had basically told me about Neferure, but I assumed that it was old news. I was so swept off my feet by his declared love for me that I couldn't even imagine that he had felt this way before with anyone. Now I wondered if I was second best...and just how much of my husband's heart was mine.

By the time Moses returned that day I was a wreck. He seemed in a better place until he saw my face. "Come here," he said, opening his arms wide. When I didn't move, he repeated in a stronger tone, "Zipporah, come here!" Reluctantly, I walked within the circle of his embrace, but my head was down. Moses put his finger under my chin and tilted my face up, observing the tears in my eyes. "What is it?" he asked, tenderness in his voice.

"Do you love me?" I whispered.

"You know how much I love you."

"Do I? What of Neferure?"

"Don't be jealous of a dead woman, Zipporah."

My face colored. That sounded so awful. "I'm not jealous," I muttered. "Are you very unhappy?"

"I'm not unhappy, but I am upset. I hate to think that my actions hastened Mother's death."

"You had said that she wasn't doing well physically."

"And to hear of Neferure. She wasn't that much older than you." He tightened his arms around me. "I couldn't bear to lose you, Zipporah."

My heart lightened at this declaration of love. "You won't lose me, Moses," I promised.

"The baby..."

"We'll be fine," I said confidently. "Gershom was easy."

"A lot of prayer went into that birth. Let's make sure we pray for Elohim's favor for this birth as well and don't grow complacent."

"Yes," I whispered, overwhelmed by my love for this man.

*

Moses mourned for his mother forty days, after which he appeared to be back to his old self, only occasionally lapsing into a quiet sadness that I knew meant he was thinking of his mother, or possibly Neferure, though I learned my lesson and wasn't going to look for trouble, as Mama said. I gave birth to our second son, to Eliezer, and He Who Sees blessed this birth as he did the first, bringing us through safe and healthy. This time we circumcised our son on the eighth day, as per the Hebrew custom handed down from Abraham, Isaac, and Jacob.

Gershom was fascinated by his baby brother, continually studying him and asking when he would be able to play. I thought that one baby was a lot of work, but it was nothing compared to the two boys together. My days were full, my nights sweet. Life was good.

About six months after the visit from the Syrian traders, Moses and I took the children on a little daytime adventure in the wilderness (and by wilderness I mean anything within a twenty-minute walk of our home). I packed a meal of water, dates, bread, and goat cheese, which we ate under the shade of a date palm next to a spring. It was a favorite spot of ours, our own oasis.

Moses liked to hoist Gershom onto his shoulders and point out the different plants and aspects of the landscape, while the little guy held onto the back of his daddy's hair. They were adorable, bouncing around like that. I sat with my back against the tree and nursed infant Eliezer, looking up every so often to watch my husband and son in the not too far distance.

We had already eaten, and a full stomach, a little breeze, the comfortable shade, and the intermittent sucking of the half-asleep baby all conspired together such that I soon dozed off, only to be awakened by Moses' lips on my neck.

"Hey." I opened my eyes, smiling at my husband. "Where's Gershom?"

"Asleep." Moses gestured with his thumb at the quiet form of our older son, carefully placed within the confines of the available shade.

"So is the baby. I think we have some time for just us."

We smiled at each other. Moses leaned back against the tree, and I leaned on him. Eliezer was totally passed out now, a trickle of breast milk escaping from the corner of his tiny mouth.

I don't know whether enough time had passed, or whether it was the peacefulness of our time alone with the boys napping, but Moses was extremely talkative that day. "I want to thank you for giving me time to process the news about my mother," he said, his arms around my hips, his chin in my hair.

"How are you with that?" I asked, a bit tentatively.

"Much better. I've been spending a lot of time with Elohim" (I nodded, I knew), "a lot of time in prayer, and I believe He's been telling me things."

"Really?" I asked, in my interest sitting up a bit, though Moses held me against him. ("Stay right here," he whispered in my ear.) "Like what?"

"Like even though I was wrong to take on the Egyptian slave masters before Elohim had specifically told me to, He forgave me and led me here, to you."

My heart swelled with these words. "You believe that I'm the one He Who Sees intended for you to marry?"

"I'm convinced of it." Moses brushed his lips against my hair.

"So," I said, trying to keep my voice from shaking, "you're okay with He Who Sees marrying you to me and not to…Neferure?" I felt awkward saying her name but needed to ask this question, and I had not seen Moses in so receptive a mood for such questions in many months.

"That's one of the things He's been talking to me about, Zipporah. I was wrong in my love for Neferure. It went where it shouldn't have gone, and I've repented of that."

"Did you…?"

"Did I what?" he asked, not making this easy.

"You know."

"Lay with her?"

I nodded.

"No, but my love for her never should have gone in the direction it did. It soured my relationship with Thutmose and caused difficulty between me and Mother at the end."

"What else did He Who Sees say to you?"

"That I'm where He wants me, and I should enjoy this quiet season with you and the boys. He said it won't always be this quiet."

I shifted my head in surprise so I could see his face better. "What do you think that means? Do you think we're going to go somewhere else?"

Moses shook his head. "I have no idea. He didn't say."

"Do you think we're going to go to Egypt?" I persisted.

"I would not expect that, barring Thutmose's death. Why? Do you want to go to Egypt?"

"It would definitely be intriguing. I mean, I've lived in the wilderness of Midian my entire life. I think it would be fascinating to see the culture and civilization of Egypt."

"You know, Zipporah," said Moses, "I'd like to tell you a little secret." He paused dramatically.

"Yes?" I urged, curious. "What?"

"As long as you're not starving or in some sort of pain, one basically gets used to one's environment. So whether you're taking care of your children and husband in a two-story villa with art on the walls or you're doing the same thing in a goatskin tent under a big sky, your life is your life and you get used to it."

"Are you saying that I wouldn't enjoy servants and exotic food and a small dipping pool in a garden filled with fruit trees and flowers?"

Moses laughed. "I'm very much sure you would enjoy those things, but after a while they merely are what they are, and those externals do not bring joy."

"Tell me what brings joy," I said, suspecting the answer.

"Elohim," he replied, confirming my suspicions.

We ceased talking and snuggled together, watching the occasional bird swoop, listening to the gentle, even sounds of our babies breathing, secure in the knowledge that He Who Sees did indeed see us and love us despite our faults and foibles, despite our sin. I closed my eyes and felt the joy of which Moses spoke. *Thank You, my God*, I silently prayed. *Thank You for this life.*

*

Our boys grew, our life proceeded. One by one my sisters got married. Some stayed with our community; some left with foreign husbands and forged new paths. My little brother Hobab grew up with my boys and got particularly close to Moses and me. We drew closer to He Who Sees, and He grew closer to us. The years slipped by.

Before I knew it, I wasn't young anymore. Moses reassured me this wasn't an issue since, as he so eloquently put it, I was as beautiful as ever. Gershom and Eliezer became fine young men, though neither one seemed in a rush to find a wife, something I worried about.

"Relax," said my husband. "If I had gotten married before I turned forty, it would have been to the wrong girl." This soothed me, but only temporarily.

I looked forward to expanding my family; I looked forward to grandchildren.

Father and Mama seemed as vital as ever. Our community had expanded to over one hundred people, and Father was continually in demand: leading people in worship, teaching, counseling, arbitrating, helping. Mama cooked nonstop, bringing food and comfort to any who were ill or distressed. I aided her as I was able.

Moses still shepherded the flocks. I noticed that every five years or so he got restless, at which point he took a week, loaded up on supplies, and went off into the wilderness by himself to seek He Who Sees. When he returned, I would pounce on him.

"So what did He say? Are we staying?"

Always he replied the same: "Elohim hasn't told me to move on. This is where He's called us for now."

I was never sure if I was disappointed or relieved by his answer. In the earlier years I occasionally thirsted for adventure, but as time went on I grew more and more settled. Still…

Years continued to drift by, folding into one another like pleats in a robe. One day I turned around and I was halfway through my fifties: my hair streaked with gray, wrinkles tracking my face like so many caravan routes. Moses laughed when I pointed this out, saying I had to reach eighty before I got bragging rights. Father was over ninety, always active, though Mama had slowed down considerably.

Moses was as handsome and vital as ever. I have to admit I had some concerns about marrying a man close to twenty-five years older than me, not for the beginning but for now, the later years. It was my happy surprise that, much like wine, he only improved with age. Lately, he had showed signs of restlessness again, something I hadn't seen in him in close to six years. By the second week of classic unsettled behavior—attention wandering, foot tapping, patent answers to anything I said—I told him, "Go! Go graze the sheep at Mt. Horeb."

A three-day journey from our semi-permanent village area towered a stony mountain called Mt. Horeb. Moses had often gone there, claiming he found it easier to communicate with He Who Sees at this particular site. I had only been there one time, and that briefly, the stark intensity frightening me, my own sins emerging more pronounced.

"Just repent if you're convicted," advised Moses when I haltingly shared my feelings. "Elohim loves you, but He *is* a holy God."

"Do you feel like this?"

"Like what?"

I lifted one shoulder and let it fall back. "Unworthy. Afraid."

"Yes. No."

I gave him a wry smile. "Why and why not?"

He squinted at the sun for a moment as he collected his thoughts, before turning back to me. "Zip," he said affectionately, "we're *all* unworthy, every person on the face of the earth: you, me, your parents, Pharaoh, other shepherds, artists, priests, Hebrews, Egyptians, Midianites, small children. All of us. We've become like one who is unclean, and all our righteous acts are like filthy rags. We will shrivel up like a leaf, and like the wind our sins will sweep us away. It's only through Him that it can ever change."

"How?" I cried. "How?"

"I think faith plays a big part," said Moses slowly. "There's more, but I don't have that piece of the puzzle yet."

"Will you ever?"

"Yes." It wasn't an arrogant *yes* or even a confident *yes,* but rather an "I've been assured of that knowledge; we're just not there yet" kind of a yes.

"But you're not afraid?"

"No. I know He whom I love, and I'm convinced that He loves me and will only accomplish that which is for my ultimate benefit."

I nodded. "I do love Him, Moses."

My husband tucked a lock of my hair behind my ear. "He knows that, Zipporah. Spend more time with Him. Sit in front of Him and listen for His voice. Don't do every chore perfectly and don't attempt to squeeze every extra minute out of sleep. He's waiting for you."

"Yes, you're right," I said, convicted. He knew me, my husband did.

Though I hadn't been back to Mt. Horeb, Moses went regularly. Each time he returned, he was deeper in love with He Who Sees, after which followed greater spiritual understanding. Even Father stood in awe. So it didn't take a brilliant wife to encourage him to go there once I saw he was looking for answers. While it was true that he could talk to He Who Sees anywhere, that mountain was a special place, a holy place.

"I was thinking that too," my husband admitted when I (strongly) encouraged (I never ordered) him to go to the mountain. "I'll head out tomorrow."

*

Early the next morning we kissed good-bye. "When will I see you?" I asked.

Moses pursed his lips. "A week, maybe ten days tops. I'll try not to be away long."

"I miss you already," I said, reaching up to stroke his cheek. "I love you."

"I love you too." He kissed me before swinging himself onto a donkey loaded with enough provisions to last on this short trip to the far side of the wilderness. "Say good-bye to the boys for me."

Our sons were out shepherding different flocks two days to the east. Moses was heading northwest.

"Yes," I said, waving as he rode away. When he was a little figure on the horizon, I yelled, "I'll be praying for you!" though by this time he was so far away I wasn't sure if he heard me.

I stood there for a while, praying to He Who Sees that He would bless Moses mightily and provide the answers he was looking for. I had no idea the degree to which my prayer would be answered.

* * *

Part IV

Moses

13

1445 B.C.

THE BUSH WAS ON FIRE, great flames of orange and yellow shooting dramatically into the sky. Not more than a third of the way up the mountain, it caught the man's attention when he emerged from the other side of the mountain, shepherd staff in hand, sheep in tow. His first response was fear, as in what if the fire spread? How fast could he get the sheep away? But as he stood there staring at the fire, debating his choices, he noticed a very odd thing: the fire hadn't spread, nor had the bush burned up. It was a large, brambly bush as bushes go, its foliage apparent even from the safe distance of a hundred meters, and so the man could clearly tell that though the brambles were enveloped in flame, their size remained undiminished and their color did not blacken.

Intrigued, he walked closer, expecting at any time to be halted by the heat of the flames. When this did not happen, he came even closer until soon he was within a few meters of the strange sight. It was then that he heard his name called from within the bush:

"Moses! Moses!"

Startled, the man took another step toward the bush. "Here I am," he said, amazed.

"Do not come any closer!" cautioned the Voice. "Take off your sandals, for the place where you are standing is holy ground."

Dropping to his knees, Moses hastily removed his sandals.

Then the Voice said, "I am the God of your father, the God of Abraham, the God of Isaac, and the God of Jacob."

Realizing this was Elohim, Moses hid his face in his sleeve, afraid to look at Him. His mouth felt dry, and he trembled with excitement. Elohim spoke to him, as a man speaks to another man, telling him those words he had longed to hear forty years ago, those words that spoke of His awareness of the suffering of the Hebrews, and of His desire to save them from their oppression. He told Moses to do that which Moses had determined to do when still in Egypt. He said, "So now, go, I am sending you to Pharaoh to bring My people the Israelites out of Egypt."

Moses' heart quaked within his chest. How desperately he once wanted to hear those words. He had acted impulsively, before God had actually said them, and had spent the last four decades circling the desert with the sheep. Now an old man, his sons grown, his young wife herself approaching old age, was it still to be?

"Who am I that I should go to Pharaoh and bring the Israelites out of Egypt?" He faltered, knowing even as the words left his mouth that the dream was rekindling in his heart, igniting a small spark into a great fire not unlike the flames erupting from the bush out of which resounded God's voice.

The voice of Elohim assured him that He would go with Moses into Egypt; that they would deliver the people out of bondage and gather on this very mountain, this holy place of Mt. Horeb. Inexplicably, in the midst of this unbelievable encounter, Moses remembered that long ago conversation with Zipporah; he thought about the name of God and how even they, a married couple closer than most, even they did not call God by the same name. Would the elders of Israel believe him when he said he had heard from Elohim?

"If the Israelites ask me Your name, what do I tell them?"

God said to Moses, "I AM WHO I AM. This is what you are to say to the Israelites: 'I AM has sent me to you.' My name is sacred, too holy to pronounce. They are to call me Yahweh." He proceeded to inform Moses of His plans: plans to strike the Egyptians down with many wonders; plans to enable the Hebrews to plunder Egyptians on their way out of the country; plans to bring Pharaoh to his knees; plans to bring the Hebrews to a land flowing with milk and honey.

Pharaoh. The name still had the power to freeze Moses' blood. "But El—Yahweh," he cried out. "What of Thutmose?"

"Thutmose is dead. His son Amenhotep, is now Pharaoh."

"Amenhotep? Not the son of Neferure?"

"Thutmose's son by Neferure died several years ago. This son's mother is Merytre-Hatshepsut. He inherited the throne five years ago, at age eighteen. He is a brash young man who will learn to fear My great name."

Moses continued to have objections. "What if they do not believe me or listen to me? What if they claim I didn't really see You?"

Yahweh took these protests seriously. He gave Moses three signs by which the Hebrews might believe: the ability for Moses' staff to turn into a snake and back into a staff; the ability for Moses to put his hand in his cloak and have it turn leprous and back to normal; and the ability to take water from the Nile, pour it on the ground, and watch it turn to blood. Still, Moses wasn't satisfied. He protested to Yahweh that he had not the speaking ability, to which Yahweh tried to comfort Moses, telling him that He would help him speak and teach him what to say.

But the forty years in the desert had beaten Moses down such that he still doubted his ability to carry out Yahweh's plan, even with Yahweh's help. "Pardon your servant, Yahweh," he begged, eyes downcast, trembling. "Please send someone else."

That was too much. Yahweh grew angry with Moses, saying, "What about your brother, Aaron the Levite? I know he can speak well. Look! Already he is on his way to meet you, and his heart will be glad when he sees you." He told Moses that he and Aaron were to work together; Yahweh would be with them. "Don't forget to take your staff in your hand," He warned, "so you can perform the signs with it."

At this point, Moses' heart shifted, and he accepted the commission he had received, excitement and resoluteness replacing the fear.

Quickly, he traveled the dusty, rutted path in the wilderness back to his home, back to Zipporah and Gershom and Eliezer, back to Jethro and Mama and Hobab, back to all that had grown familiar and comforting. As he traveled, he marveled over what had just happened, over his actual encounter with the one and only God, the great Yahweh. His heart swelled as he replayed again and again in his mind all the words that were said, his face growing warm upon remembering the hard time he gave Yahweh about going to Egypt. *Why did I argue with Him, the greatest One in all the universe?* he agonized, repenting, vowing to be obedient always, in all things.

He thought too about seeing Aaron, thrilled to know that his brother was still alive. What also of Miryam? Pawero? Their children and their children's children? He hoped to see them, but Yahweh had given no indication of their fates. Other names and faces popped into his mind—people he hadn't thought about in decades. "Forty years!" he said aloud, to the bushes and thorns and wadis that he passed by; to the sheep who kept pace. *So much has happened in forty years, so much has changed. To think that I'll be facing a young son of Thutmose from a mother I never met, that I'll see a court of Egypt without Mother presiding. How odd, how unusual.*

So occupied was Moses with his thoughts that the trip back seemed like it took no time. He arrived at the outskirts of the compound late one afternoon, leaving him enough daylight to water and pen the flock. He greeted several people, one who immediately headed back to the tents to tell Zipporah about his arrival.

*

When Zipporah heard of Moses' return, she took a few minutes to freshen up in anticipation. Excitedly, she brushed and re-braided her hair, washed her hands and face, and cleaned her teeth.

"Mama," she called to the now quite elderly lady napping in the fading sunlight, "Moses is home! I'm going to meet him."

The old lady opened one eye. "That's wonderful, my dear. Go and be blessed."

Zipporah blew a kiss her mother's way and hurried along the path that led to the sheep pens. She didn't have long to walk before coming face to face with her husband, who was heading toward her.

"Moses! Oh, Moses, you're home!" she shouted joyfully, picking up her pace so that she was practically running. He smiled broadly upon seeing her, scooping her up with his hands around her waist, swinging her around. "I missed you so much," she said, arms around his neck when both feet were finally on the ground.

"I missed you too," he replied, eyes sparkling.

Zipporah looked closely at him. "What happened? You look about twenty years younger."

His grin widened. "It's incredible!"

"What? What happened?"

"First feed me. Then let's talk." Arms around each other, husband and wife walked back to the camp. At least five people tried to speak with Moses before Zipporah gently but insistently guided him to their own tent. Once seated outside under the pink glow of the setting sun, she plied him with stew, bread, and goat's milk until he finally pushed the bowls away.

"Are you good?" asked his wife, "because I've been patient…"

Moses laughed as he wiped his mouth. "You're a wonderful, patient wife whom I adore." He grew more serious as he studied the woman in front of him. *Still beautiful,* he thought, admiring her heavy, dark hair, dusky complexion, intelligent, clear eyes and full, soft figure. *Yahweh, thank You for this woman, my love.*

"What is it, Moses?" asked Zipporah quietly, the intensity of his stare puzzling. "What are you thinking?"

"I'm thinking that I have the most beautiful, amazing, perfect wife in the world!"

"Oh my," said Zipporah, blushing slightly but obviously pleased. "What did happen at Horeb?" She laid her hand out, palm up, and Moses put his hand on top of hers.

"I encountered Yahweh."

Zipporah frowned. "Who's Yahweh?"

"You know how we talk about God's name? How I call Him Elohim and you call Him He Who Sees?"

"Yes..." She stared at him expectantly.

"We were both right..."

"...which we knew," she inserted.

"Yes, which we knew. What we didn't know was that He has a specific name in addition to the litany of names that describe Him. He wants to be called Yahweh, and He calls Himself I AM WHO I AM."

"How do you know this?" asked Zipporah, her voice quivering.

"Because," Moses said, leaning forward, grasping her hand tighter, "He spoke to me!"

"He spoke to you! How? Where?"

"I saw a bush on the mountain that burned but wasn't consumed. When I got closer, He spoke to me from out of the midst of the flames."

"You're sure it was Him?"

Moses gazed at his wife in disbelief. "Are there lots of voices that speak out of burning bushes? Do you have something to tell me?"

Zipporah laughed nervously. "No, it's just..."

"Trust me. We spoke for a long time. I know this is He whom I have worshiped all my life." Moses got a faraway look in his eyes.

"Tell me more."

"He gave me a commission. He's sending me back to Egypt—Aaron's on his way to meet me—it's time for the Hebrews to be freed—there's a new Pharaoh." The words spilled out, faster and faster, as Moses shared with his wife the wonders of his encounter with Yahweh.

Zipporah listened: fascinated, amazed, struck dumb in parts by the intensity of the tale. Her eyes glowed as she listened.

When he finally slowed down, pausing to take a drink, she somewhat shyly said, "This is the most amazing thing I have ever heard. I feel honored to know you, a man whom God has spoken to."

Moses wiped his eyes. "It is I who am honored to know you, my love." They sat gazing at one another as the last strands of sunset vanished over the distant hills and night descended. "Come," Moses said, standing up, holding out his hand. "Let's go in."

Wordlessly, Zipporah took his hand, allowing him to lead her into the tent, where they renewed their love.

*

The next day, Moses immediately sought out Jethro. He told him much of what had happened at Horeb, though not in as much detail as what he had shared with his wife. "Let me return to my own people in Egypt to see if any of them are still alive," he said respectfully, honoring Jethro's position as head of the clan.

"Go, and I wish you well," said his father-in-law, blessing him. He studied Moses. "You're taking Zipporah." It was a statement, not a question.

"Of course."

"And the boys?"

Moses hesitated. "They're grown men. It's time they made their own decisions."

"We'll miss you. Do you think you'll be back?"

Moses shrugged. "I have no idea what the future holds. Frankly, at this stage in the game, I never expected to go back there. Yahweh holds us in His hands."

"Yahweh," repeated the old man thoughtfully. "Yes, He does."

That evening, Moses held a conference with his sons when they returned from penning up the sheep. Gershom looked not unlike his Uncle Aaron, though taller and darker. Eliezer resembled Zipporah's side of the family but with Moses' lighter coloring.

"Yes, Abba?" said Eliezer after they were seated and drinking the hot concoction brought to them by their mother. "I can sense the excitement in the air. What's happening?"

His brother murmured similar sentiments.

For the third time, Moses told about his experience at Horeb. His sons listened, entranced. He finished by saying, "Tomorrow morning, I'm putting your mother on a donkey and heading to Egypt. Who's coming with us?"

"Tomorrow morning!" exclaimed Gershom. "So soon?"

"Yes, my son. Yahweh, may His name be praised, has given me a command. I cannot delay."

"But what about the sheep?" asked Gershom. "Who will take care of them?"

Moses looked at his son and loved him. "Gershom," he said, not unkindly, "others will step into the gap. We've been called by Yahweh Himself to a great and mighty task. We need to take care of God's sheep—the Israelites. Our sheep are not as significant."

Eliezer smiled at this, but Gershom still seemed a bit unsure. "I'm going to take a short walk, and I'll be back with an answer," he told his father.

"I'm in," said Eliezer. "Let's go pack."

As it turned out, all four members of the family left on donkeys the following morning at dawn. They packed lightly, only taking the provisions necessary for making it safely across the desert and west to Egypt. Parting was difficult; everyone but Moses seemed to think they were coming back. Moses made no such commitment. "All I know is that I am to bring the people to worship Yahweh at Horeb," he said, "and after that He is bringing them into Canaan, into the land of their forefathers."

"Will we be going to Canaan as well?" asked Gershom.

"I would certainly think so," replied his father. "You and your brother are Hebrews."

"It's so odd since I've never met a Hebrew apart from you, Abba."

"Well, that's about to change," said Moses. "Time to leave."

Travel in the wilderness was never easy. It was too hot during the day and too cold during the night; intermittent sandstorms were agonizing to endure. No matter how tightly head and body were covered, there was still sand *everywhere.* Food and water were carefully hoarded and stopping places few and far between. Not a lot of talking happened as people were basically trying to survive. The various routes were not always easily visible and it was possible to lose one's way, so utmost concentration was required.

Fortunately, they were first headed to Horeb, a path Moses knew well. About two-thirds of the way there a small lodging place that provided adequate food and shelter existed for travelers. It was a slapdash affair—basically a few tents, a rough wooden shelter for animals, a well, and some substandard food all for a piece of silver a night. Moses had only stayed there occasionally, deeming it not worth the money, but with Zipporah along, he determined it was necessary. The proprietor, a sullen, toothless, wizened fellow ironically named Adib (the name means "well-mannered, courteous one"), led their donkeys to shelter and provided hay after haggling over the price.

The family ate supper, exhausted from the day's travel, when Moses swayed uncertainly from a sitting position, seemingly about to topple over.

"Abba!" exclaimed Eliezer, noticing before the others. "Are you all right?"

"I...I don't know," stammered his father, a dazed look on his suddenly pale and shiny face. He put his hands on his head, bent over between his knees. "I'm not feeling well."

"What is it? What's going on?" asked Zipporah worriedly, pausing in the midst of the picking up of bowls and utensils, an activity in which she had been engaged.

"It's Abba," said Eliezer, frowning. "He's not doing so well."

"Is it the heat?" Zipporah asked Moses. She poured more water into his cup and brought it to him. "Here, try to drink."

Moses made an attempt to swallow a little water, only to spit it back up. He jerked to the side, vomiting his just-eaten dinner in the sand behind him.

Eliezer and Zipporah exchanged concerned glances.

"Gershom! Eliezer! Help me get Abba to his bed," commanded Zipporah, cradling Moses' head.

Gershom, who had been leaning back with his eyes shut not really paying attention the last few minutes, snapped to while Eliezer was already at his father's side. The two men half-lifted, half-dragged their father to the tent in which he was to spend the night. Zipporah followed behind with an empty container in case he had to throw up again and a cloth she had wet down for his forehead. Once inside the tent, they loosened his clothing and did all they could in an attempt to make him comfortable.

"He's burning up," said Zipporah, biting her lower lip, hand on Moses' head.

To their horror, Moses moaned with pain, quickly becoming delirious. He threw up again, though Zipporah was quick enough to spot the signs and had the container ready. His neck was puffy, and red spots began popping out on his face, neck, under his arms, and his groin area.

Meanwhile, Adib had noticed the confusion and stood in the entrance of the tent, arms folded, mouth drawn. "Why do you bring a sick man here?" he snarled. "What's wrong with him?"

Eliezer went out and drew the innkeeper to the side, explaining in low tones what had happened and that they had no clue what was the matter. When he described the symptoms, Adib looked alarmed and backed away, hands in the air. Eliezer came back to the tent.

"What did he say?" asked Zipporah. "Does he know what this is?"

"Didn't say," came the terse reply. "He's an unhelpful one, he is."

They spent an awful night taking turns watching over an increasingly ill Moses. He threw up again and again until he had the dry heaves but still continued to throw up, not able to even keep a few drops of water down. His fever raged unabated, the red spots on his body grew, and he thrashed, obviously in great pain.

After the hard day of traveling when all anyone wanted to do was sink into sleep, this nightmare watch over an inexplicably sick man was torturous.

Zipporah, Gershom, and Eliezer were each able to snatch a few minutes of sleep here and there, but never more than fifteen minutes at a stretch.

As dawn approached, it was Gershom who suggested they pray to Yahweh for relief.

"I've been praying continually," said his mother despairingly.

"I mean together, out loud," said her son.

So they stood in a circle and held hands, crying out to the Lord Most High, pleading with Him to save their father and husband, reminding Him of His promises and the reason for this journey, rebuking anything that was attempting to pervert the rescue of the Hebrews from Egypt. For a long time they stood thus, eyes closed, faces uplifted, until Zipporah gave a little gasp.

"What is it, Ema?" asked Eliezer.

"It's my fault," she cried.

The brothers looked at each other. "Ema," remonstrated Eliezer, squeezing her hand. "How can this sickness be your fault?"

"I didn't let your father circumcise your brother," she said, eyes bloodshot and more than a little wild. "This is our punishment!"

"I don't get it," said Gershom, a tad nervously.

"You weren't brought into a covenant relationship with the God of your fathers through my—our—disobedience. Your father is paying for that sin with his life."

"But that doesn't make any sense!" cried Eliezer. "Why would Yahweh meet Abba and give him an assignment and then try to kill him?"

"I don't know!" lamented Zipporah, her voice rising. "All I know is I heard it distinctly when we prayed."

"She's right," came Moses' weakened voice from the bed.

Startled, they spun around. These were the first coherent words he had spoken in hours.

"My love!" exclaimed Zipporah, "are you feeling better?"

Moses ignored her question. "Your mother and I sinned when we failed to follow Yahweh's covenant rule for circumcising Gershom and bringing him into the house of Israel," he said slowly and painfully, barely able to articulate the words. They came close in order to hear him, he spoke so softly. "I will not have the spiritual protection I need to stand against the demon gods of Egypt until this wrong is righted."

They were all aghast, Gershom most of all.

"What are you saying, Abba?" faltered the elder son, the uncircumcised one.

"You will need to be circumcised to save my life and the lives of our brethren in Egypt." Moses' voice grew so soft they could barely hear him, his breathing labored such that they feared for his life. His burning eyes sought out his son's face. "Help me, Gershom." He turned his face to the wall and said no more.

Zipporah, Eliezer, and Gershom stared at one another, faces white. *What in the world was going on? What were they dealing with?* Momentarily paralyzed by shock, Gershom was the first to move, jumping up and quickly leaving the tent.

His brother ran after him. "Gershom!" he yelled at the angrily retreating back. "Wait! Stop!" Running to catch up, Eliezer soon overtook his brother. He grabbed him by the arm but was savagely shaken off.

"What do you want?" Gershom glared, his eyes red.

"Hey," sputtered Eliezer, backing away. "Don't blame me. I'm not the one who neglected to circumcise you."

"Ha ha, you're so funny." Gershom smacked his fist into his open palm.

"Look," said Eliezer in that special soothing tone he tended to use when his brother was agitated, "this wasn't your fault, but we're obviously stuck. It's not just Abba's life that's at stake, though that's significant enough: it's the lives of countless numbers of people. Do you see what Yahweh has entrusted to you? What an awesome responsibility to change the destiny of the world!" Emboldened by Gershom's softening expressing, he added, "Maybe it won't be that bad," only to have his brother flare up again.

"That bad! I know about adult circumcision. I've listened to the stories about Levi and Shimon and Dinah!"

"Nothing is going to happen to you. I'll watch over you while you heal up and protect you, okay? Can you trust me?"

"Go back to Ema and Abba. I'll be there in a few minutes."

"Gershom…?"

"Just go, all right! I…I want to talk to Yahweh. Alone."

"Yes, all right," agreed Eliezer reluctantly. Concerned, he took a few backward steps, keeping his eyes on Gershom who pushed at the air with his hand. Taking the hint, he returned to the tent.

"Where's Gershom?" asked Zipporah as soon as he entered the room.

"Seeking Yahweh."

"Do you think he'll agree?" asked his mother hesitantly.

"Yes, I do," said Eliezer. "How is he?"

"Not good." Together, they looked at Moses, who lay on his side, breathing shallowly, eyes closed, a patina of sweat on his flushed face. "I think we need to do this immediately."

An hour later, Gershom returned. He looked at his mother and brother and they looked at him, expectantly, fearfully.

"Yes," he said gruffly, in answer to their silent question.

Zipporah fell on her knees in gratitude and Eliezer's face relaxed. It was agreed that Zipporah would do the actual procedure, as she was more skilled than Eliezer when it came to doing delicate things with a knife. Adib was sought out, and silver was exchanged for poppies, and more silver for not making a fuss over the surgical procedure that was about to be done on his premises. He wandered off with a fistful of coins, muttering to himself.

After Gershom had chewed enough poppies that he passed out with one still in his mouth, Zipporah and Eliezer quickly went to work. Eliezer undressed and held his brother down while Zipporah took a flint knife to his penis, staring at it and frowning but not actually doing anything.

"Ema, hurry up!" urged Eliezer. "He's not going to be asleep forever."

Zipporah took a deep breath. "Okay," she said, as much to herself as to her son. "Yahweh, help me. Here we go." Resolutely, she gripped the knife and slowly, methodically, went to work on removing her son's foreskin. All the while she prayed aloud, repenting for her disobedience at his birth, begging for Moses' life now.

It seemed like forever, but in reality the whole thing only took about fifteen minutes. As soon as she finished, Eliezer wrapped a clean strip of linen around the wound and Zipporah hurried over to the bed where Moses lay very still, barely breathing. She held the bloody foreskin in her hand and touched Moses' feet with it, proclaiming, "Surely you are a bridegroom of blood to me."

By saying this, she unknowingly uttered a messianic prophecy, referring to the time in the future when men would be saved from eternal death through the blood of the bridegroom.

The life flowed back into Moses. In the time it took for the procedure, his shallow breathing deepened, his color returned to normal, his fever fled. The red spots on his body faded and disappeared. It was astounding how fast the recovery was. In the other bed, Gershom stirred uneasily, moaning.

"Zipporah." Moses' voice, steady though weakened, drew his wife quickly to his side.

"Oh, my love!" she exclaimed, dropping to her knees by his side. "Praise Yahweh you're better!" Tenderly, she stroked the hair back from his forehead, gazing at him with love, relief emanating from her like heat from a brazier.

"I've been dreaming about Yahweh," he whispered hoarsely. "Great things are coming."

"Great things have already begun," she responded shakily. "Can I get you some water?"

*

It took close to a week before Moses and Gershom were healed and healthy enough to get back on their donkeys and continue traveling. Moses noticed a significant difference in his older son's attitude. Whereas before he had been somewhat flippant about the things of Yahweh, now he had become a firm believer. The trial he had undergone had strengthened him, bringing him into a covenant relationship with Yahweh and his Hebrew forebears not only in a physical sense but in a very real way spiritually. He rode ahead with his father, their donkeys pointed toward Mt. Horeb, the heat of the day abating as the afternoon shadows lengthened, promising the coming evening's coolness.

"Have I told you how much I appreciate your willingness to correct past sins?" Moses asked his son, eyes on the trail ahead.

Gershom smiled, a smile that held no trace of a smirk. He flicked a fly away from his cheek, the wetness of a tear staining his finger. "I love you, Abba."

"I love you too," said his father.

They arrived at the mountain several hours after sundown, the rocks and bushes that comprised it showing up as dark silhouettes under the light of the moon, the landscape eerily different at night. Zipporah shivered and drew closer to her husband.

"Look!" announced Eliezer. "There's someone out here."

It was true. On the far side of the mountain, to the west, the fire of a campsite smoldered, its smoke rising in the evening air.

"It doesn't look like a big party." Gershom peered into the distance.

"I only see one donkey," agreed his brother.

"Abba, stay here with Ema. Eliezer and I will find out who's there." Without waiting for an answer, the brothers rode over to the fire. Moses and Zipporah dismounted, standing with their arms around each other, praying.

After what seemed an interminable period of time, the brothers returned, a figure on a donkey between them. "Hey Abba," yelled Eliezer, his voice joyful. "We have a surprise for you."

Eagerly, Moses stepped forward. "Is it…?".

"What is it?" queried Zipporah.

The figure on the donkey dismounted. "Is it you, my brother?"

"Aaron?"

"Moses!"

With shouts of joy, the brothers, separated for forty years, flung themselves into each other's arms. They laughed, they cried, they exclaimed over how old the other looked, they were thoroughly happy. When they settled down, Moses introduced Aaron to his wife and sons.

"Such a beautiful family!" approved Aaron.

The whole group settled itself at Aaron's campsite, the young men tending to the donkeys and building up the fire while Zipporah prepared a late supper. Moses and Aaron sat and talked.

"And you, my brother?" asked Moses. "What has happened with you?"

Aaron talked at length. He spoke of Elisheva, the wife he had taken from among the Hebrews, and their four sons. ("What? Not a daughter among us?" exclaimed Moses, to which Aaron laughed heartily.) He told Moses that Hatshepsut had protected him from the fate of the other slaves, and that even after her death he and Miryam had been allowed to live in peace so long as they weren't perceived as troublemakers. He shared the sad news of Pawero's passing ten years earlier, and Miryam's status as a widow, her children grown with children of their own, mostly integrated into Egyptian society. He told of Miryam's daughter Abigail and her husband, Hur, whose grandson Bezalel had astounded the whole family with his superb artistry, far outstripping the talents of his great-grandfather Pawero and great-great-grandfather Hau. He spoke of the new Pharaoh, Amenhotep II, and how the Hebrews had hoped for a relaxing of their servitude under a new king, but that this son of Thutmose was worse than all those who came before, the bonds of their torment tightening.

At this, Moses put his head in his hands. "It's my fault," he admitted starkly. "I rushed Yahweh's plan. I added to their pain."

"Yahweh?" repeated Aaron, puzzled. "Don't you mean Elohim?"

At this Moses perked up. "Let me tell you what's been happening here," he said, launching into what Yahweh had done recently by appearing in the burning bush and sending them back to Egypt to deliver the people out of bondage. He told Aaron what he was to say, and about the signs Yahweh had given him that would convince the Hebrew leaders of the genuineness of his call. Aaron nodded excitedly.

"Yes, He spoke to me and led me here. A group of us have been meeting and praying for years, discerning six months ago that the time was ripe. Elohim confirmed His plan to me in a dream. I've prepared for this journey ever since."

"I'm amazed you came alone, my brother."

"I had to," said Aaron, his features hard to see in the darkness but the sad tone of his voice unmistakable. "Amenhotep is so paranoid about Hebrews, I couldn't slip away with even one other person. I had to come alone."

Moses nodded, impressed. "That was a difficult journey for me to take alone as a young man on a horse and not a donkey. You're pretty tough, Aaron." Playfully, he punched his brother lightly on the arm.

Aaron grinned. "I've tried to stay in shape," he said modestly. They looked at each other and laughed, feeling like young men again now that they were together, remembering the camaraderie of their youth.

*

Early the next morning, the brothers awoke at the crack of dawn, an exhausted Zipporah, Gershom, and Eliezer still asleep. They climbed up the mountain to the site of the burning bush, which burned no longer. Falling on their faces, they worshiped Yahweh, thanking Him for His great mercy on them and their people, thanking Him for life, for restoring family, for providing and keeping them safe even in the midst of this great wilderness.

When the early morning dew evaporated and the sun was fully ensconced in the morning sky, they returned to camp, finding the others at breakfast.

"There you are!" sang out Zipporah, catching hold of Moses and kissing him, smiling shyly at Aaron. "We have food."

"Food is always good," said Aaron kindly, gazing with approval upon the woman his brother married. In the strong light of day, they could all really see each other clearly. Aaron saw Moses' sons, strong and handsome, and his wife, agreeable and still beautiful. His brother no longer looked the part of an Egyptian prince, however.

"You look like Abba," he said. "You remind me of him now."

Moses was pleased. "You could give me no greater compliment."

After the sun peaked and it was no longer so hot, they left Mt. Horeb, traveling back to Egypt over the same route Aaron had used to get there.

*

It took close to two weeks. In that time Moses and Aaron did so much talking about their lives and were so caught up with not only the significant events that had happened but the daily nuances that they soon felt as if they had never been separated. Gershom and Eliezer appreciated their uncle's company, immensely enjoying getting to know him.

Only Zipporah hung back. At first it was shyness, a natural reserve. Once that wore off, though, she realized that she felt like a bit of an outsider—the only Midianite among several Hebrews. *It's ridiculous that I feel this way*, she chided herself. *They're my husband, sons, and brother-in-law, for goodness' sake.* Still, she had trouble getting past the invisible wall.

One night when they were practically at the border of Egypt, she snuggled against Moses, her back to him, his arm around her. Everyone else was sound asleep, the light snores of three men punctuating the cold desert air. Only Zipporah and Moses were awake.

"What is it, my love?" breathed Moses in her ear. "Why are you not yourself?"

Zipporah started to cry. She couldn't help herself—the kindness in his tone opened the floodgates of emotion.

Moses held her closer. Years of familiarity had taught him that she would speak when ready. In the meantime, he kissed her hair and prayed silently.

Finally she sobbed, "I'm scared."

"Of what?"

"Of being left behind. You've been all mine for so long and now even the boys act like they were only ever Hebrews. I don't share your Egyptian past or your Hebrew blood."

"Zipporah, Zipporah!" remonstrated Moses, gently turning her so that she faced him. "Don't you know by now that you're flesh of my flesh and bone of my bone? You're my very self! Never doubt your place in my life, never doubt your significance. After Yahweh, there is no one who is closer." He traced the outline of her jaw with his finger.

Zipporah sat up, blew her nose, and took a gulp of water from the cup she had stuck in the sand beside their bedroll. "You mean that?" she asked, more composed.

"Have I ever lied to you?"

She slid back down into her husband's waiting embrace. "Never."

"All right then," he said, his voice getting drowsier. "Now go to sleep. We have another long day tomorrow. Are you better?"

"Yes, my love." She *did* feel better. He always knew the right thing to say. What a man.

"Good. I just hope Miryam doesn't give you any trouble."

What? "What do you mean?" demanded Zipporah, alarmed. "You think I'm going to have a hard time with your sister?" But the only answer she got was the sound of deep breathing. Moses had fallen asleep and was not to be roused.

"Huh," grunted Zipporah, allowing the exhaustion of the day to pull her into sleep.

*

Three days later, after bribing border guards and traveling carefully so as not to draw undue attention, they approached Goshen. On the way, Moses was in constant amazement, pointing out landmarks old and new, saying things like, "I designed that obelisk" and "That pyramid wasn't here. I'm not so sure I like what they did with it" and "I had almost forgotten that smell of river decay mixed with lotus blossom."

Gershom and Eliezer kept exchanging open-mouthed looks. Their understanding of who their father was evolved from moment to moment in this startlingly new environment. What an adventure! Following sheep around the desert all day seemed further and further away.

They came to Aaron's home in Goshen. Warmly welcomed by Elisheva, a smiling, round-faced woman with laugh lines at the corner of her eyes and whose graying hair was wrapped up in a head scarf, they quickly felt at home. Only used to tents, Zipporah and her sons luxuriated in being in an actual house with a roof over their heads. Moses appreciated it too after his forty-year hiatus. Everyone was thrilled with a bath and a hot meal, after which they met Aaron's sons: Eleazar, Ithamar, Nadab, and Abihu. The two Eliezer/Eleazars hit it off while Gershom seemed to get along equally as well with the other three brothers.

Aaron immediately sent word to the leaders of the Israelites, requesting their appearance. He advised that utmost discretion be used, and set up ten homes in his neighborhood in which to lodge everyone. He also let Miryam know that he was back and that she should come over as soon as possible.

*

The next day, as they were reclining at dinner, there was a knock at the door. Elisheva went to answer it, encountering a tall, elegant, older woman with upswept white hair and probing brown eyes.

"I have a surprise for you," whispered Elisheva.

The woman's eyebrows went up. "Is it what I think it might be…?"

Trembling, she grasped her sister-in-law's hand.

"Come with me." Elisheva smiled.

The two women walked in to where the men were sitting. "Miryam!" exclaimed Aaron, rising. "I have someone whom I know you'll be very happy to see." Moses got up as well, and the two brothers approached Miryam.

She looked from one to the other, realization quickly dawning on her face. "Moses?" she asked hesitantly. Upon his affirmative nod she gave a little scream and threw herself into his open arms. "Moses, O Moses!" she cried. "I have longed to see you for so many years!"

It took awhile, but after the tumult of their initial encounter settled down somewhat, Moses introduced Miryam to Zipporah and his sons. She hugged each of them tightly, tears filling her eyes. "My brother's children! After so very, very long! God is good!" When she reached Zipporah, she kissed her on both cheeks and gazed intently into her eyes. "The wife of my beloved brother," she murmured. "You must be a very special woman indeed."

Zipporah gave a little nervous laugh. "Well, I like to think so," she joked, instantly regretting her flip remark. Instinctively, she was awed by this intense woman. It was clear that advancing age had not dimmed the vibrancy of Moses' older sister. She felt the power of Miryam's personality; they all did.

"I've heard so much about you," Zipporah added.

The other woman smiled. "All good, I hope."

"Of course," said Zipporah.

They looked at each other, awkwardly. Just as Zipporah was wondering what to say next, there was another knock on the door, and the first of the seventy leaders of Israel came into the house.

It had begun.

* * *

PART V

MIRYAM

14

1445 B.C.

I WAS IN SUCH A TUMULT I COULD BARELY THINK. My adored brother, my special project from Elohim, my responsibility since I was a little girl who had been gone for so many, many years was finally back. When I first found out about the death of that miserable Egyptian and Moses' subsequent escape from Egypt, I was inconsolable. It took my sweet Pawero all of his considerable skill to calm me down. Even then, I never recovered. Not ever. Oh sure, I lived a good life with Pawero, I loved my children and their children and now their children's children, but I always missed Moses. I always remembered him in my prayers. I always wondered if he thought of me.

I never doubted he was still alive. I knew in my bones Elohim had a special purpose for him that still needed to be fulfilled. I heard rumors of Midian but couldn't even begin to imagine my prince of a brother in that barren, boring wilderness, devoid of culture and good food. What would he be doing there? Surely, I reasoned, he had moved on to Syria or some other place.

The years went by, one after another. My children grew, married, had their own children. Life was full and rich, but I never stopped praying for Moses, never stopped looking forward to seeing him again. I have to admit that by the time Pawero passed away, my prayers about Moses had grown rote and infrequent. Every so often something happened that would trigger a memory and I would think, *Moses, pray for Moses.* When Aaron mysteriously left on this trip of his, I had my suspicions that it might somehow have to do with Moses, but Elisheva refused to confirm or deny anything. Despite my best efforts, her lips were sealed.

The worst part of Moses being gone wasn't at the very beginning, regardless of a few meetings with Hatshepsut which we basically spent crying in each other's arms. No, the worst part was just after the death of my beloved queen. I realized there wasn't anyone who knew and remembered Moses the way she and I did, not Pawero, not even Aaron. My brothers enjoyed a very different sort of relationship with one another. I was more of a mother to Moses than a sister. I was also the liaison between his real mother and his adopted mother, a role that called for the tact of a first-rate statesman.

If I had to guess about what Moses had done all these years, my first thought would be to imagine him as a higher up in a kingdom somewhere, his identity a secret, his many talents put to good use. Whenever I heard of an architectural achievement over the years, I always had a moment of, *I wonder if Moses....*

So imagine my surprise to finally be reunited with him and find a shepherd. Even more of a shock was meeting his wife. She was an attractive woman but so obviously not royalty. Not at all the sort of woman Moses would have married had he remained in Egypt.

I never was behind the idea of Moses marrying Neferure. That I knew was a disaster right from the start, though try talking sense to a man overcome by passion. But I did at least think that Moses was going to marry a woman like Neferure, by which I mean royalty. I also wondered from time to time if he might not marry a Hebrew woman, someone extraordinary of course, someone perhaps a bit like...me. When I saw this dark desert woman, so utterly out of place in Egypt, all my preconceptions about Moses' wife flew out of the window. I admit that I was so flabbergasted I may have been a touch standoffish. Elisheva scolded me.

"Miryam, you really need to be more welcoming to Zipporah," she said later that day once Zipporah had excused herself and the men were otherwise engaged. "This isn't easy for her."

"I was nice," I protested.

Elisheva snorted. "You spent too much time with Hatshepsut," she said, for perhaps the millionth time. As always, I ignored the comment. Really. People claim I can sometimes be imperial, but I don't see it. Nevertheless, I tried harder, making an effort to sit with Zipporah and ask all sorts of questions about her life. Granted, whatever didn't have to do with Moses bored me terribly, but I tried to subtly redirect her with carefully pointed questions.

"And you had only two children—why?" I asked her.

Zipporah blushed. "Because that's how Yahweh determined to bless us. No other reason."

Ah, yes. Yahweh. That's what Moses and Zipporah were calling Elohim these days. Aaron, too, I noticed.

After a couple of days in close proximity I felt like we were on good terms. Zipporah didn't take me up on every opportunity to talk, which was fine. I spent every moment I could with the men, listening to Moses and Aaron.

I don't know when I would have seen the signs from Elohim/Yahweh, if I weren't with the leaders. All of us were amazed when we watched Moses' staff turn into a snake, saw his hand become leprous, and upon going down to the Nile, observed the water he poured from it turn to blood on the ground. After we reassembled at Aaron's house, Moses shared Elohim's heart of compassion for the Hebrews and His desire that now was the season for deliverance. Overcome by great emotion, the assembly bowed down and worshipped.

*

I will be the first to admit that I've lived a very interesting, full life. Even though I was approaching ninety, quite frankly I felt half that age. When my beloved Pawero passed on, I tried to keep busy. Between mentoring my grandchildren, keeping a hand in the family pottery business, song writing, dance, practicing my *tof miryam*—or tambourine—skills, getting more involved in the Hebrew community, and becoming something of a liaison between the Hebrews and the small group of believers among the Egyptians, I had plenty to do. However, a restlessness niggled at me. I went back and forth between wanting to go to the next life and be with Elohim and Pawero, or looking forward to a renewal in this one. When Moses returned from Midian, I had no idea I was entering into a phase that made my life as a young girl look mundane in comparison.

Even though Moses and Aaron were the top leaders in the move to free the Israelites, and the seventy elders were just beneath them in authority, still, I occupied a very special place. I held an honored position as Moses' older sister, the woman who helped raise him and was originally used by Elohim to save him. I was allowed to be privy to council meetings; I was listened to when I had an opinion (which was frequently); I was given authority over things that had to do with women and encouraged to use my song, music, and dance anointing to lead them in worship.

In retrospect I admit that I viewed Zipporah as more of a rival than a help when it came to these things. If truth be told, I resented all the years in which she had Moses to herself whereas my time with him had been constantly held in constraint by our differing statuses. I envied her easy camaraderie with Moses and her instinctive understanding of who he was currently.

It has been told to me over the years that I can be intimidating. I may have exercised that "talent" with Zipporah. She didn't come from a culture where women have the high degree of equality that we are fortunate enough to have in Egypt. Though she had plenty enough to say to Moses and her sons in private, yet in front of other people she grew quiet and submissive. It was only when she was comfortable that her clever wit emerged. With me, she wasn't so comfortable.

But Elisheva reached out to Zipporah, getting her involved in the cooking and organization of supporting the leaders. She grew to know several of them, her popularity increasing as her personality had opportunity to shine. One of the sons of the leaders, a young man named Joshua, would sit and talk with her for hours, plying her with questions about her life with Moses. She liked him quite a bit, putting in a good word for him with Moses whenever possible.

Even apart from our interactions with one another, events weren't proceeding as smoothly as we had originally hoped. When Moses and Aaron first met with Amenhotep, that brash young man who made his father look measured and wise in comparison, the young Pharaoh not only refused the request to take Israel into the wilderness but retaliated with anger and doubled the misery of the people. No longer were the Hebrews to be supplied with straw for the making of the bricks they used in the construction projects; now in their "spare" time they had to find their own straw.

Of course this was beyond impossible. Already our people were so burdened they could barely function. Adding this crazy amount of work changed everyone's excitement to discouragement. Falling short resulted in severe beatings when the brick quotas were not met. People scattered across the land, frantic to get enough straw. Children as young as two years old were put to work. It was a terrible time. Moses was under tremendous pressure as he went from being perceived as deliverer to a huge troublemaker. Several of the Israelite overseers, upon leaving Pharaoh's presence, encountered Moses and Aaron waiting for them.

"May Elohim look on you and judge you!" they railed, furious. "You have made us obnoxious to Pharaoh and his officials and have put a sword in their hand to kill us."

Moses was heartsick over this turn of events. "Have I harmed my people twice?" he moaned. Distraught, he refused all food, locking himself away from everyone except Zipporah, seeking after Elohim.

Our God did not disappoint, meeting Moses and speaking to him. Elohim reiterated His promise to deliver the Hebrews, breaking Amenhotep's hold over them. "I am Yahweh, and I have remembered my covenant," He said. "I will bring the Israelites out of Egypt and to the land I swore to give to Abraham, Isaac, and Jacob."

Greatly encouraged, Moses and Aaron once again assembled the leaders, telling them of Yahweh's faithful promises. You can only imagine the despair my brothers felt when their message fell on stony ground. The same leaders who had wholeheartedly welcomed Moses a very short time before now turned their backs on him, discouraged by the harsh labor. With the exception of Joshua, the men would not listen.

"We thought it couldn't get any worse," they cried, "but we were wrong!"

"Don't be wrong again!" pleaded Moses. "Listen to Yahweh!"

One by one, shaking their heads, the men left, refusing to be persuaded. Among the last to go, Joshua, a handsome, well-built man in his thirties, came to Moses, grasping his hands and looking him in the eye. "I will stand with you," he said respectfully. "Count on me."

"Thank you, my son," replied Moses, a small smile on his exhausted face. "I will not forget your offer."

Despite the encouragement from Joshua, this rejection of God's word settled heavily on Moses. Only Zipporah was able to soothe him. I envied their close relationship, missing Pawero all over again. I tried to help Moses. "Let me see him," I asked Zipporah. "I know he's upset. Let me talk to him."

Zipporah hesitated. I could tell that she didn't want to out and out say no to me, but she also didn't want to say yes. "I'll mention your offer," she hedged.

Mention my offer! My ears burned with embarrassment. I deserved better than that! I got aggressive.

"Look, Zipporah," I fumed. "I have a special relationship with my brother. I can talk to him in ways...."

"What ways?" interrupted Zipporah, arms crossed, eyes narrowed. "You look, Miryam. I'm going to do what's best for my husband even if that makes me seem mean. He's got the weight of the world on his shoulders, and he needs to be protected from all unnecessary—"

Now I interrupted. "What? Are you calling me unnecessary?"

"Not you," said Zipporah, her voice shaking from the strain of our impasse, "but I firmly believe that your well-intentioned attempts to see Moses are only going to add to his stress. I know him! Please believe me about this."

We locked eyes. I looked away when hers teared up. "Fine," I muttered, turning. "If he needs me, you know where to find me."

"Yes, I do. Thank you, Miryam."

Not looking at her, I waved my hand in a half-hearted farewell, already walking in the other direction.

Within days of this encounter, Yahweh spoke to Moses and commanded him to tell Amenhotep to let the Hebrews go. Moses' self-confidence was so eroded by this point that he protested to Yahweh that he wasn't capable of speaking. Why would Pharaoh listen? In His kindness, Yahweh allowed Moses to use Aaron as his mouthpiece, but He did not let Moses off the hook. Both of my brothers were to go see Amenhotep. From this point on, Moses didn't have one spare minute.

* * *

Part VI

Zipporah

15

Egypt, 1445 B.C.

EVER SINCE I CAN REMEMBER I've wanted to travel and see more of the world. While it's true that the desire has weakened over the years, still, I was genuinely excited when Moses announced this expedition to Egypt. Not even the unexpected circumcising of my thirty-eight-year-old son while simultaneously almost losing my husband didn't completely dampen my enthusiasm.

The trip itself was difficult. My bones were not what they used to be and my stomach was acting up, but at least we had each other. When my men and Aaron were asleep and I was secure and warm within my husband's arms under the cold, starry, night sky, that closeness made up for a great deal. The camaraderie invigorated me. I loved having my husband and sons all to myself, and Aaron was easy company. He seemed to like me and was very considerate. I guess that I'd gotten spoiled. God sent me a prince and allowed me a forty-year monopoly on his time and attentions. Once we entered Egypt, that abruptly ended.

At first it was fascinating to merely look around and see the sights. Is it possible to express the astonishment one feels upon viewing a pyramid for the first time after a lifetime in which the largest manmade object is a spacious tent? Is it possible to share the bewilderment that comes from interacting with nonstop people when one's community from birth to middle age has numbered roughly one hundred? Is it possible to convey the shock of getting to know women like Miryam, who not only consider themselves every bit as good as a man but are actively involved in leadership, shoulder to shoulder with the men?

Maybe I should be a little more honest here. Actually, it wasn't women *like* Miryam; it *was* Miryam. From the first moment when she swept into my life like a whirlwind I was as awed as a small child. Admittedly, she attempted to be kind to me, but I could tell that I was merely an obstacle in the way to Moses, whose company she truly desired. I wanted to like her. Really. For forty years I had been hearing stories of her brave devotion to my husband, her many talents, and her huge role in preserving his very life. Moses sometimes laughed about her territorial attitude and occasionally domineering ways, and I laughed with him, never imagining even for a moment that those self-same attitudes would one day affect me.

When she walked into Aaron and Elisheva's house that first day, I was already in a tizzy from all the excitement. Though I knew she was older than Moses, making her *considerably* older than me, she was still a beautiful woman. There was a timelessness to her features, a classic look that belied age.

Tentatively, I held back, not at all sure in the midst of these cosmopolitan people in this cultured land. Even the slaves seemed worldly. Also, Moses was so busy that I felt like I was on my own when it came to the social end of things.

Our times together were more and more limited to sleeping. Moses was so worn out at night that he had no inclination to get involved in endless discussions as to who said what to me and what it meant. He got in bed late, fell right asleep and rose early so as to seek Yahweh. I missed our intimate meals and walks and times of companionship. I tried to be understanding, but my attitude slipped a bit. One day I complained to my husband that I never got to see him.

"Oh, Zipporah." He sighed tiredly, gathering me into his arms. "I'm trying to obey Yahweh by consolidating a huge and unwieldy group of slaves into a cohesive unit that will follow me out of the most powerful country on earth and into the desert. Oh, and the ruler of aforementioned powerful country is actively hostile to such an action." He looked at me with those warm brown eyes. "Trust me, I would much prefer taking a long walk with you than any of these endless meetings I'm forced to attend with Hebrew tribal leaders who are riddled with anxiety as to how to approach Pharaoh."

I swallowed. "You're right," I said, ashamed. "I guess I was thinking of my wants and not even considering that you might be just as upset as me."

Moses smiled. "I think you don't understand how much I love you."

"Tell me," I said, snuggling into his embrace. "I want to hear all about it."

Things improved for a few days until Moses and Aaron had their first appointment with Pharaoh. To say it didn't go well would be a massive understatement. It went so badly that at the end of the interview the Hebrews basically had their workload doubled. The leaders turned from Moses, except for the sweet young one who was always kind to me. My husband grew despondent, shutting himself away in prayer whenever he wasn't meeting with Aaron and Miryam. I was well aware what a stressful time this was for him and attempted to stay out of his way and not cause any more difficulty. I grew especially close to Elisheva during this time. We worked shoulder to shoulder in the kitchen, preparing vast quantities of food for both our men and the endless parade of people stopping by to see Moses and Aaron.

"So," I remarked casually to Elisheva as I chopped up cucumbers for a salad, "What's with Miryam?"

Elisheva paused as she kneaded barley flour dough, blowing a loose lock of hair off her face. "In what way?"

"Well, I'd like to be closer to her, but I feel like there's an invisible wall that I can't get through. Any ideas?"

"That's a hard one, Zipporah," answered Aaron's wife. She pounded out the bread dough a few times before continuing. "It's just that, well, Miryam has always been different. She's not quite an Egyptian and not quite a slave, if you know what I mean."

I snorted. "It doesn't look like she's a slave *at all*."

"No, you're wrong there. She spent her early years living in fear of Pharaoh and his decrees; she watched her parents die under slavery; she's always known that if not for the special unmerited favor of Yahweh, her life would have been very different. It's been hard to live between two cultures. I think that only Moses and perhaps to some extent my Aaron have truly been able to understand the unique place in which she finds herself. Also," and here Elisheva lowered her voice although we were the only two people in the room, "she and Moses' adoptive mother were unusually close. Being privy to the seat of power does something to a person. How can it not?"

"Okay," I said, slicing another cucumber with perhaps too much vigor, "I understand what you're saying. But can't she just accept that I'm Moses' wife? That we are one in the eyes of Yahweh? That he's no longer the young man who fled Egypt forty years ago?"

"Oh, Zipporah!" Elisheva walked over to me and hugged me, a little awkwardly as she was careful not to touch me with her dough-covered hands so it was more like an elbow hug. "In the short time I've known you I already love you like a sister. I can see why Moses is so crazy about you."

"Thank you." I blushed.

"No, don't thank me. I'm only telling you the truth." She finished kneading the bread dough, formed it into a ball, and put it into a bowl, covering it with a clean cloth. Taking a damp cloth and cleaning her hands, she looked at me. "Don't let her demeanor throw you. Reach out. Don't be intimidated. You're both on the same side. You both want to see Moses succeed. And frankly," she added, almost under her breath, "he needs all the support he can get right now."

Elisheva was right about that. My husband was facing opposition from almost every quarter. I didn't know it, but things were about to get much worse.

*

When relations between the Hebrews and Pharaoh were still in a stalemate, one of the tribal leader's grandsons, a young boy named Joseph, came breathlessly running to the house we were staying in late one night, pounding on the door.

None of us were in bed. Instead, we were gathered around the table, intermittently praying and talking about what to do next. The knocking startled everyone.

"I'll get it," said Aaron's son Nadab, springing to his feet first. "Who's there?" he asked.

"Joseph. Open up!" demanded the voice on the other side of the door.

We all looked at one another. "Let him in," said Aaron. "He's a good boy."

Nadab opened the door, and Joseph tumbled into the room. "I need to see Moses!" he all but shouted, frantically scanning our faces.

"I'm Moses," calmly announced my husband, lifting his hand. "What can I do for you, son?"

Joseph looked around nervously. "Can we talk here?"

"Anything you have to say, you can say in front of the people here," answered Moses.

"Okay." Shakily, the boy drew in a breath. "I have just found out that there's a plot afoot to kill your wife and sons!"

What? Involuntarily, I gasped, as did Elisheva.

"Sit down," commanded Moses. "Tell me everything."

It took awhile but eventually the whole story came out. Someone overheard a palace guard who had overheard someone else who had gotten it straight from Pharaoh's court, etc. etc. The Egyptians were afraid to take on Moses himself and so the reasoning was if they killed me and our sons, it would be enough to destroy Moses.

"Can't argue with that logic," muttered Gershom, white-faced.

What should we do? Everyone had a different idea: go into hiding, take on a different persona, be in disguise, but the only plan that Moses was comfortable with was for us to be completely out of Pharaoh's reach. We all prayed to Yahweh for confirmation, after which Moses and Aaron both agreed to send me and the boys back to Midian as soon as possible.

Later, much later, after everyone had gone to sleep and Joseph was given a makeshift bed on the floor, Moses held me tightly. We didn't even speak; we were both too exhausted and overwrought for words. Instead, we clung to one another, not sure when we would see each other again; not sure of anything other than we were determined to follow Yahweh no matter where it took us or how events played out.

*

The next day, Miryam, who had not been at the house the night before, was informed of all that had transpired. I wasn't sure if she would be pleased by my absence and said a little rashly, "It'll be easier for you to get in to see Moses now." I thought I said it in a light-hearted way, but Miryam was not fooled by the obvious dig.

"You don't think very highly of me, do you?" she asked, frowning.

I sighed. "You've not been so thrilled with me either."

Miryam stamped her foot, an annoying trait that would have probably seemed cute if we were better friends. "That is simply not true," she cried. Turning her head, fidgeting with one of her many bracelets, she finally looked at me. "I admit that I've felt a certain level of…competition…with you."

"A certain level?" I snorted. "I feel like we're those wrestlers I keep seeing in all those wall pictures. Only I'm not sure who is winning."

Miryam's right eyebrow arched. "A wrestler? You're comparing me to one of those enormous wrestlers?" Her mouth twitched and a small laugh escaped, then another, and another. Soon she dissolved into a full-scale attack of the giggles, which set me off. Before I knew it, the two of us were helpless with laughter, clutching our sides because it hurt to breathe.

"Oh my," I gasped, when I could finally speak. "That is such a funny image," which of course set us off on another round of laughter.

"Zipporah, my sister." Miryam held open her arms, and I let her enfold me into an embrace. We hugged tightly for several minutes, and when we separated, she clasped my face between her hands and kissed me on both cheeks. "Forgive me for sinning against you?"

"Yes," I said, "but only if you forgive me as well."

"Unquestionably," she replied.

We smiled tentatively at one another, happy with this newfound level of intimacy but careful lest it prove fragile.

"I hope to see you again one day," I said.

"Oh, you will," said Miryam in a tone that was more than polite reassurance; it was more a prophetic "I've heard from Yahweh" type voice.

"You aren't going to get rid of me that easily."

"Good." Suddenly my eyes welled up. "Take care of Moses," I beseeched her.

"I will. But only until you're back with him. Where you belong."

Again, we embraced. I did not see her again in the land of Egypt.

*

It took two days for Moses to work things out with our unhappy but obedient sons, and then we were on our way home.

"Take care of yourself," he said, kissing me gently.

"I love you."

"I love you, too." Brushing away my tears with his thumb, he gazed intently into my eyes, cradling my face. "Don't despair, my love. We'll be together again."

Numbly, I nodded, too choked up to speak. How I loved him! How I already missed him. Giving instructions to the boys, my husband hugged them, patted the donkeys, and waved good-bye. Turning my head, I watched him until he was a speck in the distance.

Oh, the agony of that good-bye! Eliezer, Gershom, and I hated to leave, but we had no choice. We couldn't risk being an impediment to that which Yahweh had sent Moses to accomplish. I tried to be brave, but mostly I cried, until my sons became concerned and did everything they could to comfort me. With difficulty, I attempted to control my emotions. Mostly I got through the days by praying constantly to Yahweh. It was the only thing that brought me true peace.

*

It took three weeks to get home, at the end of which I was exhausted. We stumbled into the village one day at dusk just when I thought I couldn't last another hour. Mama cried when she saw me. Father helped me to my tent.

"What happened?" wailed Mama, tears running down her wrinkled cheeks.

Too drained to talk, I held her hand and closed my eyes, letting Eliezer and Gershom explain all that had transpired since we saw them last. Father was extremely interested while Mama just clucked her tongue.

"Sounds like Yahweh is about to do amazing things in Egypt the likes of which have never been seen before in this world," mused Father, stroking his beard.

"Thanks, Grandfather," said Gershom. "Now I feel even better about missing it." He was still upset about leaving Egypt.

"Now, now," cautioned Mama, "it sounds like this was the only thing to do. Yahweh will bless you."

"Abba wants us to meet up with him once the Hebrews are out of Egypt and in the desert. He said he'll need all the help he can get organizing and leading them to Canaan," said Eliezer, grinning.

Father, however, wasn't done with Gershom. "It's not going to be a fun show," he scolded. "It's going to take some pretty awful things to convince Pharaoh to allow so much of his free labor to pick up and leave."

"There's the staff, and the hand and the blood...," began Gershom.

Father snorted. "We'll see. I think it's going to take more than that." He put his hand on my shoulder as I lay resting. "I'm just glad that you're all safely home."

*

My little brother Hobab, slightly older than my sons and unmarried like them, came to sit with me one day about a week after I had returned. Born after my marriage to Moses and so much younger than me, I considered him more like a nephew or a surrogate son and less like a brother. He had grown up with Gershom and Eliezer, the three boys tumbling together like pups in a litter. Moses was quite fond of him, often remarking to me how pleased he was with Hobab's grasp of the spiritual. He had a natural affinity for the wilderness and seemed to have been born with a sixth sense of knowing his way around places that, even with my lifelong experience, all looked the same. Instead of shepherding, Hobab became fascinated with metal and fire. Suffice it to say that he was the village metal worker. I was very proud of my brother's many accomplishments.

Now Hobab sat back on his heels next to me in front of my tent, asking question after question about my time in Egypt. "I'm fascinated by what's going on," he said in his rich, low voice, a faraway look in his thoughtful eyes.

"I wish I were still in Egypt," I said wryly. "I feel so useless here."

Hobab squeezed my hand. "Don't be distressed, my sister. You were in the midst of an enormous spiritual battle, the likes of which none of us have ever encountered before."

Intrigued by his words, I turned to look more fully at him. "You think?" I asked hopefully.

"Most definitely," he exclaimed. "It is clear to me that you have been attacked harder than anyone else because of your proximity and significance to Moses."

"But why didn't Yahweh just deliver me from my would-be attackers? Why did He allow me to be driven off?"

Hobab shook his head. "Even if everything worked out perfectly, you're too much of a distraction for Moses. I know him. He would worry nonstop if he thought you were in danger. I believe that right now he is in the midst of such wildness that it's a mercy you're not there."

I tried not to look guilty at these words and failed.

Hobab laughed. "It's true, Zip. It's better that you're here."

My brother's words were like healing oil. They soothed and comforted me, helping reconcile me to being back home. With Yahweh's help, I was able to relax and enjoy my family and friends, focusing my mental energy into praying for Moses and the others in Egypt.

*

Over the next few months, Father, Mama, Gershom, Eliezer, Hobab, myself, and most of the members of our community stayed alert in prayer, waiting and watching for the news from Egypt. One fine day in spring, the messenger came.

It was Gershom who saw him first. Gershom, out with the sheep in pastureland west of our desert village, the sheep nibbling at the fresh green covering that sprang up after the winter rains, tiny wildflowers dotting the terrain. At first the man was a dot in the distance, slowly becoming more distinct with each passing minute.

"Hello there!" called out Gershom when the man was within earshot. "Do you come in peace?"

"In peace," yelled the man, plodding along on his donkey, obviously thrilled to come in contact with another human being. He couldn't have been much older than thirty, slight and short with weary eyes. He looked hungry.

"Have some water," said Gershom, handing him his own skin.

Thirstily, the man drank, head back, eyes closed. When finished, he said to Gershom, "I'm looking for the family of Moses."

"Well then you've come to the right place. I'm his son."

"*Baruch haShem*!" cried the man, whose name was Jada, throwing his arms wide open in an expression of worship and delight. "Yahweh has led me to the right spot."

Excitedly, Gershom asked, "Do you have news of my father? Of Egypt?"

"Lots of news," rejoined the messenger. "A longer story than I can repeat. Would you be so kind as to lead me to the wife of Moses and the rest of the family?"

As quickly as possible, my son led the messenger to our tents.

I was sitting in front of my tent grinding grain when they approached. Quickly, I got up and bowed to the messenger, who bowed back. "How is my husband? Is he well?"

"Very well, my lady, wife of Moses." The man grinned, white teeth very white against his dark skin, made darker by streaks of dirt, evidence of hard traveling.

"Thank You, Yahweh. Praise God!" I exclaimed, weak with relief. At my insistence, before any other news, I brought Jada a wash basin for his face, hands, and feet. Then he drank his fill and ate, after which a much happier man recounted his news to our very eager ears. Word got around and various people showed up, desirous of hearing everything he had to say.

"What was the last thing that happened before you left Egypt?" he asked me, wiping his mouth on his sleeve.

"Pharaoh doubled the load of the Hebrews with that whole straw thing," I said, remembering. "And Moses was preparing to go back with Aaron and talk to him again."

Jada nodded. "They did go back. Pharaoh asked for a miracle and Aaron threw his staff down so that it became a snake. But Pharaoh had his wise men, sorcerers, and magicians do the same thing."

"Oh, too bad," said Gershom, on the edge of his seat.

Jada held up his hand. "Not so fast. Aaron's staff swallowed up all the other staffs."

We looked at each other. *Well then.*

"Did that convince him?" I asked.

"Unfortunately, no. So Yahweh had Moses and Aaron meet up with Pharaoh on the banks of the Nile in the morning. Aaron took his staff and stretched out his hand over the waters of Egypt—the streams, canals, ponds, and reservoirs—and they all turned to blood. Blood was everywhere in Egypt, even in the wooden buckets and stone jars."

We all gasped.

"How horrible!" Mama shuddered.

"Definitely," said Jada. "The Egyptians had to dig along the Nile to get drinking water, because they couldn't drink the river water."

"So did Pharaoh let the Israelites go then?" asked Eliezer expectantly.

"Not yet. A whole week went by, an awful week filled with trauma, and then Yahweh sent Moses and Aaron back to Pharaoh to demand that he let His people go so they could worship Him. This time, Moses told Aaron to stretch out his hand with the staff over the streams and canals and ponds and make frogs come up on the land."

"Frogs aren't too bad...," I started to say.

"How many frogs?" interrupted Father.

"Millions," said Jada, grimacing. "Millions and millions of these slimy, repulsive things."

"What did Pharaoh do?" asked Hobab.

"He had his magicians do the same thing."

"Wait," said Father. "Let me get this straight: Egypt was inundated with frogs, and Pharaoh worked it out so there were even *more?*"

"Ha ha," laughed Jada. "Let's just say he's not the sharpest knife in the drawer."

"What next?" asked Gershom impatiently.

"The frogs were so awful that Pharaoh did summon Moses and Aaron and asked them to pray to Yahweh to remove the frogs, and that he would then let the people go offer sacrifices."

"Did he?" I asked.

"Moses prayed and the frogs died. All of them. Huge, stinking piles everywhere." Jada's nose wrinkled at the memory. "But Pharaoh hardened his heart once there was relief."

"This guy is too much," remarked Eliezer to much agreement and some laughter.

Jada paused in his narrative to help start an evening fire. While he had been speaking, the evening shadows had lengthened and the sun had sunk lower and lower in the western sky, streaking the sky with lines of orange and purple. It was time for a break. By mutual agreement, we got up, stretched, attended to various necessities of life, and met back in front of a roaring fire. Wrapped in a blanket, I cuddled next to Eliezer, leaning against my son's strong arm. "Isn't this fantastic?" I whispered to him.

"Totally," he said. "Beyond anything I've ever heard."

I nodded. "I don't think we've even gotten to the really exciting part yet."

"I know. I can't even begin to imagine what's coming. This is unreal."

Word had spread in our community about Jada, and it looked like everyone, including the little ones, had crammed themselves around the fire. I could see Hobab, Gershom, and Father filling in the latecomers about what they had missed.

Long into the night, Jada continued his narrative. The events which befell Egypt were amazing beyond contemplation.

The next morning, my prayers were answered. Gershom, Eliezer, Hobab, Father, and I loaded up our donkeys and went with Jada to the camp of the Israelites in the wilderness at Mt. Horeb, to my husband, to Moses.

* * *

Part VII

Miryam

16

Goshen, Egypt, 1445 B.C.

THESE FROGS ARE OUTRAGEOUS. I can't stand them another minute. *Argh!* Slimy, repulsive, nasty devils. I understand there's a lot more of them outside of Goshen, but still...I've never seen so many in my life. The Nile turning to blood was bad enough, but we got through it by digging for water. The joy that flashed through the community when the blood in our wooden buckets and stone jars turned back to clean water was indescribable. Almost immediately, however, we were inundated with more frogs than I knew existed on the entire earth. I have never been a frog fan. I think the Egyptians are crazy to worship the ugly little things.

Moses strongly encouraged, actually ordered, me to move to Goshen. Abigail, Johanan, Noa, and their families were already here, but I had remained at the house where I lived with Pawero. I must say that I was secretly relieved to pull together a few belongings and head over here to Abigail and Hur's house. My old neighbors weren't as friendly as they used to be. Something in the air had...changed.

My beautiful oldest daughter, already a grandmother for many years, greeted me affectionately at the door when I showed up one day close to sunset. "How are you, Ema?" she asked, kissing my cheek, her face kind, her hair lightly streaked with gray.

"As well as can be expected, given these crazy times," I answered, dropping my bags. Hur, my God's blessing of a son-in-law, instantly appeared and scooped up my possessions. "Thank you," I murmured to his retreating back.

"I'll put these down and say a proper hello," he said over his shoulder, already disappearing into the tiny room I called mine when I came to visit.

"How are the children?" I asked Abigail after settling down and nursing a glass of beer.

"Not exactly children." She laughed, rolling her eyes. "Uri and Rachel are fine. Bezalel (Uri's son) has been consolidating all his tools, preparing in faith that we really will get to leave Egypt."

I nodded. Abigail's grandson Bezalel was amazingly talented. He could do just about anything artistic in any medium. As a little boy, he absolutely adored Pawero, and the two of them would disappear into Pawero's workshop for hours. My husband would have been so proud to have seen the work Bezalel produced as he got older.

So anyway I was with Abigail when the plagues started. We got through the water turning to blood, but the frogs almost did me in. Thankfully, it only lasted a couple of days. I didn't sleep the whole time, I was so disgusted (though Abigail insisted I dozed off). Needless to say, I was a bit crazed when they finally died.

It took us a week to clean up the dead frogs until there were these huge piles of decaying, foul-smelling bodies *everywhere*. I didn't complain about the odor, though. In my opinion, a dead frog is infinitely preferable to a live one.

A week later, Yahweh sent a third plague: gnats. Again, we didn't have it quite as bad in Goshen as out, but it was still pretty miserable. Imagine huge clouds of tiny bugs getting in your eyes, ears, nose, covering all the food, the surface of the ground…yuck. Pharaoh's magicians tried to replicate turning dust into gnats, and they couldn't do it, interestingly enough. By the time Yahweh took away the gnats, every Hebrew's prayer life had improved enormously. We were desperate for relief, and more and more desperate to leave Egypt. It was bad before; now it was completely untenable.

Pharaoh still wouldn't relent and allow us to leave, so Yahweh told Moses to get up early in the morning and confront Pharaoh at the river bank, saying to him that next there would be swarms of flies everywhere in Egypt; on the people, in the houses, even covering the ground. But Yahweh did say that this time there would be a distinction between the Egyptians and the Hebrews, and that no flies would be in Goshen.

HALLELUJAH!

May I say that we were overjoyed? May I say it again? To see Yahweh beat down our oppressors but leave us unscathed was utterly stupendous. I also believe that to first experience the plagues and then be supernaturally protected did much to further the loyalty of a people who didn't always understand that Yahweh was not only their God but also the only God. You would think that after years of brutal slavery they—we—would have been willing to suffer anything and everything in order to escape this accursed land but surprisingly inertia held considerable sway. The plagues were not only to persuade Pharaoh but also to convince the Hebrews that they had no choice but to leave.

After the flies, the Egyptians continued to be subject to awful plagues.

Even with all these displays of the greatness of Yahweh, plenty of people scoffed, not willing to believing He is all powerful. We in Goshen couldn't believe how long Pharaoh was holding on, refusing to let us go. Finally, he summoned Moses and said he had sinned. He begged Moses to pray to Yahweh for an end to the horror. Of course, once the present horror was whisked away, he would immediately harden his heart—or Yahweh ultimately would—and not let the people go.

I found it interesting that after the first four plagues Pharaoh hardened his heart, but after that, Yahweh hardened Pharaoh's heart. I spoke to Moses, asking him why.

"Good question, Miryam," he said, locking his fingers together. "Why do you think that is?"

I hesitated. "Is it because we can't say *no* to Yahweh too often?"

"Good," said my brother. "But there's more. The more we resist Yahweh, the harder it is to open our hearts to Him. Soon He leaves us in our disbelief. But it is never too late to turn to Him," he added, unable to resist the urge to sermonize.

By now Pharaoh's officials turned on their king, saying, "Do you not realize that Egypt is ruined?"

We were just stunned by Amenhotep's senseless stupidity (though I suppose most stupidity *is* senseless). The young king finally agreed to let the men leave but balked at allowing the women and children to go. He accused Moses and Aaron of being bent on evil. He drove them out of his presence, after which Yahweh told Moses to stretch out his hand over Egypt so that the current plague of locusts would swarm over the land and devour everything growing in the fields, everything left by the hail.

In Goshen, we held our collective breath. The devastation wreaked on this land that until very recently had looked so prosperous and invincible dumbfounded us. *Locusts!* Who didn't know the capacity for destruction inherent in the locust and his billions of companions? Yahweh blew them in by an east wind, and they came in huge numbers, covering the ground until it was black. They ate *everything.* Nothing green remained on tree or plant in all the land of Egypt. It was absolutely terrifying. The Egyptians had become terrified of us and our God. I thought surely this would sway Amenhotep, but once Moses prayed and Yahweh removed the locusts with a powerful west wind, his heart hardened yet again.

Yahweh then brought upon Egypt the ninth plague: the plague of darkness. For three days a darkness the likes of which no one had ever seen descended on the land. It wasn't merely nighttime; no, it was a darkness so frightening and tangible that it could be *felt.* People started going insane from the horror of it.

Since we had light in Goshen, it seemed to me that anyone with half a brain could easily see that the Hebrew God is all powerful and not to be messed with. However, though Amenhotep initially said yes to going, he forbade us from taking our flocks and herds. When Moses protested, he flew into a rage, screaming to Moses to get out of his sight. "Make sure you don't appear before me again," he yelled. "The day you see my face you will die."

I must say, I was quite proud of Moses' cool. He told Pharaoh, "Just as you say. I will never appear before you again."

*

All told, the plagues lasted for close to six weeks. During this time, we stayed as close to home as possible, keeping out of the way of the Egyptians, whose nostrils we had become a stench in. I took advantage of the forced inactivity to play my little drum, my *tof Miryam,* as it was called. It was not the same one Abba made for me all those years ago; I wore out the original one and had new ones made. This was my sixth, no seventh, *tof.* My daughters Abigail and Noa enjoy dancing to the beat of the drum.

"Come move with us," sang out Noa, pulling me up by the elbows from my sitting position.

"Ach!" I groaned. "I'm too old."

My daughters exchanged knowing glances. "Ema, you will never be old," Noa assured me.

Giving in, I danced with my girls while simultaneously playing the drum, holding it over my head. We hooted and shouted with joy, stamping our feet in anticipation of all that Yahweh had and would accomplish. We kept going until, sweaty and disheveled, we dropped to the floor.

"Love it," said Abigail, laughing.

*

Suddenly, after 430 years, our time in Egypt ended abruptly. First, we got the order from Moses to ask our Egyptian neighbors for gold and silver.

"I feel so awkward doing this," I told Elisheva as we picked our way through the hail-decimated fields and over to a section of town that was primarily Egyptian and not Hebrew.

"Careful," she warned me, stepping far to the right of a dead cow, putrid and rotting in the hot sun, covered with flies.

"All this death and destruction..."

"...seems to be necessary," rejoined Elisheva.

"...and now taking their valuables..."

"Think of it as payment for all our labor, for our lives poured out on the soil of their monuments. We've already paid in blood."

"Yes," I agreed, slightly abashed. I know I've had a much easier time than most.

Silently, I took Elisheva's hand and squeezed it. She squeezed back, and together we knocked on doors and received riches from people who were terrified, people who knew that a huge and powerful God unlike any they'd encountered was on our side.

We had less than a week left in Egypt. More orders came from my brothers, orders to take a lamb per family and slaughter it on twilight on the fourteenth day of the month, orders to paint our doorframes with its innocent blood, using sprigs of hyssop as paintbrushes, orders to eat the meat roasted with bitter herbs and unleavened bread, orders to eat in haste, orders to stay inside under the protective covering of the blood. For this was the night of the final plague: the worst of them all. This was the night when the Angel of Death struck down every firstborn in Egypt not covered by the blood of the lamb. Many non-Hebrews saw what we were doing, asked about it, and did the same.

We huddled inside our homes, bellies full, sleepy yet alert, possessions bundled and ready to go. The younger women kneaded bread but left out the yeast; there would not be any time for the bread to rise. We heard the anguished cries of those families who watched with horrified eyes as their beloveds died—families from the most menial of servants all the way to the palace of Amenhotep himself, whose young son was stricken.

It was then that Pharaoh finally relented—only then, after his boy died, did he agree that we could go. And go we did. It was like a dam burst forth, families streaming from every home in Goshen and from other neighborhoods too. Friends and relatives of Pawero who came to worship Yahweh through our witness joined the ever-increasing throng of Hebrews. Many non-Hebrews joined themselves to us that night, eager to align themselves with this most powerful of Gods.

I was too old to carry bread dough on my head, but I had a heavy bundle of those items I held most dear, plus the silver and gold and precious stones I received the other day.

"Hurry, Ema!" yelled Hur, standing at the threshold of the house, checking to make sure all were safely out and on their way.

"Coming," I called, slipping the straps of my bag on my back, following after him. Just as I got to the door my eyes lit on my *tof,* propped against the wall. I grabbed it quickly but was not able to stuff it in my pack. It was in my hand as we fled.

All that night we pushed hard, as hard as we could with all our flocks and herds and pregnant women and little ones and elderly and sick, heading to the desert road that led to the Sea of Reeds. I kept pace with the assembly, giving thanks to Yahweh for allowing me to see the deliverance of His people. It was an amazing time. I did my best to encourage and bless those around me, keeping up their spirits by occasionally beating out a song on my drum. Something about the music made our feet lighter.

A stunning thing happened (though everything that had happened for the several weeks prior to that was stunning). Yahweh joined us! He really joined us, appearing in an intensely light dense cloud. During the days, this Yahweh-cloud led us, and when we traveled at night the cloud took on the appearance of huge flames of fire. It was not unlike how the burning bush looked, said Moses, only much bigger.

By the third day, I somehow made it up to the front of the assembly and was walking with Moses and Aaron. I noticed that we were taking the long way around to the sea. I asked Aaron why.

"You think we should go through Philistine territory?" he asked me, eyes tired, eyebrows raised. "You think this group is ready to do battle?"

I saw his point. No, of course not. We would scatter like sheep without a shepherd.

It was a hard trip. The initial euphoria wore off, and people grew weary. Babies cried, children whined, tempers flared. I was not doing quite as well bolstering spirits as I did at first. Our bread was flat, without yeast. *Matzah*, we called it.

"It's a sign," said Moses. "Eat it."

I found myself thinking about Zipporah. I wondered what she was doing. How odd that we should be caught up in the midst of such a great deliverance led by her husband and she herself was unaware of what was happening. Sorry that I didn't have more time with her, time to get to know her, I chastised myself for wasting time, for allowing petty jealousies to get in the way of knowing her sooner. I prayed that I'd live to see her again.

And then suddenly we were there, at the sea. We camped near Pi Hahiroth, between Midgol and the sea, mountains to the left and right. It was a great relief to stop and rest, to wash out a few things at the shore, to sleep, to eat.

Unfortunately, our reprieve was short-lived. Amenhotep had yet another change of heart. He could not bear the thought of his slave labor force slipping out of his hands. Furious, he took six hundred of Egypt's best chariots and horses and troops and pursued us. We felt the earth shaking from the pounding of the hooves before we saw the dust at the edge of the horizon. Everyone started to panic, wailing and crying. Moses was accused of bringing all of us to the desert to die.

"Would that we never left Egypt," the people moaned.

I feared a riot would break loose.

Moses calmed the people. "Do not be afraid!" he warned them. "You will never see these Egyptians again! Stand firm and see the deliverance of Yahweh. He will fight for you. Just stand still!"

Yahweh had Moses raise his staff over the waters of the sea. A driving wind pushed through from the east and the waters started to separate! It was astonishing. Then, as if that weren't enough, Yahweh in the cloud which had been leading us went behind and separated us from the Egyptians so that we were unreachable. We had light, and they had darkness all night long.

When the waters divided such that a path was visible through the sea, Moses sent word to follow him. I could feel the hesitation and the fear that rose. *Go into the sea! What if the waters return? Impossible!* Mothers clutched their babies.

"Come, let's go!" shouted Moses. "There's no time to lose!"

That was when the second miracle occurred. The people obeyed! We conquered our fears and followed, streaming across the middle of the sea on the strip of dry ground. I shouldered my pack and walked with my daughter Noa and her family. Tentatively, I stepped onto the newly made path, not knowing what to expect. It was surprisingly dry, though quite spongy, and my feet made a slurping sound as I walked. On either side were towering walls of water, quivering with pent-up energy. I tried not to think about what it would be like if the walls let go, focusing instead on praising Yahweh in my heart for His marvelous kindnesses and His many good deeds.

There was surprisingly little conversation. Other than the lowing of the cattle and the sheep and goat noise, it was quiet. A holy time. Even the babies were still, sucking on fingers or sleeping.

After the last person got to the other side of the sea, the Yahweh cloud that had separated us from the Egyptian army lifted and the army poured after us into the sea. It looked like they were having trouble with their chariots.

Confusion and chaos reigned. Just as the dawn broke, Moses, from a high perch overlooking the water, stretched his hand out. The earth shook, there was a terrible roaring, and the walls of water collapsed, crushing everything in their path. The Egyptian chariots and horsemen were swept away by the whirling torrents of foamy sea, drowned and destroyed.

I was appalled and elated at the same time. I had never seen death like this. Yet these were my enemies, bent on my destruction and the destruction of my people. Involuntarily, I stopped and reach for my *tof,* shaking it hard so that the bells ring loudly. I dropped my pack and broke out in dance, Noa right at my heels following my steps. Yahweh put a song in my heart and the words flowed from my mouth:

"Sing to Yahweh
For He is highly exalted.
Both horse and driver
He has hurled into the sea."

Other women joined in. Soon there was a huge procession, dancing and twirling. Many others had similar *tofs,* and throughout the shore the sounds of the ringing bells and the beating of drums mingled with these words of praise to Yahweh, moving like waves throughout the camp. It was a moment unlike any other, and I was giddy and breathless with the sheer power and excitement of it all. I felt as if I had been drawn up into a heavenly realm. Never before had I felt so close to my God! Never before had I been immersed into His presence like this! My cup ran over. I could not contain all the blessing Yahweh was pouring out! If only it could always be like this. . . .

* * *

PART VIII

MOSES

17

Mt. Sinai, 1445 B.C.

PEOPLE WERE EVERYWHERE. As far as the eye could see, the land was dotted with tents. Were there ever so many people gathered in one place at one time? And the animals, the constant sounds, and smells, the noise....

Wearily, Moses rubbed his eyes as he gazed at the teeming, shifting scene before him. What an incredible few months it had been, unlike anything he—or anyone, for that matter—had ever experienced on this earth. His relationship with Yahweh had budded and blossomed beyond his wildest dreams, the children of Israel were free, the Egyptian army destroyed, the promised land of milk and honey tantalizingly close. He needed to guide this fledging nation to their new home, needed to direct them, needed, basically, to be their wet nurse.

Moses sighed. He missed the companionship and human warmth of his wife, missed his sons. When Jada had returned a few days before with a good report of the imminent arrival of the family, Moses had been thrilled. Not only were Zipporah and the boys coming, but his father-in-law, Jethro, had sent the message that he and Hobab were coming as well. Now, with every passing hour in which they still weren't here, his concerns grew. Were they all right? He understood Zipporah wasn't all that well. Despite a heavy schedule of conflict resolution, he found his thoughts constantly straying to his wife, his prayers to Yahweh unceasing. *Bring her to me. Please.*

Suddenly, a shofar blew. One of the guards on sentry detail spotted people coming. Heart pounding, Moses squinted into the distance. *Could this be them? Let it be!* "What do you think, Joshua?" he asked, turning to the young man who rarely left his side. "Do you think that's my wife?"

Joshua squinted too, but even his younger eyes weren't able to make out specifics. "I'll find out," he said, already running down the hill, shouting to one of his subordinates. It took about an hour, at which point it was definitely confirmed, that yes, the travelers spotted were indeed Moses' family. Delighted, Moses went down to meet them. Per tradition, he showed respect by first bowing down and kissing his father-in-law, then his sons, and, finally, he swept his wife in his arms, showering her with kisses.

She clung to him, weeping softly with the joy and relief of seeing him again. Others looked away, the intimacy of their reunion not for public consumption. Then he led the whole clan, including Jethro and Hobab, into his tent, where they talked for hours. Zipporah curled up on his bed, holding his hand while he sat and shared what Yahweh had been doing, which was basically very similar to everything Jada had already told them. He spoke about the hardships they had met and how Yahweh had saved them. All the while, Zipporah's eyes feasted hungrily on Moses' face.

Jethro was delighted to hear about all the good things Yahweh had done for Israel. Again and again he said *baruch haShem*, as did Gershom, Eliezer, and Hobab. Toward evening, Moses tenderly covered up a now sleeping Zipporah and went with the men to offer sacrifices to Yahweh, one of which was a ram brought by Jethro. Aaron came with all the elders of Israel, and together they ate manna in the presence of Yahweh.

When he returned to his tent that night, Zipporah was sitting up, waiting for him.

"Did you eat?" he asked as soon as he came in.

"Yes, thank you. Joshua had one of the women attend to me, which I know was per your instructions."

"I'd like to assign two women to you, my love. I don't want you doing any extra work."

"I've never had a maidservant," protested Zipporah. "You know I've always done everything myself."

"My love," said Moses, sitting next to her and looking into her eyes, "those days are over. I need you freed up to help me, to be here just for me. I'm a bit overwhelmed, you know."

"Oh, my darling!" she exclaimed. "Tell me what I can do first."

He winked at her and laughed. Playfully, she slapped him on the arm, blushing. "Stop," she said, not meaning it at all. They renewed their love, after which Zipporah fell asleep, but Moses stayed awake for a long time, his wife in his arms.

*

The next morning, Moses left their tent and went and took his customary seat where he served as judge for the people. They crowded around from morning until evening, bringing their conflicts and problems to him.

Jethro came and found him and observed all that went on. He waited off to the side for at least two hours until Moses took a short break, at which point he approached his son-in-law. "What are you doing?"

Moses explained his normal procedure, and how it took all day.

"You've got to be kidding," exclaimed Jethro. "This is way too much work for you and you're entirely too valuable to wear yourself out like this. You've got to delegate, Moses. Why don't you teach the people the ways of Yahweh but appoint capable, God-fearing men over the people as judges? Only take on the most difficult cases."

"You know, you're right," agreed Moses. "That does make sense."

That very day, Jethro helped him set a new plan in motion that freed him up considerably. It took a few weeks to get it up and running, but it made an huge difference in Moses' vitality and ability to spend time in the presence of Yahweh. At the end of the first week, Moses encouraged Jethro to go back to Mama. "You've brought me my family," he said, smiling, "and you've helped me restructure my life. Go home and take care of those God has given you."

"It will be difficult to leave you, my son, and my daughter and grandchildren, but I am content in knowing that I have seen the great things God has done. Hobab and I will leave in the morning."

To everyone's surprise, Hobab refused to go. "Not yet, Father," he told Jethro. "I feel called to be here, to help."

"Let's ask Moses," said his father.

When they put the matter before Moses, he agreed with Hobab. "I didn't want to say anything and sway your decision," he said, "but I also believe you're supposed to stay with us, at least for the time being. Will you be all right if Hobab remains, my father?"

"Have you prayed?" he asked his son.

"Yes."

Jethro was silent for a moment, his eyes closed. Slowly, he nodded. "This must be from Yahweh. Who am I to say no?"

Jethro's parting from his family was short but emotional. Zipporah was the last to say good-bye. She hugged her father fiercely. "Will I ever see you again, I wonder?"

"Maybe not in this life," he answered slowly. "But definitely in the next one. We'll both be with Yahweh. Remember that, and remember my love for you." So saying, he gently extricated himself from her arms, gave one final wave to all who were gathered, and left.

*

Later that day, when Zipporah was resting in the tent she shared with Moses, a visitor came. "There's someone here to see you, my lady," announced her new maidservant, a sweet-faced young girl named Zahra.

"Who is it?" asked Zipporah.

"Miryam, my lady," said Zahra, looking impressed. "The master's sister."

Miryam! "Send her in."

"Zipporah, my sister!" Miryam swooped into the tent and kissed Zipporah on both cheeks. "I told you we would meet again, and here we are."

"It's wonderful to see you again, Miryam," responded Zipporah a trifle shyly. "I've thought of you."

"And I you." The two women looked at each other, eager to resume their relationship on the new level it had reached after their reconciliation in Egypt, but both hesitant lest they misstep.

"I'm so glad you're here...," they said simultaneously, then laughed. "You first," said Miryam.

"No, you."

"All right." The older woman reached out and clasped Zipporah's hands in her own. "It's so good that you're here. I can already see a change in Moses' countenance for the better."

"I'm glad. This is," she removed a hand and gestured helplessly, "intense."

"Very. It'll be easier for him, though, now that you're here. He seems to be one of those men who need a wife."

"He needs his sister too," said Zipporah generously.

"Not as much as he needs his wife," answered Miryam, shaking her head. "You complete him in a way no one else can. You're a special lady."

Zipporah smiled. "Thank you. That means a lot. But I don't even have him to myself anymore."

"None of us do. He belongs to Yahweh; he's just on loan to the rest of us." She grasped Zipporah's hand and then released it.

*

With his wife and sons by his side, Moses moved forward with a lighter step. His relationship with Yahweh continued to grow by leaps and bounds such that it was rumored that not even Father Abraham could possibly have been so close to God. From Mt. Sinai, Yahweh revealed Himself to the people in the midst of thunder and lightning, a thick cloud, loud blasts of the shofars, smoke, fire, and a continual violent trembling of the mountain. The people were warned not to force their way through to seeing Him lest they perish. Only Moses, with Aaron at his side, was allowed to see Yahweh and live.

Yahweh spoke many words to Moses on the mountain, starting with what would come to be known as the Ten Commandments. He set down instructions for a holy, set apart people—a people who would worship Him in spirit and in truth. He warned Moses that there would be severe consequences if the people were to follow other gods and that under no circumstances should they ever adhere to the detestable practices of the nations they were about to dispossess. God assured Moses that He would establish the borders of the Israelites' land from the Red Sea to the Mediterranean and from the desert to the Euphrates River. He allowed Moses to approach Him with Aaron, Aaron's sons Nadab and Abihu, and the seventy elders of Israel. They saw the God of Israel. Under His feet was something like a pavement made of lapis lazuli, as bright blue as the sky. God did not raise His hand against these leaders; and they ate and drank a covenant meal in Yahweh's presence.

Then, placing Aaron in charge, Moses went on alone with Joshua, his aide. He climbed the mountain, and the glory cloud settled on it. For six days, the cloud covered the mountain, and on the seventh day Yahweh called to Moses from within the cloud. From below, it looked like a consuming fire. Moses entered the cloud, staying on the mountain for forty days and nights. During this time, Yahweh revealed to Moses the history of His dealing with people, which would be known as *Beresheet.* He also gave Moses instructions as to the making of the Tabernacle, an earthly representation of the throne room in heaven. Finally, by His own finger He inscribed two tablets of stone with the covenant law. These tablets were supernatural in that from whichever side you looked at them, you could read the three-dimensional words from the right direction.

Unfortunately, while Moses was in the presence of God, Aaron was having trouble filling in for him. The people grew restless when Moses didn't quickly reappear, bullying and frightening Aaron, insisting on new gods, like the ones they had known back in Egypt. At first Aaron held out, but soon enough he buckled, terrified lest they kill him and his family. Thinking he could keep them loyal, Aaron came up with a compromise and made an idol, calling it Yahweh. Despite the horrified resistance of Miryam, Elisheva, Zipporah, his sons Eleazar and Ithamar, and several others, he harvested gold earrings from the people, melted them down, and fashioned a golden calf, not unlike an Egyptian idol. The next day, he proclaimed a festival to Yahweh, at which the people sacrificed burnt offerings and presented fellowship offerings. Afterward, they sat down to eat and drink, and things got out of control as they rose up to indulge in lewd behavior.

While this was going on, Zipporah grew more and more frantic. "No!"

she cried, attempting to thrust her way through the partying crowd, filled with a futile desire to topple the calf idol. Her sons and brother tried to hold her back, warning that she would be crushed by the mob. "They're out of control, Ema," said Eliezer, holding her by the arm. "We can pray that Yahweh steps in, and that Abba returns quickly. It's obvious that Uncle Aaron is in way over his head."

"Eliezer's right," agreed Gershom. "What can we do against thousands of people? It seems like only Abba can handle them." He looked around at his family. "I say we stay put."

One by one, they all nodded, though not happily. "It's too late," agreed Miryam sadly. "We're wildly outnumbered. Let's get on our knees and pray to Yahweh for help."

Zipporah, however, would not calm down. "No!" she cried. "You all know Moses wouldn't stand for this!" She slipped out of Eliezer's grip and ran back into the crowd. "Stop!" she begged, going from one person to another. "Don't do this evil thing!"

"Ema!" screamed Eliezer, "Come back!"

She kept going, heedless, intent on standing in for her husband, doing what she thought he would do. But she had not reasoned on just how wild the crowd was. Men and women who normally treated her deferentially now pushed her aside in their frenzied debauchery. When she reached a part of the crowd that was thickest, she slipped, tangled in the sweaty bodies. Falling to the ground under a stampede, she cried out for help, but her voice was swept away in the din.

Miryam dived into the crowd after her. "Zipporah!" she screamed hysterically, eyes scanning every face, her voice lost in the tumult. "Where are you?"

Meanwhile, Eliezer and Gershom frantically made their way toward where they had seen her last. Everywhere there were bodies, writhing and pulsating to the beat of some really nasty makeshift music. "Out of the way, out of the way," they yelled, pushing people from side to side, trying to see through the crowd.

"Out of the way yourself," growled a burly fellow.

"I'm Moses' son! Obey me!" demanded Gershom.

"Moses, ha!" The fellow smirked. "We haven't seen that one in a long time. Good luck seeing the old man again." He shoved Gershom aside.

"I'm ready to kill him," seethed Gershom, fists raised.

"No, stop it," cautioned his brother, laying a restraining hand on the other's arm. "We need to find Ema. Everything else can wait."

The two brothers continued to look, yelling themselves hoarse but to no avail. It seemed as if their mother had vanished. It wasn't until an hour later, crazed with anxiety, that they noticed a figure on the horizon where some of the crowd had been awhile before. It was Miryam, bent over something and howling in despair. Frantically, the brothers raced over.

"What is it, Aunt Miryam?" shouted Eliezer when they were almost upon her. "What's happening?"

Miryam didn't answer but continued to make noise not unlike an animal in pain. To their horror, they saw that what she was crouched over was the prostrate body of their mother. Dumbly, she pointed at Zipporah's chest which had been trodden on and crushed.

"Ema!" moaned Eliezer, his voice broken. "Ema?"

Zipporah's eyes fluttered open. "My sons," she said weakly.

"Shh, Ema, don't exert yourself," said Gershom, tears rolling down his face. He and Eliezer both sat beside her, Eliezer holding her head, Gershom stroking her arm, as she looked up into their beloved faces. "Tell Abba...," she whispered, the sounds of praying intensifying. "Tell Abba that I love him."

"He knows Ema," said Gershom softly, anguish distorting his features. "Come back to us!"

Slowly she shook her head, a slight smile playing about her lips, her gaze to the left and above their heads. "I see God's salvation," she murmured. "Tell Abba." Her head fell to the side, the life within her no longer on this earth.

"Zipporah! Ema!" The cries of those who loved her mingled with the shouts of the dancing revelers in the camp below.

* * *

Part IX

Zipporah

18

Mt. Sinai, 1445 B.C.

I'M DYING...GOOD-BYE, MOSES MY LOVE. I will see you in heaven, at the feet of Yahweh...He beckons to me...I see Him....

* * *

Part X

Miryam

19

Mt. Sinai, 1445 B.C.

I COULDN'T BELIEVE ZIPPORAH WAS DEAD. I was stunned. This was a nightmare. Moses had been gone forty days, and the camp had turned into a madhouse. When he returned and found his wife dead, his brother the high priest presiding over a calf idol, and the children of Israel running around naked howling at the moon he would be beyond furious. I trembled at the thought.

My son-in-law Hur stepped in and took charge, at least where Zipporah was concerned. He instructed us to wrap her in linen and spices, and lay her dead body outside the camp in a special tent. We were not to bury her until Moses returned, he said. One of his men was stationed there to drive off any wild animals that might try to maul the body. We were in a state of shock. I didn't think Aaron even knew yet; he was so busy "managing" the rioters.

Then I heard a sound . . . like Moses was coming down from the mountain. From my tent I had an excellent vantage point. I got up and peered in that direction. Yes, yes, it was Moses. I could see him, followed closely by Joshua. He had two large stones in his hands. When he spotted the calf and the wild party, he hurled the tablets to the foot of the mountain. It looked like they were smashed into pieces. Oh my.

Then he started yelling at Aaron. I couldn't hear what they said, and I didn't think I wanted to know. I decided just to hide for a while.

Hobab approached him, placing a hand on Moses' shoulder. Moses reared back in shock. That's when I knew . . . Hobab must have told him about Zipporah. Moses began running to the entrance of the camp. He shouted something. His words were repeated…what were they?

Then I heard them: 'Whoever is for Yahweh, come to me!'

All the Levites rallied to him. As fast as I could, I stumbled toward my brother, with the members of our tribe. When I got within striking distance of Moses, I heard him say, "This is what Yahweh, the God of Israel says: 'Each man strap a sword to his side. Go back and forth through the camp from one end to the other, each killing his brother and friend and neighbor.'"

As a ninety-year-old woman, I did not strap on a sword. Instead, I stood as close as I could to Moses, and watched and prayed. I saw sights I never thought possible: my fellow Hebrews run through by their brothers. Though the troublemakers had incited the people to sin and incurred God's wrath, it was still a horrible sight. The sounds of singing, dancing, and revelry from a few hours earlier quickly turned into screams of anguish and shouts of war. When the dust settled, we learned that three thousand perished.

As if that wasn't enough, Yahweh further punished us for the sin of the golden calf by sending a plague. Indeed He was serious when He spoke of purging the evil from among us.

I wasn't sure if Moses would be angry with Yahweh over the death of his wife. There was so much death, destruction, and hysteria in the camp that it was hard to tell where one anguish ended and the other began. I do know that he closeted himself in with his sons for a day, quizzing them again and again on Zipporah's last words and the details surrounding her death. I also spoke to him, though most of the hour we spent together was taken up by hugging and crying. I stressed the heroics of Zipporah's final actions—how she wanted more than anything to do what she knew Moses would have done had he been there. My brother didn't respond; he only sat there with tears pouring down his face into his beard.

Zipporah's death pushed my brother to pursue his relationship with Yahweh in ways he had not dared previously. He asked that God send His Presence with the Israelites so that he and the people would be distinguished from all the other people on the face of the earth.

After Yahweh agreed to this request, Moses pushed even more. "Show me Your glory," he demanded, a request so outrageous, so blatant, and in the end, honored. He actually was permitted to view the glory of Yahweh, though not His face.

After this, he again ascended the mountain of God and received anew another set of stone tablets to replace the ones he had broken. When Moses descended the mountain with the tablets, he was not yet aware that his face was radiant due to his encounter with Yahweh. We all, including Aaron, were afraid to go near him; such was the reflected magnificence of God in his face. But Moses called to us, loving us, telling us all the words of God that he had been commanded. From that point on, he wore a veil over his face except for when he entered Yahweh's presence.

I was surprised at how strongly Zipporah's death had affected me. I felt cheated: how I wish I had been given more time to get to know her! I bitterly regretted the time lost in Egypt by my petty jealousy and resentment and vowed to do better.

* * *

PART XI

MOSES

20

Mt. Sinai, 1444-3 B.C.

ON THE FIRST DAY OF THE FIRST MONTH OF THE SECOND YEAR after leaving Egypt, Moses stood with his aide Joshua and allowed himself to smile. He gazed with obvious pleasure at the newly completed Tabernacle. Done strictly according to Yahweh's specifications, it was a beautiful representation of God's order, from the inner holy of holies that contained the ark with the stone tablets, to the golden menorah just outside the holy of holies across from the table with the show bread, to the gold altar on which burned fragrant incense, to the altar for burnt and grain offerings and the basin with water for washing. Gorgeous curtains of blue, purple, and scarlet yarn and finely twisted linen with bronze and silver posts and bases surrounded the courtyard. The curtains around the tabernacle itself were similar in colors, only they had cherubim worked into them by skilled embroiderers, and the clasps were made of gold. Great skill had gone into every item, overseen by Bezalel, Miryam's great-grandson. He was a master craftsman filled with the Spirit of God. The ark he made was a stunning masterpiece—acacia wood overlaid with pure gold with a cover of pure gold on which hovered two cherubim made out of hammered gold, their wings spreading upward. Of course, one could argue that the golden menorah was equally a masterpiece, with its cups shaped like almond flowers with buds and blossoms, all hammered out of pure gold; or, for that matter, the table, likewise made from acacia wood and pure gold.

And then there were the priestly garments made for Aaron, woven from blue, purple, and scarlet yarn, with thin sheets of gold cut into strands worked into the yarn and fine linen. The shoulder pieces had onyx stones in gold filigree settings and were engraved with the names of the sons of Israel. The breastpiece was a work of art, with four rows of precious stones mounted on it in gold filigree settings for a total of twelve stones, for the twelve tribes of Israel. Aaron's robe had pomegranates of blue, purple and scarlet yarn and finely twisted linen around the hem of the robe alternated with bells of pure gold. The turban had a plate of pure gold attached by a blue cord on which was engraved: *Holy to Yahweh.* The clothing for his sons was similar, though not as elaborate, and without the breastpiece, shoulder pieces, and gold plate.

Truly it was a spectacular sight, filled with the glory cloud of Yahweh.

Once the work on the Tabernacle was completed, Moses had time to realize that he desperately missed having a wife. Despite the fact that his life was filled with people from dawn to starlight, and his encounters with Yahweh fulfilling beyond words, the human intimacy of a wife in his bed with whom he could share his deepest thoughts pulled at him. Others noticed as well. One day, Joshua and several of the elders requested a meeting.

"We're worried about you," said Caleb, son of Jephunneh, a trustworthy man from the tribe of Judah and a close friend of Joshua's.

"You need a wife," said Gaddi, son of Susi from Manasseh.

"You're too important to all of us. We want to help," put in Palti, son of Raphu from Benjamin.

"Zipporah would want you to move on with your life," said Joshua quietly.

Moses listened and agreed. "There will never be another like Zipporah," he said, wiping his eyes. "But I hear your counsel and I will take this before Yahweh."

"We can ask nothing more," said the men.

The next morning, Moses sat before Yahweh. "I miss Zipporah," he told Him.

The response came quickly. *Have you considered Lielit?*

Lielit?

"Who's Lielit?"

Yahweh said nothing more, but the following week Moses was sitting as judge for some difficult cases when he noticed a young woman accompanying one of the litigants. He was at an age where he didn't necessarily focus in on every beautiful woman who passed in front of his eyes, but this one grabbed his attention. She was quite dark, much darker than the average Egyptian, with braided hair in coils at her neck. Tall and slim, clad in colorful blue and green robes, her face reflected a dignity and serenity he didn't often see.

"Who is that?" he whispered to Joshua.

Joshua, who seemed to know everything, had a ready answer. "That's Lielit, the Cushite, my lord."

Moses started. *Lielit! The name Yahweh gave him.* "The Cushite," he said slowly.

"Yes, one of the people groups who joined with the Israelites out of reverence for Yahweh."

"She's...very beautiful."

Joshua shot him a sidelong glance. After a moment, he offered, "Would you like me to introduce you?"

Behind his veil, Moses' face colored. *Well, why not? This is from Yahweh.* "Yes," he said, perhaps a little too loudly. "Yes, I would like that."

And so began a very short courtship. Within a month, they married and Lielit moved her few belongings into Moses' tent. Moses was blissfully happy with his new bride, thanking Yahweh daily for the comfort she brought into his life. Others were not so happy. Miryam, in particular, who had such trouble warming up to Zipporah now became her greatest champion.

"How could he remarry so quickly?" she fumed to Aaron, agitated at this turn of events.

"It has been a year," he said mildly.

Miryam glared at him. "Barely. Aren't you upset at all?"

Aaron grimaced. "I'm not thrilled with his choice," he admitted. "I'm surprised that he chose a Cushite. Are there no Hebrew girls available that he had to choose a Cushite? First an Egyptian, then a Midianite, and now a Cushite. I don't get it."

Miryam didn't say anything. Aaron was the only one of the three siblings who had actually married a fellow Israelite. Well, at least Pawero wasn't dark like this Cushite, she thought.

"Although," said Aaron, "he did say that he heard from Yahweh he was to marry her."

"Bah," spit Miryam. "Has Yahweh spoken only through Moses? Hasn't he also spoken through us?"

Aaron looked at her, the incident with the golden calf seemingly removed from his memory. "You're right. He's also spoken through us."

Emboldened, they sought a private audience with Moses, scolding him for marrying Lielit, reiterating their positions of hearing from God. In his humility, Moses did not respond to these accusations, though he was deeply saddened that two of the people he loved most in the world were so intent on destroying his happiness. Suddenly, both Miryam and Aaron did indeed hear Yahweh's voice, as they claimed. "Come out to the tent of meeting, all three of you!" He commanded.

Trembling, the three of them went out. Then Yahweh came down in a pillar of cloud, summoning Aaron and Miryam forward. He said to them:

"When there are prophets of Yahweh among you,
I reveal myself to them in visions,
I speak to them in dreams.
But this is not true of my servant Moses;
he is faithful in all my house.

With him I speak face to face,
clearly and not in riddles;
he sees the form of Yahweh.
Why then were you not afraid
to speak against my servant Moses?"

The anger of Yahweh burned against them and when He departed, Miryam's skin was afflicted by *tzara'at*, the flesh rotting and as white as snow. Aaron was aghast, pleading with Moses to forgive them their foolish sin. Moses, shocked as well, cried out to Yahweh on behalf of Miryam. Yahweh agreed to heal her, but not for seven days, during which time she was to be confined outside the camp. "If her father had spit in her face, would she not have been in disgrace for seven days?" He asked.

Quickly they hustled Miryam outside the confines of the community, setting her up with a small tent and enough food and water for the week. Trembling and shaking at the thought of being alone in the wilderness, plus the fear that gripped her from Yahweh's anger, she begged them not to leave her.

"Seven days, my sister," Moses assured her. "You'll make it."

* * *

Part XII

Miryam

21

Mt. Sinai, Outside the Camp, 1443 B.C.
Miryam's Journal

I HAVE LEARNED MY LESSON. Never again will I attempt to compete with Moses or push my will above his. I have seen directly from God Himself that my own brother is a prophet of Yahweh unlike any other. Yahweh has given me much in this life, more than I ever could have dreamed possible when as a little girl I lived in a slave village on the banks of the Nile. I find it ironic that my skin has turned deathly white when I despised the black skin of Lielit. Now I long for my own skin to darken. *Would that it were even darker than hers, only healthy.* Yahweh, please remember your maidservant in her distress.

This has been the longest week of my life. As day passes to night and back again, I cling to Yahweh, repenting of my sin in dust and ashes. Slowly at first and then more forcefully I feel His love and forgiveness wash over me. I think my skin is improving; it hurts less. Is it less white? Hard to tell, though by the fifth day I am certain I see a definite change for the better. The relief I experience in the renewal of my Father's love is fathomless. Never again do I want to leave His presence!

Repenting of my rebellion, I sing softly to Him in the cold night air: *only one thing I ask, this is what I seek, to dwell in the house of Yahweh all the days of my life and to gaze on His beauty, to be a pillar in the tabernacle of my God. I will sing and make music to Him, seeking His face forever, worshiping Him with all of my heart both now and forevermore. Blessed be His glorious name.*

Epilogue

MIRYAM LIVED ANOTHER THIRTY-SEVEN YEARS, breathing her last at Kadesh in the Desert of Zin just before the Israelites reached the Promised Land. After her death and burial, there was no water for the community and once again the people rebelled, quarreling with Moses and Aaron. Yahweh told Moses to take his staff and speak to the rock, which would give forth water. In his anger, Moses struck the rock twice. For this sin, he and Aaron were not allowed to go into the Land with the people, both dying soon after; first Aaron and then Moses. Joshua son of Nun succeeded Moses as leader, acting as general of the Israelite army. It was Joshua who led the people in battle to physically take the land that Yahweh promised.

Gershom and Eliezer found wives within the Tribe of Levi, from which came their ancestry.

Hobab stayed with the Israelites at Moses' request and his descendants lived in the territory of Judah in the Negev near Arad. They were known as the Kenites. Years later, Hever the Kenite married Yael (see *Polished Arrows*).

Taking It Deeper
Out of Egypt Discussion and Study Guide

1. How would you describe the young Miryam? The young Hatshepsut? What drew them together not only as servant and queen but also as friends? Is there someone you are friends with who is very different from you? What drew the two of you together?

2. What kind of relationship did Hatshepsut have with her father? mother? brothers? How does this differ from the relationship you've had with your parents and siblings? The custom of royalty marrying brother to sister was entrenched in Egyptian society. How would you have responded to it, had you been Neferure?

3. How did you react to Miryam's encounter with Amenmose when he tried to take advantage of her in the gardens? From your perspective, did she handle it well or not?

4. Contrast the type of queen Mutnofret was with the type of ruler Hatshepsut became. Which queen would you rather have as a ruler, and why?

5. Was Hatshepsut's thirst for power out of bounds, or what you would expect from a ruler of her caliber? Explain.

6. Describe Moses' relationships with Miryam and Hatshepsut when he was young. What roles did each of them play in his life?

7. Was Miryam right to marry Pawero, a non-Hebrew? Why or why not? What factors would you have weighed in your decision, if you were Miryam?

8. What do you think happened in both Miryam and Hatshepsut's lives after Moses fled Egypt? Use your imagination to paint some scenes.

9. If you were Moses, would you have killed the Egyptian, who was beating a defenseless, elderly Israelite? Why or why not? Do you believe that any killing or murder is justified? If so, under what situations?

10. How did the "bridegroom of blood" incident on the way back to Egypt affect Moses? Zipporah? Gershom? How did it change Gershom's relationship with God?

11. Why did Miryam and Zipporah's relationship get off to a rocky start? Do you believe it was inevitable for two such women to butt heads? Why or why not? How might each have changed their behavior for a less rocky start? In your own life, what might you say or do to ease a rocky relationship right now?

12. In the golden calf incident, Zipporah tried to handle things herself . . . and died as a result. Do you believe she did the right thing, in principle? Why or why not? What would you have done if you were Zipporah?

13. Miryam and Aaron were clearly unhappy about Moses remarrying after Zipporah's death. How did you respond to that action of Moses? Explain.

14. Evaluate Miryam's attitude toward Moses' new wife. How was it similar, and different, from her attitude toward Zipporah? How might Miryam have incorporated what she learned about her relationship with Zipporah to ease her relationship with Moses' new Cushite wife? Why do you think she didn't?

15. Have you ever found yourself playing God—trying to make the people around you and the events around you bend to your will—like Miryam tried to do with Moses' marriage and remarriage? Did it work out in your favor, or not? Explain. How might that knowledge help you in a situation happening now?

16. The last thirty-seven years of Miryam's life are only alluded to in *Out of Egypt*. What do you think they were like? How do you think Miryam might have changed as a result of her experiences?

17. In what way(s) did reading *Out of Egypt* bring these biblical characters from Exodus alive for you? Which character, in particular, did you identify with the most? Why? Are there any characters you'd like to know more about? If so, which ones?

The Ten Plagues

1. The Plague of Blood
2. The Plague of Frogs
3. The Plague of Gnats
4. The Plague of Flies
5. The Plague on Livestock
6. The Plague of Boils
7. The Plague of Hail
8. The Plague of Locusts
9. The Plague of Darkness
10. The Plague on the Firstborn

See Exodus 7:14-12:30 for a complete accounting of the plagues.

The Ten Commandments

(#1) I am Yahweh your God, who brought you out of Egypt, out of the land of slavery.

You shall have no other gods before Me.

(#2) You shall not make for yourself an idol in the form of anything in heaven above or on the earth beneath or in the waters below. You shall not bow down to them or worship them; for I, Yahweh your God, am a jealous God, punishing the children for the sin of the fathers to the third and fourth generation of those who hate Me, but showing love to a thousand generations of those who love Me and keep My commandments.

(#3) You shall not misuse the name of Yahweh your God, for Yahweh will not hold anyone guiltless who misuses His name.

(#4) Remember Shabbat by keeping it holy. Six days you shall labor and do all your work, but the seventh day is a Shabbat to Yahweh your God. On it you shall not do any work, neither you, nor your son or daughter, nor your manservant or maidservant, nor your animals, nor the alien within your gates. For in six days Yahweh made the heavens and the earth, the sea, and all that is in them, but He rested on the seventh day. Therefore Yahweh blessed Shabbat and made it holy.

(#5) Honor your father and your mother, so that you may live long in the land Yahweh your God is giving you.

(#6) You shall not murder.

(#7) You shall not commit adultery.

(#8) You shall not steal.

(#9) You shall not give false testimony against your neighbor.

(#10) You shall not covet your neighbor's house. You shall not covet your neighbor's wife, or his manservant or maidservant, his ox or donkey, or anything that belongs to your neighbor.

EXODUS 20:2-17

Acknowledgments

This book was two years in the making. I owe a debt of gratitude to: my dad, Harry, for always taking the time to look over my in-process manuscript whenever he came to visit; Yael Galiley, for diligently reading the completed manuscript and giving me excellent advice; Yahnissi Allen, who likewise contributed to the final direction of this book with her on-target critique; my husband, Steve, who has been unfailingly encouraging and supportive; Beth Howarth, who stepped in at the last minute and did a final editing of the proofs.

None of us live in a vacuum, and the following people have contributed to my life in a myriad of ways: Josh Galiley; Shimon Galiley; Eliza Howarth; Michael Kessler; Eve Nober; Dave and Debbie Zoeckler; the community at Beit Shalom, Utica, New York; and many others. You know who you are! Thank you for blessing me.

From masterful writer

Deborah Galiley

Three gripping historical tales
that transcend centuries and hearts
to show that every life...and every life circumstance...
has ultimate purpose.

POLISHED ARROWS

It was a time of great tumult...
and even greater evil.

When the Moavite King Eglon's reign of terror ends abruptly in the fourteenth century BC, the yoke of bondage is at last broken for the people of Israel. Now is their chance for a new start...but will it be enough to turn their hearts?

Devorah, the oldest child of doting parents, has grown up beloved by her entire community. Everyone senses something different about her—that God has specially placed His Hand on her—but for what purpose?

Yael, a purchased bride, is torn from her home and plunged into a life she never wanted. Can she learn to love this man she must now call husband...or is there too much of a chasm between them? And what of her dreams? Has God forgotten her?

Little could these two women guess that their lives would become polished arrows in God's quiver, targeting an entire nation.

YOHANA

He could have been any of the men
I saw every day on the streets of Jerusalem.
But when he looked straight at me,
I was overcome with an emotion I could not name...

In A.D. 25, living in close proximity to the tempestuous Herod Antipas meant continually skirting the edge of danger.

Rumors abounded of an uneducated carpenter's son from the Galil—Yeshua ben Yosef, of Natzeret—who supposedly healed the sick. Yohana had never put much stock in so-called miracle workers. So many charlatans plied their trade in and around Jerusalem, making fantastic sums off a gullible and desperate populace. Yohana was determined not to be one of those drawn in, yet there was something different about this new miracle worker....

www.greatbiblefiction.com
www.oaktara.com

Seeking Paradise

The promise was there,
waiting, waiting,
but restlessness had a hold on me.

From the thrilling and lush paradise of The Garden, to the utter loathsomeness of evil's rampage in the Nazi Regime, to the deceptive calm of modern America—Becky Hermon's heritage and life reflects a paradise terribly and dreadfully lost. Will her spiritual odyssey bring her back to Eden, or push her to the brink of despair?

An adventure junkie's unforgettable journey through Paradise…and back.

For all those who have strayed from the path—
and those who love them.

*** Bonus Features ***

Challah Bread Recipe
Artwork by Gail Ingis Claus, ASID (www.gailingisclaus.com)

www.greatbiblefiction.com
www.oaktara.com

About the Author

DEBORAH GALILEY is a Jewish believer in Yeshua (Jesus). She grew up in a conservative Jewish home on Long Island, came to faith in Los Angeles, and has lived in Central New York since 1989. Deborah is a messianic *rebbetzin* (rabbi's wife—her husband, Steve, is the rabbi), mother of five, author, percussionist, bread baker, cancer survivor, and Boston Terrier owner. *Out of Egypt* is her fourth novel.

For more information, visit Deborah's website:
www.greatbiblefiction.com

You may write her at:
Deborah@greatbiblefiction.com

www.oaktara.com

CPSIA information can be obtained at www.ICGtesting.com
Printed in the USA
BVOW03s1842160414

350861BV00005B/141/P

9 781602 903531